Frank,
You've been . . . .
in the creation of Baobab. I
hope "Slats" joins in on the shelf
soon.

BAOBAB: a novel

Larry Hill
5/16/2019

LARRY HILL

First Edition Design Publishing
Sarasota, Florida USA

Baobab: a novel
Copyright ©2019 Larry Hill

ISBN 978-1506-908-15-1 AMZ
ISBN 978-1506-908-14-4 PBK
ISBN 978-1506-908-13-7 EBK

LCCN 2019939481

May 2019

Published and Distributed by
First Edition Design Publishing, Inc.
P.O. Box 17646, Sarasota, FL 34276-3217
www.firsteditiondesignpublishing.com

Dedicated to the overworked and underappreciated, often heroic, Foreign Service Officers of the United States Department of State

And, to the even more unsung family members and loved ones of those officers, who thanklessly travel with them to all corners of the globe.

THE BAOBAB TREE

An iconic resident of the arid Sub-Saharan Africa, especially the island of Madagascar, the baobab is often referred to as the "upside down tree." Absent of leaves most of the year, the bare branches, limited to the very top of the trunk, suggest misplaced roots.

A tall one can stand close to 100 feet and the most rotund ones have a circumference well over 100 feet. The heaviest family members will weigh upwards of 75 tons. The oldest trees are very, very old. Their rings are so faint that counting them is nearly impossible. One report claims that a South African specimen was calculated to be 6000 years old, based on carbon dating. Surely, some make it to 2500 years, offering stiff competition for the title of the planet's oldest living thing to the bristle cone pine of the American West.

They produce flowers and fruit. The attractive white flower is 8 inches wide but lasts less than a day, falling to the ground where small mammals eat the malodorous remains and disperse their seeds. The large, hard-shelled fruit, known as monkey bread, can be made into an edible powder, which has recently become accepted as a super-food, available on Amazon and Alibaba. It is considered tasty by some, but as sticky and tasteless as Hawaiian poi by many.

The baobab tree is considered at risk from the consequences of global warming.

List of Characters

US EMBASSY, Donoulu, Zinani

Holden Fairchild III - American Ambassador
       Marylou Fairchild – Ambassador's Wife
       Judy Anne Dean – Ambassador's Secretary
Ernestine Grant – Deputy Chief of Mission
       Amanda Sertoli – Ms. Grant's Secretary
Conrad Prudholme – Administrative Officer
Bernadette O'Kelly – Political Officer
Chen Wang – Economic Officer
Frank Norbert – Regional Security Officer
Michael Eisenstat, MD – Regional Medical Officer
       Gillian (Jill) Eisenstat, RN – Doctor's Wife
       Electra Sinalago – Office Nurse
       Madam Diallo – Office Secretary
Steven (Fireman) Pfund – Financial Officer
Berkeley Eaton – Consular Officer
Garson Graham – US Aid for International Development Country Director
Lori Burkitt – CIA Station Chief
Gene Browner – Public Affairs Officer, US Information Agency
Eddie DeQuervain – Communication Specialist
Anisa – Interpreter of French and Fulani
Gunnery Sergeant Billie Don Rice – Head of Marine Contingent
General Constance Fimbri, US Army – Commander US Army Medical, Europe

US PEACE CORPS, ZINANI

Willie Johnson – Peace Corps Director
Ulysses Singh – Peace Corps Deputy Director
Beth Sinova – Peace Corps Volunteer
Jenny Addison – Peace Corps Volunteer

US AIR FORCE

Colonel Martin Whipple – Pilot
Lt. Colonel Jack Nu – Co-pilot
Captain Zebulon Fellows – Flight Surgeon

GOVERNMENT OF ZINANI

Oumar Ibrahim Lassoso – President
       Mohammed Lassoso – President's Son and Heir Apparent
Minister Coulibaly – Health Minister
Minister Assisata Obode – Foreign Minister
General Saloum Traore – Army Chief of Staff and Number 2 to
President Lassoso
Dr. Traore – American Trained Orthopedist and Post Medical Advisor
to US Embassy
Dr. Tontan – Administrator of Lassoso General Hospital
General Sulieman Sacco – Commander First Division Zinanian Army
Colonel Sigfried Otobalo – Commander of Army in New Akron
General Joro – Supporter of PPD
Colonel Rashad – Supporter of PPD

GOVERNMENT OF LIBYA

Muammar Gadaffi- Dictator
Ambassador Muktar – Ambassador to Zizani
Sheik Harif Rahman – Representative of Gadaffi in Zizani

PPD (*Parti de Peuple Democratique*)

Oumou Kinsa – Leader
Jini Togola – Assistant to Leader

I

Doctor Michael Eisenstat knew that he'd have to fight falling asleep as the Ambassador entered the room for his Country Team Meeting. He often dozed, as there was rarely anything of interest for him at these regular Tuesday morning confabs.

"Gentleladies and gentlemen, we've got 72 hours to leave the country." Holden Fairchild III, representative of the President of the United States to Zinani, declared unexpectedly. Eisenstat's concern about nodding off vanished.

"The Foreign Minister called me twenty minutes ago and gave me the news. She didn't say why. But, she did say that we could leave one person behind to secure the building. That's going to be you, Chen." Chen Wang was the Commercial Officer and the Embassy's most well liked American.

The reaction in the room was like that of a group of family members at an airport after being told that the flight their loved ones were scheduled to arrive on had disappeared from radar screens -- silence and viscous anxiety. As there were just 14 official Americans on staff, nearly all of them were members of the Team. Medical attaché Eisenstat was the oldest and least diplomatically experienced of the officers.

Zinani and all of West Africa had been hotter than usual. The median high temperature that April had been 110 degrees. Nearby Timbuktu had registered 118 the previous day. Donolu, the capital of Zinani, garnered little advantage from its location on the Begoro River as local breezes hardly ever happened. The Embassy's Administrative Officer had been on a jihad against electrical wastage, vainly trying to convince the staff that ceiling fans, in both their offices and homes, offered sufficient relief. Ambassador Fairchild agreed with the conservation effort, as long as it didn't affect any room in which he was likely to spend time. The secure conference room therefore was comfortably air-conditioned.

An envoy of few words, Fairchild generally left most of the discussions up to his minions. "Take it away, Ernie. I'm gonna call State Department and let them know about this."

"Yes, Mr. Ambassador."

He pushed back his leather chair and stood up. On key, everyone rose at the same time, because the Ambassador had never told them not to. The Marine Guard Gunnery Sergeant opened and then closed the heavy steel door of the cool but claustrophobic room as the boss left and his subordinates sat back down.

Deputy Chief of Mission (DCM) Ernestine Grant despised being called Ernie. As number two at post, she was the real source of information and influence in the Donolu Embassy, although a lot of her energies were spent making the Ambassador think that he was.

She had as much in common with Fairchild as a Corvette did with a Ford pickup. Single, short, black, born in Boston with a BA from Tufts, she had joined the Foreign Service in the early seventies, almost twenty years earlier. Some considered her employment to be the result of a talent search during the early days of affirmative action. In reality, she was immensely skilled and had climbed the promotion ladder based on merit at a terrific speed, several years faster than her contemporaries.

This situation in which Ms. Grant, 44, found herself was made to order. Her visage reflected supreme self-confidence.

Ignoring more senior officers in the room, the DCM turned to the young Political Officer, Bernadette O'Kelly, known by friends as Dette. "Could this have anything to do with your relationship with General Sacco?" Lieutenant General Sulieman Sacco was one of the three most important officers in the Zinanian Army.

II

Months earlier

Bernadette O'Keefe O'Kelly, 35, was born in Lincoln, Nebraska, the third oldest of eleven children, to Frank O'Kelly, a cop, and Ginger O'Keefe O'Kelly, a telephone operator. Dette was one of two of the eleven who graduated from St. Catherine's of the Table High School and went on to college. She attended Creighton in Omaha, and graduate school at the University of Nebraska, writing her PhD thesis on fellow Nebraskan William Jennings Bryan.

Finding academics stultifying, she successfully sought a diplomatic position at State. A job as consular officer in Liberia was followed by an uneventful two-year stint at the State Department in Washington. She opted to become an Africa specialist, where the competition was much less intense than Europe or Asia, and accepted the assignment of Political Officer in Donolu. She knew of Holden Fairchild's reputation as a hands-off leader, and reckoned that she might well end up as a sizable fish in the large, sand-filled pond.

Her history of romance was meager. One of her brothers was her date to the Senior Prom at St. Cats. Creighton was a bust as well. Her first real fling occurred at grad school and led to a pregnancy after her first meaningful refusal to follow the dictates of the Holy See. The father was her thesis advisor, Morton Feldspar, a man of 52 with a wife and three children, one of whom was Bernadette's classmate. Dr. Morty denied any responsibility for the conception. Having to fend for herself, she flew to Chicago for a surgical solution.

Celibate in Liberia, she had a second romantic relationship in DC. She met Gregory "Stonewall" Sorenson, a Congressional aide and good Catholic boy from Sheboygan at the National Archives, where, for entertainment, he was listening to the Watergate tapes. He invited her to dinner. Eggplant Parmesan at hers followed chicken curry at his place the next day. Lovemaking at both flats the next week resulted in ten months of cohabitation. Her parents and his mother were brought into the picture (His father, a spelunker, had died of rabies from a bat bite.). Everybody liked everybody else, although none of the three was terribly happy with the cohabitation.

The couple enjoyed living and loving together, but Stonewall never proposed. Dette, in spite of her relative modernity, was reluctant to do so. She eventually did. He said no. She moved her stuff back from his apartment to her considerably smaller one, and they never saw each other again.

A political officer's position requires frequent contact with host country nationals, both in and out of government. It necessitates at least a working knowledge of the language and a familiarity with the religion, art, music, mythology, economy, history, anthropology, sociology, and geography of that nation. O'Kelly had all the skills and was an immediate success in Zinani. She was well regarded by the Ambassador and other co-workers, both American and local. Those Zinanians who counted, both in Lassoso's upper echelon and the tiny, well-hidden democracy contingent, accepted her.

One of her assignments was that of keeping current on the Zinanian Army, as the country was not considered important enough by Washington to justify a US military attaché. Landlocked Zinani had no navy. Two early model French Mirages and one unsound Russian troop transport hardly qualified as an air force, so the Army was the only meaningful arm of the military. It was made up of three divisions, totaling 25,000 troops, and a tiny, but elite airborne battalion through which the President of the Republic, Oumar Ibrahim Lassoso (known in the Embassy as OIL) attained his power. As far as the political officer could learn, neither the President nor any other member of the battalion had ever jumped out of an aircraft. The only truly important division in the Army was the First Division. Stationed in the capital, the First's responsibility was to assure the longevity of the revolution and its Chief of State. Bernadette O'Kelly's most important military contact was the Commander of that division, Suleiman Sacco.

Sacco was north of 40, but in his Sahelian-way, looked closer to 30.

Bernadette first met him at one of her obligatory visits to the Presidential Palace, and found him captivating, an interest he seemed to reciprocate.

Sacco proved to be a valued source for Bernadette; her steady stream of tips for her superiors raised the value of her stock in the commodity market that decides on the future of young Foreign Service Officers. Her fund of confidential data, from Sacco and others, was at least the equal to that of Lori Burkitt, CIA Station Chief, her competition for relevance of information with the higher-ups..

Sacco was a confidant of President Lassoso. His family had been Lassosoists since the coup that put the President into power. His father served as Ambassador to Germany, France, and finally, the UN, where he died suddenly of an undiagnosed illness. Several Saccos (uncles, cousins, and more distant relatives), wore the Army uniform, all with officer rank, none lower than major.

Suleiman signed up after two unsuccessful years of engineering school in Toulouse, where he never grasped the basic concepts of Newtonian physics, let alone quantum mechanics. Hailing from Zinani's second largest city, Sokimbo, the President's hometown, and being a Sacco, enabled him to enlist at age 21 with captain's bars, a position from which inclusion in the upper echelon came rapidly. He spent a year at Ft. Bragg, NC, learning the army gospel according to Uncle Sam; he returned with remarkable skills in the English language and a handful of seeds of democratic thought. He was never disloyal, in part because of all the funerals he went to of his cohorts who were. He sometimes partook in Lassoso's occasional purges, hesitatingly barking out the Fulani equivalent of "Ready. Aim. Fire." With each Swiss-cheesed victim, however, his discomfort with the ways of the President grew.

Don Juan was not a West African. Rudolph Valentino would not have been a big hero in Zinani. Romeo and Juliet would confuse and bore the most sophisticated Donolu audience. These are not romantics; the chase for a Zinanian male involves lions and warthogs, not women. While an attractive female Foreign Service Officer in Rome, Paris, or Brasilia, be she single or married, handles more passes than a rugby player, such is not the case through West Africa. Here, the rare gentleman caller arrives at a woman's door with a brother, cousin, or friend, while the visit involves a Coke and a brief conversation, usually with the TV on, then everybody goes home.

O'Kelly and Sacco had had at least weekly contact in offices, at parades or receptions, or on their official phones, for six months. The handshakes had become longer and firmer than the usual mackerel-like African version; the duration of eye contact lengthened accordingly.

Four months into their friendship, just before the elections that would, with 99% of the vote, reinforce the dictator's hold on office, Bernadette's night guard rang the bell, announcing a visitor. Most visitors, regardless of time of day, were there to sell something; cucumbers and tomatoes or tribal masks and faux antique sculptures were the usual bill of fare. Occasionally, the visitor was one of the married fellow Americans coming to complain about his wife, hoping for an invitation into Dette's disheveled bedroom. The hope was always unrequited. That night the faces were black and nothing was for sale.

General Sacco came to the door in a suit. She had never seen him in anything but camouflage. The suit was dark and fit reasonably well. A white shirt and plain blue tie accessorized. The black shoes were highly polished. A teenage boy whom he introduced as his nephew, Nisso, accompanied him. Nisso wore a white caftan, clearly meant for special occasions.

Dette was ill prepared for such a visit. She was wearing ratty beige shorts and a sweatshirt emblazoned "FIGHTING IRISH." She was braless, a not insignificant fact for the amply endowed Midwesterner. The living room was a mess. Newspapers in French and English were scattered about, the crosswords in the English ones being half done. *National Geographics* and *Catholic Digests* (a birthday gift from Mom and Dad) littered the coffee table. Her collection of primitive African paintings hung askew on the wall, as if there had been a recent trembler. She had knocked the globe off the table while rushing to the bathroom earlier and had not picked it up since. The dinner plates (meal for one) were still on the table as she had let her houseboy go home early. Half-full glasses of both scotch and soda and cheap California Chardonnay remained.

"Ça va, Mademoiselle O'Kelly? How's it going?"

"Ça va, General."

"How is your family?"

"Fine, yours?"

"Fine, thank you."

"How is your life? Your work?"

"Fine thank you, yours?"

"Ça va."

"Please have a seat. The boy can sit by the TV." Nisso spoke no English and barely enough French to get by, but a soccer match was on.

Bernadette and the General spoke in English, in part to keep Nisso ignorant, but in equal part a result of the fact that she was still not entirely comfortable in French. Sacco made up for his deficiencies in physics with an uncanny ability to pick up languages. In addition to French, English, Arabic, and Fulani, all which he spoke fluently, he could converse in four other African tongues. There was no spoken explanation of Nisso's presence so it was clear to Dette that he was brought along for propriety sake. She knew not to offer beer or wine to her Muslim guest. Both visitors chose Coca-Cola, while she showed her independence by picking up and sipping on the warm Chardonnay.

"I am sorry to disturb you this way, without calling first," a moot apology considering that she didn't have a phone. Of the Embassy personnel, only the Ambassador, the AID director, CIA Station Chief and the doctor had home phones.

"Pas de problème, General. I am honored."

"Please call me Suleiman."

"Gladly. I am Bernadette."

"Bernadette, I have been meaning to come on a visit like this for many weeks. Only this evening have I developed the courage."

"Oh," she responded barely audibly.

"Twice before, I dressed, made Nisso put on his caftan, and drove toward your house, only to turn around at the last minute. Tonight, I probably would have done the same, but my nephew made it clear that he, at thirteen, was too old to get dressed up just to take a ride in the car."

Dette chuckled, nervously.

"Miss O'Kelly, ... uh, Bernadette, I would like to be your friend."

"But, we are already friends."

"No, I mean more. I would like to spend much time with you. I would like you to go to dinner with me, to dance with me, to meet my family. President Lassoso is having a gala celebrating his election and his 21st anniversary in office next Saturday and I would like you to accompany me."

"Again, Suleiman, I am greatly honored. I assumed that you were married."

"I was. About 10 years ago, after my studies in France, my family arranged for me to marry a beautiful woman from Sokimbo. Her name was Fatou. After the wedding she got pregnant, but just before the baby was to be born, she had bleeding. We went to Lassoso Hospital, and the doctors operated. I never saw her alive again. Fatou died in the operating room and the baby boy died a few minutes later. Those doctors were butchers. No one ever talked to me, except the nurse, and she expected a cadeau, a tip. I have not been alone with a woman since."

"Not even when you were in the United States?"

"No."

"I am so sorry." Dette had never before had an emotional reaction to an African, other than those whose tragic pictures she had seen in magazines during the continent's famines and droughts. She wasn't able to tell which emotions were active at this moment: sadness, gladness, nervousness, or sexual arousal.

"So, will you go with me to the Palace next week?"

"I am so honored," she said for the third time, "but I cannot give you an answer now. Please call me in my office day after tomorrow."

"I will. *Nisso, allons-y*. Let's go. Bernadette, thank you for your kind hospitality." He had drunk about 10% of his Coke. Nisso had finished his, plus the first three Oreos of his life, and had seen his team score a goal, making it an altogether successful visit. They left her house less than twenty minutes after arriving.

III

On a typically quiet Wednesday in the Chancery, DCM Ernestine Grant was busily and uninterruptedly composing the efficiency reports for her staff. Aside from her own report, which is the responsibility of the Ambassador, Grant wrote almost all of these documents for the American diplomats. She prided herself on the quality of her writing, recognizing that promotions are based almost totally on the evaluations of a Foreign Service Officer's boss. Her record at getting her charges promoted was outstanding. Given her focus on the important task at hand, she was startled when her secretary, Amanda Sertoli, announced that the Political Officer wanted to see her right away.

Bernadette tried to spend as little time with Ambassador Fairchild as possible, finding him pompous and ponderous. He, on the other hand, felt her to be a budding talent and often wandered down to her office, ostensibly to inquire about a cable or a newspaper article, but in reality, he saw her as one who liked to hear his stories. She didn't, especially after she had heard the same one five or more times, but was not ready, willing, or able to convey that to him. Dette, therefore, opted to talk to the DCM about the previous night's gentleman visitor.

"What do you think it was all about? Is there more to it than meets the eye?" inquired Grant after hearing the story.

"I honestly don't think so. The vibes between him and me had been a lot more resonant lately, so I wasn't all that shocked when he came to the door."

"What about the story of the first marriage?"

"I had heard about it before when the Ambassador first assigned me the military portfolio. Sacco's facts match those we have, even the stuff on the screw-up by the Lassoso Hospital doctors. Apparently his wife died at the hands of the anesthesiologist. He didn't notice that the oxygen tank was empty and that he was giving her pure nitrogen. I don't think Sacco knows that detail."

"Tragic."

"Sure was. Everybody says he really loved her, and unlike most of his cohorts, there's no evidence that he messed around, even when he was out of the country."

"So, what next? Do you want to go out with the guy?"

"Yeah, I do. He's nice, good looking, and he seems to like me. Furthermore, I could use the attention."

"I know very well what you mean…let me know if he has any friends. In the meantime, keep your eyes and ears open. Running in company like that, you might pick up a few tidbits."

"Ernestine, I do not mix business and pleasure."

"Bernadette, keep your eyes and ears open."

Thursday morning, a Jeep pulled up in front of the Embassy. A corporal brought a note addressed to Second Secretary B. O'Kelly and told the guard that he would wait for a reply. Dette was on the second of her two daily croissants when Amanda brought the envelope down the hall.

The President of the Republic, Oumar Ibrahim Lassoso, requests the pleasure of the company of General Suleiman Sacco and his guest Second Secretary Bernadette O'Kelly of the Embassy of the United States of America at a reception to honor the beginning of the twenty-second year of the First Republic of the Democratic State of Zinani." Date, time, and dress code (elegant) followed.

Dette, the ever-efficient American, affixed a Post-It-Note to the expensively embossed invitation, "Tell the messenger that I accept."

Saturday night at 7:15, the doorbell rang. A black Mercedes had appeared with a driver in camouflage and a single passenger. Suleiman Sacco was dressed in the same suit he had worn on the earlier visit, obviously pressed in the meantime. The shirt was still white; the tie now was striped in yellow, blue and black, the colors of the Zinanian flag. The shoes were even shinier.

The closet in the master bedroom of Dette's small house was sparsely filled. Presidential receptions were not in her plans when she shipped her wardrobe. Saturday noon, she got the idea of checking with the Ambassador's wife, Marylou Fairchild, a woman of impeccable taste who frequented events where couture was crucial. Their sizes were similar, although Marylou's dresses were tight on Dette around the bodice. Marylou offered and Dette chose a light yellow, floor length gown. Sacco was impressed.

Bernadette's house was on the banks of the Begoro River, known colloquially to the Americans as The Big; the Presidential Palace sat, less than 30 minutes distant, on an easily defended site on a prominence above town. Despite its strategic importance, the road between them was in hideous condition. The trip, even in a well-suspended German luxury car, could be best compared with a ride on an electric bucking horse found in Texas drinking establishments.

The Presidential Palace was patterned after the Alhambra in Granada but it was built on a shoestring. OIL had it commissioned not long after his ascendancy, expecting that one Cold War side or the other would pay for it. No takers were found, so the building had to be paid for out of import duties and donor contributions intended for health, agriculture, and infrastructure.

The building was now fifteen years old, and while not as decrepit as the internationally famous sports complex in Zinani's third city, New Akron, it looked much older than that. The Moorish arch at the entrance lacked its original elegance as bits and pieces had fallen off over time. The floors were not marble but slate, much of it cracked. The walls, which in earlier pictures looked gleaming white, were now covered with the light reddish brown of laterite dust. The drapes and upholstery were similarly tinted.

On either side of the entry hall were huge portraits of the President-for-life and his family. The picture of the President suggested an amalgam of Napoleon, Haile Selassie, and Elmer Fudd. Madam President's was that of a striking and elegantly dressed lady, as one might expect from one born into wealth and educated in Paris. Her three sons appeared short, handsome, and tending toward the effeminate. Images of Siamese cats and poodles were much in evidence in the portrait gallery.

To reach the ballroom, a guest passes through the kitchen, the result of the uninspired work of a young graduate of the Lassoso University School of Architecture whom the President selected to design his palace. Finicky eaters found the path a plus, as they were able to evaluate the hors d'oeuvres before they were offered.

Suleiman and Bernadette arrived early as Lassoso expected his military and ministerial cadres to be present to greet the guests from the diplomatic and business communities. Bernadette was the first white face in the room. A pair of faux-Louis XIV thrones, one large and one small, were elevated behind a bandstand, upon which rested a collection of drums and exotic stringed instruments. A bright red carpet runner approached the bandstand, disappeared underneath it, and reappeared on the other side in front of the thrones. The remainder of the floor was slippery bare hardwood, polished so well that Dette wished that she were wearing sneakers. Enormous threadbare tapestries, showing battalions of Caucasians in a variety of warlike activities, covered the long walls. The short walls tried to pick up the Moorish leitmotif; they were covered in blue and white arabesque tiles, many of which were missing or visibly cracked. At one end of the long room, a flag stand held the Zinanian national emblem; the other end featured the newly created Lassoso family flag, which portrayed a lion (none of which had been seen in the country for decades), a baobab tree, and a propeller-driven airplane out of which jumped a lone paratrooper. Four non-commissioned officers in camouflage, stood, one on either side of each flag, AK-47s in hand.

The President, a devotee of the grand entrance, was not in attendance when Sacco and Dette arrived. Mohammed, his oldest son and heir apparent, and Mohammed's only wife, Aroos, a diminutive, moderately obese half Zinanian, half Pakistani, greeted them. Mohammed was meaner, smarter, and more fundamentally Islamic than his father. The first Lassoso to go to Koranic school, he had spent four years in Saudi Arabia, and was instrumental in persuading his father to rid the nation of most of its evangelical Christian missions. Sacco had been taught by Jesuits in the European countries in which his father served as Ambassador; he was frightened by the excesses of fundamentalism, and despised Mohammed Lassoso.

The greetings were perfunctory and the couple joined the several dozen other early-arrivers milling about. The bar served only non-alcoholic drinks. Unsalted Zinanian peanuts and stale popcorn served as finger foods for the sparse crowd.

With the arrival of the diplomatic corps and the few wealthy entrepreneurs, the hall shortly began to fill. Most of the businessmen were Zinanian; there was a scattering of Lebanese, Egyptians, Europeans, and Japanese. The Japanese had succeeded in pushing aside Peugeot and Renault in cars, Kodak in film, and both the Americans and Europeans in tires and TVs. The only American businessperson at the event was an advance man for Burger King, trying to finally steal one on their Mac-rival. The band played Zinanian favorites, interspersed with recordings of Edith Piaf, Bing Crosby, and The Eagles.

Oumar Ibrahim Lassoso had attained the presidency in meteoric fashion. He went from Corporal in the Zinanian Army to Chief-of-State and Commander-in Chief in three months.

At age 27, almost a decade after Independence from France, he was a sergeant, well situated as a staff assistant to the ranking General, and as such was seated behind one of the few typewriters remaining in the country after the pullout of the colonialists. He cut orders elevating himself to major, and then appointed himself, with the General's unconcerned concurrence, as commander of the parachute battalion. This was before he had ever ridden in, let alone jumped out of, an airplane.

From that seat of power he staged a bloody coup. He assembled, from a group of friends and neighbors, a firing squad that quickly dispatched his boss, the General, and assorted other officers, enlisted men, government functionaries, and wealthy Lebanese businessmen.

Consolidation of power was not difficult in view of the demise of almost everyone with a tertiary education. Free elections were promised, but less than a year into the revolution, OIL gave into the will of his people to be President-for-life.

He was in his third decade of his presidency. Many of those fellow members of the coup, at least those who had not themselves fallen to their associates' salvos, met regularly, with new loyalists, to practice marksmanship and insure the continuity of the revolution.

The law of the land granted the President of the Republic the salary of 20,000 Lassosos per month -- equivalent to 350 US. His annual personal expenses were estimated to be more than one thousand times that number. The money was used for tuition, room and board for children in private American universities, and his principal wife (number one of three), who spared no expense to satisfy her taste in clothes and jewels.

A likeness of Oumar Ibrahim Lassoso graced the one and five Lassoso coins, and the ten, twenty, one hundred, and five hundred Lassoso notes. There were no bank notes of greater value. As there were neither checks nor credit cards in the country, any transaction of significance required a bag full of OIL's portraits.

Lassoso's lengthy tenure had been notably free of internal strife. His willingness to shoot, or more accurately, have shot, any citizen who spoke against him and his revolution, produced an environment of quietude. As Zinani had little geopolitical interest for great and not-so-great powers, there was almost no global voice speaking against his autocratic rule. Odds had it that President-for-life was a realistic moniker.

At precisely 9 PM, a hush fell over the hall. A door opposite the entrance to the kitchen opened. A close look revealed that that portal opened directly into an enormous closet lined on one side with a collection of blue, yellow, and black dresses and on the other, a line-up of tuxedos, Brooks Brothers tropical weight suits, safari suits, and camouflage fatigues.

Mr. President sported his dress blues, a chest full of ribbons and medals, none having anything to do with combat, a plumed hat, and a long, curved ceremonial sword. Madam was bedecked in a navy blue gown, a yellow belt, and yellow shoes. The small band played the national anthem; the song sounded like something John Phillip Sousa might have written during a bout of malaria.

A receiving line formed made up of Mr. and Mrs. President, Mohammed and Aroos, and the Chief of Staff and Sacco's boss, General Saloum Traore, accompanied by a stunning Senegalese woman thirty years his junior. Dette began to get nervous. She had never met a head of state. She had, of course, observed Lassoso from a distance on numerous occasions. Up close, she noted that Lassoso was more handsome than she had expected, certainly more so than the Elmer Fuddian portrait in the entry hall would suggest.

"Good evening, Miss O'Kelly." Bernadette was not surprised by his English, having heard that he spoke it as well as he did French. She was shocked, however, that he knew her name. No one had whispered her identity in his ear as she came face to face with him. "*Bon soir, General Sacco.*"

"*Bon soir, Monsieur le President,*" responded General Sacco and Second Secretary O'Kelly simultaneously.

"I have heard a great deal about you from a number of my advisers. You are quite well known in our country."

"Thank you for your kind words, sir."

"I suggest that you be very ... uh, shall we say, circumspect during the remainder of your time in Zinani, Miss O'Kelly."

She turned bright red, not evident to others in the subdued lighting of the Palace. Her heart beat hard and fast and her fingers and lips became numb. She was unaware that she had a reputation. "I will, Your Excellency."

She and Sacco shook hands and exchanged meaningless smiles with the remainder of the line. She remembered nothing after the presidential greeting.

They walked to the bar where she longed for a scotch but accepted a sparkling water. He chose Coke. They both refused the miniature egg rolls and the fried okra slices slathered in millet paste. At a distance, she spied Ambassador and Mrs. Fairchild who were engrossed in conversation with the man from Burger King. Ernestine Grant, who, with little effort, had persuaded Chen Wang, US Economic attaché, to escort her, stood with the Moroccan and Algerian Ambassadors. Bernadette was not of a mind to discuss the encounter in the receiving line with the Ambassador or DCM, so kept her distance from both.

"What did the President mean by circumspect?" asked Sacco, repeating the unfamiliar word.

"He wants me to be more choosy about whom I talk to."

"Why?"

"I'm not sure I know. I don't want to talk about it here."

Dancing followed the completion of official greetings. The combination of 1940's big band music and 1970's rock continued to dominate the playlist. Protocol had it that no one danced until the President-for-life took the floor. He prided himself on his talent on the dancefloor. All assumed that his first partner would be Madam, who gloried in the spotlight. That night, no one would have been right. He offered to take, instead, the hand of Madam Amina Mukhtar, the stately wife of the Ambassador of the Republic of Libya. She acted as if she had not even noticed the gesture, as practicing Muslim females avoided physical contact with any male not in their immediate family. Embarrassed for having broken protocol, the President selected the wife of the Russian Charge d'Affaires, the nearest non-Arab female, with whom to stumble around the slippery floor.

The party lasted another hour and a half. Sacco could not leave until the last foreigner had left. Because of the dry bar and uninspired hors d'oeuvres, the departures happened quickly. On the way home, Sacco again broached the subject. "Why did the president say that to you?"

"I don't know. I really don't know." She had been trained well enough to know that the first person to talk to about a politically sensitive matter should not be a member of the host country government.

The road back to her house was no smoother than it had been earlier. The events of the night however, were enough to distract from the discomfort, in the same way that a headache takes one's mind off a sprained ankle. As always, the streets were nearly deserted after close of business; there wasn't much to do in the dark night of Donolu.

Sacco walked Bernadette to her door. In spite of the disconcerting exchange in the receiving line, she had had a nice time and felt good in the presence of Suleiman. She wanted to spend more time with him, both later and then.

"Would you care to come in for a while?"

"I'm sorry, Bernadette. I cannot. I must arise very early tomorrow. My division is going on maneuvers." He put both hands on her shoulders and bussed her, twice on the left cheek and once on the right,

16

then turned around and returned to his car.

She remembered the rejection by Stonewall Sorenson. "Shit," she said.

IV

Monday after the gala at the Palace, Bernadette O'Kelly asked for a meeting with the Ambassador and the DCM Grant. Having spent two sleepless nights since the Presidential comment, she knew that it would be inappropriate for her to keep it to herself any longer.

"Circumspect, huh? So you think that there is a connection between what he said to you and his thing with the Libyans?" asked Ms. Grant.

"I can't imagine that there isn't," O'Kelly answered. "Lassoso never says anything offhanded, especially if there is someone likely to take offense. And those certainly were offensive words."

"Why you?" interjected Fairchild.

"Probably because of my contacts with the PPD. Gaddafi hates the idea of democracy."

"What's the PPD?"

"Sorry, I thought I had mentioned them to you. That's the People's Party for Democracy. Pretty small and new. Most of them are women, mainly students at the University. The leader is Oumou Kinsa, a faculty member and the daughter of the import-export guy, Alpha Kinsa. You know him don't you?"

"Sure. He comes here a lot to talk about selling stuff in the US."

"Oumou spent three years in Baltimore getting a PhD in Developmental Economics at Hopkins. I've had lunch with her a few times. She is no fan of Lassoso, in spite of her father's success. OIL made it easy for him to bring in luxury goods – Rolexes, Coach bags, Mont Blanc pens – stuff like that."

Fairchild was incredulous. He had heard none of this before, not that he was terribly savvy on the political situation in Zinani. Most surprising was the fact that women were at the head of a democracy movement, an unlikely scenario in Africa.

Ernestine, who had been involved in a couple of the lunches with Ms. Kinsa, felt a twinge of pride. The idea that black African females might be involved in politics of change was thrilling.

"What is this Oumou up to?" Fairchild asked.

"She is going about this cautiously, keeping her name out of the paper and off the TV, and talking to her student friends individually or in small groups. Most are women but men are beginning to listen, too. Unfortunately for her and her movement, the believers are almost all University students. There might be an occasional high-schooler and a few middle class unemployed men, but I don't think she's made an impact on the military or the agricultural masses yet."

"There's talk that the university might be shut down soon. Do you think that Oumou and her friends are the reason?" asked Ernestine.

"Could be, but as you know, OIL gets annoyed at times and just does things like that to show how powerful he is. He is still pissed that he didn't get into secondary school and is taking it out on today's educational establishment. How else do you explain him appointing an uneducated and unintelligent millet farmer as Education Minister?"

"So, again, you think that his comments are a result of your dealings with Oumou?" asked Ernestine.

"Has to be."

"Have you encouraged her party ... what's it called, the DDT?"

"No, Sir. It's the PPD, the People's Party for Democracy. And no we haven't really encouraged them, other than to supply answers, with the help of Gene Browner at the US Information Service, as to how democracy is carried out at home. As far as I know, Lori Burkitt's CIA people aren't giving them any money."

"That's correct," muttered the Ambassador who knew the destination of every cent spent by an official American in Zinani.

"So why is Lassoso so uptight about your role? Is there more?"

"That's everything I can think of. He must be getting pressure from Ambassador Mukhtar and then the wild man in Tripoli. Their goal is to squash the democracy talk and drive a bigger wedge between us and the Zins at the same time."

"How does he know that you talked with Oumou?" asked the Ambassador.

"He has informants, lots of them, and you can be sure that some of them are college students, probably even some female ones."

"By the way," interjected Ernestine, "how do you think that OIL reacted when he learned you and his trusted divisional commander, General Sacco, were coming together to his party?"

"Good question. Remember, I told you that my name was on the invitation. Gotta think that the President knew who was invited. But, at the same time, he obviously wasn't happy to see me. Or, then again, maybe he was, so he could give me that warning.

"Remember, Dette, before you went out with Sacco, I advised you to keep your eyes and ears open. Clearly you are following that advice. But let me give you an even more important suggestion."

"And that is?"

"And that is, don't let emotions get in the way of your work. Stay cool, even when it seems like the bastards are all out to get you." Ernestine concluded with a word that neither Fairchild nor O'Kelly had heard her use before, "Don't fuck it up." The Ambassador nodded with a smile.

Bernadette called General Sacco's office and was surprised to find him answering his own phone. "How were your maneuvers?"

"There were no maneuvers. I'm sorry. We couldn't afford the gasoline even if we had a reason for maneuvering. I declined your offer because I was worried that someone was following us. If they saw me go in your house after what the President said to you, it could have been trouble for me, and for you."

"Suleiman, we need to talk."

"I agree, but I still can't come to your house."

"OK. Let's meet at the Lebanese restaurant next to the Hotel Aubergine?"

"If we really want to talk, we cannot stay in Donolu. We must get out of town. You drive out the road that goes to New Akron and park your car at the Texaco station. I will meet you there and we can go to a place I know on the river."

New Akron, Zinani's third largest metropolis with 35,000 inhabitants was called Mongo since its foundation but accepted a name change when it's Sister City, the fifth biggest town in Ohio, requested naming rights when it built what was originally the most up-to-date sports complex in West Africa.

The New Akron highway didn't resemble one from old Akron. Not only was it full of axle-breaking chuckholes, it was choked with a jalopy-derby of cars, taxis, and the ubiquitous 15-passenger minivans, slow trucks spewing toxic exhaust, motorbikes and non-motor-bikes by the thousands, donkey- and horse-drawn carts with seven-year-old drivers, an occasional small camel train, and hordes of walkers, primarily women bearing staggering loads on their heads. Bernadette was not fond of driving anywhere in Zinani, but particularly hated the New Akron road. Her predecessor had banged up an embassy vehicle and killed a donkey, costing the US taxpayer several hundred dollars to the aggrieved donkey owner.

The Texaco station was a landmark, at least for Americans starved for signs of home, about 15 kilometers outside of the center of the capital. Dette pulled up at the appointed hour, her nerves, already on edge, now further shattered by the driving experience. Sacco was not there. She waited in her car with the motor and air conditioner running. Employees of the station came up to her to ask what she wanted. She waved them off with a smile. An old blind man led around with a stick held by a young girl, presumably his granddaughter, stood at the side of the driver's window until Dette gave him a couple of coins. Salesmen with fruits, cassette tapes, and small plastic bottles, full of unidentifiable liquid, failed to make any sales.

The General, dressed in street clothes, arrived ten minutes after Bernadette. He drove himself in a small rusty Peugeot that showed unmistakable evidence of having been on the Zinanian roads for many years. This junker, more than anything, convinced Dette that Sacco was not on the take, unlike many of his superiors, equals, and inferiors.

He motioned to her to come to his car. Having sized up the Peugeot, she gave him a "Not-on-your-life" look. Sacco was not accustomed to any form of rejection, especially from a woman, but hesitatingly acceded to her unspoken counter-order and climbed into the front seat of her Toyota Camry.

"Where to?" asked Bernadette, as if she was a cabbie talking to a fare.

"I know a place on the river where we can talk alone. Follow that road behind the station."

To call it a road was a stretch. What they drove on was merely a track of sand, packed harder than the surrounding sand, on which many thousands of donkeys had pulled many thousands of carts but very few motorized vehicles had ever traveled. They slalomed through brush and termite mounds standing as tall as the top of the car. Dette wondered where all the termites were. These construction geniuses appear to build and leave behind insect castles like tiny speculating contractors.

As they approached the Big River, neem trees and baobabs became common. They passed four Fulani villages, each comprised of ten to twenty small houses, made of the ever-present red laterite clay, and populated by several dozen children and a few women pounding millet in a huge wooden mortar with an equally large wooden pestle. Often two, or even three women ground as a team in the same mortar in perfect unison, one never interfering with the strike of another.

The children played happily, usually a game involving a hoop, a tire, and a stick. Bernadette was taken by the apparent contentment of these people who had nothing - nothing in the same sense that rich Americans have everything.

She was also struck, but not surprised by the total absence of men and boys over the age of thirteen. Most men leave these villages to seek work in the city, often unsuccessfully. Many then leave Zinani for more promising possibilities in wealthier nearby countries like Ivory Coast or Senegal. Thousands of Zinanian men live in France, where they take menial jobs, but jobs paying enough to allow them to send money home to support their one, two, or three wives and gaggles of children.

Ten kilometers later, after hitting bottom several times, the Toyota arrived, mostly unscathed, at the river. Sacco motioned her to turn upriver, toward Donolu, after which they traveled another five kilometers to what could best be described as a baobab forest. The fabled baobab usually is seen and worshiped singly. The strange shaped tree looks like its roots are in the air and branches in the ground, and has leaves when all the other deciduous trees are bare, and is leafless when all the rest are green, is rarely in sight of other members of its species. In this case, there were probably fifty within three or four acres. There was no sign of humanity - neither cans or bottles, nor any example of the blight of West Africa, the blue plastic bag.

Bernadette stopped the car under one of the larger baobabs. The sun shone brightly and she knew that the Toyota would become oppressive without shade. They got out of the car and she extracted a cooler from the trunk; no expat ever went on any road trip in Africa without cold liquids. They sat down on a pair of large boulders at the riverside. She gave him a Coke and took for herself a local beer, reputed to be rich in formaldehyde.

Neither was anxious to start talking. Her opening gambit, involved the weather, something about it being cooler than she remembered it last year at the time It fell on deaf ears. Africans don't talk about the weather, except as it has a direct influence on crops. Sacco asked her a series of questions about her family, knowing no more about them than he had learned on his visit to her house. Americans don't talk about family like Africans do.

Finally, both got around to the topic that led to this meeting. "So, what is your opinion about President Lassoso's comments the other night?" She asked it first, although he was about to pose the same question.

"Bernadette, please be careful. I have heard since that the President is not happy about your involvement with the PPD, especially with Oumou."

"But why? I have only listened to her. I haven't encouraged her or the movement. Hell, I haven't even taken her in to meet the Ambassador. He can't possibly be worried about the PPD. They only have a few dozen members, most of whom are college girls. Oumou is the oldest and she's not even thirty."

"Please don't say hell, Bernadette." African women say very little to men, let alone expletives. Sacco hated that part of his stay in the US, especially hearing "shits" and "fucks" from pretty young coeds. He avoided most American movies to spare himself the unpleasant sights and sounds. She blushed and promised herself never to swear in front of him again, a promise about as keepable as one to not breathe again.

"There is a lot more to it than you know, he continued. "Oumou is not just another woman who has ideas that he doesn't like."

"What do you mean?"

"Oumou Kinsa's father has been close to Lassoso for many years."

"I'm aware of that. I know that they have had business dealings that have benefited both of them -- to the disadvantage of the rest of the country, I might add."

"True. But more importantly, Lassoso was very much taken by Oumou when she was growing up. She was beautiful, smart, and as far as he knew, a young woman who would make a perfect, loyal wife; in other words, she was everything that his first wife was not. She was only sixteen when Lassoso started talking to Alpha Kinsa about the possibility of marrying his daughter."

"He was going to dump Madam?"

"No. As you know, any man in this country is allowed to marry four women."

"Oh, yeah. I knew that. So, what happened?"

"Even as a teenager, Oumou was different, very different, from most Zinanian women. She had a mind of her own. Most girls' parents make the decision on who they will marry. That's true for boys too. The parents set up the match, mainly as a business proposition. It was a real compliment for the Kinsas when the President asked for their daughter.."

"Some compliment from that jerk."

"The merchants and business people of the country do not think of him as a jerk. He made many of them very rich. In any case, Oumou defied her father's wishes and refused the marriage, remarkable considering she was so young. Her father was upset. They say he made threats to cut her out of his will. She was unrelenting, claiming that she was not ready to marry anyone, even the President.

"What did she think of OIL?"

"What do you mean *oil*?" Sacco had never heard his glorious leader referred to that way, even though newspaper headlines occasionally used the three letters

"Monsieur Le President, Oumar Ibrahim Lassoso, O-I-L," she answered with sarcasm.

"As far as I know, she didn't care one way or the other. He was to her just an old man who often had his picture in the paper, who her father constantly praised, and who was entirely too friendly to her with hugs and kisses.."

"How did her father let Lassoso know of the rejection?"

"I don't know. What I do know is that her father had to pay much higher customs duties. Fortunate for him, he was already rich with most of his money in Switzerland. He was never again invited to the Presidential Palace."

"And Oumou?"

"She left Donolu and went to university in Dakar. She did very well there, became known to your United States Information Service, and was offered a scholarship for a year at Johns Hopkins. She did so well that the University offered her the resources to get a PhD. She did a thesis on the crimes of Mobutu in Zaire. She wrote about what everybody knew but was reluctant to document, that Mobuto and his cabinet were putting most of the USAID money into their own Swiss accounts. Parts of it were published in a European foreign affairs journal."

"And, I assume, that's how she recognized the problems here - that Lassoso and Mobutu were birds of a feather?"

"What do you mean?"

"That they were the same."

"Of course. She obviously had to keep that quiet or she would never have been allowed to return. OIL, as you call him, was delusional enough to think, even seven years after being told no, that this beautiful girl, now educated, might still marry him."

"*That's amore!*" Bernadette said, immediately thinking, "Why did I say that?" Sacco let it pass, having no clue what she meant.

"Then what happened?" she chimed in hoping to make amends for her idiotic statement.

"Oumou came home to Donolu to work in her father's business, which was doing well in spite of being one of the few importers paying full fare. She also taught one course at the university and started talking to students about democracy and began organizing the PPD."

"And when did Lassoso find out about that?"

"I hear that one of the President's security people infiltrated the PPD."

"Why didn't OIL just arrest her? He certainly has done that and worse in the past."

"He did put two or three of her fellow party members in jail, all male, even though there are very few men in the party. As to Oumou, he was not about to start arresting women, and more importantly, he still longed for her."

"That's an amazing story, Suleiman. I had no idea. Any time that I have talked to her she has said that she was a democrat in an autocracy, not someone who had rejected the marital offers of the Chief of State. How about another Coke?"

"OK." She was now on her second beer and the combination of the alcohol, the hot sun and the fascinating revelations had significantly altered her sensorium. As she handed him the Coke, she sat next to him on his boulder, having moved from her smaller but smoother one a few feet away. As there was only a small saddle of indented granite on which to put one's bottom, two bottoms were a tight fit and hips met. Neither said anything nor moved for several minutes. They both stared at the slow moving Begoro and the dugout pirogues fishing a kilometer or more down river. Bernadette recalled the way she felt the first time she was at the movies with her thirteen-year-old boyfriend. What seemed like an eternity later, he took her hand in his; she provoked the intertwining of fingers. Suleiman, eons afterwards, turned to her and kissed her, this time not once on the right cheek and twice on the left, but very centrally, on her lips. Centuries later, he slowly and gently unbuttoned her blouse, her main thought being that no one had ever done it so skillfully before.

During both of her orgasms she spoke, not quietly, not loudly, the two words that she always utters in similar situations, "Oh, shit." She had violated the promise that she had made to herself less than an hour before.

V

Bernadette recalled nothing of the drive back from the baobab forest to the Texaco station, to her home in Donolu. The final part of the tête-à-tête forced into the deeper reaches of her memory the incredible information that she had learned before they went from two boulders to one. As she had not made love to a man in ages, she felt a strong sense of physical and emotional gratification. As she had never been made love to by a black man, she experienced a mixture of sensations including liberal satisfaction that she had been so open to a member of an oppressed race, guilt because of what her parents would think, and anxiety because she knew that once would not be enough.

She recognized immediately the ramifications both for her psyche and her job. She knew that sleepless nights lay ahead. She did not know what she would do about work. Who could she tell and what could she tell them? She had no real confidants.

Ernestine Grant was someone she enjoyed talking to, particularly on political and women's issues, but there was no way she could talk to her about sex with the General. Judy Ann Deane, the Ambassador's secretary, would bring Jesus into the picture, a confusion that Dette was not prepared to confront. Dr. Eisenstat's wife Jill had become a good friend. The Eisenstats often had her to dinner and were part of her tennis foursome. But Jill was too much like a mother; there were sixteen years between the two. Finally, she decided on the doctor himself - have a problem, see a doctor, especially when he's free of charge. She borrowed her next-door neighbor's phone.

"Mike, its Bernadette. I need to see you."

"How about in the office tomorrow? We have the Saudi Ambassador and the Singhs over for dinner." Ulysses Singh was the Deputy Country Director of Peace Corps. The Eisenstats were constantly having guests for dinner, trying to match unlikely people to make for scintillating evenings about which they could write their friends and relatives in

Beverly Hills. An Arab bigwig and a Sikh were going to make for a great letter.

"I'm really sorry but I need to see you tonight. It's very important."

When an individual calls his or her physician insisting on an immediate visit, but does not say something like, "I am having chest pain," or "I am bleeding," or "I have a high fever," it has something to do with sex or violations of the law or both. Michael liked Bernadette a lot and he liked getting involved in matters of great sensitivity. "Let me finish my profiteroles and sauterne and I'll meet you at the clinic in 45 minutes."

When he pulled up to the Embassy gate, he could see that her Toyota had arrived immediately before. He waited his turn patiently as the guard opened first her, then his hood and trunk, and used his long-handled mirror to check under the chassis, all to rule out the unlikely possibility of an explosive device being unknowingly carried onto US Government property. Zinanians did not have bombing as part of their culture, although one could not be positive that employees of other embassies like the Libyans or Iranians did not have some way of booby-trapping official American vehicles. The heavy steel blockade with its massive gates creaked open slowly. The Marine Security Guard, standing behind an inch of bulletproof glass, welcomed them. He seemed not at all interested in why the two of them should show up together at this hour, with her not looking sick or wounded.

The doctor's clinic was on the second floor of the Chancery, a story beneath that which housed the offices of all the sensitive officers of the institution like the Ambassador and DCM, the Political and Economic Sections and the CIA Station. Lesser luminaries like Budget and Finance (B&F) and General Service (GSO), the people who made sure that everything at the Embassy and in the diplomats' houses worked well were also located on the second floor.

Michael's office bore no resemblance to the high rent high-rise on Wilshire Boulevard that served his practice for nearly two decades. Every two years since the establishment of relations between the Americans and Zinanians in 1960, there had been a new American physician on the second floor. Each doc had his own favorite books and equipment without which he feared he wouldn't be able to save lives. The finance office and the Ambassador would never prevent the doctor from buying whatever he wanted, so lots of new stuff was brought in and none was ever moved out. The Health Unit grew gradually, mainly to store the stuff that the outgoing doc left behind. When Michael arrived in country, he found among other things a Smithsonian-vintage EKG machine, enough expired IV fluids to refloat a Begoro River boat, long-expired pills that had been proved not only ineffective but unsafe ten years earlier, adequate plaster for casting all of the broken bones in West Africa for a generation, and a complete embalming kit.

Lots of money was spent on drugs and supplies; almost none was spent on interior design. Rattan furniture, dangerously splintery, served the rare patient who had to wait to see the doc or the nurse. Rust was the primary color of the previously gray metal receptionist desk and file cabinets. Wall decoration consisted mainly of terrifying posters advising people how to avoid such scourges of mankind as AIDS, herpes, and emphysema. Alcoholics Anonymous had generously displayed its literature, not an inappropriate addition for the members of the diplomatic profession that had more than its share of alcohol abusers.

Eisenstat's consultation room was not likely to end up in *Architectural Digest*. One large room served for both consultations and examinations. A small metal desk and bookcase, a cheap desk lamp, a chest to store and display instruments for looking in a variety of orifices, and a rickety old wooden examining table, with stirrups for pelvic exams, were the sum total of furniture. A tattered curtain was available to pull around the table when a female patient was changing into a Government Issue paper gown. He had covered some wall space with Californiana, such as Hollywood movie posters, and photos of gray whales and the Golden Gate Bridge.

"So, what's the problem, Ms. O'Kelly?" He called her that not out of formality but a reverse informality.

"I fucked the General." No beating around the bush for this political officer.

Michael, unaccustomed to hearing such expositions from his patients, squirmed in his wooden, cushionless captain's chair. "Oh," he responded nonchalantly, "what General?"

"General Sacco, Suleiman Sacco."

"You mean the guy who runs the Palace Guard?" In his attempts to learn French, Michael read the daily paper and was reasonably knowledgeable about the military.

"Right."

"Is he married?" A stupid question because he couldn't think of any non-stupid ones.

"No."

"What happened?" A good question, taking him off the hook for the ten or fifteen minutes that it took her to talk about Texaco, baobabs, boulders, and blouses.

Prior to the Foreign Service, Michael dealt almost exclusively with patients with high blood pressure, diabetes, obesity, arthritis and the like. The heart and the blood vessels were his main bailiwick. If one of his heart patients happened to have a bladder infection she would be referred to the urologist two floors down. A splinter would require a surgeon. Fucking the General would clearly have engendered a stat call to the psychiatrist. The nation of Zinani had one psychiatrist who spoke no English, had no phone, saw no private patients, and was a cousin of General Sacco. Eisenstat had no place to refer; he was now a general practitioner.

"And how do you feel about it now?" He remembered from psychiatry rotation at medical school to ask about feelings.

"I feel great. I enjoyed every sweaty minute of it and hope it happens again ... and again." Not the answer the doctor wanted to hear. He wanted guilt; that was easier to deal with. Between a Catholic patient and Jewish doctor, both had ample knowledge of the guilt-ridden condition.

"That's too bad. It would certainly be more diplomatic if you could just write it off to experience and make it a one-time deal."

"True."

"Can you do it, Dette? Can you say, 'Thanks a lot but it's over?'"

"Probably not. I really like the guy and I sure liked the screwing for a change." Eisenstat squirmed a bit more.

"I presume you used a condom?"

"Jesus Christ! I hadn't even thought of that. Hell no, we didn't use a condom. I had had two beers and it never came to my mind ... but not

30

to worry. He hasn't been with a woman for years. AIDS isn't a concern."

"Bernadette O'Kelly, for a smart person you are unbelievably dumb. First, you're in Africa for god's sake. AIDS is everywhere. Yeah, even in Donolu. Second, you can't buy everything the guy says, even if he is Mr. Wonderful. Tell me that he's giving you the straight scoop when he says he hasn't been with a woman since his wife died. How many men do you know who could do that? Somewhere near zero I would guess. Second, HIV is not the only thing we wear condoms against. Herpes maybe? Gonorrhea or syphilis? Maybe babies? You ready to have a little mixed-race infant to lug around from post to post, or an abortion perhaps?"

Bernadette sat expressionless except for the glisten that appeared in the whites of her eyes. Two silent minutes later, she spoke softly. "Michael, I was stupid, but it's going to be OK. I really believe he doesn't have any diseases and my period just got over a few days ago. But next time, I'll be safe. I promise."

The doctor shook his head in dismay. "There is nothing I can do to either reassure you or talk you out of continuing it. I can ask that you look at all the ramifications of the relationship, not only as it affects you, but how it would be seen by the Ambassador, the Zin government and even by Washington, should it ever become public, and you know it will."

"I have thought about all that and it does scare me."

"So?"

"I don't know. I know that I will have to talk to the Ambassador, at least to tell him some things that I have learned from Suleiman. But I don't see how I can stop seeing him."

"And what did you learn from him?" asked the doctor with a wry grin.

"Cut it out, you lecher." Her tears were drying and she had forced a miniscule smile.

Michael Eisenstat became father-like. "Bernadette, you are a good friend and a respected colleague. Both Jill and I feel very close to you. I am really worried about you. I know that it feels good now and probably will continue to for a while, but I cannot imagine that it will not eventually cause you, and him, a great deal of pain. Be careful, will ya?"

"I love you guys and god knows, I respect your opinion. I wouldn't have taken you from the profiteroles and the potentate if I didn't. I know that the relationship is brand new and I've let the stars get in my eyes. I don't know if you have been overwhelmed by the feelings of new love, but it isn't easy to let go of."

Michael recalled the days of his "open marriage" and its occasional moments of incredible teenage-like euphoria and mumbled a noncommittal, "Uh-huh." He stood up as a sign that the discussion would not go further tonight and when she followed suit, he gave her a bear hug and then a kiss on the same cheek that Sacco had originally kissed twice.

The car with the Saudi ambassadorial flag on its front fender was gone by the time he reached home. He hoped that Jill would be able to embellish the letter home with fascinating African/American/Arab trivia. That letter would have contained nothing about what he just learned, in spite of the fact that most of his doctor friends in Southern California would have drooled over that kind of stuff.

Ambassador Holden Fairchild III was part of a dying breed, that of the old school diplomat. He was a graduate of Princeton, Class of '50, where he majored in Politics, and was a member of the Ivy Club, when that had some significance. He attended graduate school at both Harvard and Johns Hopkins, completing a PhD in African Affairs at the latter in 1957. After passing the Foreign Service Examination on the first try, he did well on the oral interviews, (administered by Yale '42 and Dartmouth '48,) and found himself posted to Guatemala City as a consular officer. Tours of duty in political jobs in Upper Volta, Senegal, Hungary, Laos, and Malawi, two years each, with stints in the unfriendly halls of the Mother House in Foggy Bottom, dotted his CV. Prior to getting an ambassadorial nod, he was Deputy Chief of Mission in Bamako, Mali. There he spent much of his time running the show as Chargé d'Affaires while the Ambassador (Cornell '41) was home taking care of his dying wife (Wellesley '41).

"Holly," as he was called in the bedroom by his wife, and behind his back by his staff, had hoped for a more significant post for his Ambassadorship than Zinani. He had taken the Bamako job, considered a burden, not a plum, with a promise of Pretoria, South Africa, to follow. Shortly before the White House sent his name to the Senate, a pizza baron who had joined the "Give a High-Five to the President!" Club by contributing half a million to the reelection campaign, suggested that a couple of years in South Africa might be the perfect thing for his wife's budding textile import business and his golf game. Fairchild was left with a choice of Bissau in Guinea-Bissau and Donolu. He couldn't speak Portuguese and thought he was too old to learn it, so that left French-speaking Zinani.

Three months and a half-hearted grilling by the Senate Foreign Relations committee later, he landed at Keita-Coulibaly International Airport on one of the twice-weekly Air Afrique flights from Charles de Gaulle. He had the great misfortune of following in the footsteps of the legendary M. Turner Fredrickson, Jr. (Brown '48), uniquely popular, eminently effective, and now the Deputy Assistant Secretary for West African Affairs. Fredrickson made regular trips around the region, including biannual stops in Donolu that undermined his successor's credibility and diminished his self-confidence.

Marylou Fairchild (Rider College, Trenton, New Jersey, five years, no degree), Mrs. Ambassador, was perceived by most as the wearer of the family pants. When young Holden entered his senior year at Princeton, he, like many of his classmates in those years of the Silent Generation, was still a virgin. Marylou, only two months younger than Holden, had lost that status at 15 and by the age of 21 had developed quite a repertoire. Marylou wisely offered up her basket of goodies in a way that made Holly feel that he was the conquistador. Their first carnal episode led to pregnancy, so they married. Statistically the chance of a good result with this beginning wasn't great, but they beat the odds. Holly and Marylou had been married 31 years, and had raised two children (Ralph, Princeton, '88, now assistant Head Master at a prep school in Connecticut and Holden IV, Staff Sergeant, US Army), who gave them four grandchildren.

To say that Fairchild's career was illustrious would be an overstatement. It was workmanlike. He had been a good political officer. His expert glad-handing and backslapping guided him up the ladder of success, with progressively more interesting jobs of greater and greater responsibility. No one ever accused him of being innovative. Nonetheless, he knew that he would be an Ambassador someday; all Ivy Leaguers knew that. He accepted the Zinani assignment, recognizing that declining would close the door on getting the name he sought -- Mr. Ambassador. Once he was so titled, they could never take it away from him. It was like Judge or Senator; give it to someone for a day, it's his or hers for life. He assumed that the assignment would be one of a figurehead -- lots of receptions, golf tournaments, and visits to exotic tribal villages. But real politics --no way. Zinani had been a stable dictatorship for more than two decades. They always voted the American way in the UN, except on the more contentious Arab/Israel issues when they sided with their coreligionists. The tour of duty was surely going to be a no-brainer.

"Bernadette O'Kelly wants to see both you and the DCM this morning," announced Judy Ann Deane, Ambassadorial Secretary, when Fairchild arrived at 10 AM. He often came in late, figuring that his cocktail partying qualified as work and that he could therefore compensate himself. Plus, Marylou had decided that he was killing himself with inactivity and made him accompany her and the Boston terrier on a one-hour walk, along the polluted riverbank and open sewers each morning.

He was surprised by the second request for an audience by his bright young political officer in a week, but remembering the surprising information of the last visit, quickly asked that she be brought in.

As drab as the doctor's office was, the Ambassador's was that elegant. Decisions about expenditures for furnishing and redecorating were the task of the Administrative Officer. Neither Conrad Prudholme nor his predecessors were anxious to tell an Ambassador that he or she did not need new Chinese and antique Persian rugs, new Henredon couches or new Stifle lamps; they merely cut back on washers and dryers in the houses of the communication specialists and secretaries.

The room was the length of a bowling alley but no wider than four or five lanes. Two electricity-guzzling air conditioners kept the occupant comfortable and the visitors chilly. His walls were lined with Princeton memorabilia like pictures of old grads from Aaron Burr and James

Madison to Bill Bradley and Ralph Nader, as well as the usual collection of the second-rate work of third-rate artists and artisans of countries in which he had previously served. Forty-watt bulbs were screwed into all the fixtures, a tidbit thrown to Administrative Officer Prudholme's energy conservation program. Chen Wang once brought a flashlight into a meeting to protest the darkness.

"Something big, Bernadette?" asked Fairchild.

"Yes sir. I had a meeting with General Sacco."

"Again? Where, in his office or yours?"

"He thought that it was too public to go to either of those so we drove out of town."

"Where?" asked Ms. Grant, a stickler for detail.

"Oh, someplace along the Big, toward New Akron." Not wanting to get questions requiring other extraneous details, she continued, "He told me some most surprising information about President Lassoso and Oumou Kinsa." She proceeded to relay the news about the proposals and the rejections.

The DCM was the first to speak up, "Incredible. I'd never heard a word of a connection between the two."

"Neither had I," responded Dette.

"The most bothersome part of this is that a man scorned is a man unpredictable," said Grant. "He may get really tough on the PPD because of it, or, then again, he might take it easy on them because he has a thing for her."

"I couldn't agree more, Ernie ... er, Ernestine."

Grant continued, "Don't let on to Oumou that you know any of this and, in fact, cut down on your contacts with the PPD. This can of worms is too big. "

"You got that right," chimed in the Ambassador.

"Did you learn anything else, Bernadette? Anything else to report?" asked the DCM.

"No, nothing," responded the love struck O'Kelly, lying through her teeth.

VI

Doctor Michael Eisenstat, prior to his days in the diplomatic corps, spent 18 years as an internist in Beverly Hills. He had been educated both as an undergraduate and medical student at UCLA. The son of a famous cardiologist at that med school, he finally tired of being known as the Professor's kid, left his practice to his younger brother, and sought a second career that would combine medicine and travel. The State Department seemed just right, so he brought the idea home to his wife, Jill.

"Great idea," she said. "Tell them that you want to go to London."

That's not how it worked. Getting a job as Regional Medical Officer involved surmounting multiple bureaucratic hurdles. Several doctors and administrators interviewed Michael to determine whether he had the skills and temperament for a job different from that of the usual American physician and very different from that of a Beverly Hills internist. Both husband and wife underwent medical exams to prove that they were healthy enough for assignments in any country in the world; no asthmatics were acceptable for Bolivia nor were HIV-positive patients offered a position in Saudi Arabia. A provisional offer was made. They then needed security clearance to prove that neither was a spy, a felon, or an addict; friends, neighbors, colleagues, and relatives were interviewed and all gave them high marks. He, and they, were pleased to learn that toking of a few marijuana joints years before was not a reason for exclusion.

Ten months after having told his patients and staff that he might be leaving, he was on his way, not to England, but Zinani. While they had an awareness of the country from rare mentions in newspapers and on TV, neither knew anything of consequence, not even the name of its capital.

Jill, a Chicago native, Stanford graduate, and burned-out hawker of high-ticket medical devices, was ready to get out of Southern California.

36

Their two kids were both in college and only came home for holidays. She was not terribly disturbed to learn of the absurdity of her request to be stationed in London, as she was reasonably fluent in French and had a soupçon of knowledge of Francophone Africa. From application to acceptance, to pack-out and departure, a mere six months, they were Donolu bound.

Oumar Ibrahim Lassoso General Hospital (LGH) sits in the center of downtown Donolu, between the French Embassy and the Foreign Ministry. The Health Ministry, which the hospital must consult every time it wants to buy anything more costly than a tongue blade, stands on the hill near the Palace. Driving by the LGH, one would not mistake it for the Mayo Clinic. Like the rest of the capital, no building is more than two stories in height. The structures were built by the French in the early part of the twentieth century and appear to be still sound. The entire complex covers some five acres and includes eight separate buildings, only two of which house patients, the remainder being the kitchen, laboratory, X-ray, pharmacy, etc.

Lassoso is the major general hospital in the country and, because of its location, treats most of the acute illnesses and accidents in this infection and trauma-plagued capital. The metropolitan region boasts two other hospitals, one associated with the nation's sole medical school, where the AIDS, TB, and psychiatry patients are treated, and a second one several kilometers out of town that caters to the wealthy and well connected. Throughout the rest of Zinani, a patient has only a slightly greater chance of getting a Band-Aid than he does a CAT scan.

The Soviet Union had adopted Lassoso hospital in the mid-sixties in its attempt to collect chits to be called in for crucial UN votes. At the height of the cooperative effort, twenty-five Soviet citizens, including fifteen physicians, served in professional capacities at the institution. The Chinese responded in kind by sending several doctors, including two acupuncturists, to the rich man's hospital out of town. The French, with ten professors and support staff, continued to play a role at the Medical School they had founded well before independence. Aside from Dr. Eisenstat, there was no American, nor other English-speaking doctor, within two hundred miles of Donolu.

In early 1992, the Soviet medical contingent left Lassoso Hospital and Zinani on a midnight Aeroflot flight with no advance warning. They had conceded the Cold War and saw no reason to continue spending rubles in Africa. Patients were left without doctors or nurses, interns and residents were left without instructors, and hospital administration was left with nothing. What was left was a rag-tag collection of equipment from East Germany, Czechoslovakia, and the Soviet Union, all without spare parts or anyone who knew anything about maintaining or fixing them. Within weeks, the facility had ground to a near high-tech halt. X-rays could not be taken, nor lab tests run. The few air conditioning units had broken down. The operating room lamp was often replaced by a gooseneck, with a flashlight as secondary back up. Sterilization was not a functional concept.

A motorcyclist hit Michelle Graham, the six-year-old granddaughter of AID Director Garson Graham, two months after the Russians left. She was visiting her grandparents for the summer while her parents climbed Mt. Kilimanjaro. The house nanny was taking her to the *Grand Marché* to buy material for a new dress, when a small Honda loaded with firewood lost control turning a corner and hit the 50 pound child head on. She lay motionless. In Donolu one cannot call an ambulance. There are no phones. There are no ambulances, except an old Peugeot that had been purloined by the Chief of Surgery for his personal use. The nanny found a taxi driver willing to accept the fare after getting advance payment, and transported them the ten blocks to Lassoso General.

An iron gate blocked the entrance into what was called the emergency room. An old man stood guard against entry by anyone without a stethoscope and a white coat. Dozens of bedraggled citizens pleaded with him to let them in to see their injured or sick relatives; they were rebuffed. At first he turned away the white child and black woman, but the nanny convinced a young intern to open the gate.

The emergency room was hellish. The narrow halls were filthy, with discarded food, papers, and insects, both flying and crawling. In spite of the 105-degree day, the ceiling fan hung motionless. The emergency ward had a series of rooms meant for two patients each. Most were filled beyond capacity, primarily with Zinanians appearing either moribund or not sick at all. A room was set aside for nurses; it was filthier than the rest. Several women with white smocks sat silently, not smoking, not reading, not talking, not moving. There was no apparent connection between these nurses and those who would be their patients.

In spite of her comatose status and ethnicity, Michelle's arrival initially did little to stimulate activity. She was deposited in the hall where she continued to bleed slowly and breath rapidly. The nanny began yelling but not until she shouted the word *tubab*, white person, did anyone move in her direction. The realization that they had of a Caucasian child in distress finally produced the on-call provider, a young man, barely 20, and a student of the local medical school, plus two of the previously immobile nurses.

Michelle was wheeled into what was generously called the "treatment room." An emergency room physician's main responsibility is to be able to differentiate sick from not sick. Even the youthful trainee was able to make the call in this case; he immediately sent for the surgeon, who had both a phone and transportation, the purloined ambulance. In the meantime, an IV was started and a sample was sent to the blood bank to prepare for a blood transfusion.

No one had done anything about notifying Michelle's grandparents. Neither the nanny nor any hospital employee had the presence of mind to track them down. A witness to the accident at the *marché* had initiated a chain of conversations that finally led to the question being asked of Garson Graham, "Why, Sir, are you not at the hospital?" He quickly learned of the event, called his wife Millie, grabbed Dr. Eisenstat, and sped to Lassoso General.

By the time they arrived, Michelle was in what served as the operating room. It was a dark, dingy, unscrubbed, partially tiled square space with a creaky old hand-operated table, a nonfunctional ceiling light with a gooseneck replacement, and a chair for the anesthesiologist. A nurse anesthetist squeezed a black rubber breathing bag fifteen times per minute to substitute for the Russian anesthetic machine that sat inoperative in a storage closet. Nothing prevented the family from marching into the operating room in street clothes; the operating team doing the exploratory abdominal surgery never looked up or acknowledged their presence.

As horrific as the entire event was, the most frightening sight for the grandparents was a plastic bag of blood dripping into an IV tube attached to the right arm of their granddaughter.

"My God, you are giving her AIDS!" screamed Millie to a room of people who spoke no English.

Thanks to the Moslem mores, Donolu has a lower HIV prevalence than many of its African neighbors, but higher than that of any American city. Screening for the disease was done on the donated blood but "mistakes" were made. Hepatitis B, a viral illness much more likely to be transferred by transfusion than HIV, was not even screened for.

Michael Eisenstat spoke some medical French and was able to express Mrs. Graham's concern to the surgeon.

"He said that he has no option; Michelle was bleeding to death from the ruptured spleen he discovered when he opened her abdomen."

"But she'll get AIDS."

"She probably won't, but let's worry about that later. And let's get out of the OR and let the doctors take care of her. The surgeon is trained at one of the best hospitals in Paris. Let's let him do his job."

Michael remained in the OR while the Grahams stood in the unclean, unlighted, un-air-conditioned hall, where there was no place to sit. He knew the splenic rupture was only Michelle's second most important problem, as the removal of the broken organ was straightforward and curative. One can live normally without a spleen. Her major medical issue was her brain. Her coma, while not suggesting brain death, was deep, and the sign of major intracranial trauma. The total number of CAT or MRI scanners in Zinani was zero. The total number of neurosurgeons in Zinani was the same. In other words, there were no doctors to treat the diagnosis that could not be confirmed with equipment that didn't exist.

Michael passed the word to the parents in the hall.

"What can we do?" sobbed Millie.

"We can pray," answered Dr. Eisenstat who had not done so since his Bar Mitzvah. "And we can call for an airplane to get her out of this goddam continent."

SOS, the pre-eminent medical evacuation company serving West

Africa, was a phone call away ... in Geneva.

Dr. Eisenstat rushed to the Embassy, where he could make contact with Switzerland. An air ambulance was dispatched. Within twelve hours she was on her way to Paris, with a doctor, a nurse, blood, fluids, drugs, and machines on board.

An MRI diagnosed her with a brain contusion, not treatable by the surgeon's scalpel. Only time would tell whether she would live or die and what the long-term consequences might be. The bedside vigil began. Over eight weeks, she slowly regained her consciousness and mobility. But she was, even after a more impressive recovery than anyone had expected, not the Michelle of before, nor was she likely to be the Michelle of the future that everyone expected. She did get Hepatitis B, but not HIV, and will, for the rest of her life, be a carrier of that potentially cancer-causing virus, so tiny that only an electron microscope can see how ugly it is.

The experience of six-year-old Michelle Graham made Ambassador Fairchild decide that if he accomplished nothing else during his tenure in Zinani, he would help pull Lassoso General Hospital out of the medical dark ages. At the time he had no way of knowing that his decision would possibly lead to a phone call from the Foreign Minister ordering him and his mission to leave the country in 72 hours.

Eisenstat was not surprised when Judy Ann Deane called, asking him to come to the Ambassador's office, as such calls came regularly. Fairchild was both a hypochondriac and a self-styled student of medical science. He had developed a real fear of cholesterol and couldn't go for more than a month or two before requesting a blood test, being fearful that a diplomatic diet was a sure cause of heart attack and premature death. Any cholesterol result more than his usual 190 nearly brought him to tears. Attempts to reassure him were countered by a batch of articles from what few books and journals were avaiable. Michael gave serious consideration to purposefully disabling the apparatus that made the measurements, but ultimately decided otherwise, as it was the only one for several hundred miles.

"Doctor." Even though the two were confidants, Fairchild always used the title when they were on Embassy grounds, in great part because he wanted to make sure that he himself was addressed by his title. As he put it, "I like to be called by my given name: Mr. Ambassador."

"Doctor, we have a great opportunity."

"Oh, what, sir?"

"You know how I feel about the thing with the Graham child."

"Of course."

"As you know, the Army is closing bases in Europe because we won the Cold War. When bases close, so do hospitals. There will be a lot of disposable equipment and supplies. None of it'll be sent to the US or any other American facility 'cause American docs only want new stuff. The old will be declared excess and tossed out."

"Right," said the doctor, obligatorily.

"Well, there is no reason that we cannot get some of that stuff here and improve that fucking hospital. No way am I going to stand still and let the State Department send me any other diplomats, especially ones with kids, when the only hospital in town is more likely to kill you than cure you."

"Do you really think the Army would send any equipment here? Our hosts are not exactly popular in Washington," said Michael.

"I'm well aware of that," the tone of which made Eisenstat wish that he had limited his comment to a single word. "But if I sell it as a combination of a humanitarian gesture and a move to improve the health care for our people, it might fly."

"Maybe."

"I'll check with some people I know in Germany. In the meantime, you try and lay the groundwork in the Health Ministry."

VII

Less than two weeks later, Fairchild received a confidential cable from the European command of the US Army.

"Judy, please get Dr. Eisenstat down here. I have to show him this cable."

Michael was busy in the "Abattoir," the name he bestowed on his hideously ugly office. He was seeing his fifth strep throat of the week, had an athlete's foot in the reception room, as well as an impatient family of five waiting for government-mandated hepatitis A vaccinations. A call from the Ambassador requires an immediate response, delayable only if the doctor is in the midst of CPR, and then only if the cardiac arrest victim is someone the Chief of Mission deems worth resuscitating. A quick bottle of penicillin tablets was doled out to the strep throat, the Marine with the foot fungus was asked to wait or return, and the family was turned over to the nurse for their injections, much to their relief.

The doctor nearly always walked up or down the steps, not for the exercise, but because of a realistic fear of getting stuck in the elevator. Electricity in Zinani was notoriously unreliable with blackouts and brownouts experienced as near daily events. The Embassy has a backup generator that almost always worked, but it looked like something Robert Fulton designed and Dr. Eisenstat, accustomed to the luxurious Otis Elevators of his Wilshire office building, was not about to test his luck.

"Doctor, I received a cable from the Commander in charge of all of the medical care for our Army people in Europe, General Fimbri. She tells me that they are, as I predicted, going to close some hospitals and that they are looking for worthy recipients of their excess material. So far, we are the only ones that have put in a bid on the stuff. I'm sure we are going to get something."

"That's good news." The doctor, who was accustomed to answering his educated colleagues with EKG readings, oxygen saturation levels, and beta-blocker doses, had sunk to this type of inane, but essential response.

"What have you learned from the Health Ministry?"

"They are interested in getting whatever they can. They know that they are terribly underequipped. They will be appreciative of any help that we can offer. I get the opinion, however, that they've heard this song and dance before -- promises of stuff that either never comes or is of little value. What we cannot afford to do is send boxes of expired medicines, broken down electrical equipment without spare parts, or a bunch of bedpans and urinals that no Zinanian patient or nurse would have any idea how to use. What we need to bring in are things like hospital beds. At the General Hospital, patients are sharing beds, or lying on the floor, often times without mattresses. Chairs, filing cabinets, storage cabinets, desks, stethoscopes, and blood pressure cuffs -- those make sense -- few, if any, moving parts, and no such thing as obsolescence.

"The Minister sent around a memo to the heads of the departments of the hospital to find out what they want. I saw the results the other day. You'd think they were trying to restock the Mayo Clinic. No one mentioned beds or lamps. They asked for CT scanners, MRI's, radiation therapy units, and surgical instruments for operations like kidney transplants. Pretty unrealistic. Our overseas Army wouldn't have them and they wouldn't be able to plug them in and maintain them. Almost everything in our hospitals is 110 volts; their place is wired for 220."

"Michael, you know that we won't have much control over what comes or when it comes. Somehow we'll have to get the idea across to the Zins of mouths and gift horses.

"Incidentally, I have my monthly audience with President Lassoso this afternoon, and I'm planning to tell him about General Fimbri's cable. Care to go with me?"

"Sure."

"You'll have to go home and put on a suit."

Michael liked that he could usually wear a polo shirt to work, but a change into his blue seersucker suit was a small price to pay for the chance of entering Zinani's answer to the Oval Office. "I'm on my way."

The Ambassador's car was a Ford. Other Ambassadors, even in places like Donolu, were transported in Mercedes, Cadillacs, Lincolns, or Rolls-Royces. The Secretary of State had declared ostentation inappropriate and offered embassies Fords, Chevys, or Plymouths. When the Ambassador is in his car, a small version of Old Glory flies on the left fender. Protocol requires that the Ambassador sit on the right in the back (unless the car was right-hand drive.) Michael knew where to sit only because the Ambassador's driver, Bubacar, hopped smartly out of the front seat in his crisply pressed livery and opened the left rear door for him. Anisa, the Ambassador's half Zinanian, half Belgian, Vassar-trained interpreter, sat stunningly in the front passenger's seat. Michael was surprised to hear a Chuck Berry CD coming from the four speakers. *Roll over, Beethoven.*

There was no conversation on the short trip to the Executive Office. The Ambassador tapped his foot and patted his knee to the cadence of the rock and roll, while glancing at the list of talking points made up for him by his political and economic officers. Fairchild looked like the prototypic Ambassador should look. His full head of white hair was recently trimmed and neatly in place. The bifocals had real horn rims - no plastic for Marylou. The lightweight gray pinstriped suit was a custom job. The impeccably pressed white shirt had no buttons on the collar. The silk tie sported the Princeton Ivy Club stripe; he ordered a new one every couple of years. The outfit was bottomed off with black wingtips, scuff-free. Michael felt dumpy next to this splendor. His suit had cost $49.95 at an outlet (he had stored his more expensive ones when he left the USA) and his shoes had lots of scuffs. UCLA didn't have club ties.

The Executive Office was in a heavily fortified part of town. OIL reportedly was always concerned about a coup d'état and demanded strong military security. The Ford and its passengers passed three checkpoints where the flag on the fender gave them instant access. The soldiers, each of whom packed an automatic weapon, looked frighteningly young. More than once, an expatriate had mistakenly driven where he shouldn't have and died in a barrage of bullets, with apologies later being sent to and accepted by the appropriate embassy.

The building itself was not impressive. French colonial in style, it was two stories high, with a broad, covered portico on the second floor.

From there, the President-for-life could make pronouncements to the masses, when the budget could afford the gasoline to bus them in. Like most every building in West Africa, it needed a paint job. The surrounding flora reminded no one of Versailles.

The three visitors were welcomed at the door by Lassoso's executive assistant, a short bald white man with a Fu Manchu moustache. Although the Ambassador spoke excellent French after several tours in Francophone countries, he followed protocol, allowing the formalities with both the assistant and the President to go through his interpreter Anisa. Even at the Presidential level, the initial conversation stressed the health of the family members of each participant, with the answers having little basis in truth.

Lassoso's office was large but not grandiose. Expensive carpets lay on the floor, gifts from other Islamic nations. In the faux-French chandelier, only half of the bulbs were alight. The desk was oak, obviously imported from afar, and the black Presidential swivel chair was raised to its highest notch, making OIL look taller than he was. A tan leather sofa and matching chairs served as seating for both toadies and dignitaries. Most striking was the picture gallery on the walls. Hundreds of photographs, both black and white and color were hung, in no apparent order. Without exception, all contained the President himself; the great majority featured one or more subjects, many of whom Eisenstat could not recognize. Presidents Reagan, Bush, and Carter were there. So were Gorbachev, Mitterrand, Deng, Suharto, Mobutu, Mugabe, Arafat, Gaddafi, and Saddam Hussein. Muhammad Ali had obviously stopped by. So had Barbra Streisand, Mother Theresa, and Hillary Clinton. Madam Lassoso was pictured in many of them, often with the wives of luminaries; she and Imelda Marcos made a striking contrast in color prints. Behind his chair was the largest photo, a near life-sized black and white one of himself, in Arabic mufti, atop a camel, with a single baobab tree in the background.

OIL reminded Michael of Fidel Castro. They both sported fatigues and smoked cigars. The demeanor of the Zinanian was much like that of the oft-televised Cuban. They shared haughtiness, self-righteousness, and an overblown sense of self-worth. The body language of each said, "I know that I am right. You are probably wrong. Try to convince me that we are both right."

"Let us speak in English today, Mr. Ambassador." Lassoso spoke it well but had not previously done so with Fairchild. Anisa was disappointed. Dr. Eisenstat was delighted. His French was passable in the operating room, not so outside of it.

"Very well, Mr. President. Congratulations on your recent celebration once again and thank you for the splendid reception. All of the Americans that went had a wonderful time."

"Even Miss O'Kelly?"

"Yes, of course. Why do you ask?"

"I may have been a little abrupt with her. Did she not say anything to you?"

"No, she only said how much she enjoyed the event." A diplomatic white lie.

"I am sure that Miss O'Kelly is a fine officer in your Embassy, but sometimes she may be a bit more aggressive, shall we say, than she should be."

"I understand, Mr. President. I shall talk to her."

Dr. Eisenstat, of course, knew about Bernadette's encounter with the General. He was unaware of the encounter in the receiving line.

Anisa, who considered Bernadette a special friend, had absolutely no idea what the discussion was about. She was worried.

The Ambassador changed the subject quickly. He had received instructions to make a very definitive request to the President regarding a desired NO vote in the UN. No penalties for voting the wrong way were made explicit, but the nature of the demarche made it clear that a YES would not be looked on favorably. Lassoso's response to the entreaty from Washington was simply an undecipherable nod of his head.

The mood in the room had quickly changed and the Ambassador was feeling more relaxed. He brought up commercial issues, asking for favorable responses to the requests of Burger King and other US enterprises. He petitioned for more humane treatment of the tiny Berber community in the North, and asked the President to look into the reasons for the unpleasant treatment Americans were getting as they came into the country by plane or car.

"I have asked Dr. Eisenstat to join me in this meeting to talk about some ideas that he and I have to help you, shall we say, modernize Lassoso Hospital."

"I know we have fallen behind the times. Quite frankly, and I would ask you not to repeat this, I wouldn't go to that hospital myself, even with my name on the door and my picture in the entry hall. When any member of my family gets sick, we go to Paris or even New York. What can you do to help us?"

"Dr. Eisenstat would be better able to answer that than I."

"Eisenstat ... isn't that a Jewish name?"

"Yes, Sir, it is."

"We used to be very close with Israel, until 1967. That so-called Six Day War changed everything. We had to shut down their Embassy here and ours there. Sadly, some of our most useful advisors left then. They were excellent in training our military, both the pilots and the infantry. Also, they were of great assistance in our irrigation and power development. I never felt anger toward Israel and hope that we can eventually reestablish diplomatic ties."

The words were fine but Michael was disturbed that the connection had been made in the mind of this unpredictable leader. "I agree, Sir," he said, as if what he said on the subject had importance. He looked toward the Ambassador who gave him a nod of approval and a second nod suggesting he discuss the matter at hand.

"Mr. President, as you know the Cold War between the Soviets and the USA is over and our President has begun cutting back on our military presence in Europe. With fewer American troops, there is less need for military hospitals and therefore some of them will be decommissioned. There is a great deal of hospital equipment that will no longer be needed for our personnel. It is likely that the President will allow a distribution of some of that equipment to places where it will be of use.

"Ambassador Fairchild has contacted General Fimbri who will likely be responsible for the distribution if it happens. She cabled him this week that she might well look favorably on a request from Zinani."

"We would, of course, be most pleased with such help," responded the President with a gratified look. My wife had surgery at your

Columbia-Presbyterian Hospital in New York three years ago and we developed a great respect for the level of hospital care in your country. As we are so poor, our hospital, which the people kindly named after me, has none of the modern equipment needed for even basic care." This expression of poverty came from a man who owned a fleet of luxury cars and a private airplane.

Both the Ambassador and the doctor were concerned by the mention of Columbia-Presbyterian and its suggestion that similar quality gear would be on its way to Donolu.

"Please be aware, your honor, that military hospitals are not the same as large private urban medical centers. The comfort and safety of our troops, while important, is achieved less lavishly than that of private patients in New York. In addition, we do not know what exact equipment, if any, will be available as part of the process. It is likely to be beds, desks, and other less sophisticated equipment."

"We have very sophisticated doctors in Donolu, especially at Lassoso hospital. Most of them have been trained in Europe and a few have gone to your country. I know that they would be able to take advantage of whatever you send."

"I understand that, Your Excellency."

"When will our new equipment arrive?"

Michael was concerned both about the question and its inclusion of the word "new." "Sir, I can't answer that yet. As we mentioned, it is still just an idea. Much depends on Washington and Headquarters in Germany, as well as the requests of other developing countries."

"Please keep me informed through my Health Minister, Mr. Coulibaly. By the way, Dr. Eisenstat, did you know General Moshe Dayan?"

"No sir, I did not have the pleasure." He was stunned by the fact that this national leader would think that all Jews would know one another.

"General Dayan and I were close friends. Too bad about that nasty little Yom Kippur war." A quick perusal of the pictures on the wall revealed no one with a patch over his eye.

The half hour allotted to the American visit concluded with niceties including wishes of good fortune for the various wives and children. The mustachioed Caucasian who walked them in, walked them out. He had never introduced himself. The music on the way home was of a different genre from the earlier Chuck Berry rock – the Grand March from Aida.

VIII

The Ambassador called his political officer into his office. "Bernadette, this has become a big deal. The President brought up your name during our monthly visit yesterday. He described you as aggressive. In fact, he said 'too aggressive.' That's not something we like to hear."

"Did he mention General Sacco or Oumou Kinsa?"

"No, just you."

"Any advice, Mr. Ambassador?"

"Not really. Just like the other day, I suggest you lie low for a bit. You sure that there is nothing that you are not telling me about either Oumou or Sacco?" Fairchild was fishing; he wondered whether O'Kelly might be lesbian.

"No sir, nothing to report.

There was plenty to report. It wasn't reported.

Several days had passed since the magic moments in the baobab forest. There had been no further contact between the General and the Officer. She hoped he would make the first call. She stayed in her office during working hours so as not to miss him. She declined dinner invitations on the chance that there would be another visit, with or without the nephew. Not a word.

Dette had never visited Sacco's home. He resided with his extended family in a moderately upmarket concession -- a group of interconnected freestanding buildings, often of only one room, accommodating different branches of the family. She had driven by his house twice on the hope that she would find him or Nisso walking outside the walls. No luck.

Finally, she decided to try to find him at home, after work but before sunset. Zinanian weekends start mid-day Friday and end Sunday

51

morning; Friday afternoons are meant for prayer. Like Sunday mornings in the US, most do not use the time for religion. While she knew Sacco to be an avowed Muslim, she was aware that he rarely attended mosque. Bernadette opted to make her foray on Friday. She left work an hour early, justifying it by mentally counting the number of hours of overtime she'd spent uncompensated in the past pay-period. A quick shower and shampoo and a change into a less drab outfit than the beige dress she had worn to work made her feel just a bit more appealing.

His neighborhood was upscale, but did not compare to the collection of villas populated by high government officials, successful merchants, and foreign diplomats. The neighborhood roads were unpaved and deeply rutted, true of most all of the streets in the capital. There was electricity and plumbing. Most roofs sported antennae or dishes. The modest single-story whitewashed houses, usually of concrete building blocks, sat right on the street as Zinani lacked sidewalks.

As Dette drove by for the first time, she saw the General's rusty Peugeot. Cautiously but excitedly, she parked the Toyota behind it.

The concession had no front door. Instead, an opening in the front wall allowed direct access into a courtyard where a bevy of toddlers were frolicking with a soccer ball. Scattered about were several chairs of rusty metal and colorful rubber tubing, plus a series of plastic pots containing a variety of tropical plants. A chocolate-colored dog, the size of a Dalmatian, greeted her with a burst of yapping and a thorough sniffing. It was a clone of the hundreds of other Zinanian curs she had seen on the highways and byways of the country.

The barking brought an elderly appearing woman to the courtyard. Dette had given up guessing the age of Zinanian citizens since she rarely came close. Constant childbearing and arduous housework, without labor saving devices, aged women quickly. Men, on the other hand, who benefited by the society's willingness to have most of the hard work done by the women, often looked younger than they were.

This woman had obviously seen many rainy seasons. Five feet tall at most, she was clothed in typical West African garb, a bright orange and blue floral sarong and a loose fitting orange turban

Dette spoke no Fulani. Since the beginning of her fascination with the General, she toyed with the idea of picking up the language, reputed to be fairly easy to master. She guessed the lady spoke no French, as very few women and girls were taught to do so. Nonetheless, Dette tried, *"General Sacco est là?"*

"Sacco?" She pointed to herself and the playing children. "Sacco." She motioned to each of the doors that faced onto the courtyard. "Sacco, Sacco, Sacco, Sacco."

"Oui, oui, Sacco. Mais, je voudrais voir General Sacco. Suleiman."

"Ah, Suleiman."

The old woman sauntered toward one of the doors, opening it without knocking. She leaned in and yelled an unintelligible command containing the word "Suleiman." Moments later he appeared, obviously waking from an afternoon nap. He wore a grey T-shirt and loose fitting trousers of material much like that of the lady's ensemble. He was barefoot. By then, Dette had come to the conclusion that the General was her son.

"Miss O'Kelly, you have come to my house. *Ca va.*" She couldn't tell if he was surprised, angry, pleased, or some combination of all three. He kissed her on both cheeks.

"Ça va, bien. Yes, General Sacco, I have. Like you, I have come by more than once, but only today mustered the courage to come in."

"Welcome. Let me introduce you to my mother, Madame Sacco." A simple gesture in her direction caused the elderly lady to break out in a broad, nearly toothless smile and offer her hand in greeting. "Those noisy children are my nieces and nephews. There are fourteen of them who live in our concession. I have four brothers. Two have two wives each, one with just one, and the last, like me, none."

"You have no sisters?"

"Of course I have sisters. There are six, but as you must know when they marry, they move to their husband's concession. The last one moved out more than a year ago."

"Your father?"

"He is dead. It has been three years. We think it was malaria because he had a high fever but refused to go to the hospital. He ate herbs that obviously were not the right ones because one morning we found him dead in his bed. My oldest brother, Saloom, who drives a taxi, became head of the family at that time. Please, Miss O'Kelly, may I get you something to drink? I must apologize for not having any beer but you can have tonic, Coca-Cola, or Fanta."

"A tonic would be very nice, General." Both continued to speak formally because of the presence of the mother, who had no clue what they were saying.

He sent one of his nephews to the nearby boutique to get the drinks. "Please come in to my part of the concession."

The three of them, including mother as chaperone, entered into a moderate-sized room, lit with three low intensity bulbs. The floors were concrete; a red and black imitation Persian carpet lay in the center. Shiny maroon Naugahyde covered two easy chairs and a short sofa. Seven of the ubiquitous iron and rubber cord chairs sat empty in front of an old Korean television that had been granted a central, almost alter-like position. It was not on; ZTV, the only local channel, was unpredictable in its hours of broadcast. A clicking ceiling fan almost imperceptibly stirred the air; there was no AC. The walls were virtually unadorned except for an old calendar page with a landscape featuring a bend in the Begoro, and two photographs, one of a man who looked strikingly like an older Suleiman, and the other of President Oumar Ibrahim Lassoso. Dette doubted that the latter was indicative of respect or loyalty.

Two doors led off the main room; one went to the kitchen, the other the bedroom and bathroom. She decided against asking to see either, although she was more than a little bit interested in the latter.

Sacco motioned for her to sit in one of the easy chairs, while he sat on the couch. Madam Sacco took a seat in the other upholstered chair. The General's expression suggested that he was resigned to his mother's presence. A moment later, his nephew, Nisso, came into the room and shook Dette's hand. Bernadette had had the foresight to purchase a package of Oreos from the commissary, and gave them to the boy while asking that Suleiman insist on them being shared with all the cousins.

After another round of "*Ça va's*", Bernadette plunged into meaningful discussion. "It seems like such a long time since we were together." It had been less than a week.

"Yes, it does. I have been very busy, and I am sure you have, too."

"Actually, work has been very quiet lately. I have been spending much of my time in my office reading. Ambassador Fairchild has not given me any new projects. "

"I see." Sacco did not seem anxious for the discussion to become substantive.

"Suleiman, I enjoyed being with you very much." She tried to play down the emotion, both of voice and body, to make the mother think that she was talking business. Madame sat expressionless.

"And I with you, Bernadette."

"I hope that we can spend more time together."

Just as she was to hear his response, the whole purpose for her visit, his nephew came in with the newly purchased soft drinks. As if he was the Pied Piper, five younger children followed him in. All filed by the pale guest, offering their hands in high-fives. The two youngest each muttered a single word, "*Tubabu*," white person. Madame offered Bernadette ice cubes for her tonic. She declined, recalling Doctor Eisenstat's admonitions to avoid liquid or frozen water. To avoid pathogens, Western diplomats in Africa always made ice with boiled or bottled water and consumed beverages without ice when they were outside the diplomatic community.

Suleiman's mother brought in some stale, pale beige biscuits and equally over-the-hill peanuts. Bernadette wished that Nisso would reappear with the Oreos. That didn't occur so she forced down one biscuit and half a dozen peanuts, countering their unpleasant flavor with the warm, bitter, local tonic.

After a few minutes the children filed out and to Bernadette's pleasant surprise, their grandmother followed. Whether she had become bored by a conversation she couldn't understand or wanted her son to have some privacy was unclear.

Sacco spoke up before O'Kelly had the opportunity to repeat her suggestion for more visits. "Bernadette, I am very worried about what is going on in this country."

"What do you mean?" she responded, fearful that this was a lead-in to his saying there would be no further meetings.

"There are many things that are happening at the same time, maybe unrelated, maybe not."

"Like what?"

"You saw two of them at the gala, and were part of one. The President's comments to you about being, what was the word ... circumspect, were alarming. I had never heard him make such an undiplomatic statement. Plus, I'm concerned by his closeness to the Libyans. They have always been very much in evidence here, at least since Gaddafi took over. It was their money and our labor that built the dam near New Akron. But Lassoso has never before shown preference for the Libyans over your country or the Soviets or the French. For him to say that to you with Ambassador Mukhtar standing next to him was troubling.

"Just yesterday, three members of the Executive Committee of the People's Party for Democracy were arrested without charge. Oumou was not one of them. He told the newspapers and the TV not to report the arrests. That's rare. The media has been fairly free here, til now."

"We have heard none of this at the Embassy."

"The only reason that I know about it is that the Chief of Staff of the Army called each Division Chief into his office this morning to warn us that there may be some demonstrations soon. Plus, I know the owner of *La Presse.*"

"And how about you, Suleiman? Are you worried about yourself?"

"Not yet. As far as I know the President and the Chief of Staff still trust me. They are counting on me for protection should there be any trouble. Fortunately, they recognize the loyalty between me and my troops and know that sacking Sacco would be a mistake." He chuckled at his little joke. She did, too.

"And what do you think about us? Are you concerned about being seen with me, the American rabble-rouser?"

"What does that mean, rabble-rouser?"

"Someone who causes trouble."

"No, I am not concerned. I love you for it. We need rabble-rousers here." The L word gave her an all-over tingle, even in its platonic context. "I am a little worried for you however. If you are seen with me often, important people might get nervous. Lassoso would have little trouble finding a reason to get you out of the country."

"I understand. I agree. But that gets me back to the comment I made before the drinks came. I would like to spend more time with you."

"Me, too, and we will. We must, however, be … circumspect. We can't be too public." With that, he stood, took her hand and led her through one of the two doors, the one to the bedroom. Afterwards, the only thing that she remembered about the room was that it sweltered, that the ceiling fan didn't work, and that the bed was meant for one.

IX

In Beverly Hills, Jill Eisenstat was known to most of her acquaintances as the doctor's wife. She hoped that the change of venue would allow her to enhance her personal identity.

She had taken up batik before leaving California, and was pleased to be assigned to Zinani, a country known for its textile tradition. She brought the equipment necessary and an ample supply of cloth and dyes, and set up a studio to start a small business in their spacious, Embassy-owned house.

Jill quickly learned that producing pieces of cloth adorned with thatch huts, elephants, and baobab trees was not going to satisfy her. She could make only so many pillows and scarves in those designs before reaching the saturation point. She had hoped to sell in the US and locally, but had little success. Her sister-in-law was able to unload a few for five dollars each to friends, but that outlet dried up quickly.

She tried making bigger pieces to fashion them into dresses and skirts, and ordered several dozen elaborate labels reading "Jillian de Zinani." She received effusive compliments from those to whom she gave them, but failed to find a market to justify her efforts and investments. "Screw this," she exclaimed one day, while Michael was watching a four-week old pro football game on a tape that his brother had sent. He had succeeded in not having learned the results in advance.

"Screw what?" he responded, pushing the PAUSE button.

"This art stuff. I am no artist. I never have been and I never will be."

"I think your work is wonderful. I'm sorry you haven't gotten into men's clothes. I'd wear nothing but Jillian's. Don't give up. It took Ralph Lauren and Calvin Klein years to get started."

"You don't know a damn thing about Ralph Lauren or Calvin Klein!"

Appropriately rebuked, Michael wanted to push PLAY, both to get out of the discomforting discussion and to see if the Raiders could hold on to their slim lead. He wisely decided otherwise and held his thumb motionless. "You are right, honey, I don't. But, I love your work and think you are really talented. If you quit doing that, what will you do?"

"Damned if I know. Maybe I'll get a job at the Embassy."

"Even if the nursing job was open, you couldn't have it. The regs say you can't work for your spouse."

"There are two things in the world that I have absolutely zero interest in. Those are, in reverse order, getting back into nursing and working for you." Michael's urge to press PLAY became stronger. "Maybe I could get that position as head of the commissary."

Embassy Donolu had a reasonably well-stocked commissary to sell American goods to the official American community, at a price which reflected the high cost of shipping to a land-locked Saharan nation. No matter how expensive, there were Americans who would pay any price, drive any distance, shoulder any load, to get Fruit-Loops, Baby Ruths, Miller Genuine Draft, and Diet Coke.

The job as head salesperson was neither burdensome nor highly remunerative but it was popular with the spouses of officers without children, as it got them out of their houses to see their fellow country folk. The position was open at that time, as the incumbent had flown to Ft. Worth to give birth to her fourth child.

Jill applied for the barely more than minimum wage position. Her only competition was Scott Uveal, the 21-year-old son of an IT operator. He had just failed out of a Florida junior college and had come to Africa, for want of a better alternative. Jill got the job. Scott, reasonably skilled in the construction trades, eventually joined the Peace Corps and relocated to Uzbekistan.

"Hi, Hon," said Michael, looking up from his French grammar book and taking off his headphone. Much of his free time was spent trying to improve this language that, unlike Italian and Spanish, sounds nothing like it should sound. He had beaten her home, having seen only two patients that day, both with itchy rashes.

Jill had taken on a laterite hue. Her day had been devoted to inventory, counting bottles of A-1 Sauce, boxes of Tampax, and cans of Campbell's Cream of Mushroom Soup. She flopped on the couch. "I'm wiped out." Mamadou, the attentive houseboy, placed her usual drink, diet lemonade, in front of her. Michael was well into his second Heineken, bought at Champagne prices from the local Lebanese market.

"Tough day?"

"Pope Catholic? Bear shit in woods?"

"Guess where I went today?"

"Redondo Beach."

"Wrong. President Lassoso's Office."

Jill's eyelids elevated slightly. She was not one given to bursts of enthusiasm when it came to Michael's work-related exploits. "Oh, why?" she asked, a query more verbose than he had expected.

He told her of the meeting with the Ambassador, the cable from Gen. Fimbri, and the twenty minutes with OIL. She was particularly taken by the Jewish/Dayan part. "What do you think about that?"

"Nothing much. He probably hasn't met many Jews in his life, let alone his last several years. I didn't feel any animosity. I'm not unhappy that he knows who I am. Probably not many State Department doctors are recognized by the Chief of State.

"You know, Jilly, I'd like to have a dinner party about this hospital deal. Maybe six or seven couples." "Jilly" usually preceded any requests he made for something that he was fairly sure she would rather not do.

"OK, who?" He was pleasantly surprised to get a positive response.

"Obviously the Fairchilds will be there." That was almost enough to risk withdrawing her acceptance. She liked them well enough; she did not like to entertain them, especially Marylou. She was constantly worried that Mrs. Ambassador looked down on everything that Mrs. Doctor had, said, or did. The silverware was never sufficiently polished, the carrots not crisp enough, the wine needed more time to breathe.

"Coulibaly, the Health Minister, and if he can decide which, one of his wives. Dr. and the first Mrs. Traore and Dr. Tontan; I'm not sure if he has any wives."

Traore was an orthopedist who served the Embassy as Post Medical Advisor. He had done his training in Missouri, married a nurse from East St. Louis, Illinois, and then returned to Donolu, where he took two more wives. Jill had befriended her fellow American RN, Maggie, the first wife, and was constantly amazed that she showed little unhappiness over being one of three.

Dr. Tontan, a Romanian-trained pathologist, was both the Lassoso General Hospital administrator and the only person in the country with the skill to differentiate benign tumors from malignant ones. He had one wife, a Romanian, who had rarely been seen outside of her modest home where she raised half a dozen biracial children.

"Chen Wang and the DCM should be invited. And Bernadette. She may bring that General you're hot for."

"I'm tired just thinking about it," said Jill, tiredly. Michael took that as approval of the list. "When do you want this to happen?"

"Next Friday."

"What shall we have?"

"We've got a case of a good Bordeaux."

"Not the wine, bonehead, the food." He loved it when she called him bonehead.

"Are you OK with Beef Stroganoff? Mamadou makes it well. We could start with zebra liver pate, then onion soup, and the main course with a vegetable, salad, and finish off with your zabaglione. We could serve champagne with the pate, white wine with soup, the red with the beef aa cheap Sauterne for dessert. "

"You are an incredible dilettante, Michael Eisenstat."

"But you love me ... anyway," he responded in song.

"Right," she said.

All the invitees responded positively. Coulibaly brought the same wife that always appeared at his side in newspaper photos. Nurse Maggie came with Traore. Tontan came alone. Ernestine Grant entered with Chen Wang, their hands furtively intertwined. And General Sacco, in his suit and plain tie, walked in with Bernadette O'Kelly. Ambassador and Mrs. Fairchild drove up in the beflagged Ford, an ambassadorially acceptable thirty minutes late.

The Zinanians, except for US-trained Dr. Traore, chose alcohol-free beverages, while gin and tonic headed the list for the expats on the sweltering evening. Marylou Fairchild opted for a wine cooler. Her husband insisted on a listing of available beers before settling on Jack Daniels, straight up.

Both Jillian and Michael recognized from the first moment that this was not the most compatible group of guests.

Mrs. Coulibaly, who looked like an African Ethel Merman, spoke no English, and spent the evening in near total silence. Minister Coulibaly, very cordial in one-on-ones, was stiff and virtually as uncommunicative as his wife. He was obviously not happy in the company of General Sacco.

Dr. Tontan showed as much enthusiasm as he would have examining PAP smears under the microscope.

The Traores reminded Michael of Lyndon and Lady Bird Johnson. He was the tallest guest and spent much of his time with his arm on the shoulders of others. Maggie smiled demurely, but her non-verbals made it obvious that she was the decider in her house.

Chen and Ernestine seemed wrapped up in each other. He told a couple of jokes, in French. His accent was so bad that neither the Anglophones nor Francophobes understood. Not even the DCM laughed.

Bernadette O'Kelly was the most ebullient guest. She wore a broad smile and a new dress that she had had made from local material, a mango tree print. Michael had never seen her look so attractive. Sacco seemed pleased to be present but made quite sure to avoid getting close to the Health Minister.

Ambassador Fairchild's basso profundo voice stood out above the rest. Most of his observations were preceded by such phrases as, "When we were in Burkina Faso ..." or, "Our house in Budapest ..." or, "My boss in Malawi ..." When he started one out with, "When I was a senior at Princeton ...," Jill and Michael stared at each other surreptitiously questioning who should lace his next Jack Daniels with a sedative.

Marylou Fairchild spent much of her time in the kitchen, checking out the fare. She even took a taste of the zabaglione and suggested that Mamadou add more sherry.

While the pre-dinner conversation was stultifying, the meal was a smashing success. The pate was extraordinary, but both Eisenstats were disappointed when no one questioned its contents. They had brought back the zebra delicacy frozen from Tanzania and held it for a special occasion.

The soup was perfect, with just a hint of brandy, unnoticed by teetotalers. The beef stroganoff was tender, oniony, and mushroomy. About half of the guests' left little log piles of anchovies on their salad plates. The Italian finale engendered oohs and ahs from even those for whom ooh and ah were foreign words.

To Michael's further disappointment, this was not a wine appreciation assemblage. Neither Coulibaly, nor the General, nor Dr. Tontan imbibed.

Dr. Traore bragged about his knowledge of American wines, expressing his preference for the varietals of Gallo and Paul Masson. Maggie took only sips of each pour, leaving several dollars' worth of unconsumed vintage behind.

Chen, Ernestine, and Marylou cared little about what kind of wine he or she was drinking, but all consumed their full share without going through the ritual of sniffing, tilting, and twirling, before drinking.

Holden Fairchild gave a dissertation on the wine growing countries of the world, quoting numbers of cases, hectares, and average consumption. If it had been possible to express displeasure at such an event, guests and hosts would have treated him to a chorus of boos.

Only Bernadette knew what significance wine had for Doctor Eisenstat. She asked all the right questions and offered just the right words of praise.

Michael's choice of a cheap Sauterne proved prescient when phrases like "Yuk, I don't like sweet wine," and "May I have some more water," resulted.

Michael opened the toasting with the champagne. "I would like to propose a toast to our honored guests, and to the reason that we have all gathered, the improvement of Lassoso Hospital."

"Here, here," all answered in unison, some hoisting flutes, others clinking water goblets.

Minister Coulibaly was the next to speak up. "President Lassoso has asked that I convey his best wishes to this group, regretting that his schedule did not allow him to join us tonight." That was reassuring to Jillian, as Lassoso's name had never come up as a potential guest. "He is honored that our humble country is being considered as a recipient for some of America's fine hospital equipment. He hopes that Lassoso Hospital will become one of the great health care facilities in Africa ... with your kind help."

Michael felt a pang of that same anxiety that he had in Lassoso's office the previous week. Expectations were clearly too high. The Ambassador spoke before Michael could comment. "Yes, I am sure that should this equipment come, and I have strong reason to believe that it will, Lassoso will be helped on its way to becoming a hospital about which you can be very proud."

Ernestine, Chen, and Michael all cleared their throats at the same time, as if they were about to start choir practice. Ms. Grant took the floor. "But, sir, let us remember that it is material from a decommissioned military hospital that we are seeking."

"Yes, of course, Miss Grant. Your worst equipment is better than our best," stated Dr. Tontan matter-of-factly, for his only contribution of the evening.

"Will they be doing transplants?" asked Maggie Traore, who had been a surgical nurse in Illinois.

"Certainly not!" her husband stated. "Let's get to the point where we can do routine surgeries without killing anyone before we talk about transplants."

"I agree," said Eisenstat, pleased by the touch of rationality.

"President Lassoso doesn't want just any hospital. He wants the best in West Africa," interjected Mr. Coulibaly. His wife continued to stare into her water glass, expressionless.

"It would take a lot to surpass the ones in Abidjan and Dakar," said Chen.

"There is no reason we can't."

The Ambassador and the DCM were both shocked that this level of discussion was going on over beef stroganoff and red wine. They couldn't tell if Coulibaly had gone off the deep end or whether he had instructions from above. "I would suggest that we discuss this at another time." Fairchild said, changing the topic from hospitals to the quality of this year's cotton crop.

General Sacco had been silent throughout the dinner. Ever the concerned hostess, Jill directed a question toward him, "Why does this country have such a large army? It looks to me that there are military men posted on every corner. And all of them carry very large guns. It makes me nervous. What are they guarding against?"

The grade school quality of the question surprised everybody that was listening, especially Bernadette and the Ambassador. Dr. Tontan was near falling asleep in his half-eaten portion of zabaglione, and Mrs. Coulibaly had no clue as to what was being discussed. The remainder perked up and trained their eyes on Suleiman, as he opened his mouth to respond.

Bernadette acted like a political officer, speaking up before the General could answer. "It's a very complex situation, Jill, what with the French colonial period and the unsettled times of early independence."

"I am able to answer the question, Miss O'Kelly," Sacco interrupted. Dette turned crimson, never before having been scolded by him.

"Yours is an excellent question, Mrs. Eisenstat. As Miss O'Kelly started to say, the French, in order to avoid another Algeria, created a large Army in Zinani in the 1950's. After independence, we were concerned about our neighbors" aggressiveness, so we armed ourselves, with help from both the Americans and the Soviets.

"Eventually, the threat was understood to be minimal, and donors stopped sending us planes and tanks. But the military was clearly a way of life for us. We spent much of our wealth on new technology. Now, we have no external enemies; the military is directed toward internal security. Some feel we should spend less on the Army and more on health and education. So far, that idea has not been adopted."

Jill felt vindicated. She despised having put her foot in her mouth and felt that Sacco's reasoned response enabled her to extract it.

The General surprised the Ambassador and DCM with his thinly veiled criticism of the President. Dr. Traore was seen to nod affirmatively, while Health Minister Coulibaly was unmistakably displeased.

Adnan Coulibaly was not a prototypic Health Minister. He had neither a medical nor a public health education. He went to school in accounting, at Lassoso University, where he was not remembered as an academic standout. He was, however, loyal, especially in menial tasks in the Finance Ministry, where he gradually worked his way up to Deputy Minister. Some creative accounting was needed to explain to donors why the Presidential Palace came in at twice budget. Coulibaly was a very creative accountant. As a reward, he was offered his choice of several ministries after a spring housecleaning of some less loyal ministers. Finance was not open, so he chose Health. He was thrilled by the idea that Mercedes-driving doctors would have to come to him to get the OK for the smallest of purchases. Coulibaly's word on matters of health was, without doubt, the word of the President.

A brief, heated discussion followed, in Fulani, pitting Coulibaly against Sacco like an African wild dog versus a cheetah. Tontan paid attention for the first time in half an hour. Even Mrs. Coulibaly became alert. Most of the Americans gawked, understanding the significance of what was unfolding before them, even if they couldn't divine the meaning of the words.

Beads of sweat dotted the forehead of the Minister. Sacco remained dry. Half a dozen comments from each, none a question, were the sum total of the encounter. The denouement involved a rapid, nearly simultaneous push back of the chairs by Minister and Madam, a shake of the hands with the Ambassador, a kiss on the cheeks of Mrs. Ambassador, a nod in the direction of the non-combatants and an exit. West Africans usually leave immediately after the completion of a meal, but this was a record rapid departure.

Dr. Tontan followed. Despite Maggie's obvious desire to stick around for the post mortem, the Traores departed at the same time. Uniformed drivers in long, black Mercedes transported both doctors. Both Sacco and Bernadette knew it was not appropriate for him to remain; he left in his Peugeot a few minutes later with his date remaining behind.

The Fairchilds, the Eisenstats, Ernestine, Chen and Bernadette sat around a lazy Susan upon which Michael had placed bottles of Remy Martin VSOP and Grand Mariner, and the correct glasses for each.

"I wish that the State Department had taught me Fulani," said Chen, who was fortunate to qualify for his posting with his meager French.

"You didn't need a degree in Fulani to figure out what was going on in that debate," answered the DCM.

"What did happen?" asked Jill.

The Ambassador decided that it was his responsibility to answer. He and Michael by this time had lit up a couple of large Dominican cigars, bought by the Ambassador out of his entertainment budget. "You may have seen an early skirmish in a turning point in the history of Zinani."

"Huh?" responded the doctor.

The DCM intervened, "This is not a contented country. Except for the students, especially the women of the PPD, most people are quiet, but that might not continue. There have been lots of arrests. And most importantly, the Army is not solidly Lassoso.

"General Sacco is in a very strong position. As head of the division that controls Donolu, he is nearly as important as the Chief of Staff. And Sacco, as you could tell tonight, is no great fan of the current regime."

"Are you saying that there's going to be a coup?" asked Jill.

"Not any time soon, I don't think," answered Ernestine. "As far as we can tell, the generals of the other two divisions are still in the President's camp. I do think that what we saw was significant in that a general was willing to make negative comments about his president, in the presence of important others. As we speak, Coulibaly is talking to Lassoso about the events of the evening.

"His options are one, to call Sacco in and tell him to cut the crap; two, to demote or fire him and maybe put him behind bars; or three, to get him out of Zinani, with an ambassadorship to Honduras or Bangladesh or some other shitty little country."

"Don't talk about shitty little countries that way," interjected Marylou, "my husband is the Ambassador to the shittiest little one of them all." Everyone except her spouse laughed, and Marylou bristled with pride.

"So where does that put us?" asked Chen. He knew that he and Bernadette would have to draft the cable to Washington describing the dinner party.

"No place special," said the Ambassador. "Obviously, we watch closely. We favor changes toward democracy, but we can't play an active role. Our meddling could set that cause back rather than help it. Agree, Ernestine?" She nodded.

The Political Officer, for obvious reasons, remained silent during the party post-mortem.

The Ambassador and the Mrs. walked out to the waiting Ford, with Bernadette who had accepted their offer of a ride. To Jill, Marylou gave special praise for the dessert, "Just the right amount of sherry." To Michael, "Remember, I love dry white wine. Hold the sugar." The evening ended a few seconds later when Ernestine and Chen departed in his Renault. Jill assumed that the first comment was, "Your house or mine?" with either a Boston or Shanghai accent.

Mamadou had gone home, at Jill's instructions, immediately after dinner. Jill refused to go to bed without straightening up. Michael, as usual, trying to avoid feeling guilty, attempted to help by hauling loads of glassware into the kitchen.

"Some evening," he commented when they finally got into bed.

"I loved it."

"The food was spectacular. Don't you wish that someone had mentioned zebras?"

"Who cares?"

"I guess I do."

"Forget it."

She continued, "Don't you think that Dette and the General are getting it on?"

"I don't know. Why do you think so?" Michael was very careful about breaking medical confidentiality, even to his wife.

"She has a satisfied look about her that I haven't seen on her face before."

"Maybe she's loving her work and has made a good friend out of an important local guy?"

"No way, José. That is a lady getting laid."

They were too tired to follow suit and turned off the light.

X

"Rodeo Drive, Rodeo Drive, this is Big Daddy." The walkie-talkie radio in the Eisenstat's bedroom blasted the doctor awake at 7AM on a Sunday they had hoped would start much later. As most of his patients were perfectly healthy because of the strict screening to keep sick folks, like diabetics and asthmatics, out of medically underserved posts, emergency calls were rare.

Each American in the Embassy was supplied with a walkie-talkie radio, mainly for security reasons, in case rapid communication was necessary in time of personal crisis or political upheaval. Since only the Ambassador plus a small handful of others had home phones, everyone else relied on the radio for day-to-day communication. The obvious downside was that everybody in the mission could hear what all the others were up to.

Each radio-holder was required to choose a unique handle. It usually had something to do with his origin, her job, or a place that he had lived before. This use of monikers, rather than real names, dated back to Cold War days when Americans didn't want Russians to know who was who and where they were. Big Daddy was the Marine post at the Embassy, the switchboard for the system. Tiger's Den was the Ambassador's, Boston Blackie the DCM's, and Shanghai, Chen Wang's. Wisconsin-native Fireman Pfund, the business and finance officer (BFO), was pleased with his choice of Cheeseman. Judy Deane was not embarrassed to call herself Church Pew. Administrator Prudholme was Penny Pincher.

"Go ahead, Big Daddy. This is Rodeo Drive."

"I have Big Red on the line. Go, Big Red."

Michael of Beverly Hills knew that Nebraska Cornhusker Bernadette O'Kelly was calling.

"Rodeo Drive, I need to see you. Over."

"Medical problem? Over."

"Sort of. Over."

The Regional Medical Officer didn't think that this would be just another report of fornicating with the General. He also knew that asking for a postponement until Monday office hours would be a mistake. "I'll meet you at the Abattoir in an hour. Over." Any eavesdropping, fluent, English-speaking Russian listening to the discussion would have been confused.

"Roger that. Big Red out. Thanks, Big Daddy."

"Rodeo Drive clear. Thanks Big Daddy." All officers quickly learned to be effusive in their thanks to the Marine on duty. If they failed to give thanks, they could expect a 6AM wakeup later in the week, ostensibly in the name of checking the working order of their radio.

Jill had developed a talent for staying asleep in her California King bed when Michael was called on the phone by a patient, colleague, or nurse. She carried this over to radio communication in Africa. She grunted unintelligibly as he walked out saying he would be back before their 10 AM tennis date with the Italian DCM and his mistress.

The drive to the Embassy on a weekend morning was easy. Almost no buses, cars, or pick-ups were on the street. The most significant hazards were the cattle, sheep, or goats being herded through the city. The vegetable ladies had not yet begun to set up their stands, the gas pump jockeys hadn't brought out their whiskey bottles full of fuel, and the lepers weren't in their usual places where the more affluent Zinanians and expatriates were likely to hand over a lassoso or two.

Once again, the Eisenstat car proved bomb-free. The doctor drove into the parking lot, climbed the steps and opened his office. The morning was cool enough that he had no need to turn on his air conditioner. He had come in his tennis togs of cutoff jeans and an old "SAVE THE WHALES - BOYCOTT JAPANESE GOODS." Dette was waiting for him outside the Abattoir. Her shorts were brief, enough to make the doctor take notice. A tight tank top emphasized her most remarkable physical characteristics. She had put on a baseball cap to cover the lack of grooming and dark glasses made it difficult to decipher her mood.

70

Michael could not deny that he found Bernadette attractive. He knew that he would never do anything about it, but fantasy was fun. In addition, he had never picked up the tiniest inkling of expressed interest on her part. He was afraid that he was really over the hill, of no interest to the younger, appealing Nubians. He still felt like a thirty-five-year old, but his infrequent looks in the mirror confirmed the fifty-year-old date on his birth certificate.

They sat in the waiting room as there was no chance that any other patient or janitor would interrupt them. Bernadette started, "I threw up this morning."

His immediate concern was food poisoning from the dinner party. His stomach was fine and Jill had not grumbled about nausea. On the other hand, only the salad was suspicion-free. The zebra pate was a couple of weeks old, and both the Stroganoff and the zabaglione contained cream, great for growing salmonella. "No one else at the party has complained. Probably it was something you ate earlier in the day, or maybe a virus."

"Michael, I wouldn't have called you here for anything like that."

"What do you mean?"

"I am more than a week late with my period and my breasts ache. That's what I mean."

"You mean you think you're pregnant." This was not a diagnosis often made by internists.

"Correct."

"Oh, I wouldn't worry yet. It's probably just stress. You've had some tough times lately."

"I really wish that I could buy that, but I have been pregnant before and it felt just like this." Michael had not been aware of the Dr. Morty incident. She reached in her tote bag and pulled out a jelly jar half filled with a yellow liquid. "This is this morning's urine."

"The lab tech will not be here 'til tomorrow."

"Come on. If a woman can do the test at home, the Regional Medical Officer can sure as hell do it in his lab."

"OK, I'll give it a try. Be aware that I have never done it before."

"I have great trust in your intelligence and your skills, Dr. Einstein."

The pregnancy test kit contained a sheet of instructions that could have been followed by anyone who had mastered See Spot Run. Three wells, a few drops of one liquid from the kit in the known positive, a few of another in the known negative and some pee in the test well. Wait five minutes. A negative test either means that the woman is not pregnant or that she tested too early. A positive however is a positive.

During the five minutes he asked her about birth control. "How come you're not on birth control pills?" Her alluding to a previous pregnancy made it quite clear that papal dictates were not the issue.

"Quite frankly, I never thought that I would get into a sexual relationship here. In fact, I was more than a little worried that my screwing days were over."

"I can hardly imagine that." He purposefully avoided eye contact with that statement. "And how about condoms?"

"The first time we did it, I had just finished my period so there was no worry. The only other time, at his place, I asked but he said he'd never used one, maybe never seen one. So, I took one out of my purse."

"Never seen one? Even with all this talk about AIDS?" asked Michael.

"Remember, this is a guy who says that he has not slept with a woman since his wife died. Whether you do or not, I believe him. But, we used one of those blue Atlas ones that USAID is selling and it broke."

USAID was sponsoring a program to market condoms throughout the country, using TV and radio ads to spark interest in and demystify them. Attempts to do the same by handing out free condoms were not successful. Conventional wisdom was that only something paid for would be used, so AID initiated a program in which they were sold for a few cents each. The sales were great but the Atlas brand was getting a bad name because of a reputation for fragility.

"Not you, too. I have been hearing the same from the Marines."

"I think they have been bringing condoms in that were meant for Caucasians or Asians. They don't seem big enough for Africans, or at least one African." Had Michael been sitting, he would have started squirming in his chair.

Five minutes elapsed. The positive well had a bright red dot, the negative well, nothing. The test well had a red dot, just as bright as its neighbor. "Yeah, Dette, you're pregnant."

"Mother of God." He had never before heard that epithet before.

"Now what, Bernadette?"

"Jesus, I don't know. I certainly can't carry the child, so I guess its abortion number two for this good Catholic girl. Can I get one done here?"

"Zin law says no abortions. I have heard of people having them, but they sound like the back-alley jobs that our country knew so well before Roe v Wade. I wouldn't let you do that."

"Couldn't you do one here in the office?" she said in all seriousness.

"Come off it, Bernadette. I am a goddam internist. For me doing a PAP smear is complex stuff. I wouldn't know where to start."

"How about that French pill?"

"You mean RU 486? I looked into that for someone else. It's illegal in Zinani and the US Government doesn't allow us to stock it in an embassy."

"Can you send me to Paris or London for an abortion?"

"You are well aware that the Department is not about to allow one of its embassies to spend two thousand bucks sending one of its officers four thousand miles for an abortion. Imagine what the Pro-Lifers would do with that information. If you want to go up there, and I think that it's probably your best bet, you'll have to pick up the tab yourself."

"I am going to need time to think about this."

"You have some time. You're only a few weeks into it. Who are you going to tell? Sacco?"

"Oh, Michael, I just don't know. I really do love the guy and I could imagine worse things than marrying him, but I know that I won't. There is too much standing in the way for both him and me. And if I am not going to marry him, there's nothing to be gained by telling him I'm pregnant. I'm certainly not going to expect him to pay for the trip. I just don't know." He saw tears on her cheek for the first time since he met her. He put his arms around her and held tight for several seconds.

"I hate to bring up another subject, although it is related."

"What's that?"

"Don't you think that it's time to let the Ambassador know that your thing with General Sacco is more than just friendly and professional? What we saw last night at the dinner table was a little scary."

"Yeah, I agree. I had already decided that I couldn't keep lying. The word was going to get out sooner or later, and it might as well come from me, rather than from Lassoso's people. But, I am not going to say anything about today's developments. And please, please, Michael, don't say anything, even to Jill."

"You know me better than that." He hugged her again.

Ernestine Grant's office was just down the hall from the Ambassador's. On Monday morning, her secretary, Amanda Sertoli sat out front, like a sentinel protecting the gate to a castle. The door to the inner chamber was closed.

"Is she in?" asked Bernadette, looking like she hadn't slept in days.

"Mr. Norbert has been in with her for half an hour. I'm not sure what they are talking about. I'll let her know that you are waiting." She buzzed and let her boss know that her Political Officer wanted to talk to her. "Just a few minutes, Bernadette. Please have a seat."

Dette was convinced that the entire Embassy was talking about her and that the conversation going on behind the door between the DCM and the Security Officer had something to do with her and Sacco and maybe even the pregnancy.

She observed Amanda closely and for a minute wished that her own mind could be as vacant as that of this Foreign Service Secretary. She had heard of Amanda's four failed marriages, each childless, and especially the last one to the Italian-American communications specialist at the US Embassy in Moscow. Word had it that she had been the victim of spousal abuse and left him only after she suffered a broken clavicle. Dette found it hard to believe that Amanda was only a few years older than she; she looked like she was near the age of mandatory retirement. No one ever saw Amanda outside the office. She was a major customer of the Video Club and the Commissary, but was never at either the Snack Bar or the American Club. She ate her lunch at her desk while reading romance novels. She declined essentially all invitations to the point they almost never came her way any more. There were those who worried that she was clinically depressed and that she was a suicide threat; she didn't even have a dog.

Frank Norbert, the officer responsible for insuring the security of the diplomats and families, came out about ten minutes later. He nodded and smiled at Bernadette but said nothing, further deepening her concerns that she was the subject of the just concluded discussion. "Go on in," said Amanda.

DCM Grant's office was the most tastefully decorated one in the Chancery. Her appreciation for art was obvious, with some excellent paintings from Africa and America. Tomes about painters dominated her bookshelf. She had a pair of Dogon masks from Mali and an iconic butterfly mask from Burkina Faso. Behind her desk were signed photos from her two heroes, Bobby Kennedy and Martin Luther King. Simply designed African carpets were on the floor and the furniture was covered in plain blue fabric. Her lamps had 100-watt bulbs as she refused to kowtow to the Ambassador and the Administrator

"Good morning, Bernadette."

"Good morning. We've got to talk."

"Go ahead." The formality was uncomfortable for both, who were accustomed to cordiality.

"General Sacco and I are more than just friends."

"Are you sleeping with him?"

"Yes. I have … twice."

"And?"

"And, what?"

"Where does it stand now?"

"We haven't done it in a couple of weeks"

"It sounds like the General may be a little wiser than you."

"I guess you're right. I haven't been exactly a genius. But, as you and I discussed even before that first time we went out to the Presidential Palace, I was lonely and frankly, horny. It just sort of happened, on that trip to the river where I learned about Oumou and Lassoso. The next time, I made it happen; I made a house call.

"And what's next?" The air was one of mother to daughter rather than colleagues in diplomacy.

"Christ, I don't know," said Dette, getting testy, as she might have with her mother. "You know, I really like him. I have been happier in the last few months than in a long time. I shudder at the thought of breaking it off."

"Cut the nonsense! Look, you are the_Political Officer in this Embassy. He is the general of the most important Army division in the country and the man most likely to be central to any move against the government. Just look at the events of Saturday night. Your friend Sacco is a gutsy fellow; either he is going to disappear from the country or the planet or he is going to be making headlines before too long. And you are going to bed with him! Be realistic. You have only one option and that is to stop."

"I could marry him. He hasn't asked, but I know that he wants to."

"Wrong. First, your career ends, *tout de suite*. Marry him and you are either an unemployed ex-Foreign Service Officer wife of a General, wife of the President, or widow of an ex-General. Second, you are not exactly the type to be the loving wife of a Zinanian VIP. About three weeks after the wedding, you would be going crazy, wishing you were a single Political Officer again. And, young lady, my guess is that he is not about to propose nor accept a proposal from you. He has obviously got more lofty things on his mind than his own personal love life."

"But, I don't want it to stop."

"Stop, it must. There are no other choices, other than sending you home."

"I'm sorry that I told you."

"You know that's nonsense. You had to tell me. I am a little concerned that you didn't do so earlier, and I know the Ambassador is going to be pissed. But I don't think it's too late. I think that we can keep you around. Both he and I think you are a very good political officer. We don't want to lose you."

"You have to tell the Ambassador, don't you?"

"I sure as hell do. If he learns of it from elsewhere, not only does your career bite the dust, mine does, too."

"All right, I'm convinced. No more sex in high places. I don't know how I will communicate this to Suleiman. Probably, I'll just not get myself into a position where sleeping with him is possible."

"No, I think you have to be proactive and let him know that it's over. Done."

"Do you think it is OK if I still see him professionally?"

"As far as I'm concerned. You still may be able to get some good information from him," concluded Ernestine, ever the professional, dryly.

As Bernadette left her office, she heard Ms. Grant ask Ms. Sertoli to find out if the Ambassador could see her right away.

XI

The wheels of an Air Force C-130 touched down precisely at the scheduled time of 1500 hours on a scorching Wednesday afternoon. Michael Eisenstat, MD, accompanied by Administrative Officer Prudholme and Consular Officer Berkeley Eaton, was there to represent the Ambassador. At the moment of touchdown, Hospital Administer Dr. Tontan pulled up on the tarmac in his chauffeur-driven Mercedes.

Michael had recognized long before that Keita-Coulibaly was no exemplar of the advances in airport security. Any terrorist prepared to spend a few days in Donolu could, with ease, get a bomb aboard most any plane or shoot an airliner out of the sky. The fact that no American or Israeli airlines landed there, coupled with the typical terrorist's unwillingness to put up with a few days in Donolu, made such an episode exceedingly unlikely.

The 2000-meter runway, the longer of two at the airport, was lined on both sides by tiny farms up to the macadam, cultivating peanuts, millet, and sorghum. Dozens of mud huts were within a wing's breadth of either side of the runway, such that an errant landing, not even noticed by the passengers, could make several people homeless. Only three or four planes landed daily, making the nuisance factor worth the risk for the nearby residents.

The plane, about the size of a 707, was the only large craft at the airport when it pulled up. The first person off the stairs was a short, fiftyish gray-haired woman whose US Army uniform sported a single silver star on each shoulder. Her black plastic nametag read FIMBRI.

"Welcome General Fimbri. I am Dr. Michael Eisenstat, the Regional Medical Officer here in Zinani. I am here representing Ambassador Fairchild, who is under the weather. This is Conrad Prudholme, our administrative officer, and Berkeley Eaton, the consular officer." Being under the weather in this case meant that Fairchild thought it was too hot to go outdoors.

"Please call me Connie." Brigadier General Constance Fimbri, RN, had made it farther in the US Army than any other nurse. She had enlisted during Vietnam and was rewarded for her tireless work at the hospital in Da Nang. She spent several years as chief nurse at Walter Reed Hospital and a year earlier had been appointed, over several MD candidates, as head of all things medical in the European theater.

Michael introduced her to Dr. Tontan. "He is the Chief of Staff at Lassoso Hospital, where this equipment is headed." Tontan presented a limp hand and one word, "Welcome," to the important visitor.

Eaton headed off with the passports of the General and her staff, plus aircraft crew, and Prudholme, after pointing out that she could call him Connie too, sought shade beneath a wing and set about organizing the unloading.

"So, Connie, what did you bring us?" The Embassy had no cargo manifest before the landing, and Michael was anxious. Looking at the massive size of the flying machine he said, "Whatever it is, there is a lot of it."

"I hope you don't think all of that is for you." Only a small part of what we are carrying is to get off here. We will be making stops in four neighboring countries before we are finished: Mauritania, Mali, Burkina Faso, and Niger. Plus, we are carrying some military hardware for Niger, in addition to the hand-me-down medical stuff ... excuse me, the surplus medical equipment." She belatedly recognized that Dr. Tontan understood English even though, aside from "Welcome," he had the presence of a deaf-mute.

Recognizing that shade was not enough to offer comfort for the wool-uniformed general, Prudholme guided them into the terminal building. They moved to the so-called VIP lounge, a dark, mildewed room with torn carpeting, a cheap sound system playing an endless loop of martial music, and barely serviceable couches and chairs. Someone from Zinanian protocol brought them bottles of Coke and Fanta. Nurse Fimbri chain-smoked her Camels.

"You will be getting about one hundred beds and mattresses, quite a bit of lab equipment including two refrigerators, some desks and lamps, and storage cabinets. Then there are crates and crates of disposables and smaller stuff. I noticed on the manifest that you are getting a gross each of bedpans and male urinals, lots of syringes and needles, test tubes, some small surgical instruments, and several hundred pounds of medicines."

Eisenstat's first thought on hearing the list was that neither the Ambassador nor the President and his minions were going to be thrilled. More significant questions then came to mind. "The lab stuff and refrigerators, are they 110 or 220 volts?"

"One-ten like all American electrical appliances. Our hospitals in Europe are wired with 110 even though 220 is standard in most of the countries."

"Two-twenty is standard here. Did you bring any transformers to adapt them?"

"No, we don't stock transformers."

"Yikes." He recognized that they would have to come up with the money to buy transformers or anything electric would be of absolutely no value.

"What do you know about the medicines? Are they usable here and is there some time left on them before they expire?"

"I have no idea. The manifest just says drugs. I would hope that those that packed them up would have given some thought to that issue, but you know the Army."

"No, I don't but I can guess what you mean."

Eaton came into the lounge announcing that the papers were in order and that the unloading process was about to begin. The General bid good bye to Dr. Tontan. He grunted and fled to his car.

As Zinanian employees of the US Embassy, supervised by GSO Chief Ralph Fleming, began moving the containers from the plane to a truck, the four other Americans piled in the Cherokee and made the ten mile, forty-five minute drive into the heart of town.

Fimbri and her entourage were booked into the *Hotel de la Liberté*, one of the two buildings in the city of more than three stories. The *Liberté* had been an impressive structure when the construction enterprise that put up many of the world's Hiltons in the late 60's finished it. Like nearly everything in the Sahel, its majesty had fallen dramatically in the ensuing decades. The gleaming white facade had taken on the omnipresent laterite red-brown. The marble floors were cracked and dangerous. Re-upholstery was an unknown art and twenty years of public use created a distinctly ramshackle lobby. The fact that it was still the choice for most important visitors was strictly due to the lack of competition.

The Ambassador knew that he must give recognition to the arrival of a US general in his country and hosted a cocktail party that evening at his residence. The same group that came to the fateful dinner at Chez Eisenstat was invited, in addition to a few more members of the medical and military communities. Minister Coulibaly brought a different woman, presumably another wife, this one much younger than the previous and possessing more *joie de vivre*. Maggie Traore was again present and, as before, Tontan came alone. The usual libations and crackers spread with processed cheese made up the consumables and the whole thing was over in ninety minutes.

Jill and Michael were asleep under the mosquito net when the phone rang. As night calls from his small fit patient list came by radio rather than phone, the ring heralded either a call from the Ambassador or one of the Marines on duty in the Embassy, or a call from a friend in Beverly Hills who forgot that there was a nine-hour difference between the two cities.

"Dr. Eisenstat, this is Sergeant Rice at Post 1."

"Uh-huh."

"We have just had a call from the Liberté Hotel saying that the General is very sick. She would like you to come over right away."

Probably just a case of diarrhea or vomiting from the new environs, thought the doctor. But he recognized that he would have to get up and go, something he had not done since his last month in private practice. He threw on his cutoffs, a lime green Lacoste, and Birkenstocks, and jumped in the car. It was 3:15 AM.

A cattle drive was occurring on the street in front of his house. He had heard mooing before the phone rang, but thought it part of a bovine dream. He had to weave through the animals that showed no sense of urgency to avoid being hit by his Peugeot. The trip that should have taken ten minutes at that hour took more than twice that.

His Nigerian nurse, Electra, was waiting for him in the lobby, as a result of an urgent radio message from the Sergeant. She had wisely stopped by the health unit and picked up the emergency drug and equipment valise. General Fimbri's room was on the fifth floor. Michael, as usual, declined the elevator ride and ran up the steps while Electra rode. He was pleased that he made himself stay in shape on a stationary bike, since jogging was next to impossible in this hot, crowded metropolis.

The door to room 507 was open. He entered and saw on the bed a woman looking very different than the one he had left at the Ambassador's a few hours earlier. Her face was ashen, not just as a result of removing her make-up. Beads of sweat rolled off her as if she had just played full court basketball.

"What's wrong General?"

"I think that I'm having a heart attack," she answered between labored breaths.

"What do you feel?"

"Like someone dumped a load of bricks on my chest."

"When did it start?"

"About two hours ago. I thought it was indigestion. But the chest pain went into my arm and jaw and I knew that it was my heart."

"Do you have a history of heart problems? Any angina or high blood pressure?"

"I'm on blood pressure meds and my cholesterol is pretty high." Michael wanted to point out the speed with which she went through a pack of cigarettes but realized there was nothing to be gained at this point.

Michael Eisenstat, Internist with special interest in cardiology, had plenty of experience with this sort of patient. There was almost no doubt that her initial diagnosis was correct. Everything for a textbook diagnosis of myocardial infarction was present. In Beverly Hills, this was a straightforward situation. Call the ambulance, transport the patient to the Coronary Care Unit at Cedars-Sinai, prove the diagnosis with an EKG, give the drugs to try to dissolve the clot, or catheterize the arteries and put in a stent before the damage becomes irreversible, then monitor in the cardiac care unit and be prepared for complications. Donolu was a different story, especially starting from the fifth floor of the *Liberté*.

"Start an IV Electra, please." He was praying that the General wouldn't develop any heart rhythm problems before he could get her to the health unit where he had Zinani's only heart monitor and defibrillator. But he would be as prepared as possible if she did. He had the nurse give her a dose of Xylocaine to diminish the chance of a possibly fatal arrhythmia and morphine to lessen the excruciating pain. Calling an ambulance never entered his mind. The one they had was probably home with the surgeon and it was no better equipped than an Embassy Cherokee, except that it had a gurney. The hotel brought its wheel chair and the patient was loaded into it with Electra acting as a human IV pole. The elevator was called; under these circumstances Michael could not refuse to get in. The ride down caused him to break into a sweat not quantitatively or qualitatively different from that of his stricken patient.

He was afraid that getting into the Jeep and across town to the Embassy might touch off a cardiac arrest. Having no defibrillator with him could mean the demise of his patient. Except for the bucking bronco ride, the transport proved uneventful. He kept his finger on her pulse the entire time. An occasional premature beat caused short-term concern but she was generally in a good steady rhythm at a rate neither too fast nor too slow.

His second elevator ride of his stay in Africa brought out nearly as much perspiration as the first, but resulted in the patient and staff arriving in the relative safety of the Abattoir. Oxygen was started although he knew that his supply would only last two or three hours. Electra quickly slapped on the EKG leads and handed the recording to Michael. His diagnosis was accurate; she had irrefutable evidence of an acute myocardial infarction. He wished that the clot-busting streptokinase he had ordered had arrived, but knew that was too much to expect since he had only sent the request six weeks earlier. No facility within a thousand miles had either streptokinase nor any of the other medicines used in the first world to dissolve clots, so he couldn't just borrow a dose from a nearby hospital. He would have to hope for the best. He was comforted with the knowledge that a large majority of

LARRY HILL

patients who get to medical care with heart attacks survive them, especially if there is a defibrillator present to deal with the life-threatening arrhythmias. His office was no ICU but he was going to do everything in his power to make it just as good as one.

His old defibrillator had an adequate cardiac monitor attached; unfortunately, it had no alarm so that someone would have to watch every heartbeat. "Electra, please call Maggie Traore and ask her if she would be willing to come down and act as an ICU nurse for a few hours. We are going to need to spell each other." He was glad that he had done some training with both Electra and Maggie in continuing education of arrhythmia recognition.

Connie Fimbri was feeling much better, surrounded by the best medical team Zinani had to offer and drugged with a total of 15 milligrams of IV morphine. The pain was controlled and the sweat had dried. Her respirations were no longer labored.

But, she had to get out of the country, ASAP. State Department had long ago decided that Donolu was no place to take care of a sick patient and had committed itself to evacuating any of its employees and their families to either Frankfurt, Paris, or London. Since General Fimbri was Germany-based, it made sense to direct her to Frankfurt. C-130s don't make good hospital planes, any more than an aircraft carrier would make a good fishing boat. A call had to go out to Germany to get a plane flown in.

"Eight hours minimum, they said."

"Eight hours of ICU work for us," they responded.

After things quieted down, Michael looked at his watch for the first time since he left his house. It was 6:30 AM. He sat down and started on a cup of coffee that Judy Deane had brewed. Judy, the Ambassador, and Conrad Prudholme had all come to the scene early on and had been involved in the logistics of calling Germany, getting landing rights for the hospital plane, and other details that go into arranging an emergency medical evacuation.

"Dr. Eisenstat, come quick!" The accent was Nigerian.

He rushed to the patient's bedside and saw that his patient was in the midst of a grand mal seizure. He looked at the monitor. "Jesus Christ, she is in V Fib!" Ventricular fibrillation is the rhythm that kills most

84

who die of heart attacks and the rhythm for which coronary care units were invented.

Electra started doing closed chest cardiac massage, expecting someone else to start mouth-to-mouth resuscitation. "No, no, not that! Charge the defibrillator!"

The nurse fumbled at the machine, having never used it in an emergency and having not trained on the unit in many months. Michael leaped to the defibrillator and punched the orange button. The light went on and the indicator needle quickly moved to the ready position. He pulled the paddles out of their holders, placed one under Connie's left breast and the other on the upper part of the right chest.

"Stand back!" He pushed the deliver-a-jolt button causing the General's torso and arms to jump partly off the bed. A look at the monitor showed no change in the lethal rhythm.

"Three hundred sixty watt seconds!" As high as the defibrillator could go. This time Electra made the appropriate adjustment and recharged the machine. "Stand back!" The extremities flew higher. Another glance at the monitor. "Sinus rhythm." Normal, standard, good old garden-variety sinus rhythm, the kind most all humans have most all of the time.

The seizure stopped and the officer, who had been out for about ninety seconds, awoke, moaning, and rubbed the part of her chest that had just been the sight of the discharge of a very large amount of electrical energy. "What happened?"

"Just a little problem with your heart rhythm." Even nurses don't need to hear that they have just been brought back from death.

"Electra, please start a Xylocaine drip." Xylocaine can be dripped into an IV line to prevent a recurrence of the awful event.

The remainder of the day was as tranquil as could be with an unstable heart attack patient a continent away from appropriate care. The heart rhythm stayed normal sinus throughout. The blood pressure never dipped below 100 and no evidence of shock or lung congestion appeared. For the day, the health unit played the single and solitary role of a dedicated coronary care unit. The rashes and sore throats and coughs and minor bruises and sprains and gamma globulin candidates were asked to return the following day. The phone lines were kept open to serve as the nerve center for the logistics of getting the evacuation plane into the country.

At 3:15 PM, twelve hours after Michael received the first phone call, he received another one telling him to get his patient to Keita-Coulibaly International at 4 PM for the flight to Germany. He was too tired to be bothered by his third elevator ride of the day; he was certainly not going to take his eye off the portable monitor until she was safely ensconced on the air ambulance. General Fimbri had actually gotten a few hours of sleep; her only complaint on the ride out was the discomfort in the areas of the electric shocks.

When they pulled up on the tarmac, the military air ambulance had just arrived and was parked next to the C-130, like a dachshund puppy standing beside a Great Dane. Having been presented the case report by Dr. Eisenstat, the traveling military emergency physician saluted his wheel chair-bound patient and boss and supervised getting her aboard.

Michael boarded the craft to see what it looked like. He was impressed. The value of the equipment aboard clearly exceeded that of all the medical hardware of Zinani. He shook hands with the patient who owed her survival to him, and parted with words that he did not later regret, "Think about maybe giving up those cigarettes, General."

XII

Lassoso General Hospital has a large storage facility on the backside of its two-hectare (five-acre) lot. Half a dozen large pallets of boxes had made the trip from the belly of the C-130 to the front of the building and a media event was scheduled for the grand opening.

Representing the United States were Ambassador Fairchild, Ernestine, Michael, Chen, and the interpreter, Anisa Larue. The President-for-life was there with Health Minister Coulibaly and Hospital Administrator Tontan, plus an assortment of unidentified others. ZTV, the only channel in the country, was represented, as were the radio station and *Les Nouvelles*, the official print organ of Mr. President.

Under the shimmering noontime heat, the Ambassador gave a brief speech in surprisingly good French, complementing the Zinanian people, its doctors, politicians, electricians, nurses, military leaders and troops, sick folks, and even the residents of the morgue, who would soon be able to lie in more comfortable repose with the arrival of the American medical supplies. OIL responded with a prepared statement, obviously written by Coulibaly, thanking the US for taking Zinanian medicine out of the 19th century and helping make Lassoso General one of the finest health care centers in Africa. Anisa gave an under-the-breath translation to Michael who was the least likely to understand. He became progressively anxious with each comment about "finest," "best," and "modern."

Eisenstat's anxieties were soon to be justified. The pallets, each supporting one or more shipping boxes, stood front to back. One by one, the heavy-duty wire cutters opened the weighty containers. The first four contained nothing but beds -- non-electric bedframes on legs (usually but not always four) with wheels and mattresses -- 115 beds. Unidentifiable liquids had dried and soiled several of the mattresses. No doubt that the hospital needed beds; its capacity was rated at 405 beds but they owned just over half that. Many were mats on the ground, springs without mattresses, or complete beds containing more than one patient. But beds, they could get anywhere. They could even make beds.

There were two pallets to go to turn this haven of death into one of the finest health care centers in Africa. Number five had the two refrigerators. New, they weren't. Good size, 25 cubic feet, but dusty, well scratched-up, with frayed electrical cords ending in 110 volt plugs. The packers in Germany hadn't bothered to take off the nurses' working schedules that had been taped to the door of one.

Behind the refrigerators were pairs of steel gray desks and swivel chairs, some bookshelves, six gooseneck lamps, a surgical ceiling lamp, and a variety of lab equipment more appropriate for a high school biology class than Mayo Clinic Africa. There was a centrifuge adequate for urinalyses but little else, a counting device for hand enumerating the various types of white blood cells, lots of pipettes and test tubes, plus six Bunsen burners, of World War II vintage.

Michael studied the face of President Lassoso. He looked like a child who had been expecting a pony from Santa, but who had just opened the biggest box under the tree and found new shoes and OshKosh B'Gosh pants. That same child might still harbor the hope that the pony was in the back yard; Lassoso's look said that the CT scanner, the arteriogram machine and the advanced computer system just had to be on pallet #6. The situation called for a brass band; there was none nearby.

Container number six was full of boxes. Unless they were making CT scanners a lot smaller than Lassoso remembered from his visit to New York, or CT scanners could be broken down into multiple small components, there was about to be one disappointed dictator.

One at a time, the cartons were removed from the pallet. The first contained tongue depressors, 144 boxes, each with 250 wooden tongue depressors. Cotton tip swabs followed, thousands of them. Vaginal speculums filled the next one, hundreds of dozen plastic speculums, disposable, size small. For a variety of reasons, not the least of which was that Zinanian women have on average eight children, small was not big enough, but who knew? The male urinals and the bedpans were bulky and steely so took up a lot of room and weighed much more than the plastic and wood stuff. Syringes and needles, microscope slides, and bandages -- several boxes each; Michael knew that they were sorely needed in this hospital where hygiene was a barely known concept, and the chances of transmitting infectious disease via used syringes or secondhand bandages were very high. But they weren't much good for creating a computerized tomographic image.

The drugs came next. Big cartons filled with small boxes. Nervously, Michael looked in one with Dr. Tontan looking over his shoulder: sodium bicarbonate solution, of little use; chloramphenicol, an antibiotic often used in the third world but considered to have too many serious side effects for any but the rarest use in the US; cold pills numbering over 100,000, good but hardly a reputation-booster for the hospital; ampicillin, a tried and true antibiotic, but six months expired, all of it; athlete's foot cream and athlete's foot powder; water purification tablets, a concept totally beyond Zinanian comprehension; Retin-A for the prevention and treatment of skin wrinkles, just expired; aspirin, aspirin with caffeine, aspirin with buffers.

One very large box remained in the far end of pallet #6.

Dr. Eisenstat and the other Americans knew that it was not a scanner, nor anything else worthy of being featured on the nightly news. Lassoso's gang hoped otherwise. Six large Zinanians were required to move it out of the container. Opening the carton revealed an eight-foot metal and glass refrigeration unit with a large red cross on each end -- a blood bank refrigerator, 110 volts, of course. Nice, much needed in this land of primitive blood banking, but not newsworthy.

The President's face lengthened perceptibly, reflecting neither obvious anger nor glee. He hurriedly whispered something in Coulibaly's ear and walked to his limo, tumbled through the open door, and motioned his driver to leave. No thanks to Mr. Ambassador, nor comments to the press or TV cameras - he just left. The Health Minister shook hands with the American contingent, saying au revoir and pointedly not merci. Dr. Tontan shuffled away unobserved. There were urinalyses to perform.

"I'm not sure that we overwhelmed Lassoso with our generosity," said Fairchild on the short drive back to the Embassy.

"That's certainly an understatement, Sir," responded the DCM. "I'm surprised that he didn't tell us to call the C-130 back and get the stuff out of town."

"Obviously, the hospital is going to be able to take advantage of the stuff, especially the beds, and the electrical equipment, once we buy them the transformers," commented Eisenstat. "The fact that we didn't impress the President is hardly a factor, as your goal, Mr. Ambassador, was to make a difference for the hospital."

"You're right, but I would have hoped at least for a neutral response rather than the one we got. We have not put any diplomatic IOUs in the bank with this one. We aren't going to be able to say, 'Remember the hospital equipment,' when it comes time to get them to vote our way in the UN."

"I can't imagine that it won't help us with the people. It's going to look good on TV tonight," said Chen.

"Don't be so sure that it will be covered," cautioned Ms. Grant.

"I wonder what Lassoso whispered to Coulibaly?" asked Chen.

"Who knows? We may find out about that on ZTV."

They did. The lead story was an announcement that Libyan Ambassador Mukhtar had promised the gift of a new Phillips CT scanner from Holland, which would arrive within two months. The American beds, refrigerators, drugs, and blood-banking equipment were not covered at all, nor did an article about the American gifts appear anywhere in the following day's *Les Nouvelles*.

When Dr. Eisenstat returned to his office, there were a number of patients sitting in the waiting room, including Political Officer O'Kelly.

His secretary, Madam Diallo, the only person in the Embassy whom he did not call by first name, had gotten her job during the reign of a previous Regional Medical Officer. An earlier Ambassador had to repay a favor to one of his friends in the cabinet and gave the Minister's wife the position, in spite of the fact that she was totally without secretarial skills. Her typing speed hovered in the single digits, her English was barely understandable, and her ability to organize her work and finish it in a timely fashion non-existent. She would not greet patients when they arrived, reacting only after they either spoke up or stared in her face long enough to engender a response. Michael had been asked to replace her by several of his patients, and wanted very much to send her packing, but the DCM made it clear that doing so would not be politically advisable.

"Whom should I see first, Madam Diallo?"

"I don't know. They all came about the same time."

"Does anyone have an appointment?"

"No." This was not unusual. He was rarely busy enough to require advanced arrangements. Nonetheless, he would always take a patient with an appointment before a non-emergent drop in.

He went back into the waiting room and asked, "Who's first?"

Francine Osler, a young missionary mother with her three-month-old raised her hand, much to Michael's displeasure, as pediatrics was his least favorite part of the job. Passing O'Kelly, he said, "Bernadette, why don't you just go back to your office and I can call you."

"No doctor, I'll wait here," she replied, obviously holding back tears. He decided that he would see Dette second, even if it wasn't her turn.

He marched back with the mother and crying child to learn that the little boy had been fussy and feverish for a few hours. Mother was dressed in a grimy shapeless flowered dress. The child had a diaper and an equally dirty, tattered shirt. Both looked and smelled like bathing was not a regular event. Mom offered a fever as young Gabriel's presenting complaint. "How high was his temp, Francine?" Michael started.

"I don't know. We don't have a thermometer." He had heard this answer more often than he could tolerate but successfully held back lambasting the worried mother.

He did all the right examinations, the ears, the throat, the chest, all the while knowing that the child was not particularly sick. He attempted to reassure Mom that this was just a minor virus that would pass in a couple of days. She broke down in tears. "It's so hard doctor with my husband gone all the time."

Michael was aware that the family lived in a tiny village two hours south of Donolu, with no electricity, no running water, and no other English speakers within 50 kilometers. Her husband, the pastor, traveled from village to village, often spending two or three nights away from home. In view of his patient's obvious depression, Eisenstat wished that he had time to help, but he knew that he had to see the equally tearful pregnant Foreign Service Officer in the waiting room. His job description and his personal choice required that he give preference to an official American employee over an unofficial patient. He gave Gabriel Tylenol and his Mom an hour appointment for the next week.

"Please have Ms. O'Kelly come into my office, Madam Diallo."

She mumbled what he interpreted to be a condescending acceptance of the order. He was never sure that his secretary heard, understood, or was willing to carry out his requests. Her answers were nearly always unintelligible. The inability to fire Madam Diallo was the one thing about Foreign Service work that made him miss the private sector approach to medicine in California.

Bernadette's response to his usual greeting was, "I'm fine." She hardly looked it. She took an unusually contorted seat on one of the Abattoir's gunmetal gray steel and plastic armchairs. Her short auburn hair evidenced inattention. She wore no sunglasses, so the redness of her eyes could not be hidden.

"Sure you're fine."

"OK, I'm not fine, I'm crappy."

"Why?" Michael recalled his Psychiatry 101 drills - short answers and questions; let the patient do the talking.

"I'm pregnant, I have to fly to Paris to get my second abortion and now my sex life is over. Other than that, I'm fine."

"You decided to go to Paris?"

"Yes, I heard what you said. There's no way I am going to carry the baby and no way that I would have it done here. Paris is a lot cheaper than London, so I've made a reservation to go on tomorrow's UTA flight. I guess that I'll just drop in at the closest hospital to the airport."

"Come off it, Dette. That won't be necessary. You aren't the first woman of the US Foreign Service to have this problem. We have a way of helping, even though Reagan made it impossible for us to be involved financially. I can call Trudy Bechet, the Embassy nurse in Paris, and she can set the whole thing up for you."

"Thanks, Michael."

"No problem. Now what's this about an end to your sex life?"

"After we met the other day, I saw Ernestine. I just couldn't face the Ambassador directly and talk about my sex life."

"I understand."

"She said just what I knew she would say, and the same thing I would say had our roles been reversed."

"That was?"

"End the relationship. So, I did. Now, I might as well just enroll in a nunnery after the abortion."

"Sure. Good idea. I understand the pay's not bad and they feed you well. The outfits are just your style, maybe a little nicer than what you usually wear."

Bernadette didn't smile.

"How did you end it?" Michael continued.

"Suleiman called the office the next afternoon and asked if he could come to my house for dinner. I accepted, trying not to let on what I would have to tell him. He came over, carrying a large bouquet of flowers. Michael, no one has given me flowers since college, and that was my own brother."

"Uh-huh." Psych 101.

"I cooked a nice meal. Believe it or not, I used those Army Surplus rations that the Ambassador had brought in for the hospital patients. The canned chicken breasts were fine with the curry sauce I put on them. I had had a couple of scotch and sodas before he arrived and finished most of a bottle of white wine at dinner, trying to calm my nerves and soften the devastation of what I knew I would have to say."

"Uh-huh."

"After dinner, he asked for me to show him my house. He had only been inside once before, that for less than half an hour, with his nephew. I really felt stupid showing this army general my kitchen and storeroom, when I knew that it was just a lead-up to the bedroom."

"Right."

"When we got into the bedroom, which I had left a mess for who knows what reason, he put his arm around me and I forced myself to say, 'Not tonight.' He sort of pushed me toward the bed, I guess thinking that a little force would succeed. I had to say that I was serious. I couldn't believe the look on his face. Not anger, just sadness, like a little kid not getting what he wanted."

"Then what happened?"

"He made a beeline for the front door. I asked if he didn't want to know why and he reluctantly sat down. I told him that the Ambassador had been hearing rumors about us and that he felt that our continuing would jeopardize relations between the two countries, and that I would be asked to leave Zinani if I didn't break it off. He reacted more strongly than I had seen him before, cursing President Lassoso, and the Ambassador, but claiming that he understood my position. He said something about us staying friends and I agreed, but I suspect that I won't be hearing from or seeing much of Suleiman anymore."

"Don't be so sure. It sounds to me like the guy really is in love with you."

"We'll see."

"You didn't say anything about being pregnant?"

"God, no! That's all I would have needed to screw things up even more than they are. He would not have been pleased to hear that a child of his was about to be scraped out of my uterus. I might have had his entire division surrounding my house."

"I hear you. By the way, what are you telling people as to why you are going to Paris?"

"My brother is going to be there for an International Cash Register trade fair."

"Sounds good to me. I'll take you to the airport."

"Thanks, Michael. You are a good friend." She bussed him on the cheek and left, more sprightly than she came in. Dr. Eisenstat was sure that his old psychiatry professor from UCLA would have been impressed. He asked Madam Diallo to send in the next runny nose.

The next evening, Michael and Jill took Bernadette to Keita-Coulibaly International for the midnight flight.

The usual madhouse greeted them. The massive crowds made one think that dozens of airliners would be leaving within the hour. The schedule board, updated by hand like a theater marquee, chronicled only the Air France flight to Paris, via Bamako, Mali. Dozens of young men, hoping for a few coins, had dashed toward the car to carry luggage, which in this case involved a single, small carry-on. Bernadette's "brother" was only going to be there for a couple of days, so her trip was

94

to be short. The men's services were refused, resulting in a mumble that the threesome interpreted to be an anti-American diatribe. They then ran the gauntlet of shoeshine boys; all three *tubabs* wore running shoes

It took one of three things to get into the airport departure facility: a ticket, a few lassosos, or a white face. Bernadette flashed the former and the latter, Jill and Michael the latter only; all three were quickly over the threshold. It was obvious that many local citizens had shelled out the money, as the Americans were greeted by a mob of additional bootblacks and salespeople hacking masks, statues, batiks, and beads. Their English was limited to "My friend," and "Good price." Michael unsuccessfully attempted to immunize himself from such people by claiming that he only spoke Latvian.

There were three check-in windows for the Air France flight, one of which was for premium class customers. The other two were overwhelmed by a chaotic mass of humanity. Zinanians do not recognize the concept of standing in line. Most of the ticketed passengers were men with large black trunks, obviously empty, as they could be moved toward the window with a minimal kick. These men were representative of Zinani's entrepreneurial class, the import-export people. They were on their way to Paris to pick up a load of consumer goods, usually at retail price, to bring back to their luxury-starved homeland to sell at a handsome profit. A couple hundred lassosos slipped to the customs man on the way back usually obviated the requirement for duties.

The decision as to who gets checked into economy next is based on speed, guile, and most importantly, girth and muscle power. Bernadette was gutsy but neither big nor strong enough to guarantee her place on the plane. Overbooking in Africa makes the same in the US look almost rare. If you aren't among the early check-ins you are likely to spend a few extra days in town, unless you freely distribute some large denomination lassoso notes. Michael, doing the heavy work for his patient, had learned the ropes and succeeded in getting to the window well before the allotment was filled. Plus, he had a white face.

Bernadette and the Eisenstats eventually filed into the waiting room, having not had to prove to anyone that they weren't carrying a handgun or plastic explosives. An exit tax was required, as were half a dozen stamps on the passport and boarding pass. Michael wished that he could have taken the women into the VIP lounge that he had used during General Fimbri's visit. The mildew and dankness of that lounge were a paradise compared to the noise, rubbish, and body odor of steerage.

The flight was called only 90 minutes late, amazingly prompt for a West African departure. Another mad rush ensued as no one had assigned seats. Bernadette ended up in a shabby center seat, between two heavy smoking import-export men. The food was barely edible, the wine not bad. She wanted to sleep but had not taken a sleeping pill. She was concerned about its effect on the fetus, in spite of the fact that she was about to have an abortion.

"Honey, what is wrong with Bernadette?" asked Jill on the trip home.

"What do you mean?"

"That was not the Bernadette O'Kelly that you and I know. Something is very wrong with her. I can't help but think that her General friend has something to do with it. Either she is pregnant and going to Paris for an abortion, or she is carrying some secrets for either the General or the Fairchilds, or that she is looking at another job on the advice of the Ambassador. You know damn well that her brother didn't just learn that he would be coming to Paris for a convention that has been on the books for months."

"I don't know. She didn't tell me anything." Lying to one's wife should be included in the revised Hippocratic Oath.

Somewhere over Algeria, Bernadette began having abdominal cramps. Her initial thought was airline food poisoning. None of her neighbors appeared, however, to be in any distress. The pains became more frequent and more severe. She waited in line for the one functioning toilet, finally entered, and found that she was bleeding, not heavily, a bit like one of her periods. Having figured that she would not be in need of tampons for some time, she had brought none. She used a wad of Air France toilet tissue and did her best to tolerate the pain for the next three hours, at which point the symptoms abated. Upon arrival in Paris, she immediately took a taxi to the American Hospital, where they were waiting for her on the instructions of Nurse Bechet. A quick examination followed by an ultrasound and a meeting with the doctor, who in perfect English said, "Mrs. O'Kelly, you have had a miscarriage. It is complete. We do not need to do anything more." He wrote her a prescription for birth control pills, iron tablets, antibiotics and pain capsules; French-trained doctors love to prescribe medicines. Bernadette cried steadily for two hours in the hospital waiting room; she had no one to talk to; she had been in France for less than five hours.

XIII

Bernadette wanted to return the following day but instead she stayed in Paris for the originally budgeted four days to avoid embarrassing questions. After unenthusiastically touring the Louvre for the third time, scouting the apses of the Notre Dame for her fifth, and taking her second float on the Seine, she flew back to Donolu on Air Afrique, with things looking a little bit rosier, as she'd been granted a complimentary business class upgrade. Brief stops in Dakar, Senegal, and Ouagadougou, Burkina Faso, preceded the always frightening landing at Keita-Coulibaly International. As she had not gone on official diplomatic business, she assumed that she'd not be greeted on arrival and feared that she'd need to argue over the price of a taxi. She was therefore surprised and pleased when Ernestine Grant and the Embassy expediter, Salif, met her on the tarmac. It was 2:15 AM.

"Hey Bernadette! How's your brother?" shouted Ms. Grant. They moved to the bedraggled VIP lounge while Salif got her black diplomatic passport stamped.

"Oh, he's fine. It was nice to see him, even though he was in meetings most of the time." She had worked out an elaborate set of falsehoods to deal with her absence. "What brings you out to the airport at this hour? You can't have missed me that badly."

"A lot's happened since you left. Have you heard any of it?"

Zinani does not get mentioned in papers printed elsewhere, unless scores are dying of natural disasters. Further, Dette had not glanced at a newspaper or communicated with anyone in the know since she left. "No, what's up?"

"First of all, your friend General Sacco has been demoted. They took the home guard division from him, took his star away, made him a colonel, and put him in charge of the Quartermaster Corps. His biggest decisions now are how much rice to buy and how many helmets to order.

"Jees, when did that happen?"

"The day after you left. He has been trying to get in touch with you ever since. He has no interest in talking to anyone else in the Embassy. He wants you to call him tomorrow, actually today," she said, looking at her watch.

"Where?"

"I don't know. Probably the supply depot."

"What about his troops in the division that he said would be loyal?"

"Nothing so far as we know. Lassoso elevated an unknown Captain from Sokimbo, a sycophant of his, giving him a star and command. We think that the new guy, General Joro, will have a hard time getting support from his troops."

"You started with, 'first of all.' What else?"

"Plenty. The students are getting active, more so than at any time in years. There have been demonstrations in front of the Education Ministry calling for more scholarships and a voice for students in curriculum choices. There's talk of a strike unless they get what they want, including the release of the five PPD members jailed in the last couple of weeks.

"Is Oumou Kinsa involved in this?"

"Not publicly, but it's hard to imagine that she's not. We're hoping that you can get through to her."

"It sounds like I'll be busy tomorrow."

"Yeah, it does. You were wrong; we did miss you that much."

For the first time in two weeks, Dette was thinking about something other than the fetus.

An hour later, the Embassy Cherokee pulled up in front of Bernadette's riverside house. She was greeted with a round of "*Ça va's*" by her night guard who told her that Colonel Sacco had been to see her the previous afternoon. Colonel, not General. She found herself too tired and distracted to doze off; an Ambien allowed for little more than a couple of hours of unsatisfactory sleep.

Salam Noro was the Zinanian member of the Embassy staff whose job it was to know about and make contacts with government ministries, the National Assembly, and the military. He had been a mid-level functionary of the Foreign Ministry before being offered the US Embassy job at several times his previous salary. He was every American's favorite Zinanian; his English was impeccable thanks to a USAID-supported stint at the University of Indiana. He seemed to know everybody, and was related to at least half of the nation's nabobs. When Dette walked the streets of Donolu with Salam she compared it to being seen at home with Michael Jordan or Paul Newman. Although he professed no interest in politics, Americans from the Ambassador down felt that he would be a most logical choice for President or Prime Minister should democracy ever come to Zinani.

Salam's office belied his level of competence, his intelligence, his respect, and his importance. Windowless, it was barely bigger than the room's two metal desks, his own and that of his male secretary, a man whose employment was successfully promoted by the Zinanian government.

"Welcome back, Bernadette!" effused Salam when the bleary eyed Political Officer stepped into his office at 8:30 AM. "How is your brother?" Apparently everybody had bought the story.

"Very well, thank you. How are you? Your wife? Your new daughter?" Salam and his only wife had just had their first child a week or so before Dette's trip.

"*Ça va.*"

"Let's get a cup of coffee at *40 Voleurs?*" *40 Voleurs* was the Lebanese-owned café across the street from the Embassy. Most importantly, it was out of Salam's secretary's earshot.

As usual, hawkers selling masks and magazines, shoe shines and sex, even at 8:30 AM, surrounded the coffee house. They took a table inside, to avoid the harassment and get out of the heat.

Bernadette relayed to Salam what she had learned from the DCM earlier that morning. "What more can you tell me?"

"Not too much. I have heard that Sacco is lucky to still be employed; others tell me he's fortunate to be alive. The Health Minister was very angry and suggested to the President that Sacco be jailed, but Mr. Lassoso recognized the possible consequences and just demoted him."

"Where is Colonel Sacco now?" As far as Bernadette knew, Salam was unaware of the details of their relationship.

"He is in charge of the Quartermaster Corps and has an office in some big warehouse on the river, just outside of town."

"Do you think I can see him?"

"Of course. Take an Embassy car and go to his office. But watch out; he is probably being watched closely."

"What about the student uprisings? Are they significant?"

"I really don't know. The President is just playing a waiting game. He saw what happened in Niger last year when the dictator used a heavy hand in controlling student demonstrations. He's hoping that the students will get hungry and bored and leave. Some of the students I know say that they won't stop until Lassoso is gone."

"Can you get the word to General … I mean Colonel … Sacco. Plus Oumou Kinsa -- I would like to see her today, too?"

"No trouble with Sacco. Oumou has not been answering anybody's calls lately. I'll try."

No one should confuse the Begoro in Donolu with the Seine in Paris or the Thames in London. Instead of Big Ben and the Houses of Parliament, the banks are lined with piles of garbage. In place of the Quay d'Orsay, there is a graveyard for the rusted bodies of old cars, trucks and buses. No tree is in evidence; all have long since been felled for firewood. The stench of the riverfront makes the smell of the rest of the capital almost tolerable. Aside from numerous pirogues carrying everything from passengers to passion fruit, there is no evidence of this being a port in any first-world sense. There are no large boats or barges, no cranes or forklifts, no stevedores or customs agents.

The Quartermaster Depot of the Zinanian Army is a single one-story wooden building, surrounded by a chain-link fence, topped by two layers of razor wire. Multiple holes in the fence made the security concept superfluous. Equally ineffective were the guards at the gate, attentive primarily to their domino game. The Cherokee entered the premises with a minimalist flick of the senior guard's wrist.

A handful of fatigue-bedecked soldiers sat on sagging benches under the tin eaves of the building, their only evident activities being sun avoidance and cigarette smoking. Dette often wondered how these lowly paid, uniformed functionaries could afford cigarettes at the street price of nearly a dollar a pack. Extortion maybe. None reacted in any way when Bernadette exited the car and entered the building. The electricity was not functioning; the inside of the storage facility was lit only through a pair of glassless windows and multiple cracks in the wooden walls. "*Ou est le chef?*" Bernadette asked a sullen young man, seated motionless at a desk near the entry. He shrugged in the direction of a closed door a few feet away.

She knocked lightly on the door. "*Entrez.*" She recognized the voice but heard in it less fervor than she remembered.

The Colonel's office had a good-sized window; the late morning sunlight poured in, in stark contrast to the dungeon-like atmosphere of the rest of the structure. Suleiman was seated at his desk, resting stooped-shouldered on both elbows, pencil in hand. The once sharply pressed uniform had given way to a limp rag-like outfit, as much a result of the lack of air-conditioning in the office as of its owner's lack of concern. The silver star of his generalship was gone and non-descript colonel's bars were sewn onto his epaulettes. He did not look up as the door opened and his visitor entered.

"Hello, Suleiman." He stopped writing, straightened up and turned his head toward the door, all in slow motion.

"Bernadette, you have returned."

"Yes, I arrived last night. I had gone to Paris to visit my brother."

"Yes, I know. And you know what has happened to me?"

"I do. I am very sorry." She desperately wanted to embrace and kiss him but hesitated. He made no motion toward her. "Can we talk?"

"Not here." He motioned toward the door, a sign that she interpreted to mean that the friendly greeter was probably assigned the task of keeping an eye and an ear on his boss. "Let us take a walk."

Walking the banks of the Big was no easy task. The trash dumps were frequent and hazardous. The smell of rotten food and plant waste, combined with human and animal urine and excrement, was overwhelming. One had to constantly play dodge ball with motorbikes, bicycles, and pedestrians and be constantly vigilant for an automobile passing on the right or out of control; Zinani issued few drivers' licenses.

"Please tell me what happened." To overcome ambient noise, Dette had to speak at about twice her normal intensity.

"There is not much to tell. After that night at the doctor's house, when the Health Minister and I had our disagreement, I was always followed. I could tell that some of my own men had changed the way they reacted to me and that they must be on orders from someone important. Then, the night I returned from having dinner at your house, there were two men waiting in front of my concession when I got home. One told me that I should report to the Chief of Staff the next morning. It was obvious to me that I was going to be fired ... and probably put in prison. That morning, I went to the Defense Ministry. They treated me courteously, but General Stogolo wasted no time in telling me of my demotion. When I asked why, he just said that it was on the orders of President Lassoso."

"Why do you think that they demoted you and put you in that grocery store, rather than fire you or jail you...or worse?"

"Probably because of my troops in the Division. They are very loyal to me and probably would not have accepted a bigger penalty without getting violent. But, I am not sure that we have witnessed the finale of their plans for me. Lassoso, Stogolo, and the rest may think that I will be quickly forgotten, so that they can really get rid of me in a few weeks. And, they may be right."

"Why don't you just leave Zinani and ask for asylum, in France, or even the US?"

"No, I can't do that. Zinani is my home and it will soon have great turmoil. I must be here."

"For what? Is something about to happen?" He turned his eyes from her and said nothing.

"Do you know what is happening with the students and the PPD?" she asked after a moment of silence.

"I know that I know less than you do. The television and radio have not mentioned the disturbances, and the paper has only warned people to stay away. No one would be stupid enough to come see me in view of my present situation. You, my dear, are taking chances with this visit."

"But I have diplomatic immunity."

"Only as long as the government grants it to you. They could tell you to leave tonight."

"No way that would happen."

"It has happened. It can happen again."

"I'll be careful ... Suleiman, I am very sorry about the time you came to my house for dinner. I wanted the same thing that you wanted. I still want it. I want you, but for reasons that you must know and accept, I can't have you, at least for now."

"I do know and, sadly, I accept it. I am sure that your Ambassador had something to do with it and I can understand that. I, too, hope that all will change in the future. My loss of you is very much worse than the loss of my Division."

"But, I am not lost to you forever."

"If only that were true. But, you will be leaving Zinani in a few months and I must stay. There is no way I'm going to America.

"I could leave my job and stay with you."

"No, you can't."

"I love you, Suleiman."

"Thank you, Bernadette." She waited in vain for any more words.

When they returned to the Quartermaster facility, the guards were still playing dominos, the bench sitters had not moved, but the man sitting outside the office of the Chief had left.

Oumar Ibrahim Lassoso University occupied a dusty piece of land some ten miles from the heart of town. One two-story building housed the administration, while classes were taught and faculty billeted in the dozen or so single-story edifices scattered around the three-hectare campus. No leafed tree was present. Goats had denuded the small ones that had been replanted more than once; the budget never allowed for chicken wire protection. Bushes and flowers also met their rapid demise, as during most days, goats outnumbered students. The buildings were actually handsome. The architects, unlike that of the Presidential Palace, were skilled foreigners. The lack of maintenance had taken a toll and all of the structures were in dire need of replastering, repainting, and reroofing.

A fountain had been the showpiece of the central plaza. Sculpted horses and muscular men reminded one of Rome's Trevi, but the plaster figures had peeled and the fountain had not seen water for many academic years. The centerpiece had become the campus disposal pit, choked by discarded blue plastic bags. From an airplane, the fountain would appear to be full of water. Three coins pitched into Lassoso's fountain would never again be seen.

The driver stopped the Cherokee outside the Social Studies building. A handful of students walking between buildings indicated that school was in session. The great majority were men. Many sat on benches doing, as far as Dette could tell, nothing. They weren't reading or writing or even talking; several smoked. To her knowledge, transcendental meditation had not yet made an impact in Zinani. It was as if they were majors in Just Sitting There, a field with multiple devotees throughout the Sahel.

Bernadette pushed open the squeaky main door and asked the first student she saw where she could find Oumou Kinsa. She was directed to an office labeled ECONOMICS. Oumou was the only person in the room, sitting behind a corner desk in great disarray. The opening of her creaky room caused her to look up. "Miss O'Kelly. What a surprise to see you here!"

Oumou was short - less than five feet. Her eyes were wide spread on a flat but pretty face. John Lennon glasses lent the air of a high IQ. Her T-shirt said HOPKINS LACROSSE, and being XL, detracted from a much better than average figure. Levis, rarely seen on Zinanian females, and leather sandals completed the outfit. The coiffure was cornrows, representing hours of work and pain.

"I tried to call from the Dean's office, but apparently the lines to the school are out," said Bernadette. She lied, having not wanted to hear that Oumou didn't want to talk to her.

"Not as far as I know."

"Can we talk, Oumou?"

"Of course. What about?"

"You know what about."

"I'm sorry Miss O'Kelly, I don't know what you mean."

"I mean about you and the PPD and the government."

Oumou looked around the room toward corners, ceilings and floors, making obvious her concern that others were listening to the conversation. With uncharacteristic delay resulting from the lack of sleep, Bernadette caught on.

"How is your family Miss O'Kelly."

"Just fine. I have just returned from Paris where I spent four days with my brother. And your family?"

"Except for my father's business troubles, all is well. Fortunately, my salary from the University helps keep the family in food. Would you care to go for a walk with me? It's nicer outside than inside today." February in West Africa can find days with lows in the sixties and highs in the eighties. Zinanians generally wear stocking caps, quilted jackets, and scarves in February. They gather around small bonfires at night.

This was Dette's second walk invitation of the day. Based on the importance of the information gleaned on the first, she could hardly refuse the second.

As she ambled through the barren, litter-laden campus, she couldn't help but remember the beauty of most of the campuses that she had explored in the US. Class sections under the shade tree, Frisbee on the lawn, lovers strolling the walkways hand-in-hand; these were laughable to contemplate at Lassoso U.

The French had foisted on West Africa the tradition of paying scholarships to all students regardless of need, even considering that many enrollees came from the nations' richest families. The scholarships are not nominal; in many countries, a college student gets as much as a primary school teacher. As a result, the education budget has little left for painting, planting, and beautifying. For their chat, the two young women walked to the dirt running track in the University's effort at a sports facility.

"Can you tell me anything, Oumou?"

"I can tell you one thing. Soon Zinani will not be the same country."

"What do you mean?"

"The people are not going to put up with it much longer."

"Put up with what?"

"With President Lassoso and his band of criminals, who are pushing us deeper and deeper into the last century."

"So, what's different? This has been going on for years."

"What's different is that he's jailing people without charge, firing competent people like General Sacco, and playing games with Libya.

The country is seething."

"Tell me more."

"I can't. I can say that something will happen and that we hope that your country will look favorably on changes when they happen."

"When will something happen?"

"Sorry, Miss O'Kelly."

They had finished four revolutions of the track, the conversation of the last three involving nothing sensitive, before returning to the Social Studies building. Both noticed that a medium sized, fairly well dressed, middle-aged man had been strolling behind them at the same speed. Bernadette recognized him as one of the Just Sitting There majors.

The following day, Bernadette reported on her visits to Sacco and Kinsa. There was no doubt that both were willing to have what they said go further. O'Kelly's information and concerns expressed by CIA's Lori Burkitt led to a tightening of security at the Embassy. American employees were told not to venture far from home without notifying the Marine Security Guard. There was nothing on TV or in the papers to suggest that revolution was in the wind. Many column inches and TV minutes were devoted to making Zinanians knowledgeable about CAT scanners. The obligate front-page picture of OIL had him turning spades of dirt, addressing visitors, or smiling at children. A planned trip to Europe was canceled at the last minute, ostensibly due to a Presidential virus.

On a quiet Wednesday morning, Holden Fairchild III was in his office doing a crossword puzzle. Each time Judy Anne Deane came in to give him a cable or a document to peruse and sign, he would slip the puzzle under his blotter and turn his attention to matters of State. He never needed to prepare for Wednesday morning's Country Team Meeting, as he would merely relate stories of wars from the Peloponnesus to Iraq, and then turn it over to the DCM and others for more salient information.

At about 10 AM, Judy Anne buzzed him.

"The Minister of Foreign Affairs is on the phone, sir."

Fairchild had had several meetings and phone conversations with

Assisata Obode, as her portfolio required that she be the government's representative to the foreign diplomatic missions. He actually liked her in spite of her sycophantic demeanor toward Lassoso. She had been sent by USAI to the University of Illinois for a master's degree in International Politics, and was more comfortable in English than any one else in the cabinet. The Ambassador was not at all surprised that she was calling -- probably to ask for some tanks or planes, or to announce a briefing for all missions on her country's problem with the World Bank.

"Good morning, Madam Minister," said the diplomat.

"Good morning, Ambassador. I have some important information for you, sir."

Fairchild knew that she wasn't jesting. Normally, they would have exchanged a few words about families, at least. Not today. "Yes, Minister."

"I regret to inform you that you and the remainder of your embassy staff, with the exception of Mr. Chen Wang, will be asked to leave this country within 72 hours."

"What? But, why?, Madam Minister?"

"I am not at liberty to say."

"Why the exception of Mr. Chen Wang?"

"He is not married and is a male and should be able to care for himself better than any of the rest of you. If we were to expel him as well, relations would be broken and that is not our intent."

"Well, what is your intent?"

"I am not at liberty to say.

"You are aware that we will be required to do the same to your Embassy in Washington."

"They are already making preparations to leave. You may choose one to remain if you please."

"I am not at liberty to make that decision," he responded with sarcasm that he knew she wouldn't pick up.

"Can you guarantee the safety of our property in our absence? You know that we cannot ship all of our household effects out in that period of time."

"We will do our best, but you are certainly aware that our police resources are limited and the emotions of our people can be very high. I might suggest that you keep guards on your houses in your absence."

"Anything more?"

"Nothing, Mr. Ambassador."

"Good-bye."

"*Au revoir*, Mr. Ambassador."

"Fuck!!!!" he yelled, loud enough to bring Judy Anne running into the dark office, presuming that she would find either an injured Ambassador or a shattered heirloom.

"Sir, what's wrong?"

"Get Ernestine and Prudholme in here, immediately! And, let the Country Team know that it imperative that all attend, and arrive on time."

XIV

The day after the telephone conversation between the Ambassador and the Foreign Minister and the memorable Country Team meeting, an article appeared on the third page of the six-page *Les Nouvelles*. Translated in its entirety:

COLONEL SACCO DIES AT 43
Colonel Suleiman Sacco, head of the Quartermaster Section of the Donolu Garrison and previous commanding officer of the First Division of the Zinanian Army, was found dead in his bed yesterday. He was 43 years old. The cause of death was a heart attack.

Bernadette O'Kelly, Sacco's one time lover, was responsible for keeping up with the newspapers in her capacity as political officer, and as such ran across the article while she was sitting at her desk with coffee and croissant. At first, disbelief. She had misread. It was some other Sacco. A dream, maybe. No. No. It couldn't be real. The dry eyes of the Foreign Service officer were flooded by the tears of the woman who had lost the most important person in her life, and read about it in the paper. Grief would follow, but she had to react as a servant of the President of the United States. She sprinted the twenty feet between her office and that of Ernestine Grant.

"She is with Gene Browner," Angela Sertoli tried to stop Dette from going right in, unsuccessfully. She entered and found the director of the US Information Agency and the Deputy Chief of Mission in muted conversation.

"Bernadette, we were just talking about you," said Ernestine in a voice more somber than Dette had ever heard. *She saw a copy of Les Nouvelles* open to page three, on the spacious desk.

"You know."

"Gene came across it just a few minutes ago." The US Information

Service not only disseminates information, it accumulates it.

"I'm very sorry, Bernadette," said Gene. Dette sensed that Browner, almost always morose due to his own unhappy existence, was_even sadder.

"Thank you."

The DCM broke the brief silence. "Bernadette, you know that as despondent as you must feel, we cannot sit silently back with the Sword of Damocles over our heads. We have to stay focused and find out what is going on. I'm concerned that there's a connection between the Colonel's death and our situation. You knew him very well. Did he have heart trouble?"

Dette flashed to the baobab forest and his bedroom. "I'm no doctor, but he gave me no reason to believe so."

"You mentioned that you visited him at his house and met his mother. Would you go over and find out what they know? "

She knew that she would want to make her call of condolences in any case and therefore answered, "I'll try."

"I am sorry for you, Bernadette, and I feel bad that you have to be an investigator." Dette remained silent.

The spring day was bright, and still reasonably cool. Several local citizens continued to wear their down jackets and woolen scarves. The traffic was typically snarled. It was carrot season and many of the women sported shallow aluminum pots on their heads with their carrots intricately arranged, green inside and the orange splayed around in a half sphere, making them look like orange porcupines. Dette was delayed for more than twenty minutes due to a collision between an ancient truck carrying melons and one of Donolu's green and brown "Zinibuses." Although the collision caused little damage to either, local law stated that neither vehicle could be moved until the authorities had asked their questions and made their measurements. She sat in her car, listening to an old Sly and the Family Stone tape. "*I Want to Take You Higher!*" "*We've Gotta Live Together!*" She turned it off; the songs were too upbeat.

She proceeded to the Sacco concession once the police completed their investigation. The immediate area seemed no different from the time she had visited two months earlier. Suleiman's corroded Peugeot was parked in front; she wondered what would happen to it, as there were no other drivers in the family. Only one other car was in evidence about thirty yeards away; an antique Citroen with a man sitting alone inside, dangling a cigarette out the window. Dette presumed that Lassoso was covering all bases.

Islamic custom requires that a body be buried within twenty-four hours of death, and based on the article in the paper, Sacco had been found in bed more than a full day before. She would never see him again.

There was little activity in the courtyard with no evidence of a recent family loss. Children rolled their metal hoops. The chocolate-colored dog, with tail wagging, approached Dette like an old friend. And like last time, Mother Sacco appeared from one of the doors, a faint smile on her face.

"*Mademoiselle!*" She offered her hand. Bernadette wanted to hug her but held back, not knowing the etiquette. She was surprised by the buoyant nature of the welcome, showing no outward signs of sadness. Knowing that Mama spoke essentially no French, she sought out Nisso, the nephew who had eaten Oreos at her house. The boy proved a capable translator.

"I am very sad about the death of your son, Madam."

"Thank you." Her eyes filled with tears.

"Can you tell me what happened?" She felt like she was prostituting herself, asking questions of her lover's mother about her son.

"I don't know. They just told me that he died."

"You mean he didn't die here, in his sleep?"

"No. He hadn't come home in two nights, and had not said where he was going. We thought maybe he was traveling for work, but with his good new job at the storehouse, that wasn't supposed to be necessary."

"Did he have any sickness? Did he have a bad heart?"

"He was the healthiest of all of the children. He hardly ever had malaria and never missed a day of school."

"What do you think happened, Madam?"

"Only Allah knows. His purposes are beyond our knowledge. To ask is an affront to God. We will miss him; he was such a kind person who loved everybody and whom everybody loved. But he is with the Angels now."

Bernadette recognized the incredible gap between the ways the two cultures deal with death. She refused to judge which was preferable, but prayed that she might develop some of the equanimity of Madam Sacco. *"Au revoir, Madam."*

"Au revoir, Mademoiselle."

She was hardly aware of the road or the traffic on the trip back to the Embassy.

They killed him. There was no other explanation imaginable. The paper says he died in bed. Mother says he was not at home. They must have killed him. Lassoso obviously ordered it or maybe had done it with his own hands. They probably tortured him before killing him. God, how he must have suffered.

Bernadette was livid. Anger had replaced sadness. Since her miscarriage and the discussion with the DCM about the inadvisability of a relationship with Suleiman, she had dropped the idea of a life or even a romance with him. The intense passion had waned a bit over the couple of weeks prior to these tumultuous last two days. Nevertheless, her emotions were charged and pure.

Obviously, this information needed to be shared with the Ambassador and DCM. A meeting of the key players in the present crisis was scheduled for 1 PM. It was 12:15.

Jill had learned of the imminent departure the previous day when Michael called home after Country Team. He spent the remainder of the day, well into the night, preparing for his medical role in the evacuation. Not only did he have to assemble a few medicines and some first aid equipment for the long trip, he also had to batten down the hatches in his health unit. The Abattoir stocked thousands of dollars' worth of medicines with expiration dates. He could not take them all and did not want them to go to waste. In his instructions to Chen Wang, he planned to donate them to Lassoso Hospital, as the expiration dates neared, should the Embassy personnel not have returned.

Jill awakened upon her husband's return shortly after midnight.

"Mikey, this isn't going to be so bad. A trip home would be real nice. Maybe we could go to Mammoth and do some spring skiing." Mikey and Jillsie were remnant nicknames of the Eisenstat's courting period. She only used the name now in times of marital uncertainty; he couldn't remember the last time he uttered "Jillsie."

"Jill, you are missing the picture. This is going to be so bad. Real bad. Bad things are going on between our two countries that may take years to repair. Remember Cuba? We left there in the early 60's and haven't gone back yet. Remember Somalia? We left there under the gun and the Embassy was turned to dust and all the possessions of the American contingent disappeared into the hands of the warlords. Remember what Prudholme told us - one suitcase each and as you recall, we brought almost 7200 pounds of stuff when we moved here. Yeah, love, it is going to be bad."

"Don't you think it'll be OK until we get back? We're going to keep paying Mamadou to keep the place in order. He won't have a lot of cooking and cleaning to do."

"Who the hell knows? Lassoso is not going to lose any sleep over our possessions. He may even have a plan for taking a few things for himself. Mamadou won't be of much value if the President sends soldiers over on a scavenger hunt."

"OK, I got it; it is awful. So, what are we going to take in the suitcases?"

Like everyone else, they had given some thought to what they would save in case of a fire. They had the foresight to put the passports and the photo albums in a small box in case of emergency. But now they had two days to choose, making it, if anything, harder. Prudholme had not said anything about a size restriction so they pulled out the giant duffel bags that they received as going-away presents from Michael's Beverly Hills partners.

The pair had brought their lifetimes' worth of photos with them to Africa. They each put some of their favorites in their duffels. Jill put her jewelry and some batiks she made, as well as two dresses, a few pairs of pants and blouses, lots of underwear, and five pairs of shoes, mainly athletic ones. Michael packed some polos, khakis, tennis togs, and his $50 Outlet suit. He had plenty room left and remembered his wine closet. There were a few old Bordeaux that were worth about as much as all the furniture in the place. He wrapped each in a white stocking and a Lacoste. His favorite polo, the royal blue one, cushioned the Chateau Mouton Rothschild.

Two hours after the initial panic, they looked at what was not included, which involved about 98% of everything they had. All the masks, all the sculptures, all the rugs, the Ghanaian bench, the Togolese glass painting, the Malian bogolan - they could live just fine without them. In fact, their loss felt good, almost virtuous, and worth bragging about in the future. "Oh, the stuff we left behind!"

Five minutes after they finished packing, the phone rang.

"Michael, this is Holden ... Holden Fairchild." Eisenstat was relieved that he was specific about which Holden it was. Since he read *Catcher in the Rye*, in high school, he had never come across another

"Yes, Sir."

"She's really sick!"

"Who, Sir?" There were only two strong possibilities, Mary Lou or the Boston terrier. Although the dog was named Gatsby, she was a she. Judy Anne Deane was a distant third in the betting.

"Mrs. Fairchild." The Ambassador had never been heard to use the first name of his wife in public.

"What's wrong?"

"She's stopped making sense."

"What?" After the big dinner and the response to the Sauterne, Michael had not given Mary Lou credit for making much sense under the best of circumstances.

"She's just babbling and she's sweating and very hot."

"What's her temperature?"

"I don't know. We don't have a thermometer." Michael slapped his palm into his forehead in an exaggerated show of frustration.

"She has been taking her malaria prophylaxis, hasn't she?" Michael asked, fearing that he knew the answer would be negative.

"No, she hasn't. She heard about the bad dreams and some friend told her that it would rot her liver, so she never started taking the stuff."

"But, she always came for her refills."

"She didn't want you to know, especially with me yelling at the mission all the time about how malaria would keep them from work. She would just get the bottles and give them to the maid." At three dollars a tablet wholesale, Michael was not pleased to hear this.

"Sounds, Sir, like she may have cerebral malaria," Michael said, disguising the terror in his voice. He had never seen a case, but knew the prognosis of malaria once it involves the brain is grim. Nearly half die, in spite of treatment. "I'll be right over."

He arrived twenty minutes later, carrying a bag with IVs and the spectrum of medicine required for malaria and other diseases that might cause one to stop making sense. He was surprised to find Mary Lou in the living room, on the couch, covers pulled up high. She was watching a scratchy old tape of Mary Poppins. He noted tremors beneath the comforter, but wasn't sure whether it was the rigors of malaria or her keeping time to "Supercalafragalistic Expialodocious."

"Hi, Mary Lou." He chose to be cheery and informal, in spite of the stern countenance of His Excellence stationed a few feet away. "How do you feel?"

"Better than I did a few minutes ago. I think I was out of my head for a while."

"Out of your head?"

"Yeah, I've been pretty upset since Holly brought home the news yesterday, mainly because of the dog. Gatsby has never been without us, and leaving a Boston terrier behind in a country where they don't know if she is a cat, a rat, or a ferret, is stressing me out. Then I've had that nasty sore throat and fever, so I took a Benadryl and two aspirin with the Valium that I take when I'm stressed."

"I don't remember ever prescribing you Valium, Mary Lou."

"You haven't, Michael. I have a nephew in New Rochelle who is a diet doctor; he supplies me all the Valium I need. Free, too."

"We need to talk about that, later. So what happened after those pills?"

"Since we are leaving here tomorrow, I had to say good-bye to some friends, so I invited the wives of a few of Holly's colleagues for lunch."

"Did you have anything to drink?"

"Just a toast of champagne and a couple glasses of wine." For the doctor, cerebral malaria dropped well down on the differential diagnosis.

"Then what?"

The Ambassador spoke up. "I came home to say my good-byes and found Mrs. Fairchild sprawled out on the couch. The other ladies had all left. She was mumbling something about flies in the room."

"No honey, I was saying how I didn't want to fly out of here tomorrow."

"That's not what I heard, doc."

"Probably not too important what she said. She doesn't look too bad now." He took out his digital thermometer and it beeped at 99.5 degrees -- not normal, but not cause for an addition to the critical list.

"Do you have a headache?"

"Ooh la la, what a headache I have! My whole head feels like it's going to explode. It has to be a migraine." Michael was sorry he asked, but as headache was part of the malaria syndrome, he had to prove to himself that she didn't have it.

He poked her finger with a lancet and let a drop of blood fall onto a glass slide. She reacted as if he had taken out her appendix without anesthesia. He regretted that he had come without Band-Aids but excused himself to go to the office to run the test.

The microscopic exam for malaria takes fifteen or twenty minutes and Michael had gotten fairly good at it in the past year. Mary Lou's blood failed to reveal any parasites. He was gratified not to have to sit vigil on a potentially terminal patient, but was not looking forward to castigating the Ambassador's wife for the multiple crimes of combining Valium with alcohol, not taking malaria prophylaxis, and not having a thermometer.

He called the Ambassador's residence to tell them the good news, suggesting that Madam eschew booze for a while, and maybe sedatives as well, even if she experiences stress. She responded with a harrumphing acceptance. In the background, he heard the familiar tune and lyrics of *"A Spoonful of Sugar Makes the Medicine Go Down."* He swore that the next video he would watch would be either *Scarface* or *Deep Throat*.

The evacuation team meeting started right on schedule. Besides the Ambassador and DCM, its membership included Admin Officer

Prudholme, Political Officer Bernadette O'Kelly, Willie Johnson from Peace Corps, Berkeley Eaton from Consular, Gene Browner from the Information Agency, Garson Graham from USAID, Security Officer Frank Norbert, Lori Burkitt from the CIA, and, of course, Chen Wang.

Fairchild started the discussion by asking Ernestine Grant to start the discussion.

"Lots has happened as you know, but the bottom line is that we're still ordered to get out tomorrow. The Ambassador and I spoke to the Foreign Minister, in her office this time, but she was no more forthcoming than she had been on the phone call. She smiled the whole time, as if she was asking us to come over for dinner. We asked about the role of the Libyans and she feigned shock that we should even mention them. We didn't bring up the hospital equipment.

"As you have all heard by now, the paper reported the death of General Sacco, saying he died in his sleep of a heart attack. Bernadette, would you tell the group what you learned?"

O'Kelly proceeded to relay what Sacco's mother had told her and her own certainty that he had been murdered. She amazed herself at her ability to speak of this in a professional tone.

"Are we sure that he is really dead?" asked Graham, ever the skeptic.

Dette admitted that no one she had spoken to had seen a body, but added that there was little reason to suspect that the story was a lie. What would Lassoso and his henchmen possibly have to gain? Sacco had information that they'd find valuable; maybe they got some of it, maybe not.

"And why kill him?" asked Prudholme.

"That seems obvious," responded Ms. Grant. "He is, or was, the likely heir apparent in case of a coup. There is no other person in the army or the political class that can command the respect that he had, either domestically or internationally.

"The powers hated him," said Bernadette. She described the scene at Dr. Eisenstat's home involving the Health Minister and her later visit to the warehouse.

"Lori, what have you learned about the Libyan connection?" Lori Burkitt looked less like a CIA agent that she did a Yves St. Laurent model. The 33-year-old Smith graduate was tall, slim, blond, and dressed in a lightweight plaid suit and three-inch heels; she stood out in staff meetings as Magic Johnson might at an actuarial convention. Donolu was her first foreign post. She impressed by her ability to make contacts at the highest and lowest levels. Her French was barely passable but none of her contacts, at least the males, seemed to care.

"Quite a bit. Gaddafi is in the pie with both thumbs. He's made a deal with Lassoso to supply the Army with T-7 tanks, the Air Force with the money to go buy MIGs or Mirages, and most importantly a free credit card to fill the friggin' things with gas, ad infinitum."

"What does Gaddafi get in return?" asked Fairchild.

"A friend for one. His guest lists have been shrinking of late, and he seems to genuinely like the son-of-a-bitch Lassoso. A vote in the UN, for another. Remember that Zinani's turn on the Security Council comes up soon. Also Libya might be about to make another stab at Chad and would love to have a few troops from another Islamic Republic to internationalize his incursions. Maybe most importantly, he wants to embarrass us. He is still seething over Reagan's bombs. I hear, by the way, that the CAT scanner gambit is part of every discussion he has these days. He loved it."

"So, you think that he forced Lassoso to kick us out?" queried Ernestine.

"I haven't heard yes or no on that one. Whether he asked or not, Lassoso is clearly kissing up to him and thinks the rewards from jerking us around now will be even bigger later."

"What do you hear from Oumou Kinsa and the PPD, Lori?" Bernadette felt a slight stab of pain on hearing the question directed to someone else.

"I had a chance to talk to her last night in my car. She seemed to know a lot about Sacco. She heard that he had been tortured." Bernadette cringed.

"How did she hear that?" asked the Ambassador.

"I didn't ask. She did say that the PPD's really upset by the killing and even more by the order kicking us out."

"So, do they make a move?"

"She wasn't specific, but reinforced her request that we support whatever they do."

"What did she mean by support? Are they asking us to send weapons or give them intelligence reports, or what?" asked Garson Graham.

"Again, nothing specific. She didn't ask for guns, bullets, or tanks, nor did she request any secrets. Her purpose clearly was to pass on information. I think she pictures Lassoso falling soon and wants to have some friends lined up. Oumou says she's talking to French intelligence as well.

"Any predictions, Lori?"

"I don't see how the PPD could possibly see itself as the major player in a coup. They're mainly school girls." The irony of that statement from a spook who was also a Sports Illustrated Swim Suit Issue candidate was lost on no one. "We have no information that anyone in the military is getting ready to make a move. In fact, there is some talk that Sacco is not the only officer to be silenced."

"Thanks Lori. USAID? Anything from your vantage point, Garson?"

"No new request for money; we normally get several a week."

"Yesterday, Mr. Park, the new assistant, said he would look into the activity around New Akron. Anything?" Ernestine was clearly in control of the discussion, as the Ambassador remained silent.

"As a matter of fact, one of our Zinanian employees told him that both the Zin and the Libyan military are clearing some land and pouring concrete. We have a couple of photos." Graham handed them not to the Ambassador, but to the DCM.

"Barracks maybe."

"Hell no, missile pads. SCUD's most likely."

"And why would anyone put SCUD's in this shit-hole," said Fairchild, breaking his silence. "More importantly, why, Mr. Graham did you wait til this meeting to tell us this? This is a very big deal."

"I just learned this a few minutes ago, Mr. Ambassador. Park just got those pictures. As to why, there's no way to guess what either of the two fearless leaders is up to. Maybe Gaddafi wants to have them here in case full-blown war does break out in Chad and the French intervene."

"Lori, what do you know about this?" asked Ernestine.

"Not a damn thing. This is the first I've heard of it and our folks in McLean rarely spend much time studying photos of New Akron and environs. We'll cable right away."

"Sounds like the Cuban Missile Crisis, revisited," interjected Chen Wang for his first contribution of the meeting. He did not much like the idea of being the only American left in a country where missiles were flying back and forth.

"Don't worry, Chen. Lassoso is not going to lob, or let Gadaffi lob, a missile into his capital." Chen was hardly assuaged, surmising that a SCUD in the neighborhood was not much better than a ICBM, and unlike his fellow committee members, he would still be in the neighborhood.

"Gene," said Ms. Grant, to the Information Service man who followed newspapers and television for his pay, "what's up with the news blackout?" There had been no word about the United States on the TV news. *Les Nouvelles* was also devoid of mention of the Americans. Muammar Gaddafi and his Libyans were prominent on both - nothing about any concrete or SCUDs.

"Absolutely nothing. It is, indeed, a blackout. No one is calling me. No one is answering my calls. Hell, I can't even get Space Shuttle pictures on ZTV."

"Voice of America is broadcasting the news, isn't it?" asked Ernestine.

"Sure, so is BBC, but these aren't reruns of 'I Love Lucy.'" The only people likely to listen to them are those with expensive short wave radios that are listening for the government, or are so dead-set against Lassoso that they need no further influencing."

"Willie, what's happening with your volunteers?"

"We've reached all but a couple by radio and told them to get into town right away. We told them that we may have to get out of the country and that they should bring important personal belongings. We didn't get any more specific than that."

"And what about the couple you mentioned? Why haven't they been contacted?"

"We haven't been able to raise them. Incidentally, they live just south of New Akron."

"The concrete slabs are just south of New Akron," said Garson Graham matter-of-factly.

"I was afraid of that," said Johnson.

"Who are they?" asked the Ambassador, who worried that problems with Peace Corps volunteers would play very badly at home.

"Beth Sinova, from Pittsfield, Massachusetts, and Jenny Addison, from San Diego. Jenny's Dad is Mr. Republican in the area, and was absolutely against her joining the Peace Corps in the first place. Incidentally, they are both excellent volunteers, working together in agriculture projects, both hoping to extend their stay for a third year."

"I hope they are alive to extend," lamented Fairchild. "Get a team out there to find them, Willie."

"Four of our Zinanian employees are there now, two of them natives of the area. I doubt anything sinister is up." His words were the opposite of his thoughts.

"Conrad, where do we stand on the operation to get us out?"

"Unlike the rest of you, I have no surprises," said the Admin Officer. "All is on schedule. The DC-8, chartered from Sabena Airlines, will be here Saturday morning at 0900 hours. Although, the locals don't know it, there will be a platoon of commandos aboard to secure the area as we get on. They'll be dressed up as stewards, but with no coffee, no tea, just an Uzi." He waited, in vain, for a chuckle.

"At 0700, we will be meeting at the three designated spots: the Embassy, the Ambassador's residence, and Doc Eisenstat's place. My secretary will have a list later today of who goes where. Obviously, the major factor will be where you live. The Peace Corps Volunteers will assemble at their office, hopefully all of them. But even if we don't have all of them, Willie, we'll have to go as scheduled.

"Buses will take us to Keita-Coulibaly International at 0730. We already have the buses rented. We have to hope that there won't be any difficulties on the way to the airport; we sure can't get the government to supply a motorcycle escort. We'll be spending almost no time on the ground. Remember, one suitcase and one carry-on only. Most of the luggage space will be taken up with equipment from this building. If you bring two, we'll leave one behind, our choice. Wear whatever you want, but remember, we're going to Washington and it can be chilly. The stop in Tenerife will be short, for refueling only. You'll be off the plane for thirty minutes, max. Fireman Pfund has lots of dollars and will exchange them for your Lassosos, before we go, not after. Surprisingly, the exchange rate has not worsened as this has been happening."

"I assume that all of you have made some arrangements for having your houses watched. The Embassy will continue to provide night guards, but the days are your responsibility. Payment will be difficult. We have asked Aminata of the Fireman's staff to serve as a paymaster, so that your employees can come see her monthly for their salary. I would give her the equivalent of six of their month's pay, if you can. Hopefully this whole episode will have blown over well before then and we will return to peace and tranquility. By the way, the Embassy cannot guarantee salaries for your people. If Aminata doesn't have the money from you, they won't get paid.

"Lots of you have expressed your concern about animals. As I told you, they will not be permitted on the plane, and therefore will have to remain behind when you leave. But ... we might be able to do something a bit unusual. After we're out of here, we might be able to stage a pet-lift and take all the cats, dogs, birds, and monkeys out on a truck to the Burkina Faso border. Then, with a few dollars to grease the skids, we will slip them into Ouagadougou for transshipment to the US. Chen, you will have to play a major role in this, even though the Zins from the travel section will be doing the dirty work." Chen Wang's eyes lit up as he finally saw a task for himself for the period during which he would be a one-man embassy.

"Rumor has it that some of you have weird pets. You heard the kinds that will be allowed: cats, dogs, birds, and monkeys. Yes, Sir, Boston terriers qualify as dogs. No snakes. No rodents. No goats, sheep, or cows. No rabbits, chickens, or ducks. And especially, no fish. We are not going to be responsible for keeping water in the aquariums on the truck trip to Ouagadougou.

"If you expect to send your animal on this adventure, make sure that you have a cage. This is not Noah's Ark and we will not have a truckload of loose animals. By the way, this isn't going to be free. Figure a hundred bucks or more to get Poopsie or Spot to Ouaga, then the usual ungodly sum for the plane trip. If you decide not to involve yourself with this, make arrangements with your employee or friends and figure on long-term arrangements. Any questions?"

No one responded, but there was a palpable increase in respect for

Precocious Conrad. A pet-lift was not something his colleagues thought he could have conjured up.

The Deputy Chief of Mission took the floor again. "Frank, any security issues we need to discuss?"

"Uh, nothing really different." Nothing has come to my attention. No reports of attacks, break-ins or robberies from the diplomatic corps."

"That's good news. Thanks, Frank. Anyone else have anything to add? Mr. Ambassador, any subjects we haven't covered?"

"No Ernestine, you've covered it all." He was still distracted by the strange behavior of his wife and had paid little attention to what had been said.

Ernestine concluded, "So, in summary we have a dead General, SCUD missiles, two missing Peace Corps volunteers, a bunch of girls talking about a coup d'état, and an order to leave town. Other than that, it's pretty quiet.

"Our tasks are obvious. First, find the volunteers. Second, get ready to leave. Third, try to make it so that we don't have to leave. Fourth, keep your ears open for rumors of an attempt against the President, and fifth, get your pets in their cages." Everybody chuckled nervously as Ambassador Fairchild stood up and turned to depart, more obvious than ever, a figurehead.

XV

Although they had become nearly inseparable friends, Beth Sinova and Jenny Addison had not really liked each other all that much when they first met. Jenny was a Stanford grad from a wealthy politically active family and spoke like the proper, accent-free San Diegan WASP that she was. With long, blond, straight hair on a tall slim Southern California body, she looked very sixties with jeans, a plain white T from the Gap, and blue rubber Taiwanese flip-flops. Beth, on the other hand, was second-generation Italian-American, daughter of a laundryman. She went to a junior college before graduating from UMass after six years. At least six inches shorter than her fellow volunteer, her hair was black and curly. Her hips were wide, and Reeboks accessorized her jeans and Senegalese print shirt. Her accent and vocabulary were as distinct from her partner as a Cockney from the Queen.

They were thrown together in the village of Korikono, about thirty kilometers south of New Akron. Both had majored in fields of absolutely no relevance to their new careers as community development specialists. Beth graduated with a degree in Psychology, Jenny in English Lit. Both joined the Peace Corps, ostensibly to see the world, but really because they couldn't find anything better to do with their degrees.

Jenny, in addition, was trying to find a way to escape the grasp of her so-called boyfriend, Joe Clarkson, Attorney-at-Law, an obvious comer in the Republican Party. Her Dad loved Joe; she found him a bore. So she joined the Corps, and though she sought a slot on a Pacific island, she was sent to West Africa. She wrote no letters – just postcards. Joe made noise about coming to Zinani. Jenny pleaded overwork and emphasized the squat toilets, lack of running water, the need to take a slew of vaccines and malaria prophylaxis, and a diet of rice and millet seed. The noise stopped.

After living on opposite sides of the village of about 1000 people for a few months, they decided to move in together in a reasonably large house, built like everything else in town out of the mud and thatch mixture called *banco*. Their work, with the children in the one small local school, involved the usual Peace Corps approach to community development, with gardens, basic health care, and education, especially of women. The World Bank had shown that the best investment that could be made was in schooling women and girls, who, after all, did nearly all of the work in the developing world, while their men and boys made an art of Just Sitting There.

Beth and Jenny, *les Tubabs*, became locally important. Many women in Korikono, and a few men, looked up to them and used them as confidants. They were treated almost on a par with the village shaman, being asked to offer advice on seed planting, child rearing, and husband disobeying. When the functionaries in New Akron or Donolu failed to deliver on promises, Beth and Jenny knocked on doors, often loud enough to make a difference. When tax collectors arrived, Beth and Jenny made sure that villagers were treated equally. They helped secure loans. They founded a women's cooperative.

Not everyone was pleased with the importance of *les Tubabs*, especially the majordomos. Some were not happy to have their doors knocked on frequently. Some did not particularly appreciate equity in tax collection. Others were especially displeased with the idea of a cooperative. The men of Korikono were not at all delighted that their women had changed. Peanut yields were up and new crops like broccoli and cauliflower, salable to expats in the capital, were introduced. More money was coming into the village but the men found they had little say in its use. The complaints about Beth and Jenny found their way to the mucky-mucks in Donolu.

Jenny was deep in sleep. Beth was reading by the light of kerosene when their plain brown dog, Alien, started growling, then barking. Two Jeeps pulled up in front of their house. Two uniformed men, with guns, left the lead car, came to the door, and knocked. The occupants of the second vehicle stayed behind.

"Jenny, get up! We've got trouble!" Twenty-two-year-old Beth yelled to twenty-three-year-old Jenny.

Beth opened the door, recognizing that she had no alternative. The two men, in fatigues and looking less than twenty, pushed their way in. Both volunteers spoke fluent Fulani and had no trouble comprehending the gruff orders of their uninvited guests. Alien kept barking.

"Come with us, now!" bellowed the soldier with two stripes. The single- striped one nodded his concurrence.

"Where?" asked Jenny exiting her bedroom in a Stanford T and gray gym shorts.

"You will learn soon!"

"Who has told you to come get us?"

"Our superiors."

"Which superiors."

"You will learn soon."

"We will go nowhere until we find out who sent you and where we are going." Beth tried the macho approach.

It didn't work. One of the youths started to unsling his weapon and the other took Beth by the forearm and tugged her toward the door. She pulled away from him while recognizing that she and Jenny were not in a position to do anything but go along.

"Shit, Jen, we're screwed,?"

"Yup, we are."

The four twenty-somethings filed out of the *banco* building and climbed in the first Jeep, men in front, women balancing on water cans behind. Having been repeatedly warned against being on the road at night for fear of colliding with donkeys, cows, and unlit trucks, both volunteers thought they might die, even before they had a chance to figure out what real trouble they might be in.

They survived the trip, and arrived in New Akron, passing the silhouette of the Sports Complex. They stopped in front of an unsigned storefront. Each woman was grabbed by the arm and escorted through the peeling wooden door into a single large room with half a dozen desks and a lone bare bulb hanging from a cord in the room's center. Janitorial service was clearly not a major part of this institution's budget. The one wastebasket was overflowing with paper and garbage while similar detritus littered the floor throughout the room. An offensive odor of rotten food, urine, and sweat permeated the place. The walls were lined with pictures of partially clad and unclad white females.

Two men, one black, the other lighter skinned and almost certainly Arab, sat in folding chairs under the bulb. The black man was dressed in the military garb of the Zinanian Army; the Arab wore an expensive looking business suit with no tie.

The black man spoke first. "Miss Addison, Miss Sinova, welcome." The Americans did not respond. "I am Lieutenant Colonel Otobalo. This is Monsieur Sheik Harif Rahman from the Civil Cooperation Group of the Republic of Libya. We know that you would like to know why you are here."

"Fucking-A, we do!" blurted out Beth, confident that the significance of the expletive was unknown to the Africans.

"Please, Miss Sinova," said Rahman, in near-accentless English

Otobalo continued in French, interspersed with phrases of Fulani. "There are many in our government, including our President, Mr. Lassoso, who are concerned about your activities in Korikono."

"Lassoso knows about us?" exclaimed Jenny, wondering what her father, an early Reaganite, would think of her gaining fame of this sort.

"*Bien sur*, he does. He has asked me personally to have this discussion with you."

"You call this a discussion, you bastard! This is a goddam kidnapping!" Beth's macho approach was making Jenny severely anxious. The men reacted not at all.

"As volunteers for the Peace Corps, you are invited guests of the Republic of Zinani. You are expected to obey the laws of our sovereign land and to stay out of politics. You were asked to go to Korikono and help teach children and women how to grow vegetables. Instead, you foment revolution. You call it a cooperative when it is clearly a cell of the so called People's Party for Democracy, which exists for the sole purpose of staging a revolution against our democratically elected President and Assembly."

Beth and Jenny had, of course, heard of the PPD. It was the subject of discussion whenever Americans got together, especially because of the feminine bent of the group. They had never laid eyes on Oumou Kinsa or any others of the party leadership, and as far as they knew, none of the women in the coop had spoken to anyone from the party. They had never heard talk of anything except the crops they grew and the prices they would bring.

Jenny responded with a denial. She was much better than Beth at maintaining her equanimity. "No sir, we have not been fomenting revolution, nor have we violated any of your laws. We are merely doing our jobs at the school and in town. Yes, we have worked with a cooperative, but it is only there to assure fair prices for the vegetables grown by its members. We have never met or talked to anyone from the PPD and have no plans to do so. Please let us return to our home." She thought about adding, for the first time in her life, the post-script "mother-fuckers" but figured that it might backfire.

"I am sorry, *Mademoiselles*, but we cannot do that right now. There are several questions that we must ask you. Furthermore, there will be some heavy construction being performed in and around Korikono in the next few days and we feel that you will be much safer out of that town."

"OK, then let us go into Donolu to the Peace Corps Hostel."

"That too is impossible. Our questions are very important and there are some others who would like to talk to you."

"So you will be holding us prisoner?" Beth asked

"I would not use such a harsh word," answered Rahman. "You will merely be the guests of the government of Zinani and we will try to make your stay as comfortable as possible."

"Guests, my ass," shouted Beth.

"Beth, I don't think we'll accomplish anything by yelling at them. We have no choice but to go along."

"You are correct, Miss Addison," said the Libyan. "Please cooperate and you will be able to leave here soon."

The Americans were led through a door in the rear of the building to a small shack behind. Two armed men whom they recognized as the occupants of the second car at the time of their abduction sat at either side of the central entrance. One sported a cigarette hanging from his lip and both listened on a boom box to the annoyingly shrill Zinanian music that most Peace Corps Volunteers learned to despise.

"This is how you treat your guests?" Beth directed her sarcasm to Harif Rahman.

"Your security is very important to us. We would not want anyone attacking you as you slept," he said with a straight face.

Equally straight-faced, she responded, "Mr. Harif Rahman and Mr. Otobalo, please go fuck yourselves." Of the three listeners, only Jenny reacted, with a look of terror.

The inside of the guesthouse was dark for lack of windows, filthy for lack of attention, and stinky for no lack of decaying organic material. There was one twin bed with an ancient mattress, most of its springs proudly declaring their existence through rents in the material. A lamp was mounted on the far wall. A flip of the switch did nothing to lessen the darkness. "We will get you a bulb when the market opens tomorrow." The door closed behind them and a bolt was noisily shoved into its enclosure.

XVI

Akbar Market was not one of the largest in Donolu but it was the most convenient to the Eisenstat's house. Jill did most of her food shopping there.

Akbar, like most markets in Africa, is not a single enclosed structure, but a group of rickety souks, each made up of four crooked poles supporting a thatch roof. The market consisted of several score of them. The smaller shops featured women who would sit on the ground with their daily offerings of peanuts or onions or carrots or beans, or the dozens of fruits, vegetables, roots, and powders that Jill had never learned to identify. In the higher rent souks, the more prosperous green grocers plied their wares and were joined by the canned good peddlers, the hardware hawkers, the cloth vendors, the purveyors of notions, the jewel merchants, the fishmongers, and the butchers. It was to the meat counters that Jill had come; she was going to have Chen Wang and Ernestine Grant over for dinner the night before Chen was scheduled to become the only official American remaining in the country.

As usual, Akbar Market was a madhouse. Rarely did she see another white person there, but locals were everywhere. The noise level was high, punctuated by the shouts of the more aggressive sellers and underlain with the sound of hundreds of barter transactions.

The meat men, and they were all men, were concentrated in one corner of the market. Jill liked to say that she always chose the meat man who had the most flies on his product, the assumption being that flies know quality. She could have shopped and paid twice the price at the Lebanese market down the street, where the meat was protected from the flies by a 1960's vintage refrigeration unit. She had learned, however, that the Lebanese owner bought his meat from the same wholesalers that the Akbar merchants did, at the same time in the morning. She would merely buy early in the day and take her purchase home for her houseboy to clean and freeze. She felt virtuous, thrifty, and a little bit

African. Most of the meat men had gotten to know her and allowed her to think she could play one off against the other. She was not aware that they were all part of an extended family with a monopoly on Akbar's beef and pork stands.

As her salesman of the day was about to strike his rusty and blood-stained cleaver through a large filet to cut off a two kilogram chunk for the night's *filet au poivre*, she noticed that the noise level in the market had increased a little. She saw that eyes were turned toward the street behind the jewelry section. A loud speaker then made its presence known; she could hear the words, but could not understand the Fulani. She tried to go on with her business but the small man with the big knife had stopped paying attention to her and headed toward the commotion. His fellow butchers and most of the customers followed. Neglecting her security training, she trailed behind. She had been taught that diplomats killed or injured during insurrections are most often victimized by being caught in a crossfire; they were rarely targets. The maxim of Diplomatic Security is "get down and get the hell out of there."

Boulevard de l'Independence was, in spite of its grandiose name, like all other semi-paved streets in Donolu, two lanes wide, cluttered on both sides by horse carts, donkey carts, and push carts, plus the usual mélange of bicycles, cars, taxis, trucks, buses, and unpredictable pedestrians. At the best of times, one can drive no more than five miles per hour on the Boulevard. This was by no means the best of times.

To Jill's right was a mass of some two hundred young people. They chanted slogans and shook their fists in the air. She was reminded of the newscasts of the 444-day hostage crisis in Tehran. In Iran, however, she remembered seeing almost no women. This group was predominantly female. To the left was a line of uniformed men, most with long guns slung over their shoulders, all with shields. In the middle of the group of protestors, an old Renault 205 sat stationary, a loud speaker bolted to the roof, blaring a constant cacophony of Fulani. She could pick up an occasional word of French like *"libertè."*

Jill was not comfortable in French, even with her weekly one-on-one training, and she was particularly ill at ease in a situation of frantic activity. Nonetheless, she tried. *"Qu'est-ce qui se passe?"* "What's happening?" she asked a well-dressed man standing next to her.

His response was made unintelligible by the noise and his rapid-fire speech but she did make out the letters "PPD." She was well aware of the meaning of the acronym. She looked for Oumou Kinsa, whose picture she had seen, among the crowd, but couldn't identify her. The mainly female mass moved slowly right to left, like a huge amoeba sending out pseudopods in random directions, as marchers tried to coerce observers to join in their movement. The gap between protestors and armed men narrowed. As rocks were hard to find on the main street, very few projectiles were hurled. The few that were there, glanced harmlessly off the clear plastic riot shields. Regardless, one could feel a palpable increase in the tension of the moment. The din of the chanting increased while the anxiety level of the young, uneducated military men noticeably elevated.

As far as Jill could tell, nothing specific sparked the dénouement. Perhaps the gap between protestors and military reached criticality. Maybe the protestors had a pre-set plan to provoke a reaction. Whatever, a reaction was provoked. The two groups met, then intertwined. Billy clubs were withdrawn from belts; women, and a few men, were beaten. The angry youth had only their hands with which to retaliate. Clubs wielded by men in uniform are more effective than women's fists; it was one sided -- not one sided enough, however, to prevent a fusillade of tear gas canisters from being lobbed into the crowd. One dropped not six feet from where Jill stood.

Tear gas happens on TV, she thought, not where I am standing. Police sticks and shields -- they have those in Alabama and South Central LA, not near my market. The pungent odor came first and the choking and tearing followed in quick order.

She decided to run; everybody else had made the same decision, and there was too little space. She couldn't go up or down the Boulevard. Gas was everywhere. Her only option was to retrace her steps back into Akbar Market. For hundreds of others, the same single option existed.

The two entrances were narrow; the mass of humans trying to get through them was broad. Shoulder to shoulder, back to chest, toes to heels, the bulk of humanity attempted to flee the unbreathable air. Tall ones had an advantage over short ones. Somewhat young had an advantage over very young or old.

Immediately in front of her, Jill saw a baby come loose from the colorful harness used to carry it on its mother's back and fall to the ground. Jill tried to lean over and rescue the infant, but the mass behind her shoved her quickly out of reach. The mother apparently had no inkling that she had lost her child, as she didn't stop running with the masses.

The baby was not the only casualty observed by the lady from Beverly Hills. A leper, who sat in the passageway day after day collecting a few coins from generous shoppers, could not push himself out of the way of the legions of feet, shod and unshod. His toeless feet were smashed by the hordes.

She saw an elderly, hunchbacked woman fall as the advancing mass overtook her slow shuffle. Everywhere, tables of fruits and vegetables and batteries and charcoal were toppled, making for an even more irregular surface, leading to even more people, especially children and the elderly, being trampled. Looters with quick hands filled their pockets. She witnessed an arm being relieved of its expensive looking watch. Not until she got home did she become aware that her purse no longer contained her wallet.

After some three minutes that felt like three hours, the alleys and side-alleys of the market were able to accommodate the protestors and bystanders without their fearing being crushed. The coughing and tearing lasted well beyond that, but Jill no longer feared becoming a statistic for the BBC. She had walked to the market, as she always did, and was lucky enough to be able to walk the several blocks home, uninjured. She had two thoughts as she strode through her neighborhood, where there was no sign that this was anything other than a run-of-the-mill Friday in Donolu. The first was, "Thank God we're leaving this hole Sunday." The second was, "What meatless dish can I serve for dinner?"

The phone rang on Michael's desk as he was going through files, saving the crucial ones, relegating the remainder to the shredding pile. He answered it himself, having long since learned that his secretary was barely able to say intelligibly, "Hello" and "Please hold."

"Michael, I was almost killed!"

Michael knew that his wife rarely embellished the facts so he accepted that he had nearly become a widower. "What? Tell me what happened? Are you OK?"

She relayed the events of the previous hour, including the now discovered missing wallet that had contained enough lassosos to buy the evening's dinner but little else. Fortunately, her Diplomatic Passport had been missed or possibly ignored. The VISA and American Express Cards would be of little value to the pickpocket as the Hotel Liberté was the only establishment in the nation that accepted plastic.

"Jesus!" He had heard from the Security Officer that there was some rioting going on down by Akbar Market. So as to avoid the chance that someone would inadvertently walk or drive into danger, Frank Norbert was good at informing the community when there was unrest. Clearly Norbert was unaware that an Embassy spouse was in the middle of that riot. "Are you OK now?"

"Just a little shaky and my eyes sting, but I'm all right."

"Do you want to come over to the office or do you want me to come home?"

"No. I'll be fine." Michael almost wished that she had asked him to come home. He was jealous of her self-reliance.

"I'll let the Security Office and the Ambassador know what happened. Frank Norbert might call you for more info. He'll also yell at you for getting so close to the action."

"No problem, but I sure won't do it again. I now know the power of tear gas."

Fairchild, Grant, Norbert, and O'Kelly met in the Ambassador's office. Frank started the discussion, on Ernestine's instructions.

"The town is really ugly. You have heard about the Doc's wife and what she saw down at the Akbar Market. That's the worst of it, but not all of it. There was a demonstration out at the University and another in front of the Interior Minister's office. Both were smaller, but interesting. In all three cases, people commented on how many women were involved. Some carried PPD signs and a couple had a picture of Colonel Sacco with a black border."

The other three were surprised by Norbert's performance. None had ever heard him string together more than two short sentences before. It was clear that he was energized by the unrest; they were pleased to see him performing up to his task.

"Any injuries in those disturbances?" asked the Ambassador.

"Only in the market incident where about a dozen were trampled to death, including the little baby that Mrs. Eisenstat saw. A few of the protestors had to go to Lassoso General to get their heads sewed up. None of the soldiers was hurt, as far as we know.

"Bernadette, what's your reading of all this?"

"There's no doubt that this was a PPD event. The absence of Oumou makes sense because they would immediately arrest her if they found her. She's obviously in hiding someplace. It looks like they're trying to precipitate a violent reaction from the government to rile up the public. The tear gas by itself wouldn't have been enough, but the deaths might. I suspect that they'll try to make a lot out of the funerals tomorrow."

"What do you think we ought to do now?" asked the Ambassador.

The DCM answered, "Nothing, except to deplore the loss of life and call on the government to exercise restraint. You know, the usual bullshit. We certainly won't go out of our way to find Oumou, although Dette, you ought to stick around the office in case they try to make contact. And, we have to continue our evacuation plans. About 30 hours to go."

"Any word on the Peace Corps Volunteers?"

""Willie just called and told me that there are rumors that they were taken from their house by armed soldiers. He's going to New Akron to check it out."

XVII

Peace Corps Country Director Willie Johnson came from a small Virginia farm town. His father was a mechanic; his mother cooked in and cleaned the houses of some of Roanoke's finest citizens. He did well in class and on the gridiron, receiving a football scholarship and becoming the first of his family to go to college. He was big and good enough to be drafted by the Green Bay Packers after he graduated. A spot player at offensive guard during his rookie year, he was being groomed to start the following year when, to the shock of his coaches and fans, he resigned to join the Peace Corps. Giving up a salary greater than that which his mother and father combined would be able to match in a decade, he learned French and taught citizens of Cameroon to read and write English. His success was legendary. American football, thanks to his coaching, is still played in his village, and a school carried the name William Johnson Middle School.

After graduate school, he taught Developmental Economics at a predominantly black college, but jumped when the chance to go back into the Peace Corps came his way. He served as Assistant Director of Peace Corps, Mauritania, and moved into the directorship in Zinani about a year before the events. No training had prepared him for the disappearance of two of his charges.

Johnson, his assistant Ulysses Singh, who was a Punjabi-born US citizen, and Moussa Sangare, Peace Corps' trouble-shooter and main government contact, gassed up the Corps' Chevrolet Blazer to drive to New Akron.

The trip, usually requiring three hours took just over two; drivers were staying off the road as a result of the disturbances in the capital. The three went directly to the *gendarmerie.*

Police stations in Zinani are externally well appointed compared to other government buildings outside the capital. The resources seem to be available, even when the school and dispensary in the town or village

137

are dilapidated or non-existent. New Akron's, being in the country's third city, was palatial. The architecture was African/Neo-Classical; four Doric columns stood guard over an imposing carved hardwood door. The interior of the headquarters did not live up to the palatial facade.

The strange contingent of a turbaned-Indian, a large muscular black man, and a native Zinanian entered a waiting room decorated in Naugahyde and nylon, with a massive photograph of Oumar Ibrahim Lassoso prominent over the steel and plastic coffee table. A gaunt corporal slouched on the largest sofa, dominating the piece, sucking on a neem tree twig for dental hygiene. The ashtray in front of him was nearly full. He grunted what the visitors interpreted as an attempt to learn what they wanted.

"Where is the chief?" Sangare demanded, in Fulani. One always asks for the chief, whether one visits a small village or military headquarters in Donolu. He is rarely available.

"Not here."

"Where is he?"

"Home for lunch." It was 4:30 PM.

"Get him," Sangare insisted.

"Who wants him?"

"The Embassy of the United States." The corporal did not show signs of being overly impressed but slowly arose and moved toward and through the door leading from the waiting room to the one that said in French, "Private. Do Not Enter."

Ten minutes later, the corporal beckoned them into the sanctuary. At a roll-top desk sat the West African version of an iconic Southern Sheriff: rotund, bald, neatly pressed uniform, vibrantly shined booted feet on the desk, dark wire-rimmed sunglasses, cigar hanging out of the side of his mouth. LIEUTENANT TOURE said his nametag. President Lassoso's portrait was above the desk, a younger picture.

"Gentlemen, how can I be of service to the United States of America?" Cigar smoke came from his mouth as a scudding cloud, not a ring.

Ulysses Singh answered in his serviceable Fulani. "Sir, you know of course why we are here. We represent the Peace Corps and two of our young female volunteers have disappeared."

"Ah, yes, Miss Addison and Miss Sinova. We know them well and are most distressed by their disappearance. But why come here?"

"You are the police, are you not? We hope that you would be looking for them. Furthermore, their neighbors reported seeing uniformed men take them in Jeeps the night they were last seen."

"Mr. Singh and Mr. Johnson, we do not have the responsibility of finding missing foreigners. That is the job of the military. Lt. Colonel Otobalo is in charge of that unit. And, of course you know that we have no Jeeps. We have no vehicles of any kind, except the motorbike that I must fund myself. When a citizen needs immediate help from the police, he must come to us and transport us. We do not recklessly chase criminals in black and white automobiles, like in your motion pictures."

The Lieutenant had rendered the Punjabi and the offensive tackle speechless. Moussa Sangare spoke up. "Where do we find Colonel Otobalo?"

"He can be located in an unmarked office not far from here. He does not work at Army headquarters. There is some concern for security." Toure described the location of the storefront that greeted the young women a few nights earlier.

Five minutes later, they pulled up in front of the peeling door of the non-descript single story building. A knock produced the Lieutenant Colonel, alone in the dingy, stinking room. He pulled up three chairs and pointedly dusted them off for his visitors. He opened the back door and called one of the two-armed men sitting in front of the second building, asking him to buy some sodas for the three visitors.

He spoke in French. "I am honored by your visit. I am a fervent admirer of your country and especially the Peace Corps. When I was a youngster, the Peace Corps sent a volunteer to my village. Bob was his name. Do you know what happened to Bob, Mr. Johnson?"

"No Sir, I don't. Do you know what happened to Miss Elizabeth Sinova and Miss Jennifer Addison?"

"Ah, the fine volunteers from Korikono. No, I am afraid we do not know of their whereabouts. We are, of course, anxious to find them, as they are very popular in that village. The gardens will not be nearly as productive if they are not found soon. We have every available man

139

looking for them, but you must know that our resources are limited. In addition, I am sure you are aware of the civil disturbances that are becoming such a problem for us. Most of our men are being used to assure tranquility."

Willie Johnson did not know how to swear. Even as a Green Bay Packer, his vocabulary was without blemish. He lacked the words to tell the Lt. Colonel how absurd his comments were. "Colonel, two citizens of the United States, invited by your government to help in the development of their village and your country, are missing. We have reason to believe that the military is involved in their abduction. Two Jeeps were seen in front of their house on the night they disappeared. We understand that you use Jeeps, donated by the way, by the US Government."

"Indeed, Sir, we do, but we are hardly the only ones to use them. I am sure that if you were to examine the vehicles of the so-called People's Party for Democracy, you would find some Jeeps as well. In fact, we suspect that the PPD may be responsible for this disappearance."

"Would you care to explain why they might want to do that?"

"I can think of at least two reasons. First, they might have kidnapped the young women to embarrass our President, knowing that the blame from your people would immediately be placed upon us. Your visit suggests they might be right. The second possibility is that it is a Zionist plot. We know that the Mossad is supporting the PPD and that Israel is trying to get back into Africa through a regime change in Zinani. It is possible that Mossad has insisted that the PPD take the women hostage to stimulate a strike against President Lassoso by your government. Just look at Grenada and Panama; it doesn't take much to get your people to invade."

"You will pardon us, Colonel, if we are unconvinced by your suggestions."

"Mr. Johnson, you must trust me when I say that neither I nor my superiors have any idea where your volunteers are, and that we are doing everything within our power to find them. It is clearly in our interest, as well as yours, to assure a satisfactory ending to this unfortunate incident."

"Colonel, this is not a matter of satisfaction. Our concern at the moment is not who is responsible, but that these two young women be found and returned to us, in good health, immediately. The President of the United States holds the President of Zinani personally responsible for their safety and has communicated that by letter. I communicate the same to you in your position of head of the military branch responsible for such affairs."

"I understand. We will continue to work diligently in the search."

About twenty yards from where the comic opera was being played out, Beth and Jenny were asleep, Beth on the bed, Jenny on the floor, as the single bed was truly single. The light bulb, promised more than two days earlier, had not been delivered. The lack of windows and the tightly fitting door, coupled with the fact they had no watches, in true Peace Corps tradition, took away their perception of time.

On each of the two nights since their original incarceration, they had been handed meals that were to suffice for twenty-four hours. The meals were identical - rice with okra and peanut sauce, served cold, the sauce congealed. Water, in plastic bottles, accompanied. Fortunately, the women could see neither the food nor drink. The brown hue to the water would have turned their stomachs and made them sick, even before the bacteria in the food would have the time to duplicate in numbers large enough to cause dysentery.

Toilet facilities were not of Hilton standard. Shortly after the meal delivery, they were invited out of their room to a grotesque outhouse. The ten steps between it and the door to their cell was the sole outside exercise offered them. At other times, their amenities included only a steel bucket, already fouled by what they assumed was a previous prisoner.

For the first several hours of their abduction, they screamed. The guards gave no hint of response. Even during the walk to the john, there was not a word exchanged between the guards and the guarded. Questions, complaints, insults, offers of oral sex, in French, English, and Fulani -- all were ignored. For all the Americans knew, their captor's henchmen were deaf mutes. The futility of noisemaking became evident and silence descended over the 200 square foot, splintery wooden cell. Only the sounds of countless crickets filtered under the thin crack between door and ground. The women rarely spoke to one another. What was there to talk about? Smells? Humidity? Hunger? Silence? Death? Occasionally, they hugged. Both thought of making love to the other, but neither did anything about it. Neither could initiate it. Either would have responded.

XVIII

Jill Eisenstat had not been successful in her attempt to get meat for dinner, but she was nothing if not resourceful. She and Michael had been given an allowance of 2500 pounds of consumable items to bring with her to this post where everything but millet, sorghum, peanuts, and a few truck vegetables was imported and ridiculously expensive. Forays to Costco, Safeway, and Pep Boys had them purchasing and preparing for shipping everything from toilet paper, to light bulbs, to Cheerios, to brownie mix, to motor oil., and for tonight's dinner, two cases of canned albacore.

She decided to serve Tuna Wellington to Chen Wang and Ms. Grant as her farewell to them and to Zinani and, as she progressively hoped, to the US Foreign Service. The scene at the Akbar Market had brought to the surface her love for Beverly Hills and her lack of enthusiasm for the drudgery and danger of the Third World.

She had never heard of Tuna Wellington. She thought Beef Wellington the pinnacle of the chef's art and felt that her abilities to adapt in the kitchen would allow her to pull this one off. They still had some of the zebra pate to slather around the tuna loaf that she would concoct for the heart of the dish. She planned Velveeta on Wheat Thins as hors d'oeuvres and canned asparagus as the side. Michael would break out a couple of fine vintages.

While the doctor's wife was slaving over her stove, Bernadette O'Kelly was sitting in her office as the DCM had instructed. She didn't really expect a call from Oumou Kinsa. What she most hoped for was contact from ex-General Suleiman Sacco. There was no report of a body being found; she held tenuously to the idea that her beloved would be discovered and that he would return to her arms and she would give up the Foreign Service and he would become President of the Second Republic of Zinani and ... The sing-song ring of her phone interrupted

143

the daydream.

"Miss O'Kelly?"

"Yes, this is she."

"I cannot tell you my name." The language was French; the caller was clearly educated, the voice of a young woman. "I cannot tell you for whom I am calling. It, however, is very important that you listen closely. I may have very little time on the telephone."

"I am listening," Dette said apprehensively.

"You will remember the place on the Begoro River where you and General Sacco visited some weeks ago?"

Bernadette was shocked that anyone left alive other than she knew of the baobab forest. "Yes, yes, of course, I do."

"Please go there immediately. Someone is waiting to talk to you."

"Who?"

"I'm sorry, Ms. O'Kelly, I cannot say. You will learn as soon as you get there, but please go now." The caller hung up.

Dette raced down the hall and burst into the office of the DCM who was seated with Gunnery Sergeant Rice, the chief of the Embassy's marine detachment, and Frank Norbert, discussing the plans for evacuation. She described to them the phone call she had just received.

"You know, it could be someone from Lassoso's mob trying to compromise you," suggested Grant.

"How would they know about that spot?"

"If they had, or have, Sacco, it's not unlikely that they tortured him to get information. They want to do whatever they can to embarrass the US for the benefit of their Libyan friends."

"He would never talk about that!"

"Don't be so sure. Torture has extracted far more sensitive information than where a man made love to a woman." Bernadette was perturbed that she would make a comment of that sort in front of the Gunnery Sergeant, an upstanding, uptight Christian.

"Ernestine, it's got to be him!"

"Who?"

"Suleiman."

"Don't get your hopes up. Everything we know tells us that he's dead. Either he told someone about the place, or you were followed. It goes against all rules of command, but I am going to leave the decision up to you. Go. Don't go. You make the call. He'll shit bricks when he hears about it, especially if the news is bad, but I'm not even going to mention it to the Ambassador until you return."

The drive to the Texaco station on the New Akron road felt twice as long as before, since Bernadette had no clue what she would find at her destination. The chuckholes of the unpaved stretches of the trip had proliferated and deepened. She recognized the turn at river's edge and drove the remaining five kilometers to the one place in Zinani that she would remember long after all others were forgotten. The baobabs were leafless. The forest was deserted. There were two pirogues in the middle of the river, their occupants languidly tossing their nets to catch an occasional *capitane*.

Bernadette had left within ten minutes of getting the call. Perhaps the caller had not expected her to arrive so quickly. Maybe something had happened to whomever it was that was supposed to meet her -- arrest, accident, nerves. She waited. She waited, half expecting a helicopter to descend, James Bond style, with her missing hero Sacco at the controls. Thirty minutes. An hour. She sat on the same boulder that had brought her and her lover together. Nothing.

She was beginning to consider giving up, the victim of a hoax, when she saw one of the pirogues making its way from mid-river toward the upstream bank. The person in the stern was propelling it with a fifteen-foot bamboo pole. The occupant of the front of the boat, who she took to be a small boy, bailed with half a coconut shell. The boat reached land and both passengers jumped out. Bernadette then noted that neither was as she expected. The skipper was a large, muscular man; the occupant was a tiny woman -- Oumou Kinsa.

"Miss O'Kelly! Thank you for coming!"

"Oumou. What are you doing here? What are you doing in that pirogue?"

"I had to be certain that you had come alone. I did not want any others from your Embassy, but more importantly, I wanted to make sure that no soldier or policeman followed you. I am so sorry that you had to wait for such a time." She introduced the pilot of the boat as a fellow

PPD member, Jini Togola.

"I understand Oumou. How do you know of this place?"

"Suleiman Sacco told me about it, just before Lassoso took him. He told me how much he loved you and how meaningful these baobab trees were to both of you."

"So, it's true. He is dead?"

"I'm pretty certain that he is. We have a source that was present during his torture. He said that Sulieman wasn't breathing when he left. It was terrible, but we are certain that he revealed nothing about you ... or about us."

Bernadette had cried as much as she could. The fragile spark of hope, ignited by the mysterious phone call, was all but extinguished. She quickly reestablished her persona as Political Officer O'Kelly. "You called me here for a reason, certainly."

"Yes, we have." She nodded toward Togola who resembled a professional athlete. He stood six foot seven and had the muscles of a weight lifter. Although he towered over Oumou, he clearly deferred to her. He uttered the hollow West African click of affirmation -- the equivalent of "uh-huh."

Oumou continued. "Events are moving very quickly in Zinani and we want you and your Embassy to be aware of our role in them. We, of course, would solicit your support, but most importantly, we want your understanding. We would not want you to learn of this after the fact. You have heard of the demonstrations of the last two days?"

"Yes, of course we have. The wife of our Embassy doctor was in the middle of the big one near the Akbar market."

"We are very sorry about the injuries and loss of life that occurred there. Those demonstrations, as you might have guessed, were not spontaneous. We in the PPD, along with other organizations, have done our best to stimulate ... what do you call it ... unrest?"

"What other organizations?" fact-finder O'Kelly queried.

"We cannot say. It is difficult enough for us to talk like this to you. Some on our committee fear that doing so will jeopardize everything; they, however, were outvoted." The evidence of structure and democracy in the upstart democracy movement impressed Bernadette.

"You can trust us with your information. You do know that I must discuss what you tell me with Ambassador Fairchild."

"Yes, we know that, expect it, and count on it.

"Miss O'Kelly, it is our plan to continue to keep the pressure on Mr. Lassoso and his government. The demonstrations of today and yesterday were small; we expect them to grow. There are thousands who support us and they will come to the streets when they know they are not alone."

"Will there be violence?"

"We have asked our people that they bring no guns, no knives, not even rocks or sticks. The Army and the Police are different. They all have guns, usually AK-47s. The soldiers are young and lack confidence. Any one might start shooting at any time. Their leaders have little control. They are such cowards! They are never at the front lines. They stay behind, with their big cars and teenage whores, and let the children in uniform defend our glorious President.

"You ask if we expect violence. Yes, we expect it, but we will not start it or respond to it with our own violence. Do you know what happened in Mali in 1991?"

"Yes, of course, the dictator was overthrown."

"More than that, he fell because he couldn't control his troops when they were asked to shoot their own citizens. The military turned on him."

"Do you expect the same?" asked Bernadette.

"Lassoso knows as well as we do that shooting and killing could lead to his downfall, so we expect him to be cautious. Tear gas, maybe some rubber bullets, and many arrests. But, he has troops that are poorly trained and easily frightened. We must prepare for the worst."

"Will they stay loyal to the government?"

"We don't know. General Sacco and I discussed that. He was convinced that their support was thin and that they would quickly turn to a leader who gave them hope of something new. But then he was demoted and nobody protested. He died and there was no reaction. We can't expect that the soldiers and police will automatically come to our side."

"So, where does the PPD go from here?"

"We will continue to organize peaceful demonstrations. We will look for support from the labor unions and the small businesses. We may shut down the schools and perhaps block the bridges and highways."

"Our government can't approve of that," said Bernadette.

"We know that but must consider those actions regardless."

"What are your goals?"

"We hope to get the President to accept democracy. That means elections. That means a real constitution. That means judges who would give someone like me a chance."

"You do not plan a revolution?"

"Free elections would be revolutionary. We do not expect to imitate Mali or Russia or France. We expect Oumar Ibrahim Lassoso to leave by being voted out, not jailed or beheaded."

"You really mean that, Oumou?" Miss Kinsa did not answer. "What would you like of us?"

"We want you to remain silent. We would ask that there be no outward support for the government and that you be prepared to call for democratic reform."

"You know that we always support democracy, Oumou."

"I wish that were true, Miss O'Kelly."

"I will convey your comments to the Ambassador. He will transmit them to the State Department and the President."

"That is all that we can ask of you. Thank you."

"By the way, Oumou, do you know anything about our two missing Peace Corps volunteers?"

"No, we do not know if they are safe, although both have been very supportive of our cause, especially Miss Sinova."

"Oh, what do you mean?"

"She has been very helpful in getting people to join our party and has spread the word of democracy through her village."

"Please, let us know if you hear of their whereabouts."

"We will."

Tiny Oumou Kinsa and massive Jini Togola boarded and refloated the pirogue, poling themselves to the middle of the Big where they tossed the fishing net in the current. With the dwindling light, Bernadette drove to the Embassy with the dramatic new information.

XIX

Dinner was called for seven o'clock. The Tuna Wellington smelled like tuna noodle casserole and looked like a loaf of bread. Jill felt that the three hours spent forming the loaf, layering the pate and shaping the puff pastry were probably a great waste of time.

Ernestine Grant was usually late for social events. Chen Wang was always prompt. Since they had become an item, it had become a subject of wagering as to the time of their mutual arrival for invitations. They had been on time for the dinner with the Health Minister. Jill thought they would be at least a half hour late for this occasion, while Michael bet on punctuality. He won.

Michael answered the doorbell in a mauve shirt and white trousers. Ms. Grant wore a *boubou* with a watermelon print and a bright red tank top. Economist Wang had also chosen to go African, sporting a powder blue *boubou* with gold embroidery and a maroon fez. Jillian had decked herself out in a lawn green dress and string of yellow beads. The sum of all this finery would have made an unknowing observer think of an accident in a Sherman-Williams paint factory.

The guests entered with hands joined. Among Embassy colleagues, they had become very open about their relationship.

Two years earlier when Chen Wang had arrived at post, his wife Sue accompanied him. Sue came from a wealthy San Francisco Chinese family. She and Chen met at Berkeley. She aspired to the law, but accepted his proposal, which included the role of "trailing spouse" of a Foreign Service Officer. She assumed that that meant years in the splendor and affluence of embassies in Paris, Rome, Tokyo, and Singapore. It proved to mean assignments in Yemen, Poland, Guyana, and a consulate in Surabaya, on the island of Java. She stayed in all of them, complaining often and working as a secretary occasionally. But the camel's back broke when she stepped off the plane at Keita-Coulibaly International. Less than a month after arriving at post, the heat, the garbage, the French, and the ennui got to her and she fled. Divorce papers arrived by diplomatic pouch a month later.

Wang and Grant had coupled up two months after Sue left. Ernestine invited Chen to dine on hamburgers at her place. He reciprocated with pasta primavera, having never learned to use a wok. A few weeks into the relationship, they slept together; they couldn't remember who seduced whom, but set up plans to repeat the activity twice weekly. As systems-oriented officers, they kept to schedule.

Michael and Jill, ever the avant-garde in race relations, were gleeful at the relationship their co-workers had created. The two couples were closest of friends.

"What can I get you?" asked the host. "I'm featuring a fine champagne."

"Sounds good to me; I want to tie one on tonight," said Chen, uncharacteristically but understandably.

"Not for me Michael. Do you have a Diet Coke?"

"Do we have Diet Coke? Ask me if Silicon Valley has microchips or if Peace Corps Volunteers have parasites. Of course we do. That lady in green drinks a couple of six-packs a day."

"Please, Michael." Jill denied her addiction, claiming that she could stop any time she wanted, but that she didn't want to now.

"Mr. Wang, may I take your fez?" The dark red hat was doffed and placed on the female head of a West African sculpture. Mamadou came from the kitchen with the prized bottle, two tulip glasses, and two red and white aluminum cans from Atlanta.

"Fssss," went Ernestine's can. "Fssss," Jill's followed. "Pop!" went the '76 champagne, the cork barely missing Mamadou's right eye.

"A toast to an enduring friendship and the hope that we all be able to meet again, here if possible, but if not, in some other armpit of the world. And also to you, Chen Wang, as the only American diplomat to remain in this, the world's number one armpit."

"Hear, hear."

"Clink," went the two Waterford champagne flutes. "Tonk," went the full cans of Diet Coke.

"Did the two of you hear about Bernadette's visit from Oumou Kinsa?" asked Ernestine of her host and hostess. Strictly speaking, she knew that she shouldn't disclose such sensitive issues with Jill, who had not undergone the close security check that directly hired employees had, but with the immediacy of everyone's departure, she ignored that particular tenet of the profession.

Neither Eisenstat had heard about the visit, so she proceeded to tell the story. Michael was well aware of the significance of the baobab forest. Jill was not, but did not inquire.

"What do you make of it, Ernestine," he asked.

"It sounds real and significant. Oumou said that she wasn't after a revolution, just a change of policies, but that's unrealistic."

"Do you think it's imminent?"

"It sure sounds that way. That demonstration that you got caught up in Jill was well planned and we've got to expect bigger tomorrow, when the funeral for the victims happens."

"Will OIL let the funeral go on?"

"No way he can stop it. Muslim culture demands a burial within 24 hours on the passing of any believer. To interfere would cost him his friends in the mosque and probably Gaddafi as well."

The Wheat Thins and Velveeta were a big hit. Neither Grant nor Wang was a real gourmet; the humor of the working class choice was lost on them. The champagne and coke were appreciated accompaniments. Dinner was called. At around the same time, crowd noises began filtering in from the main street a couple of hundred yards from the doctor's house. No one paid any attention to the clamor; it was nothing unusual.

Mamadou brought in the first course. Michael opened a fine white and poured, while Mamadou passed the asparagus, just out of the can, and spooned the hollandaise, squeezed from a hermetically sealed packet. "Wonderful." "Delicious." "Please give me the recipe, Jill." "Nice white wine, Michael." "Dry, isn't it?" An '83 Puligny-Montrachet. Retail price, $120.

The Wellington followed. The pastry had the color of a roan pony, and was shaped with the pleasing appearance of an uncut Jewish rye. The unfamiliar, though subtle aroma was that of the zebra pate. Like a turkey at Thanksgiving, the creation was placed in front of the host who proceeded to cut into it, releasing the unavoidably fishy juices and odors. The pieces were not uniform, leading to the comments all physicians hear at such times, "Glad you're not operating on me, Michael." The reviews were all rave, even from Michael, not a tuna aficionado.

Everyone asked for seconds of the Wellington. There was no trouble finishing the red wine, an expensive Burgundy that he had stored at varying temperatures in California and Zinani for 15 years. It was so sad that his guests thought of it as just red wine -- like thinking of a Rolex as a watch or Nijinsky as a dancer.

"Let's go in the living room for dessert," Jill suggested as Mamadou was taking the licked-clean plates away. The noise from the street had increased, but not yet enough to interrupt conversational flow.

Mamadou brought the dessert. Chocolate cake on Flintridge plates. Litchi nuts out of a can in elegant Venetian bowls. The cake was a bit dry and the frosting uneven; Jill could never get Mamadou to bake well, and she refused to bake herself. Whoever had grown and canned the litchis had done just fine.

"Chen, what are you going to do with all of us gone?" Michael asked.

"I'm not sure. Ernestine, the Ambassador, and I have been talking to some of the other Embassies about my holing up with them. None of us thinks that it would be a great idea for me to stick around the US Embassy on my own. The memories of Tehran are still acute. So far, the responses have been promising. The most open to us have been, of all places, the Armenians. They have a new building with some unused rooms and seem to think that it would be good PR for them to help the US in a time of crisis. The Taiwanese have really romanced me – they seem to think of me as a cousin. You know, I feel like a six-foot-eleven basketball player about to graduate from high school. Everybody is so nice, but you've gotta wonder about what motivates them."

"You don't really want to live with a group that speaks Armenian or Hokkien, do you?"

"You're right. I'll probably go into the Canadian Embassy. At least they speak English. It's no big rush. We've got more than 24 hours to change the entire nature of the American presence in Zinani. Long live the Zins! They make life so pleasant."

"How about some cognac?" Michael and Chen had both consumed industrial doses of great vintages, but the gracious host offered the after dinner drinks, expecting no takers. All took, even the Diet Coke drinkers. As Michael poured, a loud noise came from the street. Backfire of a motorcycle was the first impression. Then there were more, from multiple directions.

"Sounds like gunshots," Michael, the renowned diagnostician, opined without emotion.

"I'll check." Chen Wang darted to the window and looked down from the second story living room to the street just a couple of hundred yards away.

"Jesus Christ, get down!" Grant had lived through rioting in Zaire, including the revolt of the unpaid soldiers that resulted in the French Ambassador being killed by a so-called stray bullet. Rule number one in security training is get down when bullets fly.

Chen Wang didn't. "They're not going to shoot this way. Wow! There's gotta be a thousand people down there, most of 'em women and girls. And there are probably a hundred soldiers shooting. I don't know if they are shooting at the women or in the air but there are a lot of people on the ground." Because of the presence of so many expatriate diplomats, the neighborhood was well lighted, allowing him to call the play by play.

Suddenly, the plate glass window shattered.. Seconds later, Chen Wang fell to the floor. The three other diners were far enough way to avoid being cut by flying shards.

"I've been shot." Chen spoke flatly, almost as if he were asked to name the provinces of Canada.

Michael crawled toward him, brushing the shards of glass away with his hands, sustaining several lacerations for his efforts. "Call an ambulance Jill!" he commanded, momentarily forgetting where he was.

Michael had forgotten where he was. There were no ambulances for picking up the sick and injured. The one that did exist carted senior level doctors to and from the hospital. And even if there were a large fleet, none would be able to penetrate the mob in front. "Sorry, Jill, call the Marine Guard." That she could do. "Big Daddy, this is Rodeo Drive."

"Go ahead, Rodeo Drive."

"Shanghai has been shot at our house."

"Shot? Who by?"

"Unknown. Bullet came through the window."

"How serious?"

"Don't know yet, Rodeo Drive is with him

"Tell him to get Electra over to the Abattoir, Jill," Michael yelled.

"What's her call name?"

"Come on, damn it! It's not important."

Ernestine Grant spoke up. Only she noticed that the gunshots continued, even increased in frequency. "Have them tell the Ambassador and Security Officer that there's still a lot of shooting going on."

"Already being done." The Marines, expecting trouble, had increased their security position since the announcement.

"Tell them that it will be very hard getting through the front way with all the people. They'll have to go through the gate between our house and the Brill-Simmers'". Neighbors Aileen Brill and Jeremy Simmers were USAID contractors developing inland fisheries.

"Roger that. Please keep us informed."

"Shall do. Rodeo Drive out."

When Michael reached the victim, he found Chen Wang on his back, looking pale, sweaty, but not distressed. The light blue *boubou* had a large purple spot on the right upper chest. The Persian carpet, on which he fell, was likewise stained with blood.

"How you doing, friend?"

"It doesn't hurt much, Doc, but I can't catch my breath."

Michael noticed that Chen's respiratory rate was twice the normal 15 per minute. A palpation of the carotid artery and a look at his knock-off Tissot watch found a pulse of 140. "Jill, get the emergency kit!" He kept a fairly complete set of tools of the trade at home in case of an urgent house call. He didn't expect to have to use it in his own house.

As Jill crawled into the den to fetch the valise, he put his ear to Chen's chest. The breath sounds on the left were fine; those on the right were barely audible. It had to be a pneumothorax -- air between the lung and the chest wall -- squeezing the lung into a functionless mass.

When Jill arrived, he used the scissors to cut off the *boubou* revealing the hole in the upper chest that was sucking air into the chest cavity with each shallow breath. A quick tilt of the patient revealed the exit wound directly behind the entrance one. Blood pressure 70/50; Jill took it, the first one she had measured since hanging up her nurse's cap years before. Cold and clammy, low blood pressure, fast pulse – it added up to shock.

It could be the pneumothorax alone that was causing the crisis, or maybe the blood loss was more massive than Chen's soiled *boubou* and Baluchistan carpet suggested. Michael hoped for the former but was preparing to deal with the latter.

"Chen, what's your blood type?"

"No idea."

In order to prevent air from getting in through the wounds Michael slapped on gauze impregnated with Vaseline, both on the back and front. He asked for and was handed by Nurse Jillian, a large syringe with a fat 16-gauge needle, and jabbed it between two of Chen's ribs on the right. "Whoooosh." A most satisfying sound issued forth as air under pressure escaped the confines of Mr. Wang's chest.

"Doc, I feel better." Michael felt the pulse. It was a bit slower and a lot stronger. "Blood pressure is now 110/70," Jill said with a smile. Although Chen was no longer seconds from a cardiac arrest, Doctor and Nurse knew that they he wasn't out of the woods. They had no way to tell how active the bleeding was inside his chest, nor whether the air around the lung would quickly reaccumulate and drive the pressure down and the pulse up once again. They had to get him to the health unit. First an IV was needed. A patient who has bled heavily can be sustained for some time with intravenous fluids, delivered rapidly.

"Put in an IV, Jill."

"You put it in, Doctor. I haven't put an IV in in years."

The physician was not accustomed to being talked to that way by a nurse. He was well accustomed to being talked to that way by his wife. He deftly inserted the IV. The saline and glucose solution dripped rapidly into Chen's left forearm.

The gunfire had stopped. Jill, recently educated on tear gas, recognized by a faint odor that some canisters of the gas had been used to quell the disturbance down the street. There was a knock at the back door. Mamadou, who was washing dishes as if nothing had happened, answered it. Security Officer Frank Norbert and Gunnery Sergeant Billie Don Rice entered, the teargas having cleared the way for vehicular access. Norbert had brought a stretcher; Sgt. Rice had a radio in hand describing every event to the guard at the Embassy.

"It looks like Vietnam in here," said veteran Rice, seeing the blood and scattered glass on the floor.

"Screw it! Let's get him to the Health Unit, now!" yelled the usually imperturbable doctor.

"Yes, Sir." The olive drab canvas and wood stretcher was laid on the side of the blood stained rug; the two health professionals and two security professionals gently lifted the seemingly stable commercial officer, set him upon it, and strapped him in. Vital signs were checked again before the difficult trip down the stairs was undertaken. "His blood pressure is down to 80/50 and pulse back up over 120," nurse Eisenstat reported quietly. Michael stuck the needle and syringe between the ribs again and heard the welcome depressurization.

"He's got a pretty big leak. He'll need a chest tube as quickly as possible." A chest tube would suck out the air that leaked between the lung and the chest wall. Easy concept. One problem -- Michael, the internist, had never before inserted one of the large rubber tubes.

He knew that he had a tube in the Abattoir, and he also was aware that he had a surgery textbook. He had never opened it and hoped that it would be like a cookbook, telling him step-by-step where to make the incision, how big it should be, how deep to put in the tube, and how to hook it up to the suction. Donolu had three good surgeons whom, under normal circumstances, he knew he could call on to help him. The cannonade outside suggested that these were not normal circumstances, and that those surgeons would be fully occupied at OIL General. After the scene with Garson Graham's granddaughter, Michael was not about to put any of his patients at risk in that facility, even if a revolution hadn't been going on.

Getting Chen Wang down the angled flight of steps was no easy matter. The stretcher had to be tilted almost fully vertical, but the straps held. The four bearers took him through the gate to Brill-Simmers's yard and into the waiting Cherokee, where he was stretched out diagonally. The doctor and Frank Norbert stayed in the Cherokee while

Jill, the DCM, and the Gunnery Sergeant followed in the Eisenstat's Mitsubishi. The usual ten-minute trip took longer as they maneuvered around the milling crowds and soldiers manning every corner. The green diplomatic plates offered both vehicles free passage. Even this dictatorship's barely trained soldiers knew to obey the strict codes of diplomacy.

At Norbert's command, the usual check for chassis bombs was waived. Michael and Frank had little trouble transporting the 130-pound Chen from the van into the Embassy elevator. Michael was relieved to discover that he cold ride the elevator without breaking a sweat. Perhaps all these emergencies were going to cure him of his phobia.

The door to the Abattoir was open and Electra was present in jeans and T-shirt. An IV pole was in place. The crash-cart full of equipment and medicines, in case of a cardiac arrest, was ready to go.

"Get some vitals!"

"Pressure 80/60, pulse 132." The stethoscope confirmed the reaccumulation of air on the right side. Michael had kept the syringe in his pocket and relieved the pressure with first a grimace and then a smile from his patient.

"Electra, please get me a chest tube."

"What?"

"Get me a chest tube. The patient has a pneumothorax and needs a tube. And, get the suction machine." He hoped that the machine worked; he had not tested it since his arrival.

"Is Dr. Guindo coming over?" Ali Guindo was the surgeon they always called for consultations on abdominal pains, trauma, and the like.

"No Electra, I will be doing it myself. You need to focus and help me get this done."

"Yes, Doctor." The chest tube package had a sterility expiration date that had passed during an earlier Presidential administration. Michael ignored the information.

"Open it up, please. It's probably still sterile. We can always treat infection later.

"Chen, we will be putting in this tube to drain that air that makes it hard for you to breathe. I'll be putting some local anesthetic to numb the area. "

"Whatever you need to do, do it."

Michael filled a syringe with Xylocaine and injected it in Chen's side.

"I'm going to check something out in my office while the anesthetic takes hold."

He pulled his *Principles of Surgery* off the bookshelf. "Chest Tubes." Nothing in the index. "Pneumothorax, treatment, pages 1345-1349." The pages contained photographs of a silver-haired surgeon doing the procedure. The complications section was short: bleeding, persistent pain, and infection, but nothing about death.

Having decided not to pretend that he was anything other than a first-timer, the newly self-educated surgeon took his book into the procedure room with him.

The book suggested that one could get a chest tube in place within three minutes. It took Eisenstat half an hour, but it eventually went in with nothing worse than a frown from the wounded Officer. He attached the suction machine. Bubbles appeared in the water seal -- success. Michael was bubbling too, with pride.

Electra was assigned the task of dressing the wound, checking the vital signs, controlling the IV flow, and doing the scutwork that nurses always dread, but do smilingly.

Michael went into the waiting room to notify the anxious DCM and Security Officer. By this time, the waiting room crowd had swelled to half a dozen or more, including the Ambassador. Michael's long paper gown had some impressive bloodstains. To those who knew no better, he surely looked like a competent, even heroic, surgeon.

"He's doing OK." He described the procedure in layman-like terms, not letting on that it was his first chest tube.

"Now what?" Fairchild asked.

"Good question, Sir. Obviously, he cannot stay here and he cannot go to Lassoso Hospital. We've got to get him out of the country ASAP."

"But, he's the only one allowed to be here after we leave."

"Hardly relevant, Mr. Ambassador." Michael knew no more diplomatic way to tell his boss what a stupid comment that was.

"Well, I'll have to let the Ministry of Foreign Affairs know about this. Maybe they'll change their tune now that one of our people has been shot by their thugs."

"That's already taken care of, Sir." Ernestine Grant had called directly to Madam Obode to notify her of the incident. The Minister showed no great concern. She expressed her regrets but offered no change in orders."

"We are to have no representative at all in this shit hole?" The rest of the Americans were embarrassed by this utterance made by the Chief of Mission in front of several citizens of the host nation.

"Her answer was that we could replace Mr. Chen."

"Who with?"

"Not with anyone of us. With someone from outside the country."

"To hell with them. We're closing the goddam place." Fairchild was acting less ambassadorial each minute.

"Sir, don't you think that we ought to run this by the State Department first."

"Please, Ernestine, don't second guess me. We will close the doors on Saturday morning. Fuck 'em!"

"Yes, Sir." The Zinanians quietly left. The Americans silently stayed.

After two agonizing minutes, Michael spoke up, changing the subject. "I need to call for a medevac plane." He returned to the scene of his surgical success story. The IV was dripping contentedly, Electra was cleaning up the mess, and Chen Wang was asleep.

XX

Lieutenant Colonel Siegfried Otobalo bit through his burned out cigar when the phone awakened him at 11PM. He was not happy having been assigned to sit vigil on the Peace Corps Volunteers; Lieutenant Colonels don't do that kind of work. There were two privates, sound asleep, on the chairs next to the door of the volunteers' prison.

"Otobalo," he snarled into the receiver.

"Colonel, this is Sergeant Diof, speaking for General Joro." Joro had taken over when Sacco was demoted. "The General wants you and your staff to come to the Presidential Palace immediately."

"Why?"

"He didn't say. He wants you and your men here, now."

"What are we to do with the American whores?"

"We know nothing about that. Come in immediately, Sir."

"Tell General Joro that we are en route."

"Get in the Jeep, we are leaving," he barked to the privates. He hated New Akron like most Parisians abhor the provinces, and therefore was delighted by the command.

"But what about the women?"

"There aren't any women. Let's go."

The two guards were the same ones that had been there when Jenny and Beth had been locked up. While the shorter one sprinted to the waiting Jeep and jumped in the front seat, the taller lagged behind, furtively slipping open the bolt of the latch to the women's door. Humanitarian gesture? Pro-American act? Anti-authoritarian action? No. He wanted to have sex with an American woman and reckoned that one or both would feel indebted when he returned.

Beth and Jenny slept through the departure of their sentries. They had spent three days and nights in near complete blackout and had despaired finding any escape. Yelling, cajoling, kicking, and pounding had not worked. They rarely spoke to one another, as there was nothing to say. They sang from time to time. Sinova, who had a reasonable voice, knew the entire seventies and eighties repertoire. Addison, who couldn't carry a tune, usually hummed along.

I still haven't found what I'm looking for.

Ob-la-di, ob-la da, life goes on.

You can check out any time you like, but you can never leave.

Having just experienced a dream that she had failed an astrophysics test in a course she hadn't known she was enrolled in, Jenny awoke in a sweat, finding herself on the hardwood floor. She struggled achingly to her feet and started her usual morning stroll, the second step landing her right foot in the previous night's unfinished rice and sauce.

"Let me out of here!" She went to the door to rattle it to make the guards feel guilty. The handle twisted and the door opened. It opened! Light poured in.

"Beth, it's open!"

"Holy shit."

"We're free!"

"Sure we are." Sinova was convinced that she would die in New Akron, in the dark, in a chamber of horrors stinking of feces, urine, okra, and peanut sauce. She was not about to accept that an open door meant freedom having seen too many movies in which a detainee was let out of prison only to perish in a fusillade as an escapee. "Hold on a little before you go out. They might be fucking with us."

The women had their first chance to glance at the interior of their three-day prison. The walls were a veritable zoo of small reptiles, with dozens of geckos, push-up lizards, and chameleons clinging effortlessly to the *banco*. The dirt floor was strewn with mango and papaya peelings, okra tips, and peanut shells. One corner had a pile of dry feces, presumably mammalian, probably human. The galvanized chamber pot, which they had been forced to use for all but one of their daily requirements, sat safely in another corner; they had been religious about assuring that it wouldn't be kicked over during Jenny's calisthenics. Most striking in appearance were the two prisoners. The Stanford T-shirt, once white, was now red-brown laterite mixed with sauce stains of brownish-green. Bethe's Senegalese-print shirt, spotted with the same foodstuffs, managed to keep some of its brightness. Their unwashed Caucasian skins, one originally light olive, the other Republican, indicated what felt like an eternity in sordid captivity.

"Let's get out of here!" Accepting the possible fate of being the first West African Peace Corps Volunteer to fall victim to a gunman's bullet, Miss Addison opted to go first. The vinyl and steel chairs were empty. Cigarette butts had collected around the legs of one. Blue plastic bags blew hither and yon in the large empty space surrounding the shack. One light brown and one dark brown dog slept just outside. There was no human being in sight.

They tried the door to the office. It opened rustily. The room was as they remembered it from before their incarceration: total disarray and smelly but almost pristine compared to their prison. A black dial phone sat on the Lt. Colonel's desk. Beth picked up the receiver – from it emanated a shrill, irritating dial tone, the trademark of Zinani T and T.

"Jen, it works! Let's call the Peace Corps office. They sure as hell better be worried about us."

"Right. Do you know the number?"

"No, don't you?"

"Why would I know the number? Whoever calls?"

Phone book? None since the French left in 1960. Information? An unknown concept. No phone call was made.

"Well Volunteer Addison, you and I better take a bush taxi and get our asses into Donolu. I wouldn't be surprised if we were big news on BBC and CNN."

"What do you mean, Beth? We have to go back to Korikono first."

"Why?"

"Alien. He's gotta be starving."

"Christ all mighty, Jenny, he's a dog. He can survive by eating the neighborhood shit."

"But he's our responsibility. We took him in and we have to look after him."

"You are out of your fucking mind."

"Please Beth, don't talk like that. We have to go to Korikono. It will only take a few minutes, then we can go into the office."

"Idiot! You go to Korikono. I'll go to Donolu. Don't give me any shit if I end up being interviewed on CNN and you only get a still photo.

"By the way, Jen, do you have any money?" A seat on an old Peugeot covered pick-up bush taxi cost 40 lassosos, about a dollar, to ride between the two cities.

"No. As you recall, we weren't given much time to prepare for these past few days."

Since bush taxi drivers don't collect money until the end of the ride, Beth decided to chance it that she'd find someone on the other end willing to lend her 40 lassosos. Wolf Blitzer, maybe.

"You know, Twatface, maybe it's good that you are going to feed Alien while I go to the City. This togetherness has gotten a little out of hand. I was sort of taking a hankering to you." Beth was being honest.

"Why didn't you say that before?" thought Jenny, silently.

XXI

Bernadette O'Kelly considered her fate. She now had it figured that, with the rarest exception, nocturnal solitude was to be her status quo henceforth: a married professor, a wimpish grad student, and a dead Zinanian General - the sum total of her meaningful romantic exploits.

She had left the Embassy after midnight, convinced that Chen Wang was not going to die. Her trip home was uneventful. Stationed at each corner were two or more uniformed and armed teenage soldiers. Military vehicles were positioned at major intersections; usually they were trucks or station wagons, but occasionally she saw tanks or armored personnel carriers, gifts of the Libyans if they were new, the Soviets if they were middle-aged, or the French if they were old. She had no difficulty driving through any of the fortified corners as her diplomatic license continued to allow free passage.

She had been asleep for a few hours, but it was still dark out when her radio squawked its high-pitched call.

"All personnel, this is Big Daddy. This is Big Daddy. Stay tuned for an important message."

The last time Dette had heard this announcement, an unexpected holiday was declared when President Lassoso had decided to fete his second wife's twentieth birthday. The astute Political Officer surmised that she was about to hear a less benign declaration.

"Oh, God, Chen has died," she thought, then realized that the Marines would not be so crass as to make a public announcement. She supposed that it must have to do with the situation on the streets.

Five minutes, later the cacophony returned. "All personnel, this is Big Daddy. Tiger's Den is at his location and will broadcast."

"How do you turn this fucking thing on, Sergeant?"

"You already have turned it on, Sir. You are on the air. Just speak into the microphone." Bernadette cringed at the thought that Ambassador Fairchild had just polluted the airways with his seven-letter incompetence. She also was quite certain that Lassoso had someone monitoring the Embassy's radio traffic at all times.

"This is Tiger's Den. As all of you are aware, there have been disturbances on the streets of Donolu and other cities. Some have become violent. There have been deaths; some sources say many deaths. One of our own has been seriously injured, although I am pleased to say that Shanghai is doing well. Reliable sources tell us that the Ambassador of the Palestine Liberation Organization has been killed accidentally in Sokimbo. We do not now recognize, nor do we plan to recognize in the near future, the Embassy of the Palestine Liberation Organization in Zinani."

"Glad he clarified that," thought Bernadette. She had not heard of the Ambassadorial fatality and was irked that political events were happening and being discussed without her input.

"The Zinanian forces have been fully mobilized and have been ordered to maintain the peace at any cost. They have been issued ammunition and told to use it on anyone who appears to be a threat. We suspect that they have been told not to shoot at anyone in a diplomatic vehicle, but we strongly recommend that everyone remain in their house. Do not venture outside except under dire circumstances, like your house is on fire or is being overrun by infiltrators.

"Our plans are to leave tomorrow as scheduled, although the situation is fluid and we are in contact with both Washington and the military command in Germany. Preparations are being made to get us out earlier if needed.

"The next voice you hear will be that of, uh ... who the hell are you, Frank?"

"Scotland Yard, Sir." Not a bad moniker for a security officer.

"Scotland Yard will give you further information."

"Tiger's Den has summarized most of the important info. Please recognize that the situation is extremely volatile. The major areas of activity at this time are the vicinity of the Presidential Palace and the television station. Gunshots have been reported in both locations in the last few hours. So far, the neighborhoods where you live have been quiet, except for the region around Rodeo Drive's home.

"I suggest that each of you stay by your radio and turn on your television. So far, there has been no interruption of electrical service. You won't hear the truth, but if there is an emergency announcement, at least you'll know what they telling their own people.

"In the unlikely event of further injuries, we advise coming to the Embassy, to the nurses residence, or to the Tiger's Den, where a Marine who can perform first aid will be posted. Do not, repeat, do not, go to Lassoso General Hospital as your safety cannot be guaranteed." Few missed the irony of that comment.

"Although water is running normally now, it may not be soon. We advise filling bathtubs and vessels with water. Most of you have adequate provisions in your storerooms to last many days. Please do not go on the streets for more provisions. The stores are closed anyway, and we don't expect them to open any time soon.

"Our information is as complete and up to date as it can be in these difficult circumstances. Some of our loyal Zinanian employees are in the city watching events unfold and reporting them to us as they happen. We do not know everything. We ask each of you to pay attention, within the limits of your own personal safety, and let us know if anything is going on within your sight or hearing.

"That's it, sir."

"Thank you, Yard. We will take questions from anyone listening."

"You don't mean that," thought Bernadette and others who recognized the wide listening audience that had been built up by the crazy gringos over the years.

"Tiger's Den, this is Penny-Pincher," chimed in Conrad Prudholme.

"Send it, Pincher."

"In all due respect to Scotland Yard, I would ask that you have your TVs on only when someone is watching. Just 'cause there's a revolution going on is no reason to waste electricity."

"We hear you Penny-Pincher." Even the Ambassador found Prudholme obnoxious. "Any other questions?"

"Tiger's Den, this is Big Red." Bernadette got over her reluctance to use the radio. The only times she had used it before was to arrange tennis matches or plan a get together with the doctor to talk about abortions.

"Send it, Big Red."

"Den, Sir, what is happening? Who is behind this? What is our position on the events?" Dette knew that these were not the best of questions for the open line but felt so out of touch that she had to remind her boss that she was still around.

"Big Red, please use your land line after this transmission has been terminated." Bernadette did not have a phone.

"Big Daddy, this is Shrinking Violet." Shrinking Violet was an AID contractor, Osgood Genu, contracted to teach weight lifting to a team of Zinanian athletes. He weighed about 250 and was built like Schwarzenegger. His wife, Fanny, weighed about 100 and looked like Mia Farrow. She was Shrinking Violet Alpha.

"We copy, Violet."

"Shrinking Violet Alpha has diarrhea."

"Oh."

"What should we do?"

"I would suggest that you call the doctor on your land line." The Ambassador sounded as if he was not keen on discussing diarrhea.

"We don't have a land line."

"So, give her an Imodium."

"Whatever that is, I don't have any."

"I will ask the doctor to call you as soon as he can leave Shanghai."

"Thank you, sir."

"Other questions? Hearing none, we ask that you keep us informed as to any changes in your neighborhoods, and most importantly, keep your heads down. Tiger's Den clear."

As soon as the radio went silent, the phone on the Ambassador's desk rang. "Sir, this is Bernadette. What gives?" She had gone next door to a well-connected French neighbor.

"Big stuff, real big stuff."

"What?"

"Speak to the DCM." He handed the phone to Ernestine.

"Based on word we hear out of the hospital, the body count is probably over a hundred now. It may be a lot higher. Most of the deaths are students and bystanders but at least twenty burned to death in a fire in the CARE warehouse. A group had busted in to loot the place and someone torched it, either accidentally or on purpose."

"Is there looting all over town?" Dette could not believe that the incredibly warm, passive, almost teddy-bearish Zinanians could do a

Watts or a Newark.

"All over. The Lebanese restaurant Le Comfort, burned to the ground. The cigarette plant, charred. You won't believe it, but the school for the blind was sacked; all the beds -- even the Braille books.

"What's happening with the Army?"

"Jesus, Dette, they are the ones doing all the damage, killing, and looting. The students, mainly women, tried to take over the bridge to stop all traffic from crossing the river. Lassoso's bastards just fired into the crowd. There's word of at least twenty dead and more than that critical. Lots of them jumped into the Begoro since there was no place else to go. That's a long jump, like fifty feet, in the dark, and Zinanian women aren't known for their swimming skills.

"Why? Why?"

"Only a guess, but I think that Lassoso must have given the order to shoot. A few random shots, maybe, but this looks systematic and organized."

"Right." Bernadette recalled the gentleness of her dead lover and his comments about his troops. No way that a full-scale slaughter could happen in Donolu unless the President said, "kill."

"How about the PPD."

"No word. The TV station, which is still in government hands, is calling them swine so it is logical to assume that they are involved big time."

Fairchild asked for the receiver. "By the way, Bernadette, this is crazy that we are talking about this on the phone. Why don't you haul yourself down here? Political Officers probably should be involved in our dealing with this revolution."

"But Mr. Ambassador, you told us all to stay put."

"Yeah, I did, but we need you. Be careful, but come over to the residence. We'll send a Cherokee over to get you."

There had been no gunfire in her neighborhood. A quick glance from her window revealed an empty street except for a few parked cars, normal at 4:30 AM.

Five minutes later, her doorbell rang. She had not bothered to change from the shorts and CREIGHTON BLUEJAYS T-shirt. She was pleased that the Embassy car had arrived so quickly.

She opened her door to find not the Embassy driver, but a huge black man in fatigues. She recognized him. Jini Togola, the pirogue pilot at the baobab forest when she and Oumou had last talked.

"Miss O'Kelly, Miss Kinsa would like to see you."

"Where."

"I cannot say."

"I'm sorry, I am waiting for an automobile from our Embassy. I have been ordered to go to my office."

"I too am sorry, Miss O'Kelly, but Miss Kinsa insists that you be brought to see her." His massive hand grabbed her lady-like forearm. She opted against a struggle, knowing that it wouldn't do her any good, and moreover that being taken to the headquarters of the revolutionary front in mid-revolution might be a career-enhancing move.

She was directed, gently, to a waiting car. Renault 4, a box with wheels. A woman in a colorful *boubou* and turban was at the wheel. "I apologize, Miss O'Kelly, but we must cover your eyes with a blindfold." Bright yellow and blue elephant pattern. In West Africa, even the blindfolds were colorful.

"Blood pressure 120 over 70. Pulse 88. Temperature 101 degrees." Electra gave the half-awake physician-surgeon Chen's vital signs. Michael liked the first two data points. The fever was worrisome, but could probably be explained by the reaction to the trauma itself. He knew that lousy surgeons had a much higher incidence of infections than good ones. He knew that no one would accuse him of being a good surgeon, but he also knew that it was way too early to have signs of a surgical infection. More importantly, the continuous bubbling of the tube in the water seal and the reasonably low pulse and adequate blood pressure spoke to a successfully placed chest tube.

He rose from the couch to visit his sleeping patient. To prove to himself that Chen Wang was not in coma, an unlikely result of the minor surgery, he softly tapped on his shoulder. Chen was instantly fully awake, like a fireman ready to slide down the pole.

"How do you feel, Chen?"

"Good, doc. How about you?"

"A little tired, but I'm not the issue. Any pain?"

"Just the chest. Not bad."

"How about some pain medicine?"

"Huh-uh. I don't want to get hooked." Michael was too tired to argue with silliness.

"The medevac plane is on its way. We should have you out of here by noon, assuming they let it land." There was no telling what Lassoso's crew might do at the airport. The French were apparently making noise about bringing in transports to evacuate their several thousand citizens. The Belgians and Moroccans might follow suit. Landing rights for a medevac plane might be OIL's place to take a stand.

"Big Daddy, Big Daddy, this is Shrinking Violet! Emergency!" The Abattoir had its radio on, as did all houses and offices during the crisis.

"Oh, Doctor, I forgot to tell you that Fanny Genu was having diarrhea and you were supposed to radio Shrinking Violet," said Electra, embarrassedly.

"This is Big Daddy, go ahead Shrinking Violet."

"Jesus, they have come into our yard!"

"Who?"

"About a thousand goddam Zins! Send the Marines!"

"I'm sorry, we cannot." Marines are stationed in diplomatic posts to guard the Embassy and its secrets only. Six twenty-two-year-olds would not fare well against hordes. "What about your night guard?"

"He's asleep. There are a thousand of the bastards, over our wall! What do you want us to do? Shit, they're trying to break down the front door."

"Get into your safe haven." Every official residence had a single room chosen as a safe haven, usually the master bedroom. The rooms had steel doors, quadruple locks, and windows covered by iron grating.

"We're going in, but there's no radio inside." Frank Norbert had planned to get around to that security problem a week or so later. "And my wife still has the shits!"

"Shrinking Violet, this is Rodeo Drive." Michael couldn't do anything about a thousand Zins but he could comment about the shits.

"Yeah, doc?"

"Do you have any diarrhea medicine at home?"

"Damned if I know."

"Take all your pills into the safe haven and look around for Lomotil or Immodium or Pepto or Paregoric or anything with codeine and have her take four or five. Better take a big bucket also."

"Thanks doc. Oh, Christ, they broke the glass door." Only a single iron barrier stood between the throng and the AID contractor. "Send for the cops. Shrinking Violet clear."

Under the best of circumstances, one does not send for the cops. One goes and picks them up. They've got no vehicles. Donolu only has about 150 police; about half of them have riot gear and are prepared for upheaval. Most of the rest stand at busy corners where they stop drivers and shake them down for a few lassosos. The police force, with guns but no more than six bullets each, would be of little help at the invaded home of Shrinking Violet.

There were no further communications from either member of the household.

Fairchild, Grant, Sgt. Rice, and Norbert were at the Ambassador's residence. They, too, heard the plight of the Genus. "What can I do to get the Genus out of this fix?"

"Not a thing, sir," said the Security Officer. "We have to pray a little. My guess is that mob is after loot rather than victims. Any injury is likely to be accidental. I'm a little worried that Osgood will try to fight these guys."

"Why that house?" asked the Ambassador.

"You know who the landlord of that place is don't you?"

"No idea."

"The Defense Minister Yamamoto owns the place. Our sources say that the mob is going to go after the property of anyone connected with the government, even if they aren't living in it." Hyashi Yamamoto, the son of a Japanese World War II draft-dodger, had risen quickly in the Lassoso regime. Like many of his fellow Ministers, he accumulated a portfolio of real estate in spite of a salary well under that of a McDonald's fry cook in DC. "We know that they've knocked off the Prime Minister's house, stealing everything in the place including the toilet bowls, and bodily lifting his mother out before torching it."

"Why would the PPD be getting into this kind of destruction?"

queried the Ambassador, another query that an Ambassador should not have to ask.

Ernestine answered the easy one, "Sir, it is not only the PPD that is involved. This country has a lot of unhappy citizens. Fifty percent of men in the capital are unemployed, most are young with nothing to do. The military doesn't get paid on time. Businessmen have to pay high taxes or high graft. Civil servants' salaries are so small they'll never be able to afford a bicycle, let alone a car or house. Everybody sees the tiny handful of families living high off the hog with mansions and big black cars. Look what happens when authority is challenged and weakened, be it Kinshasa, Seoul, or LA. People who could barely tell you the President's name, let alone the issues that have lead to the present situation, are more than happy to rip the society to shreds, destroying everything around them."

"Where will it stop?" asked Marylou, walking in with a plate of peanut butter cookies.

"Either when everything is destroyed and the city is laid waste, or when Lassoso is arrested, killed, or driven from the country, or when the military acts so powerfully that it scares the rioters away."

"Can the military get that powerful?" asked the Gunnery Sergeant.

"Not by itself, it can't," responded the DCM. "They have a few AK47s, but most of their rifles are WWII vintage French or Russian. We know of four tanks that run, and three airplanes. That's hardly enough heavy weaponry to scare anyone."

"Not by itself?" asked the Ambassador.

"They need help."

"From whom?"

"Not us. Not France. Not the Russians. Nobody, except Libya.

"You think Gadaffi will jump in?"

"How can he not? OIL is not going down without a fight. Gaddafi doesn't want a democracy on his flank. Don't forget the SCUDs. I'll give you odds that some very large aircraft are already on the way from Tripoli."

The doorbell chimed the first four bars of the Ode to Joy, installed by Holden and Marylou at no small cost to the American taxpayer. "It must be Bernadette." The Ambassador had noticed that his political officer was half an hour later than expected.

It wasn't Bernadette. It was Lori Burkitt, the spy.

"It's friggin' dangerous out there. Try to get a little information and almost get your butt shot off." In spite of having almost lost her ass, she looked prepared for a Parisian power lunch, with a highly tailored suit of rust-colored linen.

"What happened?"

"I was trying to locate Oumou Kinsa or someone high up in PPD to get the scoop. The usual sources were dry. Had the driver go past her house and that of Jini Togola. Cops surrounded hers; his was dark. Out at the University, I saw at least a dozen dead folks, mostly women and no live ones. I heard some gunshots but couldn't see where they were coming from. Got the hell out of there quickly. We went to see a guy in the military that is usually good with info. Surprisingly, he was home. He claimed that the Army could go over any time."

"Go over?"

"Yeah, join the side of the revolution."

"What's he base that on?"

"Says that he has talked to a number of fellow officers and he isn't hearing much support for the Oily One. Oh, by the way, you asked about the satellite photos of the New Akron area. Our guys studied them. You're right about the SCUDs; there are about twenty. More important though is the fact that they've got about the same number of new tanks and APCs, plus what appears to be 2000 or so troops."

"Libyans?"

"I doubt they're Peruvians."

"Two thousand is a lot of men for this pit," said the Ambassador, irreverently.

"Right on." Lori had adapted the sixties jargon from her left-leaning parents, who were embarrassed by the fact they had a daughter in the CIA.

"Your airplanes from Tripoli, Ernestine. Looks like they've already landed."

"Yes, Sir. Lori, how do you square all this information? On one side, your officer saying that the Zin Army may turn, on the other, the presence of a sizeable foreign expeditionary force."

"Looks like war to me."

"We're not in a good place then?"

"Right on."

"Where do you think Bernadette is, Ernestine?"

"Probably finding the usual routes blocked. She may have had to stay at home."

"She would have called."

"True. Except she doesn't have a phone."

XXII

Once the elephant bandana was removed from her eyes, Bernadette found herself in a room that made her unkempt dorm room at Creighton look kempt. Two underpowered lamps struggled to make it light enough for the dozen or so occupants to see one another. Four old wooden desks sat along the walls giving the place the aura of the city desk at a mid-sized daily. Paper in stacks. Paper crumpled. Paper on the floor. Posters on the wall. A mimeograph machine on a desk. Smoke filled. Hot. Muggy. No air.

It was noisy, cocktail-party noisy. A radio and a TV were both on, competing for auditory supremacy. No one was listening to either. The assembled, almost all less than 30 years of age, were talking to each other or reading the stacks of paper or smoking or drinking Cokes or some combination. Except for Togola, no one seemed to be paying attention to the American. As soon as he removed her blindfold, he guided Dette toward a small woman in a far corner. In spite of the darkness, she knew immediately that it was Oumou. Ms. Kinsa was in conversation with two other women, both considerably more robust and taller than she. Both, like her, had intricately braided cornrows dangling below their necks.

With a wrist flick, Oumou dismissed her lieutenants and slalomed her way through the snowdrift of paper toward the recent arrival. She wore a Bogolan -- a black and white mud cloth -- shirt and Levis. She was unshod. Bernadette had always thought her pretty, not beautiful, with a Joan Baez kind of prettiness. But now that prettiness had been overtaken by a mien of utter fatigue and determination. It had never occurred to Dette that black people could have dark circles under their eyes.

"Miss O'Kelly, welcome to our headquarters. Please accept my apologies for the process we used to get you here."

"I understand why this was necessary, but I do want to keep the

blindfold as a souvenir, she responded, trying to lighten the mood."
There was no smile of comprehension. "Where am I, Oumou?" She
knew that a good spy would have been able to ascertain the location by
the route traveled even if she were both blind and deaf. A spy she wasn't.

"I cannot say, except that you are in the national headquarters of the
People's Party for Democracy. Excuse our most humble surroundings.
We spend our money on things other than rent and furniture."

"Even though I understand your needs, remember, please, that I am
a diplomat, representing a sovereign nation, and a fairly important
nation at that. Your action can hardly improve your standing in the eyes
of our government."

"We understand the ... uh, gravity of the action we have taken in
bringing you here, but felt that it was necessary in view of what we
expect to happen over the next several hours. We could not call you on
the telephone nor meet you in any but the safest of safe houses."

"Next several hours?"

"Yes, Miss O'Kelly, we expect that Mr. Lassoso's government will no
longer be in power by 10 AM today."

"Jesus H. Christ! What do you mean?" She felt ashamed of her
epithet.

"The people were very disturbed by the events of the past two days.
Many Zinanians, mostly uninvolved observers, have died. Many more
have been hurt; they will not be able to get medical care and will also
die. The President has obviously given the order to shoot to kill and so
far the orders have been followed. They will not continue to be
followed."

"What do you mean?"

"Mr. Lassoso's military will no longer continue to shoot their
brothers, sisters, cousins, and neighbors. I have personally been told by
General Joro, who, as you know, has replaced your friend Sacco, that his
division, which includes the palace guard, will no longer support the
President."

"My God! Suleiman had told me that might happen. What will they
do?"

"General Joro has told me that he and the head of the Paratroop
Battalion, Colonel Rashad, will be going to the Palace this morning to

arrest Lassoso. They will transport him and his family to the paratroop barracks on the Sokimbo road, where he will be safe from those who would like to see him hanged or shot."

"Who would support this and who won't?"

"Everybody that counts will support us. Frankly, with the military on our side, we should have no trouble."

"What about the television station?" Bernadette knew that the control of the airways, particularly TV, was key to any coup d'état.

"I'm glad you mentioned that. We will have to tell General Joro to send a platoon to the station." O'Kelly, for the first time, realized that she was talking to an amateur.

"What do you expect will happen after the arrest?"

"A committee will act as a transition government, until a constitution can be written and a new President can be elected. The PPD will constitute a significant part of the committee, along with the Army, the labor movement, and other liberal members of our society."

"Who will be the leader of the junta?"

"Juntas are in Latin America. Ours is a committee," she said with more than a hint of anger. "They have asked me to take that position."

"But, Oumou, you are a woman!"

"You Americans are so observant. Yes, I am a woman, but just because every other leader of a revolution in the history of the world has been a man, that is no reason to say that will continue forever."

"OK. Fair enough." Tell me, Madam President, why did you bring me here to tell me this? I don't see any French or Russians or World Bankers here."

"Please do not call me Madam President. Oumou is fine, at least for now. You can answer your question yourself. No one else counts in this world any more. The Russians are out of the second world, back into the third. The French are, like you sometimes say, 'wannabes.' They have wanted to be something important ever since Waterloo, but just can't get there, except in Africa. We really don't care what they say. UN, IMF, and World Bank -- they come later. We want and need the support of the United States. In fact, we would like your Ambassador to go with General Joro and Colonel Rashad to the Presidential Palace for the arrest."

"That is the most outlandish request I have ever heard! The United States Government cannot, and will not, actively involve itself in your revolution, no matter how legitimate your cause. Imagine what happens if your efforts don't succeed. The rest of the world would laugh at us."

"Our efforts will succeed, Ms. O'Kelly. America can and must be a part, not to make us succeed now, but to help us thrive as a democracy in the future. Please discuss this with Mr. Fairchild."

"I'll try, but he will not possibly accept your offer. I'm sure that we will recognize your government as soon as it is obvious that Lassoso is no longer in power, but we will not take part in his arrest."

"Please discuss it with the Ambassador. Now, if you would kindly put your blindfold back on, Mr. Togola will take you to your home."

With a few short stops, probably to avoid military vehicles, the drive from her home to PPD headquarters took less than half an hour. In any other country those stops would have been for stoplights, but Zinani had no working stoplights.

About twenty minutes into the trip, the Toyota stopped suddenly. "Miss O'Kelly, take off your blindfold quickly!" She detected panic in his voice. Following the order, she saw nothing for a few seconds as her eyes adjusted. She then perceived two uniformed men, one approaching on each side of the Renault. They wore the uniforms not of the Army, but the *gendarmerie*. As far as anyone knew, these police were not in on the startling events that were unfolding. There would be little to be gained by the revolutionaries to get them involved, as their power was limited to nuisances like stopping cars. Suddenly for Bernadette and her chauffeur, this power was a very large nuisance.

Simultaneously, the two doors were jerked open and the two occupants were yanked out of their seats. "PPD?" yelled the man who had pulled out and was dwarfed by Togola. His rifle made the size disparity meaningless.

"No, we are not PPD. We have been at a night club and are going home."

"Your car is PPD car. By orders of President, we take automobile and jail everyone." His French reflected, at best, an elementary school education.

"My friend is not Zinanian; she is American."

"All will be arrested. All get in truck." Togola and the Political Officer were tugged toward a dilapidated pea green van.

Togola pulled away from his captor and started running. The captor brought his rifle up to his shoulder and yelled, "Stop!" Bernadette had heard that gendarmes were issued rifles but no ammunition and figured the command to be a bluff. She was wrong. The long gun spoke its one-word vocabulary. It was hard to miss from less than 10 meters, but Togola kept running. After a couple of steps he veered to the right and within five more seconds he had collapsed into an open gutter. Just prior to his fall, Bernadette saw, in the first light of dawn, that a red splotch had begun to interrupt at the level of the left shoulder blade, the all-white of his *boubou*.

"You killed him!" She had never seen anyone shot. In fact, she could never remember having ever seen anyone dead.

The two young men, or boys, said nothing and ignored the body lying only a short distance away. The one who had pulled her from the vehicle continued to hold tight, and pushed her into the back seat of the old van. She thought to herself, "I am a diplomat. How can they do this to me?" She pulled out her pink *Carte Diplomatique* that identified her as a representative of the United States Government. In the past it had gotten her through customs without her bags being opened and allowed her to wantonly ignore the so-called traffic laws of the nation. She shoved it in the face of her captor; he ignored it. She showed it then to the obviously more senior partner and said in her best French, "I am a diplomat. You cannot do this to me." The freshly blooded marksman shrugged his shoulders, not an unexpected gesture from one who could barely read or write.

She thought she'd be transported on this eventful evening in an Embassy Jeep Cherokee. Instead she rode first in the PPD Renault and secondly in the green paddy wagon. At least this time, she was able to watch the passing scene. She had been abducted for the second time, in a part of Donolu of which she had no awareness. She saw groups of Africans, gathered around their charcoal fires, making tea, acting as if they were totally unaware of the momentous events taking place in their city. Less than a kilometer from the site where Togola was shot, the vehicle stopped in front of a *banco* and tin building that had a large painted sign announcing it as the headquarters of the neighborhood's *gendarmerie*.

Bernadette was removed unceremoniously from the prison wagon. Neither her whiteness, nor her femininity, nor her *Carte Diplomatique* protected her from the manhandling. The two guards posted at the front door paid no discernible attention to the unfamiliar prisoner. She was marched into the single room, lit only with candles as the electricity was out in the neighborhood.

A woman of authority presided over the reception desk. Her khaki uniform was crisply ironed; blotters, pencils, and logbooks sat neatly arranged in front of her. A photograph of Michael Jackson in a small golden frame sat on her desk, facing out. She spoke in Fulani. The only word Dette understood was *toubab*, the pan-West African semi-insulting way of saying honkey. After a few sentences, the official asked Bernadette, in perfect French, "What were you doing in that car with that criminal?"

Bernadette ignored the question, and again reached into her purse, pulling out the pink card, throwing it on the desk with the declaration that she was a diplomat, strictly immune from arrest. The presider looked it over and began speaking once again in Fulani to the two gendarmes, except this time with anger. She flashed the diplomatic card under their noses, screaming at them like a corporal-punishing mother would before striking. The two sulked away into the dim light of the back of the room. Bernadette was sure that they had not yet heard the end of the tirade.

"Miss O'Kelly, we apologize to you for the actions of our illiterate staff. They had never seen a *Carte Diplomatique* before. You are free to leave. I would, however, caution you against associating with revolutionaries. To continue to do so could be very dangerous."

"Please take me back to my home."

"I am sorry, we cannot do that. You have seen our only working vehicle and as you know it has been very busy over the past few days."

Bernadette thought momentarily about asking that a cab be called. She noted that the station had no phone and that there were no taxi stands with phones and that taxis were not operative during the riots.

She had not thought to bring her hand-held radio, so she could not call her countrymen. She would have to walk.

"Please tell me how I might get home. I do not know where I am."

The presiding officer pulled out a piece of paper and pencil and with her single candle and the early morning light peeking through the small window in the front of the building, made a map of draftsman quality, with the *gendarmerie* in one corner, Bernadette's house in the opposite. Bernadette was taken aback by the fact that the officer knew where she lived.

The walk was, as one would expect a cross-town stroll at 6 AM in Donolu to be, neither boring nor frightening. A stooped-shouldered soldier, leaning on his vintage rifle, a Marlboro dangling from his lower lip, was the most menacing sight she saw, and she saw similar ones several times. Lassoso's military might was less than imposing and they all looked the same. She was struck by the fact that there was a plan to make all of these Lassoso backers into Lassoso haters within the next four or five hours.

"*Toubab-boo! Toubab-boo!*" Little African kids announced to each other warnings of the approach of a white lady. Some of the younger toddlers screamed in fright at the unique presence in their neighborhood. The children lucky enough to have an old tire or hoop to roll paid no attention to her.

"*Donnez-moi un cadeau!*" Give me a gift! "*Bonbon!*" Candy! "*Donnez-moi un Bic!*" Give me a pen! Bernadette had a hard time with the constant begging, even by children who looked well fed and clothed. She ignored the requests. She did respond to the ones who only wanted high-fives.

"I have been kidnapped by revolutionaries, seen a man shot, arrested, and hauled off in a paddy wagon, and made to walk miles in a nasty part of town at daybreak with a map made by a woman I have never seen before, who knew exactly where I lived, accosted by unwashed kids asking for handouts. All in three hours and all on no sleep. What would they say at St. Cat's?" She hated to admit it, but she loved it.

"You're late, Miss O'Kelly." The Ambassador made a stab at humor when his Political Officer staggered through the door looking like someone who had finished a marathon without having trained for it.

"Yes, Sir, I am. I took a somewhat indirect route to your house." She relayed the events of the evening and pre-dawn morning. Her description of the arrest and the events at the gendarmerie were a crowd pleaser. "Those bastards!" "I can't believe it!" "Oh, my God!" "Shit!"

She saved the story of the PPD headquarters for last. "Word from Oumou is that General Joro will arrest OIL at 10AM."

"Wow! We had heard that the military might turn but that's only a couple of hours from now."

"Yes, Sir. And, you won't believe it, but they want you to go with them."

"Who wants me to go with whom, where?"

"General Joro and Colonel Rashad want you to join them at the Presidential Palace as they put handcuffs on the President. I know it's absurd, but it was Oumou, the next President, that made the request to me. Obviously, you can't do it."

"What do you mean, I can't?"

The Deputy Chief of Mission responded without hesitation, "Mr. Ambassador, it is not ... shall we say, diplomatic, for a US Chief of Mission to be part of a party arresting a Chief of State of a host nation."

"But, think of the response around the world. Aside from Gaddafi, Mugabe, and maybe the PLO, Lassoso doesn't have a single backer. They all would just as soon see him dumped and who better to be involved in the dumping than the US of A? You know, I like the idea. Let's sit on it for a while before we make a decision."

"I told Oumou that you would not do this," said Bernadette.

"Miss O'Kelly, that is not within your job description to tell anyone what I will or will not do. Please let Oumou know that the decision has not been finalized."

"How should I let her know? She has no phone and these elephants were in my way when I went to her place." She flashed her prized bandana. "I'd have no idea how to get there."

"Maybe I'll just show up at the Presidential Palace at ten," Fairchild said, pouting.

The assembled diplomats recognized that Mr. Ambassador was losing it. No one bothered to respond to his comment and a ring of the phone interrupted the uncomfortable silence. It was for Station Chief Burkitt.

Lori nodded a few times. "Umm," was the only comment she made before hanging up two minutes later.

"Problems, ladies and gentlemen. The Libyans are on the move from New Akron. There's lots of activity at the SCUD sites. Students are setting up barricades both in New Akron and Sokimbo. The country is on the verge of exploding. The Director is at the White House as we speak, briefing the President. No one thinks that he will do anything. After the experience in Somalia, he is not about to commit any troops to this friggin' place. The only outsiders that could conceivably intervene are the French and with their present government, they would just as soon see the Africans slaughter each other so they won't end up on the Boulevard Saint Michel."

"And us?" asked the Ambassador.

"It's not the way we do business, but we've got to batten down the hatches and pretend that this is Hurricane Oumou and Hurricane Oumar passing over us at the same time. The storms will wreak havoc but we should be able to survive.

"I agree. We stay put," Fairchild stated emphatically, forgetting that a few minutes earlier he was prepared to play western sheriff and arrest the bad guy in his lair.

"Don't you think that we ought get to the Embassy where communication would be easier?" volunteered Frank Norbert.

"Right you are Scotland Yard." The Embassy was only two blocks from the Residence. "Marylou, I'm going to work." No one could tell if he was trying to be funny.

XXIII

Alien leapt with joy on Jenny Addison as she returned from her three-day absence. The dog did not appear malnourished, or even particularly hungry. He had either scrounged for himself or been the recipient of neighborly philanthropy.

Except for a veneer of laterite dust, the house was unchanged since the volunteers were carted off. Nothing inside or outside had been moved or removed, including the handful of small bills left on their dresser. The several neighbors she encountered said nothing about the women's absence, expressing neither concern nor relief. A few, to whom Jenny had been close, avoided talking to her altogether.

She offered the loving cur a can of Alpo, a can from the CARE package that her parents had sent from San Diego each month. The offer was zealously accepted.

Relieved that her dog was well and no longer hungry, Jenny remembered that she herself was in the midst of something out of the ordinary; she had just been a kidnap victim in a country in turmoil. She had to get to Donolu. The daily car from Korikono to the capital left in a couple of hours and she knew that if she wasn't there at least an hour early, she would have to ride in what volunteers knew as the seat of death – middle, front.

There was plenty of water in her rooftop tank as the rains had been ample. Hot water heaters were the stuff of dreams, but the daytime heat rendered the contents of the tank comfortably tepid. She peeled her stiff and fetid pants and top from her grimy and stinky body. She looked at her nakedness for the first time in several days. The difference between the reddish-brown face and arms and the milky-whiteness of the rest of her body gave her the appearance of being of two separate races. Her blond hair had become chestnut-like at first glance, grossly filthy at second glance. She momentarily looked at her small breasts and quickly sent her gaze elsewhere. Jenny was always embarrassed by her flatness and envious of Beth and others better endowed than she.

The shower was one of those cardinal moments in which one of a huge series of relatively commonplace events sticks out above all others - - a great conversation, a special haircut, a memorable bowel movement, or a unique orgasm. The water had never felt so cleansing; she could watch the caked dust leave each pore and slide harmlessly, particle by particle, down her legs, across her feet, between her toes, and disappear forever down the drain. She could feel her scalp and the transformation of her hair from cooked-pasta like masses into the fineness that Miss Clairol would be proud to display. She wanted to stay forever but the tank emptied. She stepped to the mirror again, seeing a different person than she had seen step by only a few minutes earlier.

Jenny put on a fresh shirt and pants combination and set off for the center of the village. She arrived a full hour before the scheduled departure of the ancient Peugeot station wagon and sat on a pile of cement blocks that served as the waiting room. A several-months-old Newsweek that she had read at least twice before the abduction occupied her during the wait. She was the first rider present. Within a few minutes there were ten more and she knew that the jalopy could accommodate eight at best and then only if a couple were small children. She was relieved that she had arrived early.

Fifteen minutes after the appointed hour, the green station wagon sputtered its way to the brick pile, belching puffs of gray smoke. Jenny observed the tires, deficient of tread, and the windshield wipers, which were bladeless. She silently prayed for a clear day free of the need for quick stops.

Her early arrival awarded her with a choice of seat locations. She opted for right rear window -- good ventilation and no front window to put her head through in case a sudden stop was needed. Bush taxis had no seat belts, front or rear. She forced the back door open, not an easy task because of the deep dents resulting from earlier unsuccessful quick stops, and started to sit down.

"*Je suis desolait. La voiture est complette,*" the chauffeur, an unshaven elderly light-skinned African, droned in a surprisingly literate but monotonous tone. "I'm sorry. The car is full."

"But, I was here first and I have to get to Donolu. It's an

emergency."

"I am sorry, Miss. The car is full."

The others in line were poor and dirty. Their presence would have neither made for a more lucrative nor a more esthetically pleasant journey. The logical explanation was that the driver had been told not to take her.

Jenny cried. In San Diego and Palo Alto, it always worked. It had gotten her upgrades to Business Class at airports and tickets on Broadway -- she got the last seat to Les Miserables. In Korikono, it served only to make the driver turn his head and drive away with only seven paying customers.

Knowing that there was no alternative public transportation and that almost no private traffic made the run, she decided to walk the four kilometers to the New Akron highway and hitch a ride. Less than one kilometer out of town, a fairly new blue Nissan pulled up beside her.

"Can I give you a ride, Miss?" asked the driver, a well-dressed civilian she had never before seen in Korikono. The olive-skinned man's French was faultless.

"I am going to Donolu," she responded anxiously.

"So am I. Please join me." Her host offered his hand to his passenger. "I am Jacques Lalonde." She was surprised by the non-African name.

"Jennifer Addison from the American Peace Corps."

"Enchanted, Mademoiselle Addison. I am an admirer of your Peace Corps. The well in my family's village is there only because of your dedication and hard work."

"I'm glad to hear that." She felt it inappropriate to ask him personal questions as they pulled away. His cassette deck played Whitney Houston, allowing her to remain silent.

Lalonde was a cautious driver, going no more than 40 kilometers per hour over the dusty road, gently swerving to miss the ever-present potholes. They reached the highway after about ten minutes. He turned right. Donolu was to the left.

"I think you made a wrong turn."

"Oh, I'm sorry, I meant to tell you that I have to go to a village just a few kilometers from here to pick up some papers." Lalonde sounded sincere but Jenny was not in the most trusting of conditions after the recent abduction.

"That's OK. Why don't you just let me out here then and I will find another ride to town."

"It will just be ten minutes."

"Please let me out."

"I'm sorry Miss. I cannot slow down." He was doing about 30 kilometers per hour at the time. Jenny reached for the handle so that she could jump if he went any slower. It was locked, controlled from the driver's side.

The Nissan went no faster as a result of the changed relationship of its occupants. Forty, maybe forty-five, even though the well-surfaced highway was empty except for a sporadic donkey cart and motorbike.

Twenty minutes later, her host turned right, back onto a dusty road indistinguishable from the one to Korikono. Neem and mango trees made an arboreal tunnel of the road. At the end of the tunnel, they came on to an opening that reminded Jenny of Camp Pendleton. Green trucks and tanks were everywhere. The writing on them was not French, not Fulani, but Arabic. She guessed, rightly, that they were Libyan. The car stopped at a sizable tent, guarded by a phalanx of tired looking men in fatigues. Their rifles were shiny and generations newer than the ones she had seen toted by OIL's troops.

She could see, at a distance, three tall structures with pointed tops. They reminded her of rockets from the moon program.

Jacques Lalonde exited the car and helped her out. She half expected him to kiss her hand. Running was out of the question; there was no place to go and lots of firearms in the way. She was escorted into the tent.

Seated behind a field desk was a man in a western suit, no tie. He looked absurdly out of place amongst the tanks and troopers. She remembered him as the other man with Lt. Col. Otobalo at the time of her first incarceration.

"Monsieur Raban, isn't it?"

"You are close, Miss Addison. I am Sheik Rahman of the Civil Cooperation Group of the Republic of Libya. I am very pleased to see you again. We were most upset to find that you had left the accommodations that we had fixed for you in New Akron."

"There were no guards on the door and we were hungry."

"Nonetheless, it would have been better for you to stay where you were. We consider it fortunate for us that you returned to your village. How unfortunate it is that Miss Sinova did not do the same."

"What do you mean unfortunate?"

"We cannot guarantee her safety like we can yours." Jenny hoped that the comment meant that Beth was not in unfriendly hands. Or, maybe she was dead.

Rahman looked like an Arab out of Hollywood. Standing about 5'8", he had black and silver curly hair and a broad mustache. His face was otherwise clean-shaven and the suit was expensive. The shirt appeared freshly donned in spite of the afternoon heat and two buttons were open revealing a patch of chest hair the same color as that atop his skull. Two gold chains added a luxurious touch. The nails suggested that a manicurist was not too far away. Jenny could not see his shoes but she pictured pointed-toe Italian, black with a mirror finish.

Rahman's flawless English gave her some slight, though probably false, sense of security. Anyone who spoke like that must have lived in the US, or at least the UK, and therefore must have an appreciation of the way the civilized world works.

"Please get in that vehicle," he said pointing out the front of the tent to a tracked behemoth that had just rumbled up.

"I am not riding in a tank," Jenny exclaimed

"Indeed, Mademoiselle, you are not riding in a tank. You are riding in an armored personnel carrier. In fact, this one was made in your hometown, San Diego, and sent to Israel in 1972. Our friends in Syria captured it in 1973 and gave it to us as a gift." She was disturbed that he knew her as a San Diegan.

"I don't care where it's from. I'm not riding in that thing!"

"I must insist that you do so. This vehicle will be going to Donolu as the first in line in a convoy to help in the armed struggle our friend President Lassoso is confronting. You did tell our associate Mr. Lalonde that you wanted to go to Donolu."

Further refusal would clearly be worthless. She let herself be led to the green monster, managed the tall single step and got in. The stench was like that of her site of imprisonment. Only natural light through the tiny portholes kept the APC from being as dark as the cell. There were about a dozen other passengers, none of whom looked Zinanian. They stared at the new arrival, but said nothing. The hatch was battened down and the armored vehicle came to life, crawling its way to war.

XXIV

As in all the offices on the third floor of the Chancery, the Health Unit's radio was turned on for all incoming calls in this time of crisis.

"Shrinking Violet, this is Big Daddy. Over."

"Shrinking Violet, do you copy?" No answer. The doctor and the nurse could only guess what was happening at the Genu's house. There had been no reports from others of personal threats and all quickly responded to the hourly radio checks. No one knew what was going on other than through the noise outside their own homes. Gunfire yes, gunfire no. Mobs yes, mobs no.

"Temperature is 102.5 degrees. Pulse 108 and BP 120/70," Electra relayed Chen's vital signs to Michael who was anxious that there might be others out there bleeding or fevering that could not get to him.

Chen Wang said he felt OK; the bubbles in the water revealed that the chest tube was still functioning. The combination of a high temperature and rapid pulse was another thing. Infection was more likely now. Eisenstat had been a purist; Beverly Hills doctors didn't give antibiotics unless all orifices were cultured and the output of those orifices stained to look for specific bacteria. Then, an antibiotic was chosen based on the data obtained; the right drug for the right bug. No way to do that here. No lab tech, no stain; Eisenstat didn't even know where the slides were kept. He decided to give the widest spectrum, most expensive antibiotic he had on his shelves – it would treat most any bacterium the he could imagine.

"Give him four grams stat," he barked at Electra.

She gave him a look that said, "You have never used more than one gram for anyone," and pulled the liquid gold up into a syringe.

The phone rang. Conrad Prudholme on the phone. "Looks like trouble for the medevac plane."

"Huh?"

"SOS has not been able to get landing rights. Lassoso's people have told them that the airport is too busy. We haven't heard any planes coming or going so all we can figure is that OIL is either getting back at us, or he wants the runway available if he has to flee the scene at a moment's notice. Most likely, both."

"Goddam it! We have a man shot in the chest and signs of an infection that could be anywhere in his body. He has to get out of this fucking country, today!"

"Try some of those connections of yours. Maybe one of your doctor friends can help," the Admin Officer spoke with more than a touch of sarcasm.

"There's no chance I'll find anyone with all this going on. They'll all be down at the hospital sewing up the casualties, or hiding, fearful of their own safety."

"Can't hurt to try."

Michael tried Dr. Traore, the orthopedist that had been the post medical advisor. His wife answered and confirmed that anybody who knew how to use a scalpel and sutures was at Lassoso General. He called the hospital number. Busy. No one answered at the home of Dr. Tonton, hospital administrator.

"Electra, get me the home number of the Health Minister. What's his name ... uh, Coulibaly."

Two rings and a man answered. "Minister Coulibaly, please."

"I am Doctor Coulibaly." Michael was shocked that this imperious man would deign to answer his own phone.

"Sir, this is Dr. Eisenstat from the American Embassy."

"Ah, Dr. Eisenstat. How are you and your lovely wife? Mrs. Coulibaly and I have often talked about having you come to our house after we had such an enjoyable evening at your beautiful home. But, sadly, you know how difficult things are right now. We just haven't had time. Perhaps next week." Michael could hear muffled rifle shots in the background, obviously not far from the Minister's house, a house paid for, he was quite sure, by moneys donated for vaccines and maternity clinics.

"Thank you very much for your compliment, Sir, but I am calling about something of great urgency." He told the Minister about the circumstances surrounding Chen Wang and SOS. "I ask your help in getting permission for our air ambulance to land at the airport."

"Dr. Eisenstat, you must realize that I am not the Foreign Minister, the Defense Minister, or the Air Minister. I am the Health Minister and therefore have very little control of who lands and when they land their airplanes. There is nothing that I can do for you."

Michael hung up, saying nothing. There would be no further contact with this Health Minister. One of the two of them would soon be gone. Maybe both.

The Ambassador's office had become a war room. The TV was tuned to the local station in case OIL was to make a speech to his nation or, alternatively, the rebels captured the airwaves. A French-dubbed Brazilian soap opera instead offered no political intelligence, but plenty of sex.

Ernestine Grant was, without doubt, officer-in-charge. Ambassador Fairchild was Ambassador in name only. His words carried little influence in the room, although Grant was sensitive enough to the old warhorse, that her nods, smiles, and frowns allowed him to deny his powerlessness.

Administrator Prudholme and Peace Corps' Willie Anderson had joined the group.

"Let's figure out where we are now," Ms. Grant started off. "Lori, what's the status with the military movement and the Libyans?"

"No friggin' good. Our word is that there is a sizable column of tanks and APCs coming down the New Akron road toward Donolu. Probably 15 armored vehicles and a few hundred troops. The unit is part of the Libyans 379th Armored which last saw action in Chad about eight years ago, not terribly successfully. The Zins are from the Second Infantry Division, average age about 18 and average IQ not a hell of a lot higher. I would worry more about the mayhem they could create than their military prowess. Who knows who they will shoot? Thank God they only have a few bullets each. Our AWACS report is that no more troops or flights are coming in from Tripoli."

"What has Gaddafi said?"

"He hasn't mentioned Zinani. He's yelling about Israel and Egypt and France but seems more concerned about his upcoming trip to Mongolia."

"Mongolia?" asked the Ambassador.

"Yeah, he's opening an Embassy in Ulan Bator. That will give Libya 100 missions, believe it or not the fifth largest diplomatic operation in the world. That's for a country with less than four million people, most of whom are illiterate, and a third of whom are under 16."

"Any skirmishes yet with all those tanks?"

"Who would skirmish with 'em? PPD doesn't have any anti-tank weapons to our knowledge and at this point the military has shown no signs of turning."

"When will the column get to town?" Ernestine asked.

"Probably three or four hours, like 11 AM."

"That's after I was supposed to go to the Palace with Joro and Rashad when they take over the government," chimed in Fairchild.

"You aren't thinking about doing that again, are you Mr. Ambassador?" The DCM acted like she was talking to a ten-year-old.

"I don't think we should dismiss it out of hand. It would give us some fairly good press, after Somalia and all that."

"Please, Sir, believe me that the downsides are much more likely than the upsides."

Fairchild shifted his eyes to a document on his lap and said nothing.

"Bernadette, any word from PPD?"

"Nothing, Ernestine. I doubt they are spending much time on the phone or communicating with anyone except their own guys on the street."

"Do you still think that they will go through with their plans?"

"No reason to think not."

"Willie, I hear that your Volunteers are free."

"Right. Beth Sinova came into town a couple of hours ago and told the story of the kidnapping by a Zin and a Libyan and having to spend three days in the dark. But then the guards disappeared and they just walked out. The other PCV, Jenny Addison, the politically connected one, is probably back at her site. She had to go feed her dog."

"Christ, how stupid!" barked the CIA Station Chief.

"I can relate to feeding a dog," said Fairchild, mentally referencing

Gatsby the Boston.

"I'm sure she's smart enough to stay put and not get on the highway with the tanks." Willie Anderson had great confidence in his Volunteers.

"Conrad, what's happening in the Health Unit?"

"Doc is worried about Chen. Says his fever is going up and that he might have an infection. He gave him massive doses of expensive antibiotics. Worse though is the fact that we can't get an air ambulance into the airport. They won't let anything take off or land."

"How do we handle this one?" Fairchild asked.

"Any ideas?" Grant put it to the crowd.

"How about a helicopter?" Frank Norbert contributed.

"How about it? Can we do it?"

"I don't see why not. Our people in Bamako could get the Malians to cooperate. It might take some help from the French, but we could fly a chopper in from the border, land in the compound, and take him back to Mali. The evac plane could be there waiting."

"Do we have any helicopters in the area Lori?"

"Damned if I know. Mali and Burkina and Niger all have old beat up Russian ones. The French have a couple here and there and might lend us one or even fly one in for us. Our closest might be Malta or Sicily."

"Frank, get on the line with your counterpart in Bamako and get something going. If the doc is right, speed may be crucial."

"What about air space violations?" asked Norbert.

"Forget about it," responded Ernestine. "Lassoso is hardly going to worry about one of our helicopters and he doesn't have any way to shoot it down if he did.

"But the friggin' Libyans do," said Ms. Burkitt.

"We'll have to take our chances. Get it going."

"Conrad, what's the word on the evacuation plans."

"They're on hold. We'd have a hard time getting the plane or planes in as it is and obviously Lassoso and his boys have more to think about than their deadline to us."

"Agreed. Keep the plans active but don't activate yet. I just cabled Washington and they have planes available for us in Italy. They need twelve hours' notice.

"Lori, you guys are in the business of making predictions. What will be the status of the place 24 hours from now?"

"Who knows? The best bet is that we'll be in the midst of war. Lassoso won't go down easy and Gaddafi has a history of sticking through his battles at least for a while. I don't think that the generals going to the Palace will even get there let alone force OIL to step down. If the Army sticks, the PPD has had it; if they turn, it will be Libyans and a few Zins versus lots of Zins.

"If the PPD is beaten I can just imagine what will happen to Oumou. OIL has had the hots for her for years and I'll bet he works it out that she ends up in bed with him before he has her killed."

"I don't buy that, Lori," said Bernadette. "I'm a lot more optimistic than you about PPD's chance, especially with what I heard about the Army."

"I wish that we could confirm that rumor, Dette. Our guys have said nothing to make me believe it. Don't forget what they did to General Sacco."

"What about Suleiman? Do you know something I don't?" Dette asked. She'd never used her lover's first name in a public manner, but was caught off guard at the mention of him. In spite of what Oumou told her, she still harbored hope that he was imprisoned and pining over her.

"No, Dette. It's just hard to think of any other explanation for his disappearance."

"Still, I am convinced that the PPD can win this thing. I saw and heard them just a few hours ago, and they looked pretty confident and organized."

DCM Grant interjected, "Two questions, Dette. One, is that your head or your heart talking? Two, while you have seen a room full of organized and confident women, have you seen the tanks and APCs?"

Before Bernadette had time to answer, the Zinanian National Anthem was heard coming from the TV speakers, although the Brazilians were continuing to bed each other on the screen. A few seconds later, a photograph of Oumar Ibrahim Lassoso took the place of the South Americans; it was the same youthful photo Bernadette had seen at the Palace. Twice, a high-school quality band played the anthem;

one time the lyrics were French, the other Fulani, both times extolling the virtues of millet and sorghum, Zinani's soccer team, and the President. O'Kelly hoped that someone in the PPD was working on a new anthem.

The yellow, blue, and black tricolor flag appeared next, blowing in the wind, accompanied by the sound of jet engines. The camera pulled away from the banner revealing jet planes streaking through the skies. A high-resolution TV monitor would have revealed the hammer and sickle on the tails, confirming the non-domestic source of the videotape. The tanks and mobile artillery that followed were also from someone else's file films.

Next, Lassoso appeared in person. Never a terribly handsome man, he looked more wan than usual. His uniform lacked its usual sharpness and his bearing was haggard, clearly sleep deprived. He sat in a shabby recliner with a uniformed man on each side. Bernadette recognized one as General Joro whom she had heard would be handing the President his walking papers shortly.

The President held forth in French. He spoke slowly enough, with such an elementary vocabulary, that even his less educated citizens, and most of the Americans, could follow and understand. The speech was carried on both radio and television.

"Zinanians, wherever you might be, please listen! Our great nation is in peril such as it has never been since our Independence. Civil disorder is rampant and external influences are working with a tiny minority of our population, threatening your freedom. Imperialists from the so-called Republic of France and from what is legitimately called by some of our Moslem brothers, the Great Satan, America, have manipulated some of your brothers and sisters and friends and have washed their brains with the putrid soap and water of slavery. We have reason to believe that the American Air Force is preparing to bomb us like they did a few years ago in our sister land, Libya. Remember who the victims of that raid were -- the children of the nation!

"I am very pleased to report that the world community, with few exceptions, has come to our aid. The President of the Yemeni Republic will present our story to the United Nations. More importantly, we have been granted military aid from my good and great friend, Colonel

Gaddafi. He has been so kind as to send us tanks and other vehicles with which we can quickly and permanently repel any attack of France and America and those few Zinanians who have fallen under their evil spell. Those tanks are on their way to Donolu from New Akron where they landed yesterday. Should you be on the street when they come by, please greet them enthusiastically." Lassoso took a handkerchief from his pocket and mopped his brow. He did not mention the SCUDs.

"I ask all Zinanians to stay in their homes for the next 48 hours. I have had to call a complete curfew and blackout for the next two days to assure your freedom and the failure of those who would invade us. No lights are to be lit; only candles are to be used after dark. We will not be a visible target for the cowardly pilots who take off from the huge aircraft carriers in the Mediterranean, fly over our peaceful nation, drop their bombs on our hospitals and orphanages, and return to the safety of their floating steel landing strips. Anyone seen on the street at any time, other than police or Army, will be immediately arrested or shot on the spot. Any visible electric light in a window will be extinguished and the owner of the house severely punished. You may see others on the street with our permission, but those are only the doctors and workers at the water and electric plants, who are indispensable in time of crisis.

"To those who are trying to destroy us we say, 'You will not succeed!' To those Zinanians who are trying to crush our revolution and its freedom for all, we say, 'You will surely fail!' And to those outsiders who have instigated this despicable affair, we say, 'You are not welcome! Go back! Stay away!'

"Thank you for your support." With that, the face of the President disappeared and the sexually active Brazilians reappeared, a sweat-drenched woman and a man smoking a post-coital cigarette.

"Well, Gringos, what do you make of that?" The DCM always gave others the opportunity to speak up before she did.

"I like the idea of our evacuating a little more than I did before," said AID's Graham.

"How do you like that idiot saying that people should greet the tanks as they roll by, then tell them they would be shot if they are seen on the street?" Prudholme remarked.

"Does anyone think this changes anything?" asked Grant.

"It certainly does," responded Lori Burkitt. "Not too many students, even women students, are going to brave a shoot-on-sight order. The bodies at the University made for memorable TV. The only way that this is going to end up with a successful coup is if the military does flip to the rebel side. Even a neutral stance by the Army, with the Libyans barreling down on Donolu, is not enough to energize people with guns aimed at them."

"Oumou sounded certain that the Army was on her side," said Bernadette. "She seemed very confident that Joro and Rashad are going to at least try to go through with their plans to dump the Prez." She looked toward the Ambassador, fearing that he might again make a comment about going with the officers. He was dozing.

"So, let's plan." Ernestine was prepared to set out a course of action, having heard her people plus the President. "First, it looks like we will be living here together for a while. We don't want any of our folks gunned down by some 17-year-old cop. You can go outside the house but under no circumstances outside the walls.

"Second, Conrad, get on the line and get a helicopter in to take Chen out. Also get the word around that we are bringing in a chopper for humanitarian reasons, not because we are getting involved in this shit that's happening.

"Third, Bernadette, send a cable to State updating them on all of this. They better be ready to come evacuate us if things get sticky, uh, stickier. I'll talk to the French Chargé d'Affaires and coordinate; got to assume that they are having a similar coffee klatch as we speak.

"Fourth, Gunny, get your Zodiacs ready in case we need to cross the river to get to the airport." Donolu had a single two-lane bridge across the Begoro. Under the most routine circumstances, the bridge was difficult to get across. Traffic itself was bad and Zinanians tended to buy gasoline by the cupful, or when rich, by the whiskey bottleful. Running out of gas was a frequent consequence, making for interminable waits as the driver rounded up enough pushers to get his vehicle out of the way. For security reasons, the American Embassy hard purchased two French inflatable Zodiacs that so far had only been used for training exercises and sport. The plan was to put a dozen Americans on each and ferry them across the Big to waiting buses on the other side. All those living on the airport side would congregate at the Eisenstats' place preparing to convoy to Keita-Coulibaly.

Jillian Eisenstat was watching TV, too. She didn't much like watching others copulating, particularly when the actors spoke Portuguese with French subtitles, but Zinani only had one channel and she couldn't concentrate on anything else.

Michael had not been home in more than 24 hours, although he called frequently. He had been upbeat about Chen's so far successful surgery but Jill knew him well enough to know that his voice bespoke less confidence than his words. He had often told her of his nervousness about being put into positions with which he was unfamiliar. Despecializing into general practice at age 50-plus had its downsides.

She passed the mirror in her bedroom and noticed that she hadn't combed her hair in a long time. She had on a too small T-shirt that she had slept in the night before. She had never liked her breasts; she couldn't decide if they were too big or too small or the right size with the wrong configuration. The tight shirt, and the passage of time made her like them even less; at least before they pointed outwards. Now, they were beginning to go south.

Her hair was not only uncombed, it was mousy. Even more, it was taking on the color of the mongrels that hung around her neighborhood. She had never artificially colored it. Plain brown was fine; occasionally she envied the Wilshire Boulevard blondes and the Santa Monica redheads, but she never fell to the temptation of joining either group. She prided herself on saving the money of coiffure upkeep, and justified her three-dollar per day Diet Coke habit on that basis. "But," she thought, "mongrelly is too much." There was an African lady who colors Western hair that lived just a couple of blocks away. "Maybe, if the revolution ever ends, I'll get her to make it brown again."

Michael had recently given a lecture on menopause and osteoporosis to the ladies of age in the American community. She had, hesitantly, attended. She was sure that all of her friends assumed that she, as the doctor's wife and a nurse, knew all of that information and would wonder why she was there. She knew nothing, had read nothing, and had asked nothing. Michael talked about hot flashes; maybe those episodes that woke her with a moist pillow had something to do with them. Sex was becoming a burden for her, mainly because she was dry and it hurt.

'Yeah," she thought, "maybe I'm going through it too. But my periods are perfectly regular and I'm not bitchy ... am I?" She didn't talk to Michael about it; he had always been adamant about not caring for his family. But, he was the only English-speaking doctor for three hundred miles. "Oh well, it's not fatal and I'll be home on leave before too long; it can wait."

She had eaten only three chocolate chip cookies and a Snickers bar that day, her usual diet when Michael wasn't around to make her feel guilty. She didn't much like cookies or candy, but they were easy and tasted better than day-old tuna noodle casserole. She headed for the fridge to get another Snickers. The phone rang.

"Hi, honey."

"Hi, Mom. It's got to be after midnight there. What's up?"

"Bad news, Daddy had a stroke."

"When?"

"About three hours ago. We were watching a video and you know how he will go a long time without saying anything and not even answer a question until you yell at him. So, I yelled and he still didn't answer. I walked over to him without my cane. I tripped and fell into his lap and he looked at me but couldn't move his right side or say anything. I called Michael's brother and he came over and said it was a stroke - a big one. The ambulance came and took him to the hospital. They put him in intensive care and did a scan and said it was real bad. They don't think he will make it."

Hibbard Thompson was nearly 90, but aside from his poor hearing and arthritic knees, he had been amazingly healthy. He would walk at least a mile a day, using a walking stick more for show than security. To his daughter's knowledge, he had never set foot in a hospital, other than to visit a sick or dying friend. He had practiced law until 84, served as a deacon at the Presbyterian Church, and cheered for the Cornell football team like a kid.

Jill knew that her Dad would not want to be in an ICU or a CAT scan room at age 90; he had often expressed the desire to just not wake up some morning. But Jill also knew that her Mom and Dad had never discussed any of this. No living will; no written instructions. And Mom was not assertive enough to tell doctors to keep their hands off her husband.

Jill could only hope that her brother-in-law Ralph, with the advice of Mike's brother, was willing to take charge and spare her life and death decisions.

"Honey, can you come home?" This was the question that both she and Michael feared they would hear at some point during their Foreign Service career. Unlike Mike, Jill had no sibling who could be with her folks; her only brother had died in a speedboat race and she had no sisters.

"Of course, I will come home, but Mom, there is a revolution going on in this country, and right now, there is no way to get out of here. One of our good friends was shot by a stray bullet and Michael has to take care of him. He even had to do surgery, which he has no idea how to do. We are trying to get him out, but the President of the country won't give us landing rights." Jill knew that her mother wouldn't have heard about the revolution, even if local TV or papers had carried it. She knew that her parents did little other than watch videos, many of which were X-rated.

"Can't you just tell the President that your father has had a stroke and may be dying?" Mom pictured Zinani as a place where an American could just ring up the Chief of State and make such a request.

"No, Mom, I don't think he would take my call. His war has him thinking about other things. But, this may just blow over. I'm sure that one way or another I'll be able to get out of here in a few days."

"Jillie, I don't think Daddy will be alive in a few days."

"I really hope you are wrong, but please tell him that I am on my way and that I love him."

Jillian hung up and dialed the Health Unit. The line was down. She found it incredible that she had just talked with her mother as if she were in Pittsburgh but that she could not make contact with her husband less than two miles away. She occasionally heard gunfire, often enough to remind her that she was living through something historical.

XXV

Historically, what was happening in Donolu and environs was unique -- women were behind a bloody revolution. There had been female Chiefs of State, plenty of them, since Ceylon led the way in the 1960's. Plus, there have been dozens of Queens and Empresses. But never had there been a woman who headed a successful overthrow of a government or led an army to topple a foreign power. Joan of Arc had tried, but failed.

Oumou Kinsa, in spite of her impeccable academic qualifications, had little appreciation for history. Gamal Abdel Nasser, Joseph Kenyatta, Kwame Nkrumah, Patrice Lumumba – to her, they were nothing but names on public buildings or city squares. Most of her colleagues in the PPD were no more aware of these heroes of their continent than she, although nearly all could have identified Martin Luther King and Abraham Lincoln.

The word of Togola's death at the hands of the young Lassoso loyalists had cast a pall over the dingy headquarters of the People's Party for Democracy. But, a cadre in the midst of trying to topple a dictator can little afford the luxury of being stunned for long.

"It's 9:30. Rashid and Joro should be making their move about now," one of the cornrowed women shouted from a corner of the room.

Oumou was in contact with Colonel Rashid through a female courier. She was instructed to tell the Colonel that the plan was a go and that nearly all of the officers in the Donolu sector were in favor of the move.

Another one of the revolutionary contingent hung up a phone and announced, "There's a column of Libyan tanks coming down the New Akron highway with several companies of Zinanian and Libyan infantry walking and riding behind them. Strange -- our source says that he saw a white woman in one of the tanks, sticking her head out through the hole in the top. "

"A white woman – what did they think that was all about?" questioned Oumou.

"No idea."

"What's a white woman doing in a Libyan tank in Zinani in the midst of a revolution? Girlfriend of an officer? White slave? French Foreign Legion? I guess we won't find out until we meet her ourselves, see her on TV, or find her body."

"Forget the woman; we've got to do something about the tanks before they get to the Palace. It's time to break out the guns." Seeing Gaddafi as an enemy and Lassoso as the enemy's friend, the Israelis had smuggled a cache of anti-tank guns and Galil assault rifles into West Africa. They furnished the weaponry to the tiny band that served as the military arm of the PPD. Two women had gone to the Negev Desert to learn how to fire the guns and had passed on the knowledge to a handful of others. Togola had set up a plan for distribution of the equipment should it be needed. Now it was needed.

American Embassy, Donolu, heard about the white woman at about the same time the PPD did. Their intelligence gathering was more sophisticated, thanks to the skills of Lori Burkitt and her predecessors, so they knew that the vehicle in question was an APC, not a tank, and they had a description of the girl. Blond, looked American, British, Canadian or Australian, but could have been any Caucasian, even a Russian.

"Who do you think it is, Lori?" asked Ms. Grant.

"No idea. Even Gaddafi is not that stupid to allow one of his officers to bring a bimbo with him. I gotta believe it's someone in the vehicle against her will."

"Kriminetly!" Willie Anderson spoke for the first time in hours, using one of his most vulgar expletives. "Describe that woman to me again."

"Twenty to twenty-five-years old, tall, long blond hair."

"Gee! That sounds like Jenny Addison."

"Who?"

"That PCV who had been kidnapped with Beth Sinova, the one who came to town yesterday. Remember I mentioned that the other one went back to her site to feed her dog? That's Jenny."

"And why do you think she's riding in a Libyan tank?" Prudholme asked.

"Gosh, I don't know. Maybe she's been abducted again."

"Right! And maybe I'll win the lottery twice," snarled Conrad.

"I can't think of any better explanations, can you Ms. Burkitt?" Anderson never called any woman, other than his wife and sisters, by her given name.

"Sure I can. Peace Corps Volunteers have never been above getting involved in politics. Sometimes they fall for revolutionaries, playing Bonnie to their Clyde. I wouldn't call Gaddafi and the rest of that mob revolutionaries, but who knows what love can do?"

"Gee, Ms. Burkitt, I can't imagine it. Beth said nothing about Jenny going out with anyone. And, Jenny's pretty conservative. I doubt she'd get involved with a local or an Arab."

"We aren't even sure that it's your volunteer riding around in that vehicle and whether it is or isn't, there's not much we can do about it. At this point, let's hold off action until we have more information." With that, Ernestine Grant closed, for the moment, the discussion of the blond in the tank.

Jenny felt like she was in a wet T-shirt contest. Twelve Libyans and a blond Republican in an un-air-conditioned APC resulted in thirteen sweat-drenched, distinctively ripe passengers. Her companions spoke in what she assumed was Arabic, of which she knew not a word. They occasionally stared at her, but made no move to communicate.

Not having her usual bottle of water, she was very thirsty, but thirst was not her only discomfort. Her dark conveyance had iron benches and no shock absorbers. Appalling noise emanated from the unmuffled engine with disgusting sounds from her fellow passengers, who were coughing and spitting on the floor. Her bladder was uncomfortably full and she had just started her period.

Two hours into the voyage she heard shots, not of big guns like that of an armored vehicle, but of small arms. Seconds later they stopped. The hatch opened and the passengers popped out, like bubbles from uncorked champagne. Jenny was the last to emerge. She recognized, by the billboards for hotels and restaurants, that the convoy had reached the outskirts of the capital. The APC and other vehicles in the convoy had stopped next to an Army guard station. Two guards lay next to their post, dead.

The horrific sight did not lessen her needs. Jenny headed to nearby bushes to relieve herself.

"Halt!" A Libyan menacingly pointed his rifle at her. He spewed a chain of guttural sounds that individually meant nothing to her, but collectively suggested that he thought that she was making a mistake.

"I have to pee!" That got no response, except a wigwag of the weapon. She pointed to the area above her pubic bone, jumped up and down like a small child and said, "Piss." He nodded recognition, pointed with the automatic rifle, to a nearby bush, and escorted her to it. Relief from emptying her bladder was short–lived when she recognized she had no supplies for her period. She grabbed a handful of leaves and placed them appropriately.

Her escort dashed any hope of just walking away from her captors. She meekly returned to the vehicle. The heat of the Zinanian morning was nothing compared to the interior of the APC, so her desire was to prolong the interval outside as long as possible. As she stood around watching others smoke and joke, she wondered who killed the guards. She assumed that the Libyans did it, but couldn't come up with a motive.

What she did do was saunter up to a sergeant who was drinking from a plastic jug and asked him for water. When he gesticulated that he didn't understand her, she snatched the jug out of his hand and guzzled the cloudy liquid until it was grabbed back. No ice-cold beer had ever tasted so good as that fetid water did.

When she joined the Peace Corps, she was recruited by an older Stanford grad that told her that she would have experiences that would change her forever. She interpreted that as meaning that she would learn a new language, meet people of different cultures, develop gardening skills, and learn to live self-sufficiently. She had not counted on being kidnapped twice in a week, having homosexual longings, riding as a captive in an old American-Israeli armored vehicle, and witnessing the immediate aftermath of a double homicide.

When the troops were told to file back into their vehicles, she entered first, taking a seat nearer the back, away from the heat and noise of the engine. When one of the Libyans motioned her away from the seat he had previously occupied, she screamed, "Fuck off!" He may or may not have understood the words; he did understand her tone of voice. He moved to the front. Jenny Addison had been changed, probably forever.

On the Embassy television screen, the Brazilians were in between sexual exploits, so nearly all of the eyes were focused elsewhere. Amongst the diplomats, there had been no substantive discussion for an hour; many were asleep. Others read. The television became quiet and for a few seconds the screen was empty. Bernadette happened to look at the clock; it was ten after ten.

No flag. No national anthem. The scene was that of ZTV's news desk with a huge map of Africa as a backdrop. Zinani was red, the remainder of the continent, black. Behind the desk were two young women. They were neither smiling nor frowning; they looked like nervous girls on TV for the first time.

"Jesus, those are two of the women who were at PPD headquarters last night," exclaimed Bernadette.

The more senior appearing woman spoke, reading from a single piece of paper. Speaking French, not Fulani, she did not introduce herself or her partner.

"Ladies and Gentlemen of the Republic of Zinani and our friends around the world. We are representatives of the Zinanian People's Party for Democracy and we are here to announce that, as of this date, Zinani is a republic and, above all, a democracy. At 10 o'clock this morning, President Lassoso was relieved of his position. General Ibrahim Joro of the First Infantry Division and Colonel Ibrahim Mohammed Rashid of the 63rd Airborne Battalion escorted Mr. Lassoso from the Presidential Palace. Mr. Lassoso is presently in custody at a secure facility; he and his family are in good health and there is no reason to expect that condition to change. He and his assistants will have their days in court. In the meantime ..." The TV went black. The Americans expected the return of the Brazilians, but it didn't happen.

"Friggin-A! Two women announcing the overthrow of President

Shithead on national TV! Too much! Right on!" Lori the Spy, not old enough to have picked up "right on" as a student, was beside herself; her right hand was in the air, fist tightly closed.

"Not so fast, Lori," cautioned Ernestine. All we know is that two PPDers got themselves four minutes of airtime and claimed that Joro and Rashid had taken the President into custody. We don't know if it's true. I can't imagine that they could pull off the takeover of the TV station, get the word on Lassoso, and go live that fast. My guess is that they are hoping that it happened.

"Even if it did and OIL is in the hands of the Army, why did the TV go dark? We didn't hear the usual comments about staying in our houses, or get told who and where and what the new government or junta is about. It seemed like we were going to get that info but someone loyal to Lassoso got to the lines first and pulled the plug."

The Embassy, especially the Ambassadorial suite, was well protected from bombs and bullets. It was less well soundproofed. Crowd sounds began to leak into the office.

Gunnery Sergeant Rice radioed the marine at Post 1, just inside the front door. "What's going on, Corporal?"

"There's a giant crowd in the square screaming and dancing. But there are also dozens of locals at our gates, knocking, yelling, and holding up passports, some of which appear to be American."

"Any weapons?"

"Negative. Haven't seen any."

"What happened to the police guard?" The Embassy was "protected" 24/7 by a dozen or so of Donolu's finest. They had pistols but no ammunition; the guns had little value except to keep away beggars and small children.

"Nowhere to be seen. They were there at 0945 and gone at 1000 hours."

"What about our guard staff?" Embassy Donolu, had on its payroll, several well-trained local guards surrounding the Chancery.

"We had them come inside. It looks like it might get dangerous out there."

"Good work Big Daddy. You got the tear gas ready to go?"

"Affirmative. The shotguns are ready too."

"Keep us informed."

"We have to let Washington know about this," said Fairchild.

Bernadette immediately responded. "I'm already writing a cable for you to sign and send, Sir. Give me two minutes."

"I'll do something via our channels too," said CIA.

"Any word from the Health Unit? Any news on the medevac for Chen? What's Doc up to?" asked Ambassador Fairchild.

Prudholme spoke. "Worthless bastard. He has a hard enough time keeping track of his pills and tongue blades. Hardly the person to be handling logistics." Conrad Prudholme and Michael had never been great friends, but this outburst by the Admin Officer was a surprise to all present.

The first to speak up in defense was Willie Anderson. "Gosh, Mr. Prudholme, I think that Doctor Eisenstat does just fine if we need him. He sure has been helpful when one of our volunteers has been sick."

"Conrad, you're full of shit," exclaimed Ambassador Fairchild. The remainder of the staff nearly broke into applause at the comment. They had never heard him say anything so sensible at such an appropriate time.

"Rodeo Drive, Rodeo Drive, this is Tiger's Den." The Ambassador, strengthened by the response to his response to Prudholme, took to the airways, even though the Health Unit was only a flight of steps and a short hall away.

"Go ahead, Tiger, this is Rodeo Drive."

"How is Shanghai doing?"

"Not well. His pulse is up and blood pressure down and his fever high. I'm afraid he might be bleeding in his chest where the tube can't drain it. In a real hospital, they'd be getting X-rays and probably putting in a second tube. Not possible now. Any idea when that helicopter is arriving?"

"Prudholme, what's with the helicopter?"

"I thought that Dr. Eisenstat was going to call for it."

"Hear that Rodeo Drive?"

"Please tell Penny Pincher that I expected that he would do it. I have no more idea of how to call a helicopter than I would to do a liver transplant. I guess that means that there is no helicopter on the way?"

"Affirmative, Rodeo Drive."

"Shit." Saying shit on the airways, especially when the Ambassador is on the other end, is frowned upon. "Well, please tell me how to get one."

"Pincher, get over here!" Fairchild was finally feeling in command of something. Prudholme scampered. "Tell Rodeo Drive how he gets a chopper!"

"Hey, Rodeo. To get a helicopter with medical capacity, you have to call European Command in Frankfurt. They'll probably have some ship somewhere in the Mediterranean that can launch a chopper to fly over Algeria or Libya and pick Shanghai up."

"Probably not Libya, Conrad," sneered Lori. "The helicopter would be shot out of the sky."

GySgt. Rice spoke up, "I hate to say it but you people are dead wrong on this one. No way a helicopter could get from the Mediterranean to here without landing for fuel. The range of those birds is about 300 miles and you're talking 700 from the nearest carrier." The baby-faced NCO blushed when he finished, not being used to telling his superiors that they were clueless. You didn't do that at Camp Lejeune.

"So Gunny, what do we do instead?" asked Fairchild.

"You got two choices, it seems to me. Either get some fuel along the way, maybe at some desert outpost in Algeria, or bring in a plane."

"Remember Jimmy Carter's try at getting the hostages out of Iran?" asked Bernadette. "We're not too good at arranging those complicated helicopter flights; I'd vote on the plane."

"We've already been denied a landing," said the Ambassador.

"Time the US of A threw its weight around in this hole and just tell the bastards that we're coming in and expect to be treated like a world superpower," bristled Lori. "Yes, Ma'am, and Right Away, Ma'am, is what I want to hear when I talk with them. You going to back me Mr. Ambassador?"

"Yes, Ma'am!"

DCM Grant excused herself and walked to the Health Unit to tell the doctor that he wouldn't have to call for the plane but would be expected to call Minister Coulibaly.

"You know I already tried that with the Health Minister. Mr. Coulibaly wasn't too forthcoming; all he could talk about was Zionists."

"You're too nice. Next time tell the minister I don't care if he's the Health Minister, the Air Minister or the Baptist Minister; tell him that he has no choice but to allow our airplane to land to take out a badly injured American citizen."

"Ernestine, I'm a doctor, not a diplomat."

"Wrong again. Look at your business card. It says something about your being a Medical Attaché. You are a representative of the President of the United States of America and entitled to all courtesies, including the right to put your goddam plane on their goddam runway when you have another diplomat injured with their goddam bullets."

"Yes, Ma'am."

When he learned he was getting the job with State, Michael knew that his life would be different. He would be called on to fix fractures, monitor pregnant ladies, rule out meningitis in babies, and offer his shoulder to frustrated, culture-shocked spouses, lovers, and kids. He could handle all that; he even put a chest tube in a Foreign Service Officer with a gunshot wound. But, call a Minister of government, claim to speak for the President of the United States, and tell him to open up his runway as our 720 with doctors and defibrillators was on its way? That's a different story. Medical school skipped that course. Even his orientation in DC taught him only about malaria and elephantiasis, not about browbeating dignitaries. "Well, screw it, all he can do is say no. And then I'll say yes, loudly, and he'll say no and then ..."

"Madam Diallo, please get Minister Coulibaly on the phone for me." The secretary he despised so much had somehow made it into the Embassy and had taken her seat, Sphinx-like, saying nothing to anybody. "He will be found at home and his number is 88-53-03." A look of surprise crossed her face.

About fifteen seconds later, his buzzer sounded. "Mr. Coulibaly on line one." Michael had only one line.

"Hello, Mr. Minister. It's so nice to speak to you again."

"Ah, Dr. Eisenstat, Happy Passover." Michael knew it was close to Easter and that Passover couldn't be far away. He did not know that it had started the previous evening. No Seders during the revolution. He and Jill wouldn't have had one during peacetime.

"I appreciate the sentiment, Sir, but I call once again on the issue of which we spoke last night."

"I am sorry Doctor, I do not recall the subject. As I am sure you are aware, we have been very busy in the last several hours."

"Of course, Sir, I am aware of that." Michael had no idea if the TV reports of the arrest of the President-for-life were exaggerated or if the committee had not yet come for Coulibaly. "I am calling at the request of the Ambassador of the United States who cannot call himself. In turn, I call as the representative of the President of the United States." Michael had been no big fan of the incumbent, but he felt a swelling in his chest when he invoked the name of the Commander in Chief. "We ask once again that Keita-Coulibaly International Airport accept the arrival of one of our military hospital aircraft for the purpose of evacuating our First Secretary Chen Wang who was severely wounded by one of your soldiers."

"Oh, yes, I remember. I also remember that I told you that I had no responsibility for the airport and cannot grant you or your President that right. I suggest that you contact the Air Ministry."

"Sir, I suggest that you contact the Air Ministry. My patient needs care for his gunshot wound. He cannot get care here. Therefore he needs to get out of here and the only way that will happen is if our plane gets to land at your airport. As the Minister of Health, you are responsible for this and the government of the United States will hold you personally responsible for the safety of Mr. Chen." Michael could hardly believe what he was hearing from his own mouth. He knew that his threats had nothing to back them up; he only hoped that Coulibaly didn't know it.

"I can make no promises, Dr. Eisenstat. I will speak with the Air Minister."

"Thank you. I expect a return call within fifteen minutes. In the meantime, we will be notifying our military command in Europe that they should send the hospital plane, now."

Chen's temperature reached 103 degrees and he developed a shaking chill. Michael assumed that an abscess was forming in the chest cavity --

not acutely life threatening but not something he wanted to be in charge of much longer.

"Chen, a plane is on the way to get you out of here; a big one. 720 I think. Doctors and nurses aboard. The nurses have quite the reputation; word has it they take to Chinese guys with hard rubber tubes sticking out of their chests, making lots of sucking noises."

"Thanks doc. Don't feel much like chasing any nurses now... Am I going to die?"

"What do you mean, die? You're my first big surgery. I plan on keeping my 100% success rate." Trying to be funny was of little solace to either. Chen thought he was going to die, and Michael knew that when a patient started asking such questions, especially an Asian patient who usually keeps his emotions somewhere in the great deep, there was some truth to the fear. They did die, frequently.

"Chen, you are going to need some more surgery, probably bigger than the one I did. But there's nothing life-threatening about your problem. A little drainage, lots of super-strong antibiotics, plenty of bed rest and you'll be back on the bid list. They're sure to give you Paris or London after this. No more garbage dumps like Donolu for a purple heart winner."

"Hate to say it doc, but I like it here. I'd ask them to send me back." To Michael, that statement suggested a mental rather than physical illness.

"Doctor, Minister Coulibaly is on the phone." Madam Diallo could infuse the most basic transfer of information with implied sarcasm.

"Mr. Minister, thank you so much for calling so quickly. I presume that you have good news for me."

"I talked with Minister Kitchu about your problem. He told me that our long runway that the big commercial airlines land on is out of service. They started repaving it yesterday. Only the short runway is open. I'm afraid that your Boeing could not land there."

"What makes you say Boeing?"

"You mentioned it when we spoke." Mike was quite certain he had given no information about the ambulance plane.

"And how long is the short runway?"

"1500 meters."

The doctor knew nothing about runway lengths but 1500 meters, the metric mile, sounded like plenty.

"1500 meters may just have to be enough. In the meantime, tell Minister Kitchu that he has eight hours to get the paving ready for a Boeing 720, even if he has to go run the steam roller himself."

"Doctor, what is a steam roller?"

"Ask the man who told you our plane was a Boeing."

Madame Diallo entered the room as he was hanging up on Coulibaly. He noticed how nicely she was dressed in a yellow and black *boubou* and matching head cover. Her teeth showed a sign of good luck or expensive dental care. Her makeup was extensive and tasteful. She walked with a royal demeanor in gold lamé slippers. Too bad she was such a terrible secretary. "Mrs. and Mr. Genu to see you, doctor."

Michael had had little to do with the Genu's in their few months in Donolu. Osgood, as one would expect for a weightlifting coach, looked and acted like Rambo. No doctors and no pills for him. Although Michael was sure that Genu took steroids, he was never asked for a prescription. Fanny, the wife, had visited more often, mainly to talk to Michael about her inability to get pregnant. After extensive evaluation, the doctor determined the diagnosis to be lack of sex. Osgood was not about to discuss the problem.

"Osgood! Fanny! What are you doing here? I thought you were stuck in your safe haven with a bunch of rioters trying to get at you. We didn't know if you were alive or dead."

"We're not dead, doc. But Fanny there has a hurt finger."

"What happened?"

"She slammed it in the safe haven door when we were trying to get away from the bastards. They looked like they were going to eat us. Goddam cannibals."

Michael, as always, hated it when the spouse or parent spoke for the patient. "Fanny, tell me, where does it hurt?"

"Look for yourself, Doc; it's the only one that's black."

"Please, Mr. Genu, it's important for me to hear from the patient herself."

"This'n doctor." She held out the long finger, right hand. The entire nail was black.

"Does it hurt a lot?"

"It thobs terrible."

"Time for the hot paper clip trick. We gotta get the blood out from under that nail." He broke a paper clip, heated the tip with a match until it turned red and touched it gently to the nail. A second or two later, the clip broke through into the collection of blood and a mini-gusher showed how high the pressure had been.

"Ahhhh." Her response was orgasmic. She was not to make another comment during her entire stay in the office.

"So, tell me what happened. How'd you get out and how'd you get here?"

"Those safe haven doors are not only heavy, they're thick. We could hardly hear a thing through the door, even though there must have been two hundred of the bastards in the house. No one tried to bust the door down. They weren't after us – just our stuff.

"We finally came out after a few hours when it started getting dark. The house was empty. Not a stick of furniture. Not a rug. In the kitchen, they didn't just take our food and plates and pots -- they took the cabinets. Hell, the toilets and sinks were ripped out of the walls. Camera gone. TV gone. CD player gone. They even got the Nautilus equipment out; the stuff must have weighed a ton. No phones. No light bulbs. Just a puddle of piss than one of them idiots left on the living room floor. We're damn lucky we had clothes and glasses and our passports in the bedroom.

"They took our radio -- just ripped it and the cords out of the wall. We couldn't call the Embassy so we figured we'd just spend the night. Couldn't tell if anyone was waiting outside for us and weren't about to go out of the house to look."

"How'd you get here?"

"Hell, we just walked. Funny thing -- they didn't steal the car -- didn't even bang it up. They did take the keys though -- they were in Fanny's purse, along with a couple thousand lassosos. So, we walked. Streets were quiet, amazing quiet. You could hear shots from a long way away. But we didn't see no tanks or troops. Not even many people."

"How'd you get through the crowd outside the Embassy?"

"No sweat doc. These little dipshits move aside like grains of sand if you force 'em. I had Fanny grab my belt in back and just plowed my way up to the front door. Went to the front door and waved our passports in the guy's face and he let us in. Wouldn't have done him no good to try to keep us out. Some Zins tried to follow us in, but I helped the doorman push the door into their faces. By the way doc, how is Mr. Wang?"

"Not great, Osgood. We've got a 720 coming to pick him up. We might need you to help push around a few more, uh, 'dipshits' when the plane lands. They've given us some grief about the landing."

"Can't think of anything I'd rather do."

XXVI

The morning that the Libyans arrived in the capital was unusually quiet. The streets were largely empty except for a few children laughing and combing the trash piles for loot.

Jenny was still imprisoned after nearly four hours in the claustrophobic metal box with her offensive companions, and two hours since the humiliating stop for urination and leaves. Her buttocks were numb and throbbing from the relentless bouncing on a springless steel bench. Her knees felt rusted shut as she could not stretch her long legs for fear of hitting a Libyan in the groin.

She could tell that they were getting into the city as the vehicle moved more ponderously and made turns to circumvent roundabouts. The din of the engine obscured sounds from the outside. Thinking that she heard distant gunfire, she found herself feeling surprisingly secure, somewhat confident that she would get out of this unscathed. Maybe there'll be a movie about me, she thought.

The *Gare Autobus* was Donolu's answer to a bus station and the initial destination of the convoy. It was nothing more than a vast gravel yard. Waiting facilities for passengers were limited to four tin roofs to protect them from the rare but drenching West African rains. There were no toilets or outhouses. Hawkers normally swarmed the station with their papayas, bananas, and breadstuffs. Others carried wooden cases of soft drinks in glass bottles.

That morning, however, there were no passengers; there were no vendors; there were no bus drivers. Only a couple dozen empty buses. Hidden behind the vehicles was a troop of 12 people, none older than 25. All but two were women. The leader was a plain girl, barely 20, bespectacled and acne scarred, who wore not a uniform, but Levis with rents in the knees and a T-shirt that said in English, "Save the Bamako Zoo."

The group had weapons. Each of the women carried a rifle, no two alike. The two males, both teenagers, one with a Chicago Bulls tee, the other wearing a ripped shirt with pictures of a giraffe, were in charge of the big Israeli-supplied gun, a 2.5-inch rocket launcher, big enough to penetrate the relatively thin armor of the old Russian T-24 tanks of the Libyan arsenal.

"I hear them coming!" one of the junior female warriors shouted from her lookout post inside a brown bus. Asta, the homely leader, radioed PPD, "The tanks are just down the highway. Is the plan still on?"

"Affirmative! Remember, you only have two rounds for the gun so make sure you wait until the tanks are in range. We have to make each shot count." The voice was unmistakably that of Oumou Kinsa. She added, "Tell the group, if you have time, that President Lassoso is in jail."

The rocket launcher was on top of a yellow Donolu-New Akron Express. The two boys were poised at the bottom of the ladder normally used to hoist luggage, goats, and excess passengers to the top.

Asta yelled to her platoon, "The Libyans are about to turn onto this road. Lassoso's been arrested; I don't know if the Libyans know it. Whatever you do, boys, let them get close before you fire your first round. Once you fire, get the second round ready to go as quickly as you can. You only have two shots. The rest of you have practiced on those rifles for a long time. You've got lots of bullets. Shoot them at anyone you see running from a tank or any other army vehicle. Try not to hit any civilians."

"Here they come!" yelled the woman in the blue bus. The column made the left turn off the main Donolu to New Akron highway, an armored personnel carrier in the lead. The two young men climbed their ladders to the top of the yellow bus. A green and white bus hid their view initially, but within seconds the first of the Libyan vehicles poked its barrel into view. The distance between the yellow bus and the APC was about 80 meters, too far to be accurate. The boys shot anyway, missing badly. A tiny grocery shop on the other side of the street crumpled to the ground and three goats behind it were dismembered.

The turret of the APC rotated its gun toward the bus yard as the boys were rearming their rocket launcher. The noise from the enemy vehicle coincided with the disintegration of an orange bus parked right next to theirs. The second rocket launcher shell, fired from 50 meters hit its mark. The APC ground to a sudden halt, its track disengaged from its driving mechanism. There was no fire, no explosion, and no movement. The hatch opened and men started jumping out trying to escape what they assumed to be massive enemy forces. The eight girls pointed their ancient rifles at the fleeing Libyans and shot. Asta saw that one of the Libyans was a tall blond woman. "Stop!" Her voice didn't have a chance with all the commotion. The blond fell, along with six of her companions, alongside the motionless diesel dinosaur.

Four of Jenny's fellow riders escaped into the bushes. The remainder of the column, seven tanks and APCs turned around, overwhelmed by eight young women and two teenage boys in T-shirts, and retreated toward New Akron.

It had been more than two hours since the cornrowed announcers had declared President Lassoso ex-President. Since then, the television in the Ambassador's office broadcast only static -- no test pattern, no sexually active Brazilians, no martial music.

Suddenly, the TV speakers came to life. The National Anthem was played, not on tape, but by a single bugler, not a day over 13. He hit more than half of the notes correctly, making the identity of the piece reasonably certain. At the relief-inducing conclusion, the Americans applauded as if they were at the Super Bowl. The camera panned around the studio and settled on the news desk. Seated in the middle was Oumou Kinsa, to one side of her General Joro, to the other, Colonel Rashad. The massive map of Africa had been removed from the backdrop and replaced by a hand drawn poster consisting of three letters -- PPD.

Oumou was dressed in traditional West African garb, a blue-green *boubou* and green headpiece. Bernadette had never seen her in African attire; she looked beautiful. Oumou's mouth began to move but no sound was heard. She continued, clearly buoyed by events, until the bugler delivered her the live microphone. She spoke in French.

"My fellow Zinanians and my friends from around the world. To my associates in the military, including my two colleagues sitting with me whom you all know. We of the People's Party for Democracy welcome you to the Democratic Republic of Zinani. Since ten o'clock this morning, Mr. Lassoso has been in the custody of the Army and is no longer your President. With a few exceptions, of which you will hear later, the cabinet members of the old government are also under arrest and are being held at a military base in the country. General Joro, Colonel Rashad, and I will be forming a committee to serve in a transitional period before free and honest elections will be held within one year. The committee will have representation from all parts of Zinanian life, including students, labor, military, agriculture, and professional. More than one half of the members will be women.

"I am pleased to say that the Army is in full support of these changes. About 30 minutes ago, an armored column that included tanks and other vehicles from a country other than our own, was turned back thanks to the valiant efforts of a small group of PPD freedom fighters. Many of the foreign troops have been killed or injured. Members of the First Army Division have taken others prisoner.

"The last two days have produced many martyrs. To them, we are in eternal debt. The cold-blooded actions of the previous regime will not go unpunished. But, my fellow citizens, the punishment will be served with justice. Each accused, no matter how heinous his or her crime is alleged to be, will be given a fair trial. We insist that no one attempt to take the law into his ... or her own hands.

"To those who have cooperated with us, both Zinanians and others, we thank you. Especially to the men and women of the United States and France. Be aware that your help has been crucial. To all freedom-loving nations of the world, we seek your rapid recognition. To those with missions in our country, we welcome your cooperation and guarantee your safety.

"A dawn to dusk curfew will remain in effect for a few more days. We ask you to honor this curfew and warn that those who do not will be arrested on sight.

"Zinanians, we welcome you into the world of freedom and democracy. We solicit your views, your energy, and your prayers. Allahu Akbar!"

The two officers nodded their heads in approval and Oumou beckoned the pimply bugler who took the microphone back. He retreated to his music stand and started tooting the anthem again. The Ambassador leaped for his remote control and pushed the mute button. The others assembled, including the three local employees, joined in applauding the now silent screen.

"The good guys finally win one! And they thanked us specifically. This is great! Washington won't be able to ignore us much longer." Fairchild was luminous.

"Let's not get too excited just yet," cautioned the DCM. We have three people on TV saying that he's gone and that Gaddafi's people have chickened out. A little independent confirmation wouldn't be a bad idea. Lori?"

"Can't imagine that Rashad and Joro would be sitting at Kinsa's side unless this really was wrapped up. Lassoso comes back, or isn't gone in the first place and those guys are friggin' dead meat. Joro's a real opportunist; remember how quickly he got elevated when Sacco got bumped off." Bernadette cringed. "We'll get our sources to confirm it soon but I'd go under the assumption that OIL got his butt kicked.

"What do you think Gaddafi will do now? He doesn't take lightly to losing," Grant continued.

"He's got two options. One is sitting tight at his base in New Akron, not worrying about these prisoners that Oumou claims to have. The other is to come in with lots more fire power. I imagine he'll choose the first, at least for the present. He knows that the French, especially now that the dictator is out of there, won't stand by if he brings in his big guns. Libya wouldn't stand a chance against France. I guess he could pull up stakes and leave, but that doesn't sound like him.

"He'll need some watching later. He may try to infiltrate the present power group, although there aren't a lot of women of influence in the Libyan intelligence forces."

"So you think that this really will be a femino-democracy?" said Fairchild, proud of his new word.

"Sure looks like it, even with the military flanking her on both sides. What do you think, Dette?"

"Oumou looked like she was in control. The little lady is tough.

Demands and commands respect. She'll handle it well, as long as the military doesn't get jealous. Oumou has come up on her own and has been the brains behind all this." I'd suggest that we be quick about recognizing the new government and give her our special backing. She sure was asking for it on TV."

"I agree, but this isn't something we can do here. This is a decision for the President. We've got to get a cable off fast with our strong recommendations for recognition." Ernestine was her usual definitive self.

"She closed with Allah Akbar. Is she a closet fundamentalist?" asked Prudholme.

"No Connie, she's no fundamentalist. Remember how Reagan and others always end their comments with 'God Bless'? They weren't born-agains, in spite of their attempt to appeal to them. Oumou is a Moslem, not a very devout one, but a Moslem in a country that's 90% Moslem. She's got to say 'God is Great" to reassure the populous that she's one of them and not just some transplanted European."

"What now?" asked the Ambassador, conceding the helm once again to the DCM, his first mate.

"We'll call the cops and use the PPD number that we have and make sure that we won't get anti-tanked if we drive any place. Lori, you beat the bushes. Bernadette, you try to get in touch with Oumou herself and tell her we're working as fast as we can to get Washington's buy-in. Frank, try to contact all the Americans, including the AID contractors and make sure everybody is OK. Doc has dealt with the airport situation but you better make sure that 1500 meters is enough for a 720, or if it isn't, come up with a plan for getting the thing on the ground. Willie, try to round up all the volunteers. No one should be at his site; everybody in the city. Make sure that girl from San Diego is OK."

"An me?" asked the Ambassador, sheepishly.

"Sir, we'll get some official communiqués written up for you to send out as soon as DC gives us the go ahead. You might work on a few words to say for the TV cameras. The comments that Oumou made about us are going to put us in the limelight for some time."

"Doctor Eisenstat, this is Corporal Costa at Post 1. A woman has been brought to our door in pretty bad shape. The two other women who brought her say that they think she's American."

"What's wrong with her?"

"She's been shot, Sir, in the head and in the shoulder. They say that some Libyan soldiers shot her."

"How bad is she?"

"Real bad, Sir. She doesn't move. I don't even know if she is breathing."

"I'll be right down." Michael grabbed his blood pressure cuff and stethoscope. "Come on Electra! Emergency at Post 1! Bring an IV and some oxygen." He ran through the door, noticing that Mrs. Diallo was reading the paper. Osgood Genu shouted, offering help, as Michael was leaving. "Yeah, Osgood, we may be able to use you"

The young woman looked like she was asleep on the gray terrazzo floor. Her clothes were covered with dirt. The back of the right shoulder had a dark red, nearly black spot, a couple of inches wide. Her long blond hair was caked in dry sweat. He could see what Costa had meant; her breathing was almost non-existent, except for occasional bursts of rapid, deep breaths. Cheyne-Stokes respirations -- a terrible sign in someone with a head injury.

She was face down. He rolled her over. She was beautiful but moribund. A small wound, maybe half an inch, just above the left eye. Michael felt for a second one, the exit wound. It was in the hard part of the skull, back, right. Her pupils were mid-sized and opening and shutting the lids in the bright inner chamber of the Embassy did nothing to their size. As he rolled her head from side to side, the eyes didn't move in their sockets, another terrible sign.

"Do you want to intubate her, doctor," asked Electra, with endotrachial intubation set-up in hand.

"Not here and not now, Electra." This woman's problem was not her airway. Hell, he might be able to keep her alive on a respirator for a long, long time. She was certainly young and certainly healthy looking. But, to what end? So she could spend that long, long time in an intensive care unit where the family could come sit with her for hours a day hoping for the impossible? Where they could exhaust their insurance coverage and then their personal savings and then everything else?

Eisenstat had seen too many patients kept alive because his fellow doctors didn't have what it took to play God.

"Osgood, would you help me get her upstairs?" Genu picked Jenny Addison up as if he were carrying a small child. By the time they reached the Health Unit, she was dead.

XXVII

"No, Miss O'Kelly, Miss Kinsa is not here. She is at the Presidential Palace. But she would like to see you as soon as possible.

"With our Ambassador?"

"No, just you."

Bernadette was astonished to learn that Oumou had already gone to the Palace and that she, Bernadette O'Kelly, Creighton '74, was the first foreigner called in by the first woman ever to stage a successful coup d'état.

Twenty minutes after she hung up, a Mercedes limousine pulled up in front of the Chancery. The driver was a young woman, in jeans and a plain white T-shirt. From the rear, her tiny body and androgynous apparel made her look like an eleven-year-old boy chauffeur. "Please buckle your seat belt, Miss O'Kelly." The modern age had reached Donolu.

"How long have you had this job?" asked Bernadette, just to make conversation.

"You are my first rider, Miss O'Kelly."

The quarter hour commute up the hill to the Palace made it apparent that the driver was on her maiden voyage. No one was struck by the swerving Mercedes, more as a result of the nimbleness of pedestrians than control by the driver. In Zinani, like much of the developing world, a driver's license is bought, not earned. Fifty lassosos and it's yours, one hundred if you need it today. The applicant signs a statement that he or she knows the traffic code; no test is administered. A traffic code exists but there is no enforcement. No ticket has ever been issued. Should the driver be involved in an accident and not be able to present a license, a sizable fine is demanded on the spot. If the money for the fine is not handed over, the car is impounded until the cash appears.

It had been a mere three months since Bernadette had attended the reception at the Palace with Suleiman Sacco. She was struck by how it hadn't changed a bit in spite of the gargantuan changes in the body politic of the country. The new steering committee had been in office for only a few hours. The most striking difference for Dette was the presence in the Palace Guard of young women. They carried their rifles, presumably unloaded, with the same insecurity with which the driver held the steering wheel.

The ornate entry hall was little altered since Bernadette's last visit. The pictures of the first family had disappeared and were not yet replaced.

The meeting venue of Kinsa and O'Kelly was in the Palace's living area. The maze to the first family's personal quarters was, like that to the ballroom, through the kitchen. She was escorted through a huge pantry stocked with liquors of advanced age and a wine collection that would have made Michael Eisenstat drool. The irony of all that alcohol in a Presidential Palace of an "Islamic Republic" was too obvious for comment. A spiral staircase started at the far end of the pantry, winding 360 degrees to the second floor. Both splintery banisters wobbled under the least pressure, like a loose baby tooth.

A small, rectangular landing at the summit looked on to three unmarked doors. Her escort knocked on the one to the right.

"Come in, Miss O'Kelly." The voice was unmistakably Oumou's.

The room was large, not palatial. For security, there were no windows. The electric lighting was classical Zinani - two floor lamps and a dreadful chandelier of inadequate wattage. A small-screen Sony glowed in the corner, tuned to CNN International. The audio was muted as the screen featured a panel of American Republicans and Democrats discussing abortion. Oumou had a remote control on her desk, should the producers in Atlanta decide it worthwhile covering the events in Donolu. Unfaded rectangles on the dark green wallpaper indicated where the Lassoso family photos had hung.

The new Head of State hadn't slept in two days and looked it. She had obviously not dealt with a tailor to prepare for her ascendancy since she was, like the driver and the TV personalities who made the surprise announcement, decked out in jeans and a T-shirt.

The escort left the two women alone. "Oumou, congratulations."

Bernadette offered her right hand.

Miss Kinsa did nothing to accept the offer. "I am sorry, Miss O'Kelly, you must address me as Madam President. Our committee has chosen me President of the Executive Council. " She did not smile.

Bernadette felt heaviness in her chest and heat in her face. She slowly withdrew her hand. "Madam President, I congratulate you. I am very pleased by your success."

"And your government?"

"I am not at liberty to speak for my government. My comments reflect only my own personal opinion and I must say that I cannot be quoted. And, Madam President, you invited only me."

"Yes, I did, Miss O'Kelly. I know you and trust you and in view of all you have done for us, both personally, and as a representative of your country, I wanted to see you first and ask for the support of Washington and your President. We need your recognition as the lawful government of Zinani and I would like to have an exchange of letters with the White House."

"Oumou ... excuse me, Madam President, you know our system. You have certainly studied it well. As you know, we in Donolu are in no position to make a decision of recognition. That must be made in Washington at the very highest levels. The decision may come today; it may come in a few days, or a few weeks. There are political realities other than whether or not we agree with the actions of the PPD and the arrest of Mr. Lassoso. I can only say that you have won the admiration of everyone who works for the American Embassy in Zinani.

"Please tell me what you can about the present situation."

"As you surely saw on television, Mr. Lassoso and his wife and son are under arrest."

"Under what charge?"

"For Lassoso, murder. We will never know exactly how many of our citizens became martyrs because of the orders of that evil man."

"And the family?"

"Aiding and abetting. Mrs. Lassoso supported her husband while he killed. She is guilty, too. The son, Mohammed, may be even worse; we have information that he killed several of our people with his own hand. And that vile woman, Aroos."

"How about the younger children?"

"As you know they are students in your country. Yale, I believe. We would ask that you send them back. We suspect that they too are guilty."

"You must take that up with the State Department directly."

"Each of those we have in custody is in a different place. The specifics are confidential. We are concerned that counterrevolutionary attempts will begin soon, although, so far, the Army has been very helpful. They will have a prominent role in the Governing Council."

"Madam President, our government has information that Libya may have troops in your country."

"I am pleased to inform you, Miss O'Kelly, that those troops you mentioned, and the armored column in which they were being transported toward our capital, were met and defeated by a small contingent of troops loyal to the PPD. I can safely say that they have been eliminated as a problem for us. The Libyans and their Zinanian henchmen suffered several casualties in the battle. We also have learned that a Westerner, a young woman, was injured; she may be an American. Our people have taken her to your Embassy."

"How could that have happened?"

"She reportedly was riding with the Libyan troops in an armored personnel carrier and tried to flee when the carrier was immobilized."

"And you shot her?"

"I'm afraid that our people did not recognize at first that she was anything but one of the enemy troops."

"We, and you, must hope that she will be OK. It would not serve your revolution well to have been involved in the killing of an American."

"I agree, Miss O'Kelly. I will give you my word that we will do anything we can to find out what happened. It is our stated goal to make sure everybody present in our community is safe."

"Thank you, Madam President. I will pass that on to Ambassador Fairchild."

She paused briefly. "Now, I must ask you another question that is of special interest to me personally, and to our Government. As you know, General Sacco was a friend of mine, a very close friend. What has become of him? His body was never seen, even though everyone says he is dead. My dreams tell me he is alive and is trying to get to me. Please tell me where he is."

"Bernadette ... he is dead. General Joro told me two weeks ago that he was present when he was killed. It was worse than you can imagine. Lassoso himself pressed buttons, electric ones that were attached to wires hooked to the General's most private parts. He kept turning up the current, demanding information about our movement and his role in it, but Suleiman never said a thing. Eventually, the current was so high that it must have stopped his heart. They took his clothes and burned them and threw his body into the Begoro River. He was a great man. Without him, we would never have succeeded."

"What do you mean?"

"He had been a supporter or ours since our movement was born. He gave us information that we could not have learned elsewhere, particularly about the military and their dissatisfaction with the government. Without that knowledge, our efforts would have been futile.

"After the event at the doctor's home, Suleiman knew that he'd be demoted and General Joro would replace him. Sadly, Joro is not an intelligent man and would not make a good President; Sacco would have."

"Can you trust Joro? Won't he expect to be the Head of State?"

"He says not. Rashad also says he's not interested and that they support our movement."

"That's pretty strange for Africa isn't it? A man bowing to a woman?"

Kinsa did not answer the question. "Miss O'Kelly, we will just have to watch how things develop and hopefully your country will support us. When Corazon Aquino was named to replace Marcos, you supported her."

"Madam President, I must be blunt. Zinani is not the Philippines. America has no history here. France has history. We've got a few million dollars of aid and a few diplomats to watch out for Gaddafi and that's it. No military bases, no trade other than Texaco, Coke, and Pepsi and maybe, soon, Burger King. I doubt the White House or the Congress would spend much to shore up your movement."

Oumou Kinsa stared icily. Bernadette saw her anger, her disappointment, and her fear.

After a moment of silence, she asked, "Madam President, I return to General Sacco. I do not understand why he worked so closely with the PPD. Sure, he hated Lassoso but he was in a position to take over himself. Why did he come to you?"

"You said Miss O'Kelly that he was a 'very good friend of yours.' Well, he was also a very good friend of mine."

"Oh, I didn't know that."

"As soon as I returned from my training in Baltimore, I met him. Believe it or not, he was an emissary from President Lassoso, who still wanted me as his mistress. That fool did not have the courage to ask me himself, so he sent Colonel Sacco. I just laughed when he told me what the President wanted, and he confided to me that he too was unhappy with the regime.

"Within two weeks, we were lovers. I had a child by him, a girl, who was born in Ouagadougou. I had to leave the country as soon as it became obvious I was pregnant. I gave the baby to a distant aunt of mine, who I had never met. I will never see her again. Long before the baby was born, he and I, as you Americans say, 'stopped seeing each other.' He was afraid that we would be discovered and both of us killed. To my knowledge, you are the first person who has ever known about this."

"He lied to me. He said there had only been one woman before me, his wife."

"Yes, Bernadette, I know. He told me that and felt very bad about it. He did not want to jeopardize the chances of the PPD by making you jealous of me."

"My God. How could that have happened?" She opened her arms and approached the new President. Oumou Kinsa held her arms straight out, wrists bent, palms facing forward. The Political Officer stopped abruptly, turned, said, "Thank you, Madam President," and opened the door through which she entered, finding the same pretty escort that had brought her to the office in the first place. She could tell that the escort had not failed to notice the tears on her cheeks.

Beth Sinova had never before set foot in the American Embassy. She carried the old Peace Corps fear that American Embassy was another name for CIA Headquarters.

Beth was accompanied by Willie Anderson, the Peace Corps Country Director. He had been with the Ambassador and DCM when the call came in from Doctor Eisenstat saying that a blond woman had died in the Health Unit. His first and only thought was Jenny Addison. He went to the Peace Corps guesthouse on the other side of Donolu, where he found Beth Sinova, who had come into town the previous day.

"Beth, I need your help. Someone has been killed. I'm really afraid it's Jenny. She's at the Embassy. She's been shot. May have been the PPD that shot her by mistake. Please come with me."

Beth rose in stone-faced silence from the raggedy couch in the guesthouse. She slipped into her flip-flops and followed Anderson to the Land Cruiser. "Please don't let it be her," she prayed repeatedly as the car bumped over the city streets.

She had seen many movies and TV shows in which the family member or close friend was required to identify the body. Invariably, there is ample preparation of the living for the sight of the deceased, then the pathologist, or her more sensitive assistant, takes the survivor into a sparkling clean morgue, the drawer is pulled out from a wall of over-sized, stainless steel safe deposit boxes, and a pristine sheet is pulled back. Without fail, it is the right person and the identifier nods once.

Not this time. Beth followed her Director through the Health Unit door. Jenny's body was lying on the floor of the waiting room. A makeshift drape was unceremoniously pulled back. Outwardly the injuries were minimal; she looked like she was sleeping. "That's Jenny Addison," said Mr. Anderson to the physician. Beth Sinova laid down on the floor next to her friend, put her arm over the small breasts of the motionless body and sobbed. With barely a glance, Mrs. Diallo continued filing her nails at her desk.

Berkeley Eaton had never before had to deal with a dead American citizen. Dead Americans were every Consular Officer's worst nightmare, especially those Officers in countries where dead bodies of their countrymen were exceedingly rare. Aside from the Embassy Community, the small cadre of Peace Corps Volunteers, a few CARE and Save the Children workers, a couple of dozen missionaries and their families, and an annual influx of perhaps 200 intrepid tourists and business seekers, there weren't any Americans in Zinani.

Usually, a mortician can be of vital service, but in Moslem Zinani, there were none. Moslems are buried within twenty-four hours of death; embalming and cremation are effectively unknown.

But, there is bureaucracy -- problematic in the best of circumstances, paralyzing when no one knows who is responsible for what. This, in the midst of a revolution, was just such a day.

"Mike, what do you think I should do?" The shaken Eaton had come to the Health Unit when he heard that an American woman had been killed.

"You know, when I was sifting through all the medical stuff that my predecessors accumulated over the years, I came across an embalming kit. I'd never seen such a thing -- lots of tubes, needles, and liquids in old bottles -- formaldehyde, I guess. I might as well try to use it."

"Go for it, Doc. But how do we get her body out of the country?"

"We've got a hospital plane coming in a few hours to fly Chen out of here. A 720 ought to have enough room to handle the coffin." Michael always had been able to depersonalize tragedy and inject it with gallows humor. It kept him going to a shrink. How else to deal with a beautiful dead Peace Corps Volunteer lying on the floor of his waiting room? "By the way, Berk, who's going to call the family?" he asked.

"Willie Anderson will. It won't be easy. Her parents weren't too enthused about her joining the Peace Corps in the first place, especially in Africa."

"What are they going to do about the rest of the Volunteers?"

"Hell if I know, Doc. Got to imagine that almost all of 'em want to stay, even having been told before Lassoso was kicked out that they had to leave.

"You've got to call Jenny's death accidental. It wasn't the kidnappers that killed her; it was the good guys.

"I don't think Willie will recommend pulling all the PCVs, nor do I think Peace Corps Washington will close the program, especially since it looks like a democracy is going to come out of it."

"Madam Eisenstat on the line, Doctor," Mrs. Diallo interrupted, receiver between shoulder and ear, nail file in her hands.

"Yeah, Jill?"

"Daddy died." she said, swallowing her tears.

"Oh, my. When?"

"Mother called just now and said he passed away last night about two. She wasn't even there because they told her that he wasn't critical. They called her at night and told her to come over right away, that he had taken a turn for the worse. Turns out that he was dead when they called but they wouldn't tell her on the phone."

"Gosh, honey, I'm sorry. We knew it was going to happen, but I wish you could have gotten there before it did. He was a wonderful man and I know how you loved him … and him, you."

"Yeah, me too. Now I really have to get back. Mommy can't handle it all by herself and the rest of the family is worthless. Can you get me on a plane?"

"I'll talk to Berkeley, who's here dealing with the Peace Corps Volunteer."

"Huh?"

"Haven't you heard? A Peace Corps Volunteer named Jenny Addison was killed because the PPD thought she was a Libyan soldier."

"Jenny Addison -- wasn't she a tall, blond, pretty girl? From San Diego?"

"Yeah, that's the one."

"Don't you remember, Michael? She was at our Thanksgiving just after we arrived. She came over with that brassy girl from the East, Beth something. I remember her real well - so shy, so nervous, but full of the words that Peace Corps likes to hear. I was scared to death that she would never last in this country. She didn't, I guess. But, I never thought it would be like this. How terribly, terribly sad."

She paused long enough to make her husband think that they were disconnected. "Why did you make me come here? I'm not there when my father dies and instead I'm in a place where some revolutionaries kill a fine young woman who wants to help the world. I hate it!"

"I know you do and I understand. I told you there's a medevac plane coming in to take Chen out? I don't see any reason why we couldn't put you on the same plane. You can fly to Pittsburgh from wherever it takes

Chen."

"OK. What'll I do now?" she asked with a sigh of relief.

"Just hang in there. I'll get an Embassy car to pick you up. Take everything you will need and as much of the other stuff that we don't want to lose. All hell could break loose here over the next few days so getting back might be hard."

"Like what should I take?"

"Some photos, your jewelry, wills, and maybe some tax records. You can take them to your folks' home. Leave them until we transfer to our next post."

"Our next post! I can't wait!" Their two years were nearly half done and the bidding process was beginning. Paris, Ankara, Beijing, Warsaw, and Caracas were possibilities. All were a whole lot better than Donolu; none was in Africa.

XXVIII

"The 720 has departed Sicily," said Ms. Grant, matter-of-factly. "ETA is six and a half hours from now.

"Can we land it?" asked the Ambassador.

The Gunnery Sergeant answered. "I checked with the Air Force attaché in Abidjan. He says that 1500-meters is too short. 2000 is cutting it close. Most of the big airports have 4000-meter runways, long enough to handle the heavies. On the other hand, ours is big enough to take off, if it lands. "

"No way that it's going to have enough fuel." said the security officer. "Even if they wanted to buy any, there won't be anyone around to sell it. They can't get back to Europe without a refuel. They'll have to refuel in Rabat or Algiers."

"Judy, get the doctor in here, ASAP." Fairchild interrupted the discussion. His secretary was playing solitaire at her desk, upset that she had to work, rather than attend church on a Sunday.

"Yes, Sir. Can I tell Dr. Eisenstat what it's about?"

"God damn it, just tell him to get his ass on down here!" The stunned staff could feel Judy's blushing through the wall. "We've gotta find out what the story is with Chen."

"As we were saying," uttered Frank Norbert, clearing his throat, "that plane is not going to get all the way back to Europe without a fuel stop in an Arab country on the way."

Lori Burkitt volunteered her opinion, "Rabat sounds like the place. The Moroccans like us a lot more than the Algerians do."

She continued, addressing Norbert, the RSO. "Frank, security is everything in this operation. We don't have any idea if anyone is in charge at Keita-Coulibaly. We have no guarantee that they won't shoot our plane down. We don't know if they'll shoot or arrest the crew when it lands. We don't know if they'll let it take off if it lands.

"What happens if the damn thing crashes? Are there any firemen?

God forbid we need to treat casualties."

"Ma'am, we're thinking the same thing," responded Norbert.

Michael slipped quietly into the room as the discussion continued. "Sir, you called?"

"Give us an update on Chen."

"Not great. Vital signs are a little worse every hour. The pulse is real fast and the fever has hit 103. His head's OK; he worries about everything and everybody except himself. He was really torn up about that Peace Corps volunteer."

"What's your diagnosis?"

"I think he's got an abscess. He may be bleeding internally as well, but slowly. His blood count is low, although not low enough for transfusions.

"Prognosis?"

"He's not in any jeopardy of dying right away, but I wouldn't make book on him if we can't get him to a major hospital in the next 72 hours. The man needs surgery."

"You can't do it?"

"Correct, I can't do it. Chen would surely die if I went into his abdomen."

"Ah ha. So, you're telling us that we've got to get him out of here, soon."

"That, Mr. Ambassador, is exactly what I am telling you."

"Thank you Dr. Eisenstat."

"Sir, there's a couple of other things that I should bring up. First, there is the matter of the body of Miss Addison. She is in the examining room, covered in a plastic sheet. She's been dead for several hours now and it is likely to get unpleasant. Excuse me for getting so graphic. I did my best to embalm the body using the instructions in the kit that we found in the storeroom. They didn't teach about embalming in med school."

"Regs say we need the host government's permission to ship out a body," Conrad Prudholme said, looking directly at the doctor.

"Cut the shit, Conrad!" Ernestine Grant yelled. "Screw the regs! There's not a customs officer in this country that'll stand in the way of us putting a body bag on that plane.

"I stand corrected. Sorry, Ernestine."

"Michael, you said there was another thing that you wanted to talk about?"

"Yeah, Ernestine, I want to get Jill out of town. Her Dad died yesterday and she wants to get home for the funeral and for her mother. I figured we could get her out on the plane too. If necessary, we say she's a nurse; she is a nurse, you know."

"But ..."

"Shut up, Conrad! No problem, Michael. Get Jill to pack up some stuff and be home when you transport Chen."

The Ambassadorial phone buzzed. "Yeah?"

"Please tell Dr. Eisenstat to go up to the Health Unit immediately!" Judy Deane barked into the intercom.

Michael, knowing that only a change in Chen's status could produce such emotion, leapt from his chair and ran. Ms. Diallo had put her nail file on the desk; a French romance novel was open beside it, but she was able to conjure up a look of concern as her boss bolted by. He sprinted into the holding room where he saw Chen Wang working a crossword puzzle in the Herald Tribune. Electra stood next to him.

"What's up?"

The nurse pointed to the suction bottle that until this time had small amounts of straw colored fluid. It now contained a pint or so of bright red blood. Chen looked up at Michael, "How's things, Doc?"

"Looks like some little blood vessel in your chest broke. You're bleeding. What's the BP, Electra?"

"77 over 50." Michael looked at the monitor and saw the pulse was over 120. He was amazed to see how normal the patient looked in spite of the fact that he was going into shock.

"Any idea what river Minsk is on, Doc? Eight letters starting with S."

"I'm not much of a geographer, Chen. Electra, open the IVs way up. Chen, what's your blood type?"

"B Negative."

"Crap. That's pretty rare. I gotta look at the Walking Blood Bank." The bank is the list of all the Americans in Zinani who could be called in an emergency.

The computer screen for BLOOD TYPE: B- showed four names.

CARLSON, CORRINE
CARLSON, EGBERT
EISENSTAT, JILLIAN
PRUDHOLME, CONRAD

Egbert Carlson was a missionary, who was translating the New Testament into a West African language spoken by only a handful of people. Corrine was his 17-year-old daughter who had left Zinani for a Christian college in Florida a few months earlier. Egbert lived well beyond New Akron and the only way to get to him was to send a messenger. It would take more than a day to get him in. That left the Doctor's spouse and his nemesis, Prudholme.

When Eisenstat walked back to the holding room, he found Ernestine Grant seated on a wheeled stool, holding Chen's hand. Until then, it hadn't registered to him how little he had seen the DCM in the Abattoir since her significant other became an inpatient.

"How's my main man, Mike?" Grant attempted to sound street-smart and nonchalant and succeeded at neither.

"Could be better, Ernestine. He's bleeding into his chest. Probably some small blood vessel opened up. Usually they stop bleeding on their own, and I'm pretty sure that's what'll happen here. But in the meantime, we've got to get him some blood. We've only got two candidates in the walking blood bank, my wife and your friend and mine, Conrad."

"I'll round up Connie and I'll leave your spouse to you."

Michael dialed home, finding the line busy. A second try produced the same. Ten minutes later, she called him.

"I just got off the phone with Mom. She's in bad shape. Can you call in some Ativan for her?"

"Sorry honey. You know I can't do that, even if I were home. She has a doctor; let him do it. We've got a problem here that you need to know about. Chen has started to bleed...bad. He needs blood and you and Conrad are the only B negatives in the mission."

"I've never given blood before. Remember that I had hepatitis after Brazil."

"That was Hepatitis A; no problem. You're all we got."

"OK. I'll get over as fast as I can. I'll drive; the streets are almost empty. Michael, you won't mind if I ask Electra to take my blood? Nothing personal you know."

"Michael, let's get this over with. Where do you want me?" Administrator Prudholme almost never came to the office for medical reasons. Once a week he would stop by to make sure that Michael wasn't spending any money unnecessarily and to cherry pick any good ideas that Michael or his staff had so that he could take credit.

"Electra will draw your blood. Just have a seat for a minute while she gets the equipment."

"No, Michael, I want you to do it. You know there's lots of AIDS in Nigeria; you can never be too careful."

"Jesus Christ, Conrad, the fact that Electra is from Nigeria is of absolutely no importance. You cannot get AIDS from donating blood."

"I know that's what they say, but that's also what they said about dentists. You do it."

"No, I won't."

"Yes, you will." On the operational chart, the doctor answers to the Admin Officer.

Michael thumped into the storage room where Electra was assembling a blood donation set-up. "What size needles do we usually do this with?"

"18"

"Do we have anything bigger?"

"There's a couple of 14s. We never use them." With medical needles, the bigger the number, the smaller the caliber.

"Give me one of them. I'm going to draw Mr. Prudholme's blood and I want to make sure it comes out fast. We don't want him in the Unit any longer than absolutely necessary."

"Don't let him bother you, Doctor. He's the one American in the place that none of us Africans like. He isn't worth the trouble."

"Thanks for saying that Electra. Give me the 14 anyway."

Prudholme grimaced as the large-bore needle slowly punctured the skin. Dr. Eisenstat, a veteran of thousands of blood draws, missed the Admin Officer's vein by several millimeters and had to slowly poke and prod to get the needle to the point where the blood bag began to fill. At the same time, Jill entered the Unit. She wore a blue shirt waste dress and white leather flats.

"Why that getup, honey?"

"You told me that I'd be allowed only one suitcase and I'll need a dress. I can pick up some more jeans and shirts at home.

"Lie down and Electra will take the unit of blood." He made sure that Prudholme heard the choice of phlebotomists. The nurse used the smaller caliber needle and entered her difficult veins on the first pass. With three recumbent patients, the Abattoir looked like a hospital emergency room.

Michael was the Embassy's lab tech as well as the doctor. By law, every unit of blood donated for transfusion requires an HIV test. The quick test requires no great skills in chemistry. A drop of chemicals from bottle #1, a couple of drops of serum, then a drop from bottle #2, then wait a few minutes to see if the color changes. There is a positive control and a negative control; the positive should turn bright red; the negative should stay clear, and the serum from the donated units is supposed to be clear, not red. Michael followed the instructions closely. No reason to be nervous about Jill's blood. He knew her pretty well.

Two or three minutes into the waiting period, Michael glanced at the four slides, two controls, Jill's, and Conrad's. Two of them had just a hint of red. One was the positive control, the other that of the Admin Officer. *It's nothing. Just a figment of my loathing of the man*, thought the doctor. Ten minutes later, he looked again. His wife was HIV negative. No surprise. Conrad Prudholme's, that of the church-going husband and father, matched the bright red of the known positive.

Must be a mistake. Maybe I contaminated his serum with the positive control? Do it again. Ten minutes later, bright red. No doubt about it, a positive test. The fast HIV test is just a screen but a pretty accurate one. There aren't many false positives, but he repeated it again, with another box of chemicals. Positive again.

How can he have gotten the virus? He was negative just a year ago. I've never heard of him screwing around and he sure isn't a druggie...I don't think.

After a quick cross match of Jill's blood with Chen's to make sure they were compatible, Michael hung her pint on the IV pole. A mechanical pump emptied the bag in a few minutes. Chen's state seemed to improve a bit but his pulse was still 120.

"Electra, check out who is O negative. We'll need some more units."

"What about the other unit you have, doctor?"

"Cross match problem, probably nothing, but I'd be nervous giving it. By the way, Electra, you've been wearing gloves when you're around blood, haven't you? Never can be too careful."

"Yes, doctor." She handed him the list of O negatives. Five missionaries, all of whom lived outside the capital. From the staff, USAID Director Graham, Mrs. Fairchild, and Mrs. Prudholme, the Bhutanese wife of the man whose blood has just turned the HIV test bright red.

"Call AID and ask Mr. Graham to come over and I'll call the Residence and ask Mrs. Fairchild to donate a pint."

"Shall I call Mrs. Prudholme?"

"She's so little and has those tiny veins. We'd never get a unit and we probably only need two more. The plane is only a few hours away." Michael didn't want to contemplate the idea of her being positive too.

Marylou Fairchild and Garson Graham both responded quickly; their units of blood were in bags, HIV negative, and ready to give in an hour.

The doctor called the Administrator. "Connie, would you come up to the Health Unit?"

"How come Doc? Something wrong with Chen?"

"Nothing worse than before. I just have to talk to you about something."

"What about? Not about your secretary again, is it? This isn't the best time to talk about her."

"No, Connie, it's not about Mrs. Diallo. Just come up."

"Shit man, I'm plenty busy, but give me a few minutes and I'll be there."

Fifteen minutes later Prudholme bolted into Michael's office. As always, he was dressed in crisply pressed khakis, white shirt, and tie. Michael thought he looked even thinner than his usual gaunt self.

"What's up?"

"Please sit down Connie." Conrad, not accustomed to taking orders from anyone other than the Ambassador, hesitated, then sat.

"So?"

"You know that before we give a unit of blood, we have to check it out for a variety of conditions, like hepatitis, AIDS, and the like."

"Yeah?"

"Yeah. We did those tests on yours and the HIV test was positive."

Prudholme slumped in his chair, nearly falling to the floor. "Say it again, Doc."

"Your HIV test was positive. We did it twice to make sure it was not an error in our laboratory. I did it myself both times."

"So, I've got AIDS."

"No, Connie, you don't have AIDS. You're smarter than that. But you almost certainly have the virus. There's one last test that I'll have to send to the States for 100% confirmation, but frankly, the test we do here is almost never wrong."

"How'd I get it? Shit, I bet I got it here in your unit. When you stuck me with that last vaccination. Hell, I knew that I shouldn't have let you give me that shit!" Prudholme jumped out of the chair and began pacing around the room.

"No, Connie, you didn't get the virus in this unit. We use only new needles and syringes and there is no way that the vaccine could have transmitted the disease. Please sit down." The patient paced a few more seconds before sitting. "Do you have any risk factors?"

"Huh?"

"Have you had sex with men?"

"Go fuck yourself Doctor Eisenstat!" Michael had no doubt that that sentence could be heard by Chen Wang, Electra, and Mrs. Diallo, plus anyone else who happened by the unit. "I am not a faggot. You goddam Beverly Hills rich bastards may think that every other man is queer. Not where I'm from, baby! The last thing I'd ever do is corn hole some guy or suck someone's dick!"

"Sorry, Connie, I had to ask."

"Next question, asshole!"

"Connie, let's be civil. I'm your doctor, like it or not, and we have a problem that needs a solution."

"Sorry." Prudholme reassumed the bent over, motionless posture.

"You haven't gotten any shots any place else than this unit since you've come to Africa?"

"Huh uh. Remember, I told you that they tried to give me a yellow fever vaccination when I came into country because I forgot my shot card. But I wouldn't let 'em do it. I had to slip the guy ten bucks to let me through."

"OK. So that leaves sex with women other than your wife, or your wife having sex with other men and bringing it home. Either of those fit?"

"Not Peema. She won't do it with me more than once every couple of months. She's not about to get laid by any Africans."

"And you?"

"She likes me. She had five kids with me."

"That's not what I meant. Any sex with the locals?"

"Can I trust you?"

"You just told me loud enough for all of the city to hear to go fuck myself, but yeah, you can trust me. It's part of the job description."

"I have someone on the side, but she's clean, I know it."

"How do you know it?"

"She's a college graduate and says her husband doesn't screw around. He worries about losing his big government job."

"That doesn't sound very reassuring, Connie."

"Yeah, I guess you're right."

"Condoms?"

"Most of the time we use 'em but the ones you get around here are like galoshes. I can hardly feel a thing."

"How often have you done it without condoms?"

"Not more than ten times."

"We may have a source of the problem."

"How about Peema? Could I have given it to her?"

"Let's wait on that other test before we check her. In the meantime, either abstain or use a condom. You know, we've got a lot of them here and they're yours for the asking. Probably better than the galoshes. No reason to say anything to her yet, unless you really want to."

"Huh-uh. Abstaining won't be a problem. She's not very interested. So Michael, how long do I have?" His eyes moistened. Eisenstat couldn't remember the last time the Admin Officer had called him by his given name.

"Let's not get maudlin, Con. First, it's not a hundred per cent yet. If it is, you are in an early stage. You had a negative test not too long ago when you were cleared to come. Plus, there's a pretty good treatment now. Probably good enough to keep you alive to die of something else."

"It'll fuck up my career, won't it?"

"Maybe. The Department doesn't like to have anyone with the virus in places where they can't be taken care of if they get real sick. Obviously, if it's really positive, you're out of West Africa."

"No loss. I hate this stinking place. What about my...um, girlfriend?"

"I don't know. You probably owe it to her to tell her. Obviously she meant something to you. If she tests positive and is rich, she can get out of the country for care. Unfortunately, the average African can't begin to afford tests, let alone the medicines."

"Her husband will kill her if he finds out."

"He's probably the source of the virus, unless you aren't her only boyfriend."

"He'll still kill her. He's gonna be really pissed that Lassoso is gone and take it all out on her. Where do we go from here, Michael?"

"Don't mean to sound hard, Con, but we've got more pressing problems than your blood test results right now. We've got to get Chen on the plane, if we can get the plane on the ground, then we've got to get it out of here to get him to a surgeon. Maybe we can get you on the same plane also so you can get the other tests. We could say you are needed to get the paper work done when Chen gets to the hospital. I'll cable DC for clearance."

"Thanks for your help, Man. Sorry I blew up at you."

"No problem. Let's get you diagnosed and taken care of." Conrad Prudholme smiled at Michael Eisenstat, the first time he had ever done so.

XXIX

Keita-Coulibaly International Airport lies about ten miles north of the center of Donolu. Like most everything else in West Africa, it was in desperate need of maintenance, beginning with paint. Unlike the airport's military presence before the revolution, the guards were fewer and primarily female. Bernadette had come with Mohammed Keita, her Zinanian assistant, to arrange for the arrival of the medevac plane.

A three-story *banco* and concrete control tower sat separate from the unassuming one-story terminal. The only entry to the tower was unlocked. They scaled the two rickety flights of stairs and entered the heart of the nation's air transport operations. From this one small room, all traffic of commercial, military, and civil aviation was controlled. It was empty of life, save for a gray mouse that quickly scampered under a bank of computers. Dust was everywhere. Empty bottles of Coke and Sprite created a glass mini-forest. Bernadette knew little about computer hardware, but recognized the equipment in the room as antiquated. The cubic gray boxes with their small circular screens and black plastic dials belonged in a museum of aviation history. Every piece of equipment was dialed to the off position as if the workers had gone home for the night; it was 12:15 PM.

Having found no one with whom to negotiate, O'Kelly and Keita retraced their steps to the terminal, which was also nearly deserted. Dette noticed that the massive photo of Omar Ibrahim Lassoso that had hung in the departure lounge when she was there for her trip to Paris had been removed. Two *boubou*-dressed old women flung large wet rags attached to frail ropes around the floor; the airport owned no brooms.

The arrival board was dark as there were no arrivals or departures. All flights had been canceled because of the politico-military disorder in Zinani.

A tiny souvenir shop, the only place in the city other than the *Hotel de la Libertè*, that advertised that it accepted Master Card and Visa, featured wooden sculptures, painted gourds, bright bedspreads, and dust. It obviously had not been conducting business for weeks. The bar was less dusty but equally unmanned. Aeroflot, Saudi Air, Air Afrique, Air Ivoire, Air France, and Air Zinani all had desks; all were unstaffed. Dette lifted a couple of phones -- nothing. There was no electricity although the massive windows let in more than enough light. She approached one of the cleaners. "*Òu est le director du aéroport?*"

The lady kept sweeping with her rope and moist rag. *Aw ka kene, wa?*" Bernadette uttered the only African phrase she ever learned, "How are you?" in Bambara, with Fulani, the two most commonly spoken languages in the country. She wanted to know if the lady was ignoring her, deaf, or not able to speak French. The sweeper looked up, surprised, and spouted off a quick sentence that had absolutely no significance for the American. O'Kelly patted her on the shoulder as she would a Labrador retriever, "*Merci, Mademoiselle.*" She went back to her chore.

Dette questioned one of the olive-drabbed military guards, an officer, in the arrival lounge. Her French was more than good -- probably university trained. "Sorry, Madam, I know no more than you do. We were assigned here to prevent Lassoso's people from fleeing the country. The only people we've seen are those cleaning ladies. Everybody else left when the government fell."

"How will the airport run without staff?"

"It won't. The airport is closed. For three days. We don't want any counterrevolutionaries flying in."

"Have you heard that an American plane – an air ambulance will be landing here in two or three hours?"

"No madam, I have not. That is not possible. The airport is closed to all traffic. There is no one in traffic control. There is no fire brigade, no one to deliver the passenger stairs or handle the luggage. It is impossible. I am sorry."

"No, I am sorry, Lieutenant. The Government of the United States of America is bringing in a large aircraft, a Boeing 720, to evacuate one of our diplomats who was injured during the early days of the disturbances. We insist that we be allowed to land the plane. He will die if we can't evacuate him."

"I cannot grant that permission. Only a member of the Interim

Victory Team can do so."

"Is Oumou Kinsa on that team?"

"Yes, Madam, Miss Kinsa is very much on that team. Why, do you know her?"

"Yes, Lieutenant, I know Miss Kinsa quite well. How do I contact her?"

Before an answer was possible, the sound of breaking glass rang out. Both women spun around to see a massive plate of window glass empty from its frame into a pile of shards on the sidewalk, only a few feet behind where they had been talking. Seconds later, a gunshot was immediately followed by the splintering of another window.

"They're shooting at us," yelled O'Kelly in English. She ran toward the Toyota a few feet away in which Mohammed Keita had been waiting. The lieutenant ducked behind a trash barrel and barked orders in Fulani to the half-dozen other guards. One of her charges, a small teenager with plaited cornrows barely visible beneath her army cap, lay motionless with chunks of glass on and around her. Bernadette did not wait to hear what the orders were or to learn the source of the shots or the fate of the young revolutionary guard. The car sped toward the airport exit and within seconds was on the road back to the center of the city.

"Calm down Bernadette," pacified DCM Grant. "Describe what you saw."

The still agitated Political Officer relayed the story of her fruitless tour of the control tower, the emptiness of the airport with the exception of the char force, and the discussion with the young lieutenant and its noisy conclusion.

"Could you see who was shooting?"

"Huh uh. It had to be from the parking lot in front of the arrival terminal. It wasn't from inside."

"Why not?"

"Nobody there."

"Didn't you say there were some sweepers?"

"Yeah, but they were just little old ladies.

"Ever hear of Ma Barker?"

"Sure ... you know, it was sort of weird to see sweepers in the giant room with nobody else nearby. Come to think of it, if the boss wasn't around, a normal sweeper probably wouldn't sweep." Bernadette thought, as she had often thought before, how good Ernestine was at her job, asking just the right questions to get her people to come up with the conclusions that she had come up with herself.

"But why would little old ladies in flip-flops shoot at the female guards?"

"I bet you can answer that one, Dette."

"Probably owe their jobs to Lassoso."

"Right. There isn't a government employee from Foreign Minister to garbage man that isn't beholden to OIL, and a lot of them will do anything asked, even though the old man is in jail. Gotta figure that Lassoso had a set of plans for what to do in case of a coup, and part of that involved getting guns in the hands of people whose loyalty he could count on. Not a bad job, sweeping in an airport."

"How could the women from PPD be so stupid to let them inside, without checking?"

"They fooled an American college grad, didn't they?"

"Yeah, you're right."

"It's not just the airport. We've heard reports of shootings all over town and some from Sokimbo too. Mainly innocents. A six-year-old boy died near the TV station and a mom and her baby were killed with one bullet in a market. We haven't heard the last of killing in this one.

Tell me your take on the airport. Can we get the 720 down?

"The airport is fine but there's no staff. No one to do anything, including put out a fire, move whatever it is that lets you get out of the plane or put a sick diplomat back into it. Oumou's lieutenant made it real clear that she didn't think there was any way to land our plane."

" Bernadette, I don't know anything about airplanes or airports, but I can't imagine that we can't get a plane down and back up without a bunch of Zins."

"You remember, don't you, that the longer runway is out and only the 1500 meter one is usable. Did you ever find out what it takes to land a 720?"

"I heard that a safe landing takes about twice that distance and that in a pinch you can do it with 2000 meters. Did you notice what there is at the end of the runway? Forest, I bet."

"Yeah, remember they put Lassoso's golf course with tall neem trees at the east end, meaning that all planes have to land east to west, even when the winds are behind them. But at the west end, it's a big expanse of flat land, with a few patches of millet and sorghum.

"Looks like we're going to see an east to west landing."

"You mean we're good to go?" asked Bernadette, nervously.

"Not our call. The pilot has to make his own decision. All we can do is give him the numbers. But from our viewpoint, it has to be a go; our only other option, is to let Chen die." The DCM, who had spent a significant time sleeping with Mr. Chen, spoke as if she had never met the man.

"Doesn't the Ambassador have to sign off on this?"

"Get serious, Dette. Haven't you been watching what's been going on in the last few days? The Old Man is losing it. He can't make any decisions on his own. He puts on a show to make some of the less perceptive think that he's running things, but it's crystal clear that he's retired and wants only to get out of here with respect and a pension. I'll just give him a note to sign, approving the landing. He might ask a question or two, but the answers won't mean a thing. Whatever we ask for he gives."

"Sad story. They say he was a good officer early on; he sure got promoted fast, but that was in the days of the Good Old Boys. Harvard, Yale, Princeton, and Georgetown. One of those degrees and you went somewhere; a diploma from someplace else, not so quick. Ain't the same anymore; you gotta be Black, Latino, or Native American, plus add two X chromosomes and you're in like fin."

"Flynn ... in like Flynn."

"You know, Dette, I don't like it. I'm always thinking that everyone thinks I got where I am 'cause I'm a black woman."

"You're projecting Ernestine. You know you're good at this stuff and wouldn't be DCM at your age if you weren't. If there are some that think otherwise, screw 'em."

"Thanks, I need to hear that once in a while. But, we're off the subject. We've got a plane to land. How are we going to communicate with the pilot? If what you found in the tower is still true, there isn't anyone there to squawk."

"How about our communicators?" Embassies always have at least two IT people to operate most any type of telecommunication device.

"Good idea. Eddie deQuervain knows radio. Give him a call." DeQuervain, all 300 pounds of him, including the six-inch beard and unruly red/gray hair, was a military retiree, like most of the other communicators in the Foreign Service. He had spent his twenty in the Navy, some of it in subs until he became too fat to fit. He smoked like an Eastern European factory and was the commissary's number one customer for Budweiser.

"We've got to be at the airport in two and a half hours. That's an hour before ETA. In the meantime, in addition to Eddie, we'll need someone who knows vehicles to move the stairs over to the plane when it stops. Would you get Prudholme going on that, Dette?"

Grant headed for the Ambassador's dark suite while Bernadette bounded down the steps to the Administrative Office. Strangely, the door was closed. She tried the knob. Locked. Knocked. "Just a minute, please." Prudholme came to the door, chin to his waste, looking like he had just been demoted to first year Consular Officer. "Can I help you, Bernadette?"

"What happened to you, Connie?" O'Kelly had always gotten along OK with the Administrator everybody loved to hate. Often she had tried to become a confidant for him, as few others were interested in that role. No luck.

"Nothin'. Just a bit of a stomachache. Lots of stress. I'll be better as soon as this is over and everybody is safe."

She noticed the Band-Aid on his arm and remembered that he was one that the doc had called on to give blood for Chen. "Maybe you're weak from the transfusion?"

"Yeah, maybe. What do you want?" He was even more brusque than usual.

"The plane's coming in in about three hours and we've got to get prepared. I've just come from there. There were PPD guards and somebody from OIL's crew who shot up the place, but nobody to run the services. Not even anyone in the control tower.

"We're going to get Eddie to communicate with the pilot. We need someone to move the machine that lets people get off and on the airplane. Can you round up a GSO guy who knows cars and trucks?"

"Come on, Bernadette, I'm not in any shape to do that. Get Oswald to do it." She had never seen him turn down a task; he always was asking for more, anything to add to his resume and fatten his annual evaluation.

"You forgot that Ralph's on leave? I'm just passing on Ernestine Grant's requests, Con."

"Tell her I'm sick."

"OK, Con. I'll take care of it." She walked out, closing his door with more emphasis than usual.

Colonel Martin Whipple, USAF, had graduated from the Air Force Academy, top third of the class. A superb baseball player, he planned to do his four years in uniform and then try to go pro. Getting in his way was the fact that he was shot out of the sky by a North Vietnamese gunner and spent three years at the Hanoi Hilton. At release, the major leagues showed no interest, nor did his wife who, during his incarceration, had moved in with an investment banker. Whipple decided to stay in the Air Force, developing some fame during the First Gulf War by accurately dropping bombs on two bridges, three missile launchers, and an Iraqi convoy. He got enough TV coverage that his fellow fliers called him the The Great Whip.

He had lifted off from Sicily an hour earlier and had just overflown Tunis. ETA at Keita-Coulibaly was two hours away.

The preflight briefing dealt with the runway problem. "Two runways in Donolu, the long one down for repairs, the short one 500 meters shorter than anything he'd ever landed a bird of this size on. Trees at the east end, clear on the west. Revolution in the city. No big deal that the airport is closed. We've gone into closed airports, even at night, as long as we can see where we're landing. Hell, I've been to Donolu a couple of months ago, to deliver some medical goods for the hospital - the time that woman Army General got sick and we had to haul her out."

The copilot was Lieutenant Colonel Nu Lin Li ("Call me Jack"). A first generation Chinese-American, he was reared by a journeyman welder. Jack graduated from a two-year community college, joined the Air Force and was accepted to Officers Training, where he became the Rudolph Valentino of his squadron. He was, in the words of the Eagles, brutally handsome. He sought and found women who were terminally pretty. He was thrilled to be offered the slot as #2 to the Great Whip.

"Air Force, this is American Embassy, calling. Do you read me?"

"What's this, 'Do you read me?' shit?" asked Nu of the Whip, radio off. Whipple shrugged.

"Air Force reads you loud and clear, American Embassy. Please identify which American Embassy you are speaking for."

"Sorry. This is Communicator deQuervain of the American Embassy, Donolu, Zinani."

"Ah hah, our destination. How can I help you Mr. Communicator?"

"Sir, we need to know your ETA."

"Approximately 1430 hours we will be over the airport." It was 1215. "Please tell us the situation on the runway. We understand that the longer one is out of action and that we're going to have to land in 1500 meters."

"That's affirmative. By the way, the weather here is pretty nasty. It's raining and there's a big wind out of the West."

"I thought it never rained there. But, that's no big deal. How big is the wind?"

"No idea, Sir. There's a lot of leaves being blown out of the trees."

"You say it's out of the west? We were planning on landing west to east. We'll never stop this bird doing that, and they say that there's a golf course at the other end with some tall trees on it."

"Sir, we've thought of that. The General Services Officer assigned a a couple of his locals with chainsaws to make the course a hell of a lot less challenging. You won't have any obstacles to worry about if you come in from the east."

"Thanks, Mr. Communicator. Sorry I didn't bring my golf clubs. What's the status of the ground crew?"

"No such thing, Sir. Our Political Officer visited the airport to set things up and found the place empty, except for a couple of old lady sweepers who proceeded to shoot up the terminal. The control tower was unmanned; that's why you got an old submariner talking to you, pushing a bunch of buttons he's never seen before."

"What do you mean they shot up the place? Is there a terminal there at all? More to the point, is there anyone who's going to try to shoot us out of the sky or point their guns at us when we try to deplane? I've got a horny co-pilot that doesn't want to spend any more time aboard than possible."

"No, Sir. The building is still standing. No windows but plenty of walls, floors, and ceilings. And as far as we can tell, the new government has cleared the area of any shooters. The bad guys have more pressing things to worry about than shooting down your bird."

"How reassuring. Let me put on our doctor so he can get the lowdown on your patient." Captain Zebulon Fellows, Flight Surgeon, future ENT, had been a last minute substitute for Colonel Kript, General Surgeon, who usually accompanied high-level medevacs, but had just entered rehab for his codeine addiction. Fellows much preferred ear tubes and nose jobs to opening chests and abdomens, but had had his way paid through medical school by the US Air Force and was not in position to complain about the assignment.

"This is Captain Fellows. How is Mr. Cheng?"

"Good to meet ya', Doc. Mr. Chen isn't too good. Our RMO, Dr. Eisenstat, says he's real sick.

"RMO, what's that?

"Regional Medical Officer – he covers all of West Africa." He told me to tell you that his blood pressure is 80 and 60, whatever that means and his pulse is 120 beats an hour."

"A minute?"

"Yeah, maybe that's right. He's bleeding and getting blood from some of the people at the Embassy, including the doctor's wife they tell me."

"Where's he bleeding from?"

"Heck if I know. Where he got shot I guess."

"Thanks. Tell your RMO that we're prepared to open his belly or his chest on the plane. The operating room is fully equipped and we've got a trained staff." Fellows didn't mention that he'd been the head surgeon on abdominal trauma cases only twice before.

"Willco." DeQuervain figured that still meant that he would cooperate. Whipple and Nu had no idea what he was talking about. "Captain...er, Colonel, we've got two more passengers for you to take out of here. Also a body."

"Who might they be?"

"The wife of the doctor, Mrs. Eisenstat. Her father died and she is trying to get home for the funeral. And our Admin Officer, Mr. Prudholme. They didn't tell me why he's going. Probably has something to do with money; it always does with him. The body belongs to a Peace Corps volunteer who was killed in the coup."

"Yeah, we heard about that on TV. Awful. But, we got plenty room; no sweat if the customs people don't mind."

"There aren't any customs people. At least there weren't an hour ago. We're not going to let things like exit visas and airport tax get in our way."

"How old is Mrs. Eisenstat, Mr. Communicator?" asked Jack Nu, a gleam in his eye.

"Never asked. Probably about 50." The gleam disappeared.

"I better let you get back to flying. We've got a lot to do before you land. This is American Embassy. Over and out."

"Air Force here. Yeah, over and out." Nu and the Whip glanced at each other smirkingly.

Muammar Gadaffi was not happy with the results of his incursion into his neighbor's politics. And to lose to a bunch of women? He famously had had a contingent of female bodyguards, but he was a traditional Muslim at heart. Women were not meant to be leaders.

"Mobilize the Rapid Deployment Force! We're going into Donolu! I want this woman, Kinsa, brought here." Libya's Rapid Deployment Force included one Lear Jet, four enlisted men with AK-47s, a lieutenant and a major. They had never been deployed, rapidly or slowly. The enlisted men were easy to find. It was harder to round up the officers. The Major was located cuckolding a superior officer's wife while the Lieutenant was waxing the Major's BMW.

The Force was rapidly deployed at 1245 hours, some five hours after Gaddafi's order was issued. Its ETA at Donolu was 1430 hours.

XXX

The manifest of departing passengers for the 720 included: Chen Wang, the injured; Jillian Eisenstat, the bereaved, a nurse posing as a...nurse; Conrad Prudholme, the HIV positive; and Jenny Addison, the deceased.

Chen was to be transported at the last possible minute in the Toyota ambulance with Electra and Eisenstat at his side. A gurney and an IV pole, plus an outsized red cross would be the only features distinguishing the vehicle from a garden-variety van.

The remains of Jenny arrived in a Peace Corps pick-up driven by Director Willie Anderson, accompanied by his deputy, Mr. Singh. Several of her fellow volunteers asked that they be able to go to the airport, but Anderson, anxious to avoid additional victims, vetoed the request.

Mr. Prudholme and Ms. Eisenstat rode the shaky Embassy bus, accompanied by Americans and Zinanians, who were to do the heavy lifting and paper work needed to get the plane down, loaded, and back in the air.

The streets of the city were mostly devoid of signs of everyday activity -- a few cars and bicycles, no buses or vans, and a rare, distant gunshot. Several military transports, now packed with ex-Lassoso troops, who had changed allegiance, were in motion.

Back at the Embassy, Lori Burkitt, Ernestine Grant, and the Ambassador sat around the circular table in his office. Spent Styrofoam coffee cups, half eaten croissants, and a general mustiness remained as evidence of the war room atmosphere of the previous angst-filled hours.

Burkitt had just entered the scene from her secure offices in the Chancery. There, she learned of the late breaking events from CNN, as well as their often less reliable super-spy stuff garnered from satellites and human intelligence. "Gaddafi's guys are stirring in the New Akron area."

"Same ones that the PPD stopped before?" asked Fairchild.

"Yup, one and the same. They didn't lose any tanks. Looks like they're gonna try again. But it'll take 'em four or five hours to get on the road, another couple of hours to hit the city. We've got some time before the city goes to hell."

What's the story on the SCUDs?"

"Damned if I know. None of us has a clue as to what would be done with those three missiles. Unpredictable as Gaddafi is, he can't possibly think it would make any sense to unleash terror on Donolu."

"You think we should evacuate all the Americans?" The Ambassador had to know that only he, with the knowledge and approval of Washington, could answer that question..

"Hell, no. We run and Gaddafi scores his biggest victory in years. All of our houses, our refrigerators and dishwashers, our cars, our dogs, cats, and birds enter the local economy. Plus, the revolution goes immediately to hell. The women of the PPD become a joke of history and the US is seen as a buffoon. Democracy in Africa suffers a horrible setback. We've got to hang tough." Grant nodded in approval.

"What happens if we stay?"

"Worst case scenario is that Gaddafi takes over the key places like the Palace, the Army barracks, and the TV station, and extracts OIL and family from prison. The revolution is sunk. But there's no way he's going to come after the expats, nor let the Zins do us any harm. An egomaniac he is, stupid he is not."

"OK, Lori, I'm convinced. So what do we do? Sit on our asses and observe?" inquired the DCM.

"Not if we want this revolution to succeed and not if we don't want a friggin' civil war in this country. Without Gaddafi's tanks, the PPD stays in place. With 'em, they may very well be out. Simple equation. PPD goes and there'll be some battles between the supporters of the revolution and the, shall we say, loyalists, but no way the PPD comes back, nor would any other democratic regime. Lassoso, or some other military son-of-a-bitch that Libya likes better, is more firmly entrenched than ever. And another African attempt to improve the lot of its people is blown away. Huh-uh, we don't want that."

"So?"

"So, we've got to tell Gaddafi to turn off his engines and keep the tanks in New Akron."

"Why us? Shouldn't the French do it?" asked Fairchild.

"Only one super-power on this planet. We gotta do it. And, it's gotta come from on high. Get the word to the Department that the Secretary needs to call Tripoli, ASAP.

"Plus, you should probably call your old buddy, Ambassador Mukhtar,

and tell him how we'd look on their coming to town with armored vehicles." Mukhtar had been Gaddafi's Ambassador for a decade. "I wrote a few talking points for you, Sir."

Fairchild read it and handed it to Ernestine Grant who nodded affirmatively. "Good work, Lori."

"You're really something, Lori. How'd you get so good so fast?" asked the Ambassador.

"Thanks for the compliment, Sir. It's nice to be recognized. But if I am so good at this, I've got a major question."

"What's that?"

"How come a smart, supposedly good looking woman like me can't get herself laid?"

The Air Force jet was cruising at 550 knots over the bleak Sahara. Nothing of consequence had happened, nor was anything expected to happen in the hour or so before scheduled touchdown on 1500 meters of bumpy tarmac.

Whipple had done the calculations in his head a dozen times. If they landed in the first 50 meters of the runway, and were able to activate the reverse thrusts and brakes immediately, they would get the machine stopped with maybe 100 meters to spare at the other end. If they went on beyond, they still could stop it without any damage, probably. He was going in, unless the chances of a crash were high, and at this point, he judged them to be low. He'd have to reconnoiter when he got close.

Captain Fellows was worrying about his skills. Ears, noses, and throats -- those were easy. Gunshot victims - that's something else. He had seen several during training in Chicago but was never the number one surgeon. And now, the impressively unprepared Dr. Fellows was winging his way to the bedside of a man, whom, if he died, would be the center of an international incident. Too bad Chen didn't need a nose job.

"Jolly Roger 16. This is Overseer 4."

"Go ahead Overseer." Jolly Roger was the evacuation plane and Overseer, the AWACS, the airborne early warning and control vehicle that monitored the skies for the US Air Force.

The surveillance plane, or one just like it, was always in the air around the Mediterranean. Too much of interest to the United States was always happening in the neighborhood for American intelligence not to do everything possible to be aware of it.

"We have just identified an aircraft departing from Tripoli. Its profile is not that of one of their MIGs, and it's a lot smaller than a transport, either civilian or military. It looks like a Lear Jet. It's flying on a southwest course at 18,000 feet on a line to Donolu, at an air speed of 425 knots. As you are headed in the same direction, we thought you'd want to know about it."

"We are, indeed. What's its destination?" asked Lt. Col. Nu.

"We do not know where it is going. It may be on its way to Abidjan or even Lomé, although it would have to stop for fuel along the way. However, at that rate of speed, if it's Donolu Airport, it will likely be touching down at 1430 hours."

"If that's the case, we will land on top of each other."

Marylou Fairchild had not had ten minutes alone with her husband in more than 24 hours. She had watched an old Doris Day movie, played a few hands of solitaire, read most of a sci-fi book, and changed outfits half a dozen times. As the traffic had settled and the gunshots had, for the most part, ceased, she decided to go the Embassy to express a personal opinion. Judy Ann made no effort to stop her from entering the office. The Chief of Mission was deeply involved in the business section of the Herald Tribune.

"Holly, I want to get out of here."

"Huh?"

"I want out of here. I want to go on that plane that's coming for Mr. Chen. I hate this place; I despise all the people in this country. I hate Africa and I don't want to die here. You've got a job here. I don't. I want out!"

"It's not that easy, Marylou."

"It is too. I'm the Ambassador's wife. The Ambassador can put anybody on that plane that he wants. And I want, damn it. And I want to take Gatsby. You know what happens if there is an evacuation. All the animals are left behind and the dogs and cats get eaten."

"Come on, dear. This is Africa, not China. Africans don't eat dogs, especially Boston terriers. They think Gatsby is a rat. And think, please, of how it would look if the Ambassador's wife is on this plane and all the other spouses are left behind. Forget it!"

"Damn it. That ass-kissing Administrative Officer, Prickholme, of yours is going. How'd he get on the passenger list?"

"Medical problem is all I know. Doc Eisenstat told me that he was medevacing him. My guess it's a psychological problem. An anal retentive like Conrad doesn't do real well during revolutions."

"Is his mousy little wife going with him?"

"No, she's not. Chen is going. Prudholme is going and Mrs. Eisenstat is going because her father died."

"I'm aware of that, Holly. I can claim that my father died, too."

"Don't be an idiot. The whole post knows about your father's death." Marylou Fairchild's father had long ago committed suicide after being charged with financial misdeeds.

"Goddammit, I do not want to stay. Get me out of here!" She slammed her clenched fist on the coffee table, knocking a ceramic Fulani bowl to a shattering demise.

The Ambassador uprighted his recliner, got to his feet, and with index finger chopstick straight and neck veins fully dilated, said to his wife whom he had loved, honored, and obeyed for 25 years, "Get the hell out of this room now. You will stay in this country until I tell you that you can leave or until this nation returns to its normal state. In the meantime, you will act as if you live in paradise."

Marylou Fairchild, unaccustomed as she was to being yelled at by the man whom she felt she could manipulate at will, slammed the door as she left. Judy Ann Dean nodded and smiled as her boss's wife departed the suite. Holden Fairchild, III, felt a mixture of anger and pride stirring in his soul. He kicked the pieces of the shattered brown clay pot under the table and re-reclined, fixating on the New York Stock Exchange quotes for the session of six days earlier.

The vital signs and the blood count showed that Chen continued to bleed, slowly. He had received all three available units of blood and his red cell count, while not normal, was high enough to make Eisenstat comfortable that he wouldn't die before the 720, with plenty of B-negative units aboard, arrived. His fever hovered between 102 and 103. The powerful antibiotics had no effect at bringing the temperature down. Clearly he needed more than the medicines and Eisenstat's meager surgical talents had to offer. He had to get to the airport and on the plane.

The elevator ride from the fourth to the ground floor was, as usual, a trial for Michael. He couldn't take the steps; he had to be at his patient's side until he was safely in the hands of the airborne trauma team. The patient and all the life-saving fluids and devices were loaded into the faux-ambulance.

At approximately the same moment the ambulance turned out of the Embassy driveway, the armored Chevrolet prepared to pull away from the Ambassadorial Residence. Fairchild had gone by his home to pick up his wife, figuring that it was politically crucial for her to be at the airport for the departure of the critically ill economic officer and the deceased Peace Corps volunteer He wore a dark suit, too hot for Donolu, but his only one appropriate for the occasion. Marylou was dressed in a dark green silk suit and yellow hat, as if she was on her way to a Viennese garden party. Trailing behind her, on a retractable leash, was the fifteen pound, black and white dog, Gatsby.

"What the hell is that all about, Marylou? The goddam dog is not going to the airport."

"Holly, I'm fed up with you yelling at me. Gatsby hasn't been out of the yard in days. This dog needs walks or he's going to get fat and die of a heart attack. There's gonna be a lot of time at the airport. Your driver can walk him."

"Christ, Marylou, you are out of your mind!"

"It's either the dog and me or neither, Mr. Ambassador." She could be icily sarcastic.

"OK, bring him. I hope to hell there aren't any CNN cameras there. And, by the way, dogs don't get heart attacks from not taking walks."

"How do you know?" He had no answer.

The Peace Corps Ford pick-up was fifteen years-old, with over 300,000 miles on it. It had carried everything: manure, seed, water pumps for agriculture programs; tilapia fingerlings, fish food and algaecide for the fishery programs; books, pens, paper, and desks for the education volunteers; and as many as 12 volunteers at a time. A decade before it carried a dead American. An assistant director had unknowingly driven through a military check point at night. The new recruit on duty assumed the driver was a guerilla and fired his first, and last, rifle shot.

Jenny Addison was the first Peace Corps volunteer to leave Zinani in a coffin. Willie Anderson feared that her father's political prominence would mean that no volunteer would ever again be assigned to Zinani.

Ulysses Singh, in white silk pants and shirt, and a spotless turban, accompanied Anderson, attired in jeans, sweatshirt, and cowboy boots. A strange looking pair they were, different in all respects but the color of their skin. Racially, socially, politically - they couldn't have been less alike. They were good friends and equally saddened by their cargo.

The old engine sputtered to a start with Anderson at the wheel. The unadorned coffin lay in the dirty bed of the truck, still partially filled with cold-mix tar that a volunteer had been using to patch up the road to his village.

The Toyota bus made its rounds. Gunnery Sergeant Rice and Frank Norbert rode shotgun. Each carried a firearm. Osgood Genu, the weightlifter, had been recruited to help in crowd control.

Bernadette O'Kelly's was the first house on the route. She had put on her standard brown dress with the scuffed cordovan shoes. Her hair displayed the stick-togetherness of three shampoo-free days.

Prudholme's house was the next stop. His five-foot Bhutanese wife, Peema, and the twin five-year-old girls stood at his side as he approached the bus. "Why are you going, Daddy?"

"Daddy's got to work in America."

Eddie deQuervain boarded with two toolboxes full of everything he could round up that might be helpful in communicating with a 720.

The last stop before the Embassy was the doctor's place. Jill was still clad in the blue dress in which she donated a pint of blood. Taking some liberty with the one bag restriction, she brought a massive duffel bag that could carry a year's worth of clothes for her flight home.

The bus stopped at the Chancery to pick up the half dozen locals who would be doing the real work. A big box of MREs (Meals Ready to Eat, made famous in the Gulf War) was tossed in the back. Just in case. Maybe the crew would be hungry. Perhaps the cuisine could be used as bribes.

The Chevrolet transported the Ambassador and his wife, plus DCM Grant who sat in front. The squash-nosed Boston terrier snorted between his master and mistress. Minutes after leaving the house, Grant heard from the back seat, "Ernestine, I want to get on that plane!" The First Lady of Embassy, Donolu, was requesting permission to leave from her husband's employee.

Grant was incredulous. She had never been married and had only witnessed her own, TV-sitcom-like, overtly content parents interact. She was fully aware that the last few days had made her the functional leader of the Mission, but it never occurred to her that she had the power to overrule the Ambassador in a family matter. "Please, Marylou, you know that I can't do anything about that. The decision is Mr. Ambassador's."

"See Holly, you can make the decision to let me get on the plane! Your DCM said you could."

"Yes, dear, I can make that decision. But I am not going to make that decision. You are not getting on that plane. End of discussion!"

"Goddamit, I will discuss anything I want! Don't tell me when the discussion has ended!"

Not only did her screaming startle the dog and cause the snorting to cease, it prompted the driver to turn around to see what was happening. At the precise moment, an old woman on a bike exited an alley into the path of the Chevy. Only a last second swerve prevented her being hit by the hood ornament. The left fender of the big American car struck the bike's front tire and the woman fell into a puddle of filthy rain water, her cargo of tomatoes scattered over a wide area.

"Oh, Jesus, what now?" the Ambassador yelled.

The driver quickly stopped the car and jumped out. It didn't require the trained eye of an orthopedist to determine that she had a broken right leg, nor a mechanic to diagnose a bike that was totaled. The alert woman looked over first her tomatoes, then her bike, and then her leg. Within seconds a crowd began to assemble. Conventional wisdom in an impoverished country says that if you are the cause of an accident, get the hell out of there, as quickly as you can. More than one Westerner has been killed or maimed by an unruly crowd when they stayed to check on the condition of the victim.

"Sir, give me some money to give to this lady, please," the driver requested calmly and politely, but with a sense of urgency.

"How much?"

"Maybe 500 lassosos." About $15 at the previous week's exchange rate.

Fairchild pulled out his wallet. A couple of 100 lassoso notes were all he had. Like most people of great importance, he was rarely called on to spend money on the spot. "Honey, do you have 500?"

"Honey ... what's this honey shit?"

"Just give me 500 lassosos, Marylou." She made no motion in the direction of her purse.

"I've got a thousand Lassoso note, sir," Ernestine said after checking her bag.

"I doubt the lady has change," he responded.

Grant had to suppress her shock and choke down her laughter. "Sir, I think we can afford it. Maybe we can take a few of the undamaged tomatoes as change." She regretted her attempt at humor immediately; the driver, taking her literally, picked up a few of the better looking specimens before Grant asked him to stop and give them back to the injured cyclist.

The driver quickly restarted the engine and drove away. The victim was loaded into a taxi for her trip to the hospital. The event had consumed less than five minutes.

The Embassy bus had no trouble getting to the airport. As the vehicle turned off the main thoroughfare onto the road to Keita-Coulibaly International, a large Mercedes limo made the turn from the other direction. Only Bernadette O'Kelly recognized the car; she had ridden in it the previous day when Oumou Kinsa had called her into the Palace. The tinted windows prevented identifying the person in the back seat. The driver was the same young woman who had driven O'Kelly on her maiden voyage.

Security Officer Norbert ordered the bus driver to go out onto the tarmac. There was no one at the guard post to prevent that from happening. Bernadette noticed both that the terminal was guarded by female troops and that there had been no attempt to sweep up the glass from the shot-out windows. She then remembered that the shooters and the sweepers were the same women.

It was 1:55 PM, 35 minutes before the planned touchdown of the 720. Lori Burkitt, having arrived ten minutes earlier, stood next to her agency's Range Rover, smoking a Gauloise.

Before the bus had come to a complete stop and emptied, the Mercedes Benz pulled up next to the Range Rover. The driver hopped out, went to the right rear door and opened it. Exiting was a woman in sharply pressed but ill-fitting olive-drab fatigues. The driver was dismissed with an officious flick of the passenger's wrist. Dette had to clear her eyes before she could recognize that the woman in military garb was her old friend, Oumou Kinsa. Oumou sported the bars of a Lieutenant General. Bernadette could hardly believe that her one-time good buddy and fellow lover of Suleiman Sacco had become not only the Chief of State, but also the highest officer in the Zinanian Army.

The Ambassadorial Chevy joined the two cars and one bus in what had now become a significant parking lot. The Embassy vehicle screeched to a halt next to the Mercedes and again an important person had the door opened for him. Fairchild exited, followed by his obviously agitated spouse. Ms. Grant left the front seat without assistance.

The Ambassador did a double take on seeing the short woman standing a few feet away. He had never met the new President of the Republic and General of the Army but recognized her immediately. Walking toward him, she passed within two feet of Bernadette, but paid no more attention to her than she would have a flagpole. Bernadette did notice that there were at least a hundred soldiers, probably half female, in the immediate vicinity, all with rifles of multiple sizes and shapes. General Joro had been in the back seat of the car with General Kinsa; he walked lock step behind her as she approached the Ambassador.

"Mr. Ambassador, I am Lieutenant General Oumou Kinsa. I am so pleased to finally meet you after we have shared the same land and same friends for so long."

"I am flattered, Ms. President ... or should I call you General?"

"Either is fine, sir. Please meet my Vice President, Major General Joro."

"Yes, we have met. Several times at receptions, I believe."

"Mr. Ambassador, might I ask why you are here at the airport at this time?"

As she finished her question, the ambulance came into view. The glass IV fluid bottle was clearly seen through the window. "As I am sure you had heard, General, we have a badly injured diplomat, our First Secretary for Commercial and Economic Affairs. He was injured as a bystander in a gun battle that occurred on the streets outside our doctor's house. He must be moved to Paris for surgery. We have a plane coming in to take him out. In addition, the aircraft will be removing the remains of Miss Addison, the Peace Corps volunteer shot by your soldiers."

"Ah, how unfortunate. I had heard that someone had been injured in a tragic case of mistaken identity. I did not know that she had died. Our deepest condolences ... but I must wonder why I have not heard of this plane that you have coming. Somebody should have told our Air Minister. A visit by an official airplane of the United States is a very important event for our new government and we would like to prepare a proper welcome."

Ernestine saw that the discussion had gotten to the point where she felt it necessary to step in. "General, allow me to reintroduce myself; I am Ernestine Grant, the Deputy Chief of Mission." They had met more than once, but Grant felt it important to act appropriately subservient. "We were not aware that you had named an Air Minister. Our Political Officer, Miss O'Kelly, whom I believe you have met, came to the airport to alert someone to the arrival of our plane, but found no one here. When you arrived, we thought that meant that you knew that our plane was arriving and decided to welcome it."

"No, Ms. Grant, we are here to welcome another aircraft. The Republic of Libya is sending a high level delegation to discuss the recent events with us. In view of their role in the support of my predecessor, we must try to ease the strains between our new government and theirs."

Lori Burkitt overheard the comments. As Fairchild had begun talking to the President, she pulled Grant by the arm to the outer rim of the circle. "That high level delegation is what Gaddafi calls a Rapid Deployment Force. It ain't no friggin high level delegation here to discuss anything. All they'll need to see is the little President standing there and they'll grab her by the tits and pull her into their airplane and whisk her back to their Mediterranean paradise, bringing the VP with 'em. There goes the revolution. I can't believe how stupid Oumou, excuse me Madam General/Madam President, is."

Grant returned to the discussion and spoke with authority. "General Kinsa, we have reason to believe that what you are calling a 'high level delegation' is a group of Colonel Gaddafi's men coming to cause trouble. If they find you at the airport, they may well kidnap you and take you back to Tripoli, allowing Mr. Lassoso back into power." Fairchild nodded in agreement.

"Impossible. You may not believe Gaddafi. I have my doubts, too, but his Foreign Secretary, who I have known since we trained together in the US, told me that they're just coming to talk. I believe that it's against the Geneva Convention to kidnap another country's chief of state."

"Excuse me? Are you suggesting that it is in accord with the Convention to bring down a Pan Am plane over Scotland, killing hundreds? You think your new friend Colonel Gaddafi is likely to follow international guidelines when you've got one of his puppets behind bars.

Please, Madam President, think about it!"

"Jolly Roger, this is Donolu Airport, American Embassy." Eddie deQuervain felt powerful. Only he could talk to the pilot, hundreds of miles away and 38,000 feet in the air.

"Go ahead," responded the Great Whip, curtly.

"What is your location?"

"Hell if I know. There's a lot of sand seven miles underneath us. Must be over a desert. Sorry, we are over Northern Niger, forty-seven minutes from your location. Weather's perfect, no clouds in sight. Probably been five years since there were any clouds in sight at this spot."

"We've heard some rumors about a Libyan plane coming this way. The new President says that it's a delegation of officials coming to talk. Appears more sinister to us."

"Yeah, we've had the same reports. Our source thinks it's a Lear or something like it. It doesn't look like a warplane to them. We don't know if they know anything about us. Libya doesn't have much in the way of high-tech intelligence. But, the bad news is that we're both on a course to land at your location at the exact same time, 1430 hours."

"If it's a Lear, he'll have a lot easier time getting down than you."

"Understood. We'll let him put down first and get out of the way. You tell him that."

"Not me. I just deal with our guys, like you."

"Not so fast, Mr. Communicator. You may have to let him know that we're around. I don't mind chancing it on a short runway. I sure as hell don't want to bump into some private jet on the way down."

"Roger. How do I communicate with them?"

"Same way you did with us, except call them Libyan Lear Jet rather than Jolly Roger. Anyone with a license to fly a Lear has to be pretty good in English."

"OK, Captain, I'll try to speak to them. By the way, what's your name? If we're going to be trying to get you on the ground, I better know who I'm talking to. I'm Eddie."

"Whipple, Colonel Marty Whipple. Not Captain. Colonel. Most people who know me call me Whip. Up to you."

"Got it, Whip. You'll be glad to know the rain stopped. If it stays stopped, the ground will be dry in ten minutes."

"Wind?"

"The windsock is now limper than my dick after a long night with a stewardess."

"Eddie, I'm glad that there aren't any big winds, but let's have a little airway decorum."

"Huh?"

"Let's watch our language. Anyone can tune into this frequency."

"Roger that, Sir." DeQuervain turned fire engine red, but there was no one else in the tower to notice.

The Americans and the Zinanians had split into separate groups on the tarmac. President Oumou and General Joro were in heated discussion. He would occasionally bark something into his hand held Motorola but he could tell that it wasn't working. He shook the device then banged on it, front and back, again nothing. Eventually, he handed it to one of the enlisted women at his side who repeated the bark-shake-bang ritual, with equally unsuccessful results. Something of uncertain importance would just not be communicated to someplace at that time.

About one hundred feet away, the Ambassador, DCM, CIA Station Chief, Political Officer, Acting Administrative Officer, Gunnery Sergeant and Security Officer stood under the only shade tree in sight. The doctor and nurse continued to minister to their patient in the ambulance, with the engine running to keep the AC on. Anderson and Singh, who had chugged the old pickup onto the tarmac a few minutes later than the bus, stood silently next to the bed of the truck in honor of the dead volunteer. Both the Pendleton shirt and the white caftan were drenched in perspiration. About half of the Zinanian staff had brought prayer rugs and set them in the direction of Mecca kneeling in their acts of devotion. The rest of them were smoking Marlboros.

Fairchild had thought to bring one other Foreign Service National employee - a photographer. He wanted a complete record of this event to cement his name in the Annals of Diplomacy. In the meantime, his wife fidgeted in the Chevrolet while Jillian Eisenstat and Conrad Prudholme sat silently and sweated in the unairconditioned bus.

"What are we going to do about the Libyans?" Fairchild asked, having no idea. In fairness, no one else had much in the way of a plan either. "We can't shoot 'em out of the sky. No antiaircraft guns. We can't shoot 'em as they get out of the Lear Jet. Bad for our reputation."

"We could just ignore them. No eye contact." Bernadette threw it out for discussion.

"Wrong!" shouted Lori Burkitt. "These bastards are not coming to pat Oumou Kinsa on the back. They're coming to undo what she did. And the only way they can do that is do something about her. They could kill her, but they aren't going to do that with us standing here. Kidnap her? I guess they could try and make it look like she was making a state visit to Libya."

"How can they do that with all these troops here?" asked Sgt. Rice.

"Look around you at those troops and give me an answer. No Gurkha tribesmen in this bunch. They are a bunch of girls. I doubt many of them have ever fired a gun. Got to guess there aren't any bullets in most of those old rifles anyway. The Lear is probably full of AK-47s. A few fusillades into the air, and the crack new Zin troops will lay down their weapons."

"And you think they'll whisk her off, even with us, the representatives of the world's most powerful nation standing here?" queried Ernestine.

"Friggin A, unless we do something to stop 'em."

"How do we do that?"

Bernadette O'Kelly piped in. "We could get her out of here. Kidnap her ourselves before the Libyans get here."

"Come on Bernadette; you can do better than that. The troops may not be Gurkhas but they're better than the zero that we have. I got an idea. Gunny, how many of your Marines are in country?" Burkitt asked.

"All five, Ma'am, but Corporal Peutz is due out this week. He's going to be replaced by Corporal Jaeger from Dakar, but not for a few days."

"Good, get 'em over here right now."

"They're only meant to be for guarding the Embassy. We can't use them in military operations. They can't carry guns outside the Embassy compound."

"Mr. Ambassador, you have the discretion to order the Marines out of the Embassy if there is legitimate concern for the Mission of the United States."

"I do?"

"Yes, Sir, and I would ask that you order them to come over here on the double. Leave one of them at Post 1."

"But ..." GySgt Rice tried to intervene but, Lori moved between him and the Ambassador and backed him into the trunk of the tree.

Fairchild glanced at Ernestine Grant who barely nodded, but enough for him to know that she thought he should accept Lori Burkitt's suggestion.

"OK, Gunny, get them over here." No sooner had the Ambassador handed down the order than Rice spoke into his radio triggering immediate action.

Since arriving in country, Michael had wondered how the ambulance would work in a pinch. He now knew it was OK, not great. The space was cramped, especially with nurse, doctor and critically ill patient inside. Patient Chen Wang was unchanged -- pulse and temperature too high, blood pressure too low, but none was immediately life threatening. Eisenstat knew that that status could change in a second. Tiny amounts of bleeding could become torrents, sending BP plummeting and pulse skyrocketing. He was not prepared to deal with that in a fully equipped operating room, let alone a Toyota Van. He couldn't wait to turn the care of his friend over to Dr. Fellows.

"Another fifteen minutes and the plane's on the ground, Chen. Maybe thirty more and you're outta here."

"Doc, I still think I'm going to die. "

"Absolutely no reason for you to say that. You're stable. Stably bad, but at least not getting stably worse."

"You know, Doc, I'm not afraid. Life's been mostly good. I did some good for others, probably not too many, but I didn't do anything real bad. I don't think I've ever had a real enemy, except maybe for my ex. Death for me means nothing more than no life. I don't think I'm destined to go to heaven or hell or come back as a dog or a carrot or a prince. That's not for me to worry about. But if I do die, I want you to know that I think you are a great doctor.

"You know, you had left the door open when you talked with Connie Prudholme about his blood test. When he told you to go 'F' yourself. You were a true professional, honest, caring, pulled no punches, but not brutal. The State Department is lucky to have you."

In twenty years of medicine, Michael was never more moved by the words of a patient. At the same time he was scared beyond imagination that Chen was correct in his self-prognostication.

XXXI

"Hey, Whip, isn't that another bird about 30 degrees to port?" A tiny speck could be seen, 10-plus miles away, but not far when the combined speeds of the two planes exceeds 700 miles per hour. Lt. Col. Nu Lin Li was the first to spot it.

"Yeah, it is. Probably our North African compatriots. Let's find out. Overseer, this is Jolly Roger."

"Go ahead."

"We've just made visual with a jet of some sort maybe ten miles northeast of us. Is that the Colonel's boys?"

"Affirmative," answered somebody on the AWACS. "They haven't altered their course. Seems clear that Donolu is their destination. If they were going to the coast they would have shifted south by now."

"ETA still 1430, like us?"

"That's affirmative."

"How do you suggest we make it known that we're in the sky too and maybe about to land at the same moment they are."

"We can't help you. You know that we can't give away information. No contact with anyone except our close friends - the Brits, the Israelis, the French, and the Italians. And, sure as hell not the Libyans. You better have the ground people at Donolu airport contact them; they should be doing it anyway."

"There is no ground crew at Keita-Coulibaly. We've been in contact with someone named Eddie, who knows nothing about air traffic control. From the way he sounded, we're lucky that he knows how to turn on the radio and pick the right frequency."

"Yeah, we know about Eddie. We've been monitoring your communications. That comment about the windsock was a bit much. But, you gotta tell Eddie that he needs to convey the info to the Lear Jet, 'cause there is no one else that's gonna do it."

"Affirmative. Thanks, Overseer. It's nice to know you're watching

LARRY HILL

our tail."

"Good luck, JR. Happy landings."

As the AWACS and 720 were chatting, Eddie deQuervain was attempting to establish contact with the Lear, now five minutes from Zinani airspace, fifteen from the landing pattern at K-C International.

"Libyan Lear Jet, number unknown, this is Control Tower, Donolu International Airport. Please respond." No answer. Two, three more times, no answer. On the fifth attempt, a thickly accented squawk came over the airways.

"This number WEC36LNH fly from Libyan Republic to Donolu." The accent was thick.

"We read you WEC 36. What is your plan?"

"We guest of General Kinsa. We land twelve minutes."

"Be aware that there is an American 720 in your area, prepared to land at the same time. They are here to take out a sick person and must land first."

"Negative, we guest of General Kinsa. We land twelve minutes. Tell big plane, wait!"

"Stand by WEC 36." Eddie had no communication directly with the powers on the ground. He ripped off his headphones, leapt out of his seat, took the tower steps three at a time, and ran to the group under the shade tree. He explained the situation to the Ambassador, knowing that the DCM was the most important listener.

"We've got to let them come in first. No need to sacrifice everything in the name of national pride. The 720's got plenty fuel doesn't it?" Grant thought about all aspects of any situation.

"Obviously, because they're not planning to refuel before they leave."

"OK, tell 'em to wait until the Lear lands." The Ambassador nodded his approval. "And better tell the Libyans about the short runway. I would guess that a Lear doesn't require all that much less distance to land. We wouldn't mind if they cracked up; we just don't want them doing it on the runway, blocking our landing."

Eddie sprinted back to the tower and was back on the phones less than two minutes after he asked them to stand by. "WEC 36, this is Donolu."

"Roger."

"Approval is given to you to land before the 720. Please do it fast. And be aware that you are to land on runway two-niner, the shorter one. The longer one is closed. Two-niner is only 1500 meters long. Once you land, please clear the runway as fast as possible as the 720 will be trailing close behind you."

"Roger. WEC36LNH we land runway two-niner." Eddie was sure that the Libyan pilot understood nothing about the need for speed and the short runway.

"Jolly Roger, this is Donolu."

"Go ahead."

"You're number two for landing."

"Whaddya mean number two? We're a goddam 720 and they're a Lear Jet. We got priority."

"Their pilot made a stink about being the guests of the President of the Republic and they weren't going to wait on anyone. I checked with the Ambassador and he says let 'em land first. So, we ask you to circle at whatever altitude you do such things until we get these terrorists down."

"We no terrorist! We guest of General Kinsa."

"Sorry WEC36." Eddie had forgotten that all the planes heard the same things. "Jolly Roger, you must land on runway zero-two-niner. As you know, the longer zero-one-three is out of commission."

"We're well aware of that, Donolu. Just make sure that that other aircraft is far off the runway before you welcome us in." Hard enough to land a 720 on 1500 meters of pavement. Lots harder if they have to share the pavement with another airplane.

"Got you covered, Jolly Roger. The next time you get a call from me it will be to come on down."

President Oumou Kinsa, clearly uncomfortable in her poorly fitting uniform, prepared to welcome her first official visitor. A threadbare red carpet was pulled out of dusty storage and placed more or less randomly on the tarmac. Her honor guard, 90% female, began to assemble. Oumou, having watched several similar events on TV, planned to review troops with her guest. No one had schooled her on high-level military diplomacy; she had no idea of the identity of those she was soon to greet. She assumed that it would be led by her co-trainee, the Foreign Minister, if not Colonel Gaddafi himself.

The weather had turned clear and fairly hot. While the temperature topped 32 degrees centigrade, the humidity was a deserty low 30%. The runways had dried.

The air conditioners continued to function in the ambulance and the Ambassadorial Chevy. At one point, Fairchild stepped in with his wife, ostensibly to keep her company, but actually to get out of the heat. He got out after just a couple of minutes to avoid her constant harping that she wanted to leave.

"This is WEC36LNH requesting landing."

"Permission is granted Libyan Lear." Eddie was awe-struck that he had the power to determine whether and when an aircraft of a government not recognized by his own nation could land in yet another nation.

"What is wind speed?"

"Damned if I know. Looks to me like there's no wind from any direction. Please land west to east."

"Roger. WEC36LNH in final approach."

"Willie, what is that plane that is about to land. Doesn't look like a 720 to me." Ulysses Singh and Willie Anderson had heard nothing about Libyans destined for the airport.

"Looks like a Lear Jet to me." Anderson had, since childhood, been an aficionado of airplanes and knew the silhouette of most anything that flew.

"I can't imagine whose it is. We would have heard if any VIPs were on their way. Must be the French."

The small jet, now with its gear down, was making a slow, standard descent to runway two-niner. The terminal and control tower were situated a quarter of the way down the 1500 meters of runway. By the time the plane was even with the tower, the tires were still ten feet off the surface.

"Libya, abort! Abort!" deQuervain yelled into the microphone of his headset.

The plane continued its descent. "Jesus Christ, Abort your landing!!"

About 500 meters from the end of the runway, rubber touched tar, a perfect landing except 750 meters later than required. The pilot slammed on his reverse thrusters, drowning out any other noise for a mile.

"My God, he's never gonna be able to stop!" Frank Norbert screamed, but no one else heard.

To all observers, and there were dozens, it was slow motion. The runway simmered from the heat, adding an ethereal element as the plane sped away from the helpless onlookers.

The Libyan Ambassador, who had pulled up in his limousine only seconds before touch down, saw the panic in the eyes of Zinanians and Americans and knew his countrymen were in deep trouble.

The plane slowed, but not enough. There were two hundred meters to go and there were still five hundred or more meters of momentum in the machine. There was no barrier at the end of the runway, and there were no trees or buildings immediately beyond. That was good. But could the plane negotiate the soft, sandy clay beyond the end of the tarmac?

WEC36LNH reached the end of the pavement. The sand caused the front to veer to the right. Then back to straight. Then a little to the left. The nose gear suddenly dipped, bringing the plane to a 15-degree angle, tail up, nose down. DeQuervain knew there was a drainage ditch right about that spot. Not too wide, not too deep, but not good for a five ton aircraft out of control. The rapid change from level to angled caused the left wing to dip, digging itself into the porous sand. With the wing as fulcrum, the tail was lifted off the ground, ten degrees, then forty-five. The magnificent machine, with its cargo of nine men and multiple guns, left the ground, sideways, left wing down, right wing up and nose pointed back toward the earth. Milliseconds, or was it minutes, later the airplane slammed into the Zinanian desert. As the left wing and the front of the plane accordioned, the entire steel, aluminum, gasoline, plastic, and human vehicle was converted into a giant fireball. Nothing alive had the slightest chance of survival.

The Ambassador of the Republic of Libya motioned to his driver, who dutifully opened the rear door to his Rolls Royce. Within seconds, the limo pulled away from the airport, heading back to Donolu.

"Donolu, this is Jolly Roger. What was that? "

"JR, this is Donolu. That, Sir, was the crash and burn of Libyan Lear Jet, WEC36LNH. Pilot error, Whip. He touched down most of the way down the runway and couldn't stop his airplane in time. He hit a ditch and the thing exploded. We've got a big fire now - no chance of any survivors."

"Fire trucks out there?"

"What fire trucks? Remember what we told you? There's no staff at the airport, hasn't been for a couple of days. This place is closed. I think that there are a couple of fire trucks in one of those locked buildings, but we sure as hell don't have a key for the door or the trucks."

Look, man, I want a fire truck down there when I land."

"We'll try our best." Eddie knew that an argument would be fruitless, but also knew that there was no way he was going to get any fire trucks.

"So, what's the status of the runway? Did they damage it?"

"Negative, the runway is OK. No holes and no debris. On the other hand, Whip, you better stop your airplane better'n he did. I'd advise you to put your wheels down as close to those white lines as possible."

"Hey, Eddie?"

"Yeah?"

"I really don't need that sort of advice."

"Sorry."

"Asshole," Whipple muttered to Copilot Jack Nu, who ignored the epithet.

Michael Eisenstat had jumped out of the ambulance immediately after he saw the explosion. His first reaction was to sprint to the scene to see how he could help. Seconds later, he recognized the futility of the gesture. There weren't going to be any remains, let alone people to treat. The bodies would be more than "burned beyond recognition," they would be non-existent. He couldn't help but think that the Islamic approach to death was healthier than the Jewish or Christian one. The victims, in that second or so that they knew that life was about to end, would feel no fear. The families would be comforted by the knowledge that their loved ones were with the angels and had given their lives to God's cause.

He remembered that he had a real, live patient, for whom his help was crucial. He returned to the cramped environs of the Toyota ambulance.

"What happened, Doc?"

"There's been a plane crash, Chen." The look on the injured man's face made it clear he assumed that his ride home had been destroyed. "A Libyan airplane, Chen, not the 720." Chen Wang relaxed, then his face showed his ability to suffer even when the victim was an enemy of his country.

"What's that mean for the 720? Can it still land?"

"Yes, it can. The runway is clear. Your hospital should be landing in a couple of minutes."

"Blood pressure 80/60, pulse 130," Electra said mechanically. Eisenstat hoped that the increase in pulse rate was a result of learning about the crash and not a sign of worsening bleeding. He turned the drip rate on the IV up a notch.

The demise of Libya WEC36LNH brought Marylou Fairchild out of the car for the first time since her arrival at Keita-Coulibaly. She quickstepped, Gatsby in tow, toward the group of Americans gathered under the shade tree. Neither she nor any of the officialdom said a word. The now molten remains of an American-made, Libyan-flagged aircraft and its passengers lay less than a mile from where the President and Vice President of the Republic, and the most important members of the most important foreign mission in the country, stood. Nobody, except the doctor, had made a step in the direction of the tragedy. There was nothing that could be done.

"Holly, come over here," she whispered to her husband as she firmly grasped his upper arm. She tugged him out of the circle of his employees to an area in the oppressive sunlight. "All the more reason I want out of here."

"What does that mean?" Both parties kept their voices low. There had been enough embarrassing moments already.

"Did you see that plane crash?"

"No. Which plane crash?"

"Don't be an ass."

"Then don't ask stupid questions. Yes, I saw the plane crash. First one I've seen all day."

"This is a dangerous country and I want out of here. And I want out of here on that." She pointed at the plane that was close enough to be identified as one with four engines and an American insignia.

"A plane load of dead Libyans is not going to change my mind on that one, dear. You're staying." He began walking back to the shade.

"Don't you walk away from me!" The members of the circle and the Zinanian power elite all turned their heads toward the incensed woman.

Fairchild's expression soured, but he reversed his direction.

Gatsby, a small black and white dog in the African mid-day sun, lay in the shade of his mistress's dress, panting.

"There's nothing more to say, Dear," said the Ambassador, obviously humiliated by his wife in front of the most important political personalities of the country. She spun about and harrumphed back to the car, nearly stomping on Gatsby in the process.

One of the members of the PPD delegation walked up to the circle of Americans. "President Kinsa would like a moment to speak with Miss O'Kelly." Dette looked for advice from the DCM. Grant nodded affirmatively and Dette negotiated the twenty-five meters to the group of Africans. The President separated herself from the rest and offered her hand to her old friend and confidant.

"Please join me for a moment in my automobile," she said, almost meekly. They ambled slowly to the dark green Mercedes Benz, Bernadette entering it for the second time in as many days. Oumou flicked her wrist as a sign that the driver should leave; he left the motor running to maintain the air-conditioning.

"Bernadette, I apologize for my behavior of the last two days. I wasn't thinking right. The excitement and pressure of the moment and the sense that what we did is important caused me, and our movement, to become overly self-assured and to forget our friends. You are my friend, have been my friend for a long time, and will be my friend for a long time to come." Dette was unconvinced, in view of the fact that less than five minutes before the plane crash, Oumou had passed by her as if she had not been there.

"Madam President."

"Please call me Oumou."

"No. If I call you by your given name here, I might forget when the situation does not allow it. Madam President, I was going to ask what has changed your mind. Minutes earlier, you acted as if I didn't exist."

Oumou looked down at her interwoven fingers and nodded. Dette noticed that she had not removed her military hat; she looked foolish in the same style chapeau that Lassoso wore to his official occasions. "We ... I came here to greet the representatives of Libya, a sworn enemy of our movement. I thought at the time that I had no alternative. We needed recognition. Your country hasn't recognized us, the French haven't and even those so-called democracies in the area, like Mali and Senegal, have been silent. Gaddafi, for all his bluster, was willing to talk to us."

"You think he was really sending his people to talk to you? Wrong, Madam President. We have satellite evidence that his troops are, at this very moment, on the move with some of Lassoso's men, from New Akron to the capital. Gaddafi does not recognize a government while at the same time trying to destroy it. Then again, even if he did, be aware the recognition isn't worth the paper he sent it on."

"You are probably right. We want to remain while your plane lands and welcome them, and honor those of you who are departing, especially the injured man and the unfortunate Peace Corps Volunteer."

"Do as you choose, Madam President. We are your guests, not vice versa. If you ask me to, I will speak with the Ambassador and arrange photo opportunities. You do know that this will not change in any way our process of deciding whether or not to establish full relations. The decision to greet the Libyans was yours and the fact that they all died is of no consequence."

"It will be done tomorrow. Incidentally, Bernadette, those four young men who came in the Peace Corps vehicle, are they really

Volunteers? They don't look like it."

Dette was surprised that Oumou had made the observation. "You are right. Yes, those are our Marines. They were here to disable the Libyan plane when it pulled up to the terminal. They were going to shoot out the tires so that it could not get off the ground. We were really concerned that Gaddafi wanted you kidnapped."

"I thought that your Marines were only here to protect your Embassy."

"You think correctly, Madam President, but I would advise that you not make an issue of that if you are really looking for American recognition."

Bernadette left the Mercedes and returned to the group of Americans, where she relayed President Kinsa's desire to kiss and make up.

"Have you ever heard of two crashes at one airport on the same day," Whipple asked Lt. Col. Nu, a student of airline accidents.

"Huh-uh. Never happens. We're safe. One's all any airport is allowed on any given day."

"And how often has a 720 landed in Africa on a runway too short by 1000 meters, brought down by an air traffic controller who doesn't know his ass from his oscilloscope? "

"Uh ... not often. That's a rare one. Probably not more than a couple of dozen times."

"Right. Let's not get too cocky. We aren't down yet. I won't be happy until we have rubber on the hard stuff and that air speed indicator is stuck on zero.

"Crew! Get in position for a landing. It could be a tough one. For those of you who didn't see it, we were preceded onto the ground by a Libyan Lear that couldn't stop in time and ended up doing an Einstein."

"Huh?" The question came from behind the pilot.

"Mass was turned into energy. E equals mc squared.

"All of you remember the crash landing drill. Head between your knees, Cushion yourself with whatever you have. Altitude?"

"3000 feet, Sir."

"As I recall there aren't any big mountains around here. Should be safe. Let's go in." There wasn't a mountain over 500 feet high in a thousand miles.

"Donolu, this is Jolly Roger." By now Whipple had gotten used to the unorthodox means of communicating with the ground.

"Go ahead, JR."

"We request permission to land."

"You got it, baby! All the traffic is cleared. Nothing else in the sky anywhere near us."

"The fire trucks?"

"They're in place." They weren't; they were still in the garage.

"Lieutenant Colonel Nu and I are looking forward to a tall, cold one. Coke. Maybe 7-Up. That's good for the medical staff too. The rest of the crew could go for something a bit heftier."

"Moslem country, sir. We got plenty Coke and 7-Up. We'll have to call in for the hard stuff."

"Remember those white lines you warned me about, Mr. deKooning?"

"It's deQuervain, Sir. Yes, I do remember the white lines. Why'd you ask?" Eddie was worried that he'd catch hell again for warning about the obvious.

"Watch 'em closely. I'm going to put my main gear down on the near end of the first set and by the time we get to the end of that set, the nose gear will be down. Cover your ears; we'll be making lots of noise."

"2000 feet. You can see that golf course now. There's a lot of stumps. They didn't do much of a job clear cutting."

"Wind?"

"The sock hasn't twitched a bit."

"Still dry?"

"Dry as an old lady's twat."

"Eddie ... it is Eddie isn't it?"

"Yes, sir. Eddie deQuervain."

"Eddie, watch the language, and, you're not shitting me about those fire trucks, are you?"

"No sir," he lied. Having seen the end result of WEC36LNH, he figured that fire trucks would make no difference if the runway were too short for the big plane. And, he had no way of getting them out of the garages. The steel doors would need torches to cut them open and there were no torches.

"1000 feet. Landing gear down and locked." Whipple lined up the plane with the center of the runway. He couldn't see any red fire trucks but knew the ones in Africa were often painted some other color.

"Looks like a walk in the park, Jack. Hope we can get you laid within fifteen minutes; we won't be on African soil long.

"500 feet."

"The Giants gonna beat the Redskins again? Lucky bastards."

Whipple reached for his forehead to wipe off the sweat that was beginning to obscure his vision. Lt. Col. Nu was as dry as the runway.

"300 feet."

"200 feet."

"100 feet." He didn't know it, but Whipple was right over the fairway of hole 5, at 560 yards, the longest golf hole in West Africa.

Eddie saw it. Bernadette and Eisenstat and Oumou and Joro and all the rest saw it. Whipple set the main gear down as close to the beginning of the runway as humanly possible and the nose gear touched down a fraction of a second later. Could the 60-ton behemoth with a speed at landing of 150 miles per hour stop in 1500 meters? Someone knew the physics. Nobody watching knew. Whipple, the Great Whip, thought he knew. He thought the answer was yes; otherwise he wouldn't have tried it.

"Brakes, thrusters!" Jack Nu didn't need to be told what to do, but it's in the regs; gotta say it. The noise was deafening. From the ground it looked like there was no change in velocity as the aircraft zoomed past the turnoff to the terminal. Had they looked at the panel, Jack and the Whip could have seen on the screen the results of their attempts to bring the thing to a halt. From 120 miles per hour at touch down, "75, 50, 40, 30, 20." With 200 meters to go, the plane was traveling about as fast as a marathoner reaching the finishing line.

"You can quiet the noise makers, Jack."

XXXII

Four minutes after the 720 came to a full stop and turned around, it pulled up in front of the terminal. Only a handful of other aircraft was visible: two single-engine private planes owned by Cabinet Ministers; an old F-86, veteran of several national air forces before it hit bottom in Zinani; the charred remains of the Lear Jet. A red carpet had been put in place to honor the Libyans; Whipple pulled up in the perfect position for his staff to take advantage of it.

One of the Embassy's Foreign Service Nationals had located and transported the mobile stairs that would allow the crew to deplane and the passengers to board. Keita-Coulibaly was decades from warranting jet ways that extend from terminals to suck passengers into the bowels of the airport. Like most African airports, K-C used buses to move haggard travelers from the bottom of the steps to the immigration hall. But there were no buses because there were no bus drivers. In fact, there was no need for either buses or drivers as all of the people who landed would soon be taking off.

The first person off the 720 after stairs were secured was Dr. Zebulon Fellows, otorhinolaryngologist-to-be. Two surgical nurses, Anita White, the operating room nurse, an African-American, and Rosalina Gomez, nurse anesthetist, a Filipina, followed him. Fellows began descending the broad staircase, at the bottom of which the President and the Vice President of the Republic of Zinani stood stiffly. Colonel Whipple and colleagues had not been warned that his plane was to be met by local dignitaries, let alone the President. It had not occurred to either Eddie deQuervain or DCM Grant to pass the word.

Seeing what was about to happen, Bernadette sprinted halfway up the steps where she met the doctor and nurses. "Welcome, I'm Bernadette O'Kelly, Political Officer at the Embassy here."

"Oh ... I'm Dr. Fellows and these here are my nurses, Nita and Rosy. I'm the flight surgeon here to see my patient."

O'Kelly's expression went from welcoming to blank. Fellows looked old enough to vote but not of sufficient seniority to order a drink at most Stateside bars.

The taller of the two nurses extended her hand to her. "I am Lieutenant White and my colleague is Lieutenant Gomez. We are both nurses. Where's our patient ... Mr. Chung, is it?"

"No, it's Chen Wang. He's in the ambulance. But, first we've got protocol to deal with. At the bottom of the stairs, see that short woman? She's Lieutenant General Oumou Kinsa, President of the Republic and the man next to her is Major General Joro, the Vice President.

"The three of you are the first foreign visitors to set foot here since the change of government and you are about to be treated like VIPs." She did not mention that they had originally come to greet the now-deceased Libyans.

"Stay right here!" Bernadette noticed that a major faux pas was about to transpire; the Ambassador had not been included in the ceremony. Fairchild had left the circle in the shade returning to the Chevy, where he was in animated conversation with his wife, through a partially opened window. Dette windmilled her arms in the direction of the Chief of Mission, who was paying no attention to the drama playing out on the mobile stairs: he missed the gesture. Dette did catch the eye of the DCM, motioning her to get the Ambassador over to the upcoming historical event. Ernestine Grant, no Olympic sprinter, walked as fast as she could and gently spun her hierarchical superior in the direction of the new Chief of State, Vice Chief of State, and the doctor, nurses, and pilots. Fifteen seconds later, Fairchild reached the bottom of the stairs and climbed them two at a time.

"Get out of here!" he said in a muted voice to his political officer.

"Mr. Ambassador, perhaps you should meet these people before I leave. You will have to introduce them to Madam President."

Fairchild knew there wasn't a sunbather's chance in the Arctic that he would remember names after an introduction. "No, no, stay. You do it."

"Yes, sir. First, this is Captain Fellows, the surgeon, and Lieutenant White and Lieutenant. Gomez, the nurses. I don't know these gentlemen yet."

"Colonel Whipple, the pilot, Mr. Ambassador, and this is my co-pilot, Lieutenant Colonel Nu Lin Li."

"Call me Jack." Nu's comment was directed at the Ambassador, but his eyes were on Bernadette. *Not bad. Could use a little makeup. And that dress has gotta go.*

"Good to meet you. I'm Ambassador Holden Fairchild. Welcome to the Republic of Zinani. We can't thank you enough for coming our way under trying circumstances."

"No problem, Sir. It's our job. Sorry to hear about our friends from Libya. Even sorrier to see what happened to that Lear. Good vehicle, that."

"Might help the balance of payments. Gaddafi's bound to order another." Fairchild thought it was a funny comment; irony was his specialty. Nobody smiled. "Please follow me."

As the seven-person American contingent began descending the staircase, a twelve-person military band began playing. The music was reminiscent of a beginning orchestra in an elementary school. A few bars into it, Bernadette recognized "When the Saints Go Marching In." It was very loud.

"Madam President, I would like you to meet our Political Officer, Bernadette O'Kelly."

Oumou Kinsa shrugged her shoulders and cupped a hand over her right ear. "Huh?" The lead trumpet was about five-feet distant and the Ambassador did not have a booming voice.

"Meet Ms. O'Kelly! My Political Officer!"

"I already know her! Hi, Bernadette!"

O'Kelly was puzzled that neither Kinsa nor Joro said anything to the bandleader, a plump woman in her early twenties. "Anything we can do about that band?" She had to repeat her question at a full-throated yell. Finally hearing, the President turned to her Vice President who, in turn, got the word to the fat lady. Ten bars later, silence blessed the tarmac.

O'Kelly officiated at the introductions. "Madam President, may I present to you Captain Fellows, Surgeon, from the United States Army, plus his two colleagues, Nurse White and Nurse Gomez." The RNs smiled. Fellows bowed. He had seen a movie about Japan and extrapolated to the entire non-Western world. "And this is the pilot,

LARRY HILL

Colonel Whipple and co-pilot Lieutenant Colonel Nu." The crewmen both saluted, a gesture quickly and smartly returned by Joro, slowly and sloppily by the newly festooned Commanding General.

Jack Nu sized up the distaff Chief of State. Short but well put together. A figure notable through the military uniform. Eyes that suggested fear, power, and desire concurrently. The presence of someone of significance. No way he was going to make a move, but it didn't hurt to fantasize. His mind darted back to the American in the cheap brown dress.

"Welcome, as the first official visitors to the Republic of Zinani. I trust that your stay will be fruitful and that you will learn to love our people and our land."

Dette whispered something to her. "Oh, I understand that you will not be staying long. Surely you must return sometime in the future under less hurried circumstances."

"Yes, Ma'am, we will only be here for a few minutes, just long enough to pick up the injured man and high tail it back to Italy."

"I understand," Kinsa said, although she had never heard of high tailing. "But you must review the troops with me."

General Joro signaled the portly bandsperson who with a baton called her musicians to attention. The music sounded nothing like the previous number, but within ten seconds, all knew that they were hearing "Saints" again.

Kinsa and Joro began strutting. But who was to follow? Who was the guest of honor? Not the Ambassador, he lived there. Not Bernadette, same reason. Has to be either Col. Whipple or Doctor Fellows. As the Zinanians slowed their pace to allow somebody to catch up, Bernadette poked Fellows in the back. "Walk next to the President." She chose him because he was on the ground and Whipple was still on the stairs.

The buzz-cut surgeon scampered a few paces and locked step with the hosts. The ancient red carpet separated two lines of soldiers numbering about thirty --- half female. The cadence of the reviewers was as irregular as the beat of the band's offering. Fairchild, who along with Dette, the nurses and the aircrew, trailed the more honored Fellows, nearly tripped as he tried to march to the irregular rhythm. Half way down the line, Fellows left rank and approached one of the male

286

members of the platoon. "How long you had that, soldier?"

The private spoke no French, let alone English; he stared at the doctor expressionless. He had a large sore on the side of his nose, approximately an inch in diameter. General Joro saw that his soldier had no inkling of what was happening and posed the same question in Fulani. "He says that it has been there for more than two years, since he came into the city."

"Looks like a big basal cell carcinoma to me. Didn't know you Africans got those things. Usually a white man's thing. This man's got to see an ENT or plastic surgeon soon. Could kill him if he doesn't."

"Captain Fellows, we will be happy to help this soldier, but we must proceed. You have a very sick patient lying in that ambulance over there." Joro was pleased that Bernadette had jumped in; he thought he knew English OK, but not "E-N-T" and "plastic surgeon."

"Oh, yeah. You know, I'm going into ENT myself. Love to get my hands on a case like that. Don't see 'em much in the US. Our people are smarter than to let themselves get that bad." Dette wanted to knock his teeth out.

The band finished its rendition of "Saints," then they played it again. The entourage passed by the perspiring platoon and walked back to the airplane. "Madam President, you must excuse us. These people have a job to do," said O'Kelly pointing to the doctor and nurses. Oumou and Joro spoke to each other in Fulani. Bernadette knew enough of the language to understand that the question was, "What do we do next?"

President Kinsa walked the dozen steps to her waiting Mercedes, beckoned her Vice President to sit on her left, and opened the door for herself on the right. The automobile accelerated out of sight. No good-bye. No good-luck. Bernadette hoped that the new leaders of the nation were on their way to interview a candidate for the job of protocol officer.

The two physicians met half way between the ambulance and the airplane. Six-foot Eisenstat was nearly half a foot taller than his surgical colleague; he was at least two decades his senior, but had twice the hair.

"Am I glad to see you. Dr. Eisenstat's the name, Michael Eisenstat."

He offered his hand, but was met by a salute. Michael hadn't saluted anyone since Cub Scouts when he used just two fingers. He didn't salute back, dropping his hand into his pocket.

"Captain Fellows. Flight Surgeon, but I'm going to Ohio State for an ENT residency when I'm outta the Air Force. Two months, three weeks, two days, five hours..." He pushed a button on his Casio, "and...seventeen minutes, Donolu time, har, har, har." Eisenstat saw no humor in it but smiled politely. "Tell me about your patient, John."

"It's Michael. Patient is Chen Wang, 42-year-old male, status-post gunshot wound who presents the problem of persistent bleeding and barely controllable BP and pulse. Also has a high temp, up to 104. Gotta figure he has an abscess in addition to the bleed. I put the chest tube in, so I don't know if I'm the cause of the bleeding. I'm no surgeon. Internist, in fact."

"How are his counts?"

"His hemoglobin isn't too bad; we had to give him a couple of units of whole blood earlier today. Last hemoglobin was 9. His normal is 15; just had a physical before the accident. I figured to transfuse again at 8. White count way up at 22,000. Confirms the abscess, I figure.

"How about his electrolytes?"

"You haven't spent much time in Africa, have you Dr. Fellows? Even under the best of circumstances, you don't get electrolytes here very easily. Sodium and potassium machines cost big bucks. The big bucks in a place like this go for machines that kill people, not that make 'em better.

"OK." Fellows was impressed that a doctor could take care of an acutely ill person without a first-world lab.

"X-ray?"

"Don't have those either. No machine at the Embassy and we weren't about to send Chen to the local hospital during a civil war. The films are pretty awful in peace time."

"What's his blood type?"

"B-neg."

"How many units you got?"

"None, Captain. They told us you would have blood. We used the two units we could get from our own folks. We don't use the local blood, even if we could. There's a 50% incidence of Hepatitis B and lots of HIV." Eisenstat decided not to say anything about Prudholme, even though Conrad was going to be riding home with Fellows.

"Lieutenant White, we got any blood? B-negative?"

"Yes, Captain Fellows. Remember, we put on about ten units before we took off? All we need to do is cross-match it." The nurse's tone plainly displayed her disdain.

"I don't know how to cross match!"

"Not to worry, doctor. Lieutenant Gomez and I both can do it for you."

"That's good. Good. Real good."

"John, do you think he might have an esophageal bleed? I brought along an esophagoscope.'

"It's Michael. Michael Eisenstat. And, no there's no evidence of any esophageal disease. He needs surgery."

"Oh yeah, surgery. You'll have to look at our surgery suite. Probably as good as anything you've ever seen stateside, maybe a little smaller. Problem is it's hard to operate at 30,000 feet if you hit turbulence. You know that word that you never want to hear in the OR? ... Oops. Har, har, har. You'd hear it plenty in a storm. We've either got to operate here or wait til we get back to Sicily."

By this time, Michael had concluded that he wouldn't want Surgeon Fellows to operate on the anti-Semitic Minister of Health, let alone his good friend Chen, except in a do-or-die situation. "You know, he's been like this for over two days; I'd guess that he'd be better off waiting until he gets back to Italy."

Fellows looked relieved. "Couldn't agree more Mikey. You think he's stable; we'll wait. But we'll be prepared to intervene at 30,000 if things go bad."

"Before we make that decision definitively, we'd better have you meet your new patient. Lieutenants, you come along too," Michael said to the nurses.

Eisenstat slid open the side door of the converted van. A blast of cold struck them as the conditioned air gushed out into the dry, baking atmosphere of West Africa. Electra and Chen Wang were caught playing gin rummy.

"Dr. Fellows, this is Electra, our nurse.

"*Enchanté. Comment-allez vous, Mademoislle?*" The accent was more

Denver than Dijon. Why he decided to try out his French for the first time since deplaning was unclear.

"So sorry, Doctor. I don't speak French. I'm from Nigeria."

"Sorry ... sorry, real sorry. Thought you must be a local. You sort of look like that lady President we just met."

Electra was eight inches taller, ten years older, had short, straight, graying hair, higher cheekbones, a bigger chin, and looked less like Oumou than she did Margaret Thatcher.

"And this is Mr. Chen Wang, the patient. Chen, these are the two nurses from the plane, Lieutenant Gomez and Lieutenant White, and Doctor Fellows ... what is your first name, by the way?

"Zebulon. My friends say Zeb, but call me Doctor Fellows. Air Force you know, formal and all that.

"So, how's the patient, Nurse? You don't mind if I just call you Nurse, do you? I'm no good at names."

"No problem. He's fairly stable. The BP was up to 90 and the pulse was 116 and regular. Brain's OK; plays gin rummy as well as ever. Taught me the game yesterday. He and I have been spending a lot of time together."

"Let's take a look." Fellows took the big step up into the van and kneeled at the gurney. He grasped his patient's wrist and looked at his watch. He turned around and showed his Casio to Eisenstat. "Amazing time piece. A touch of the button and you know what time it is any place in the world."

"What do you get for a pulse rate, Zeb?"

"Oh yeah, the pulse. Fast. Yeah, 116 on the button. Skin real dry. His brain seems to be intact. Must not be in shock." Captain Fellows pulled up on the hospital gown that Chen was using as his traveling uniform.

"Belly looks OK on inspection. No blue spots or big veins. Probably doesn't have pancreatitis. Let's percuss." Thump, thump, thump. "It doesn't feel like a lot of free air."

"If he had a lot of free air, he'd probably have been long gone," Michael interrupted.

"Uh huh. Right. Long gone. Sure isn't long gone. Look how he holds on to those cards. Time for palpation." The future ENT doctor pushed suddenly on the left lower part of the abdomen, jetting a short blast of air from the patient's mouth. He then moved the examining hand to the upper right, where the abscess was likely to lie. Eisenstat, the nurse, and the patient all knew what was going to happen next, but considered themselves powerless to prevent it. Fellow pushed deeply under the rigs, making instant contact with the acutely inflamed mass of tissue below.

"JESUS FUCKING CHRIST!!" Neither Electra nor Michael had ever heard Chen say anything stronger than "gee." The grimacing patient dislodged himself from the surgeon with a single swipe of his own left hand.

"Did that hurt?" the first words that Doctor Fellows spoke to the man whose life he would be responsible for the next several hours. He didn't wait for an answer, turning to Eisenstat. "Guess you are right, John. Must be a subphrenic abscess. Usually, there's no rush on these. They kill you slowly."

"That's good to hear, Doc," said Chen, as Electra was gently wiping the perspiration off his brow. "Sure wouldn't want it to kill me fast."

"Har, har, har, har. That's a good one."

"Zeb, let's let Chen rest; he's got a long flight ahead of him."

"OK. Good idea. Let him rest. Abscess. No rush ... Let me show you our operating room."

Like all passenger planes, the military version of the 720 has doors for passengers and different doors for baggage. Jenny Addison's remains were to be stowed in the baggage hold of Air Force 16. Keita-Coulibaly had the usual machine that hoists heavy things from the ground to the plane. But, it was locked away with the fire trucks.

The baggage door was close to twenty feet above ground. Jenny weighed about 120. The casket weighed considerably more. How to get it up? Willie Anderson pondered the problem. Pulleys? No way to rig them up. Ladder? Ridiculous. Levitation? Anderson knew of no levitators in Zinani.

Only the steps would accommodate the casket. The steps that the crew had just descended and those departing would soon ascend. To get the casket up would take several men. Anderson needed to find pallbearers.

In Africa, if you want something heavy lifted, you get local men. For a token sum, you can get a group of heavily muscled young men to lift, carry, dig, swing an ax, twist an awl, pound a stake, pull a stump, move a boulder, or transport a chieftain. The Peace Corps Director didn't know it, but one thing you could not get them to do was have anything to do with a dead body. He approached the men who had come on the Embassy bus. They were interested until they learned the task. No. "*Mauvaise chance.*" Bad luck. He turned to the male members of the band and a few other men dressed in fatigues. "Not us."

The Marines had left when it was evident that there was no Libyan plane to render unflyable. He was left with his colleagues, the male members of the American Mission: his assistant director, Ulysses Singh, no Rambo he; Fireman Pfund, good at slow pitch softball, nothing else athletic about him; Frank Norbert, stronger than his nerdly appearance would suggest; Marine Gunnery Sergeant Rice, the closest thing to Charles Atlas around; and Ambassador Holden Fairchild III, who had played lacrosse at Princeton, second string, junior varsity. That was thirty years earlier. Dog walking was his primary mode of exercise over the past half-decade.

Chen, Prudholme, and Eisenstat were automatically excluded.

The baggage hold was opened and the pallbearers assembled. Two hundred fifty pounds, plus or minus, to lift and six men of varying strength to do the lifting.

Should be easy. It was not easy. The stairs were narrow; the casket was three feet wide leaving the porters on the side little room to maneuver. "Sorry, gentlemen." Fairchild, who became short of breath after two steps, let go. Ulysses Singh, quickly following the lead of Mr. Ambassador, found the effort beyond his capacity and gave up. Anderson and Rice were three steps down from Pfund and Norbert and responsible for about ninety percent of the load. Twenty steps to the top. They were at number six. Then seven, eight … nine..."No. No. We won't be able to get'er up this way." GySgt. Rice was handling more than his share but could see that none of the others, including the robust Peace Corps Director, was up to the next eleven. "Back down, slowly." The other three sighed with relief.

"Gentlemen," the Gunnery Sergeant said firmly, "there's only one way to do this. Please get the crowbar out of the Marine vehicle." He took the tool, inserted the business end between casket and lid, and pried the top off with ease. He removed the shrouded body from its haven, carried it up the stairs as a newly wed husband would his bride, laid the remains near the entrance of the baggage compartment and descended the staircase. "Gentlemen, I think that the four of us can handle this empty casket without no trouble."

"Hey Chen, it's time, buddy." Michael, trying to reflect a cool and confident demeanor, was as anxiety-ridden as ever having spent ten minutes with the surgical consultant. "We need to strap you into a stretcher." The Medical Unit had a military emergency stretcher that Harry Houdini would have endorsed: two long bars of hardwood, three yards of heavy canvas, and lots of Velcro. Electra mummied him in, leaving only his face visible.

"What's going to happen to me, Doc?"

"Well, we're going to lug you up the stairs to the plane and put you in the capable hands of those two nurses and the surgeon."

"That guy who just about killed me? No way those hands are going to touch me again. Make sure of that, Doc, OK?"

"He's not going to be doing anything to you, Chen, unless all hell breaks loose with that bleeding of yours. And if it hasn't in the last two days, it's probably not gonna. And anyway, if he does operate on you, you'll be asleep. No pain, my friend. And that good-looking Filipina nurse, Gomez, will be putting you to sleep.

"You'll be on the plane for about four or five hours. Sicily. There's a big military base in Sicily, with an American hospital. You'll be tucked away this evening, probably in the intensive care unit.

"They'll do a CAT scan, and if we're right in our diagnosis, they'll be taking you into the operating room first thing in the morning to get rid of that pus.

"Let's go." Electra took one corner, the ambulance driver, the Gunnery Sergeant and the doctor, the others. With a tiny fraction of the problems of getting a coffin and body up the stairs, they succeeded in loading Chen Wang into the plane, approximately 50 hours after he was shot.

The entrance to the flying hospital led into a cabin that looked much like the first class of any commercial airliner. Wide leather-covered seats, two on either side, but only three rows of them. A thin wall separated the seats from the hospital beds, of which there were four, each equipped with state-of-the-art monitors, respirators, IV pumps, and suction machines.

White and Gomez went into action. Chen's pliant body was heaved from the gurney into one of the hospital beds. As multiple tubes and wires were placed in and on his body, Electra and her boss left the OR for the seating area, where they found Conrad Prudholme deposited in a window seat, working a crossword from an old Herald Tribune. Michael was surprised to find his immediate superior in his Brooks Brothers suit with expensive Italian shoes on, as if he was about to sit for an important executive interview.

"Hey Connie, howya doing?" Michael could hardly believe that those civil words were coming from his own mouth. Here, about to leave Africa was the man who had attempted to make his life miserable for the past 16 months and who had only the previous day told him to fuck himself.

"Oh, OK." He didn't look up from the page.

"You know what you have to do when you get back to DC, don't you?"

"Yeah, I know." There was remarkably little that he had to do. He would have to find the office of the infectious disease doctor they had arranged for him. He would go through tests -- all of a sudden all that talk about T cells and viruses was going to get real meaningful. Presuming that his recent test was not a false positive, State Department would never send him to another foreign country. There was never going to be an Ambassador Conrad Prudholme.

"Good luck, Connie."

"Yeah, thanks," said the Administrative Officer, filling in a three-letter word.

Michael heard commotion from the stairs outside the plane. Seconds later, Marylou Fairchild forced her way by the steward and plopped her sweaty body into the aisle seat across from Prudholme. She gently put her big tote bag on the window seat and stiff-armed a small suitcase under the seat in front of her. Several paces behind, the Ambassador of the United States of America followed. "Marylou, you cannot get on this plane!"

"I am on this plane! So is Gatsby." She reached into the tote bag and pulled out the Boston terrier, who proceeded to lick her mistress's face and bark ferociously at his master almost simultaneously.

"You cannot stay on this flight. I insist that you leave immediately and take the goddam dog with you!" Growl. Snarl.

"That's exactly what I am doing!"

"You know what I mean, dear."

"Sorry, Poopsie, I'm getting out of here. I spent two years being lovely Ms. Ambassador, going to those goddamn receptions, talking to a bunch of stupid, fat-assed women who never asked me any questions but expected me to entertain them. I threw parties every week, making the same cheese balls and spring rolls every time. And those shitty little brownies. If I ever see another one of them, I'll puke. That isn't bad enough: then we get a revolution. Hell, I can't even let Gatsby go outside to pee and poop for fear someone will throw a hand grenade over the wall. Huh-uh. No more. I've had it. Bye-bye baby."

"Dear, I'll make it better for you. No more parties. And we'll take a vacation."

"Vacation, huh? Ouagadougou or Nouakchott, probably. You can't buy me off with that."

"How about Dakar or Abidjan?"

"Forget it, Africa is not vacationland. Bali, Paris, maybe Rio, but not West Africa, thank-you-very-much."

"We cannot afford those places, and you know it!"

"Like hell we can't. Sell some of those stupid stocks of yours...er, ours. They won't do us any good when were dead, which might be real soon."

"OK, as soon as everything comes back to normal, if the market's OK, I'll sell some shares and we'll go to Paris."

"Wrong again, Mr. Ambassador. Mrs. Ambassador knows all about the possibility of things coming back to normal. Show me any country in this continent that is normal. You want me to wait until things are normal; I'll be a worn out old hag by then." Marylou folded her arms over her chest and started fumbling with the safety card in her seat pocket.

As Dr. Eisenstat saw it, the odds were swinging in favor of the wife. The husband, trying to look Ambassadorial, looked more like a bootblack who just noticed that people were wearing only Nikes. His expression was read by the doctor as saying, "I give up." His posture said, "I'm a loser." His suit suddenly needed a pressing.

But his words were different. "That will be enough, Marylou. I speak to you, not as your husband, but as the Ambassador and Presidential representative in this country, with the responsibility of caring for the American citizens within the borders of Zinani, and I command you to get off this plane ... now!"

"Mr. Ambassador, shove it."

"This plane will not leave until you have left it."

"It may stay a long time, Mr. Ambassador."

"Mr. Chen Wang, a citizen of the United States, is lying behind that wall, critically ill. This is a hospital plane, brought to this country to evacuate him so that his life might be saved. By your deciding not to get off, his life is further endangered. You wouldn't want to have that on your head, would you?"

"I'll take my chances, Mr. Ambassador."

"I will be required to take you off with force, Marylou. Please don't make me do that."

She flipped her safety card and followed the words with her index finger, mouthing them one at a time. She lifted the armrest between her seat and the dog's and encouraged Gatsby to wiggle into her lap. The bitsy Boston responded to the encouragement. Finally, she reached in her tote and positioned a blackout mask over her eyes.

Eisenstat had seen enough. He was embarrassed for both of them. He had observed Mr. and Mrs. Ambassador interact before. Though they certainly never acted like honeymooners, they were mostly civil.

"Shove it" was not a common public Fairchild utterance. To escape the uneasy atmosphere of the passenger cabin, the doctor retraced his steps to the hospital section. Electra, who had left before the fireworks had begun, was standing idle. Nurse White was in the process of replacing the sheet after having inserted the catheter into Chen's bladder. A plastic bag of blood was hanging above his head, dripping slowly into one of the two IV sites in his arms.

Bernadette O'Kelly's brown dress was darkened by sweat as she had been standing outside for over an hour. Her assignment was one that she hadn't counted on when she joined the Foreign Service: to convince the wife of the Ambassador to get off the plane that Marylou saw as her lifeline. But Dette had gone through a lot in the last few months; Ms. Fairchild shouldn't be any tougher than losing a lover or getting shot at in an airport.

Marylou was lying as vertically as the seat would allow, eyes covered by the black shade. Black and white Gatsby slept in her lap. Bernadette poked the motionless matron in the arm. "Yeah, what do you want now?

"Marylou, it's me, Bernadette."

"Did he send you?"

"Your husband did ask me to come talk to you."

"I'm not interested in talking to any representative of the Ambassador."

"But Marylou, Chen is in trouble. We can't wait any longer to send him for help. Please think of him and come with me. You'll be able to get out of here as soon as the regular flights start up again."

"That could be months."

"No, it won't be months. Air France knows there's lots of money to be made by flying people out of here. Lots of rich men are scared to death of Oumou Kinsa and want to leave before they are arrested. I know Oumou enough to know that she'll let them go rather than put them in jail. They will be flying in a few days. I guarantee that I'll work on getting you a ticket as soon as we get back to town."

"Sorry, Dette, I'm going on Air Force 16. I want out now, not later, and there's no way that His Honor is going to stop the plane because of me. I've lived with him for almost 30 years. I know him. He couldn't do it."

"Marylou, maybe in this case I can predict your husband's actions a little better than you can. I don't think he's going to let you go."

"Yeah, he is. He's a chicken-shit, Bernadette." Bernadette had seen him in action during the events of the last several days. He, indeed, was a chicken-shit.

"No he's not, at least he's not acting like one now. He expects me to come back with an answer he'll approve of."

"Tell him to shove it."

Conrad Prudholme had been within six feet of all the events of the last fifteen minutes and had remained mute. No one had asked his opinion on this administrative matter; he offered none. "Goddammit! Let's get this plane in the air, with you or without you, Mrs. Fairchild. Tell your husband that the Embassy will save a lot of money if you stay on this plane rather than buy a full-fare economy ticket to Washington."

Dette interjected, "Connie, that's not very important now. The Ambassador is definitive on this one. Money is not an issue." Prudholme returned to the crossword.

"So, please get off the plane, Marylou," pleaded the lady in brown.

"My seat belt is buckled. My tray is safely stowed and I will soon bring my seat back to its original upright position. I know that in the unlikely event of loss of cabin pressure, a mask will drop from the panel above me and..."

"OK, I've got the picture." Bernadette backed slowly away from lady and dog, turning to exit the plane.

A Foreign Service Officer is assigned hundreds or thousands of tasks during any tour of duty. She or he does most of them very well with little if any positive feedback. Different story for negative results; they often show up on the annual efficiency report. As Bernadette descended the steps, she felt, as would any mid-grade officer, that her chance for promotion or a prime assignment was about to disappear -- because of a marital spat between the Ambassador and his wife!

She approached the congregation of diplomats under the neem tree. She noticed that nobody was talking; instead they were staring at her. Dette guessed that her long face would be easily read; she was right.

"No go, huh?" Fairchild asked, squinting into the sun behind O'Kelly.

"She really plans on leaving, Sir. There wasn't a hint of a doubt. I thought she was going to get a hernia, she had that seat belt on so tightly."

"OK."

"You don't mean you're going to let her go, Sir," asked Ernestine Grant. She had that, "Oh, not again!" look.

"Of course I'm not going to let her go. I do that, the marriage is over and my career is over the second the wheels leave the ground. I may have no control over the marriage, although she's threatened to leave before, but I sure as hell can order her the hell off that plane. Where's that pilot? Wilson, was it?"

"No, Sir, it's Colonel Whipple. He's in the tower talking to Eddie deQuervain."

Whipple had insisted that he and Eddie get away from other people.

"Hey, Asshole, where are those fire trucks? You told me there would be fire trucks and there weren't any fire trucks. What if the tires caught fire on the hot runway, or we dipped a wing while we jammed on the breaks like that. Maybe we would have had an eency-weency fire that a fire truck might have put out before we became fuckin' news footage. You know, fire trucks aren't there just for the big crashes, like our idiot Libyan friends had. Little fires, hot engines things like that. Gotta have a fire truck when you land one of these babies, especially under, shall we say, unusual circumstances." Whipple was livid.

Eddie was silent. He, as a submariner, had learned that when an officer was screaming at you, it was best to remain quiet until the energy level had dropped. He wasn't in the Navy anymore; he was a Communications Specialist in the Department of State, but officers still put the fear of God into him.

"So, fire trucks?" Whipple's decibel level had diminished.

"Colonel, can I get you a Coke?" He knew weren't any cokes left. and prayed that the offer would be declined. His prayer was answered.

"No fucking thank you." In spite of the expletive, the decibels descended a little more.

"Col. Whipple, I'm sorry about the no trucks. See, there wasn't a way in the world we were going to be able open those big steel doors to get the truck out. Yeah, I knew it when I promised you that they'd be there. But, if I hadn't, you'd have flown off, leaving Chen behind, and he'd probably die. And, having heard you on the radio, I knew that you were a hell of a pilot. You weren't gonna have any need for any trucks."

"And if we did?"

"Sir, I was ready to pay the price."

"Uh-huh, Asshole, it was me and Jack and the doc and those two nurses and the rest of the crew that would have paid the price. Ultimate fucking price."

"Sorry. Glad you made it down, Sir. That was an amazing landing. There weren't ten feet between the start of the runway and the touchdown spot. Remind me to book one of your flights when they let me out of this grunge pot. Want me to show you around the place?"

The Whip turned 360 and saw six or seven oscilloscopes that would have looked more appropriate in a junkyard. "No, Asshole, but thanks anyway. I wouldn't know what I was looking at, and I know damn well that you wouldn't either." He had forgotten Eddie's name but thought that Asshole worked well.

A horror-film quality squeak announced the opening of the door leading into the room. Ambassador Fairchild walked in, unaccompanied.

"Mr. Ambassador," acknowledged deQuervain and Whipple simultaneously.

"Colonel Whipple, I need to talk to you."

"Anything that my friend Asshole can't hear, Sir?"

"Uh … no, I guess not. Colonel, it's my wife."

"Huh? Your wife? What do you mean?"

"She's on your plane."

"Oh, I see. Don't worry about it for a second. We'll take good care of her. She'll at least get to Italy safely; even Asshole thinks we can fly this thing OK. Right?" Eddie nodded. "Can't promise you anything about the onward connections. Probably Alitalia to DC; they're pretty good."

"Colonel, that's not what I'm talking about. Marylou … er, my wife, is not supposed to be on the plane. But she refuses to get off. Nothing I said budged her. I sent our female Political Officer. Nothing. Either you're going to have to convince her or haul her off."

"Yes, Sir. I did Vietnam in '75. I know about getting people off of flying objects against their will." We'll get her off before we leave. Wanna help, Asshole?"

"Negative, Colonel Whipple. I'll stay here and control the air traffic." Aside from the crispy Lear Jet and the $50 million flying hospital, there hadn't been an aircraft in the area for days.

Lieutenant Colonel Nu was free from any ground responsibilities, at least until it was time to go over the departure checklist. He quickly concluded that even a Lothario of his skills could not score in such a desolate place in such a short time. He decided to settle for embellishing his list of candidates for further investigation on subsequent African forays; in addition, one never knew when a woman you met in West Africa might show up in Greenland or Greensboro.

He had first planned to meet the Jewish matron that he had heard about on the radio. He had sized up the doctor, her husband, as a dipshit. He had the temerity to ask Dr. Eisenstat where he might find his wife. "I need to let her know something about the flight." He was motioned to the bus, where Jillian had spent the hour witnessing an air disaster and the knuckle-biting landing of a 720, and sweating her traveling outfit to virtual unwearability. Although she was closer in age to his mother than to him, Nu still thought her worth a second glance.

"Hey, how you doin'? I'm Jack, the copilot. You Ms. Eisenstat?"

"I am, Jillian Eisenstat. Call me Jill."

"Jack and Jill. Neat, huh?"

"How cute," answered Jill, recognizing that this was a man in a hurry.

Nu detected the early rumblings of an ice-making machine and quickly withdrew his mental offer to her of a place on his Rolodex. So as not to seem ridiculous, he continued the conversation. "We leave in about fifteen minutes. The flight to Sicily will take five hours with a good tail wind and they tell me they have connections for you to Rome then to the US. Hopefully, you'll get there for the funeral. I'm really sorry about your Dad."

She was surprised that he knew why she was flying and felt that being in a hurry was not necessarily all bad. "Thanks, Jack. I'm really glad to be flying with you. You know, I've never been in the cockpit of a plane; since there's so few of us, maybe I could come up just for a sec.

"Sure, Jill. Just wait 'til the seatbelt light is off." The address book was mentally opened to "E."

As Nu hopped off the bottom step of the bus, he noticed that there were two women in the bunch of white folks gathered under the shade tree with the Ambassador. One was the plain one in the plain brown wrapper that he had met on the stairs. The other was a blond who from a distance made him decide that a short detour on the way to the aircraft was in order. As he approached he was even more pleased that his distant eyesight was unimpaired. The blond was not run of the mill.

Nu, arm extended, inserted himself in the circle of people like a cowboy in a corral full of docile horses. "Hi, Jack Nu's the name. I'm number two on the big bird." He aimed his hand at Frank Norbert first, not that he had the least bit of interest in him, but because he didn't want to be too obvious about his real intentions. Frank, never one to say very much, grunted his response and shook hands limply. Fireman Pfund was more receptive, putting a hard squeeze on Nu's metacarpals.

"And we met on the steps, right? You're Bernadette?"

"Yeah."

"Uh-huh." He had expected a more emphatic retort from the woman introduced as a political officer. Failing to get it, he turned to the short black lady, certainly not his type. "Hi. I'm Jack."

"Hi. I'm Ernestine. I'm the Deputy Chief of Mission at the Embassy." Having thought that she was probably somebody's secretary, Nu was impressed and embarrassed and turned toward the pretty young blond. If Bernadette was the Political Officer and Ernestine was the second in command, what could this one be? Secretary of State?

"Jack Nu. What's your name."

Lori Burkitt, an expert on such matters, was convinced immediately that the Asian American was a man on the make. She decided to have a little fun. "I'm Lori. Lori Burkitt. Nice to meet you, Jack Nu. Is that N-o-o, or N-u, or N-e-w, or N-o-u-g-h?"

"You got it right the second time, Lori. It's N-u, Nu. What do you do around these parts?"

"Oh, I work in the Political Office." CIA personnel in embassies do not admit their true affiliation to outsiders "Jack, you are so young to have that silver oak leaf on your shoulder. Are you a major or something?"

"Actually, Lori, I'm a Lieutenant Colonel. A major would have a gold-colored oak leaf."

"Gosh Jack, you'd think that gold would be higher than silver?"

"Yeah, you would wouldn't you? And about being young, all us Asian types look younger than what it says on our birth certificates. I'm getting on in years; my mother's getting worried that she'll never be a grandma."

"Oh, your wife can't get pregnant?"

"Don't have a wife. Confirmed bachelor, at least til now. Care to see the plane, Lori?"

"Oh, gee, can I?"

"Yeah, I've got some pull on that thing."

"How about all my friends? I bet they'd like to see it too," she said, setting him up for the kill.

"The cockpit is pretty small. I can only take in one person at a time. If we have time before we blast off, they can come up after you."

"You know Jack, the Fireman's more interested in planes than I. Matter of fact, he told me just yesterday how he wished that he could go into the cockpit of one of those big jets. I'd hate to have him miss it. You take him first."

In an attempt to prevent others from hearing, he leaned over, whispering something in her ear. "Huh? Speak up Jack. It's hard to hear at an airport."

"I said, 'Why don't just you and I go up. Fireman will have plenty of other chances.'"

"Friggin-A! I'm not going anywhere with you, especially into something called a cockpit. Hey, Jacky, isn't there something wrong with that front tire. It might need to be inflated before you take off. Why don't you go check it out?" The rest of the group stared at the blushing officer, not the least bit surprised by the words of their favorite spook. Co-pilot Nu walked away speechless.

"Hey, Lori. Remember what you told me not so long ago?" asked Ernestine Grant so that others couldn't hear.

"What was that?"

"How hard it was for you to get laid."

The 720's sound system was playing Simon and Garfunkel. Marylou Fairchild had begun the same seat back crossword as Conrad Prudholme. Gatsby slept and snored. The handsomely uniformed officer who she had seen get off the plane while she was in the limo now sauntered up to her. "Ma'am, mind if I sit down for a moment."

"Huh? Oh, OK. It's your plane I assume."

"Colonel Whipple is my name, Martin Whipple. I'm the pilot of this rattletrap."

"And you want me off it, don't you? You've been talking to my husband."

"I can't imagine how you got that idea. But, yep, I was talking to your husband. I'd just love to have you fly with us. You know, it's not bad having an Ambassador's wife on the flight. Ground people take more notice, for what that's worth. But, Ma'am, the Ambassador is the boss here. Once we get in the air, it's all my show. But I can't taxi out there for a take off if he tells me no. And he, sure as it's hot out there, told me no. Not a little tiny Rhode Island no, but a full-fledged, economy-sized Texas no."

"Why don't you just ignore the great big Texas no? What's to stop you? That coward wouldn't stand in the runway to stop you."

"Ever hear of a court martial, Mrs. Fairchild? The Air Force is my boss and the big boss is, bless his moderate neo-liberal conservative soul, POTUS himself. Your husband is the personal representative of that very same President. I disobey the Ambassador, even of a godforsaken little country like this, and I'm not only out of the Air Force, I'm in the pokey. The hoosegow, the big house, the slammer and up the river. Yeah, ma'am, I'd love to have you along, but not that much."

"And if I refuse?"

"All I can tell you Ma'am is that this plane will not lift off with you on it. One way or t'other, that seat you are in, 3-B, will be vacant."

"Well, I refuse. I am going and Gatsby is going with me." She motioned to the sleeping dog to her side.

"The Ambassador didn't mention any dogs. Can't see any reason we can't take Gatsby along."

"Don't be stupid, Colonel. Gatsby and I are both going."

Whipple stood up slowly, like a gourmet after five three-star courses.

No rush. He ambled toward the door, leaned out part way. "Gentlemen, would you please give me a hand?"

Gunnery Sergeant Rice, Fireman Pfund and Frank Norbert single-filed down the broad aisle. The pilot leaned over to unbuckle her tightly cinched seat belt. She pushed at his forearm. "Get your hands off me!"

"My sincere apologies ma'am, but I've got a job to do and you are preventing me from doing it." The force of her resistance diminished and she let him approach her midriff, lifting the clasp, opening the belt.

"OK, goddammit, I'll get off. Gunny, bring the dog!" The four-man, one-woman and one-canine contingent lock-stepped toward and through the cabin door and down the hot metal stairs, into the waiting limo. Mrs. Fairchild and her canine were sped from the tarmac, destination Ambassador's residence, as soon as the rear door was slammed shut. The Ambassador had arranged alternative transportation for himself. When she saw Marylou Fairchild exit the plane, Jillian Eisenstat, the last of the passengers to board, left the bus, climbed the stairs, and plopped into the broad leather seat she'd just vacated.

Michael and the rest of the medical personnel were unaware of what had transpired on the other side of the partition. Chen was looking a little better. He was on his second unit of blood and his color had pinked up a bit. Blood pressure was inching toward one hundred, although his temperature hadn't dropped. The urine bag was filling at a speed that comforted Dr. Eisenstat, knowing that one of the early signs of total system failure in a badly injured patient was diminished urinary flow.

Eisenstat wondered how the staff could stand working in such cramped spaces. The little operating room, next door to the hospital ward, could accommodate a full-sized male surgeon only if he stood dead center. A move of just a few feet required shorter stature or spinal curvature. He also noticed how firmly each piece of equipment and furniture was fastened to the floor or the walls. A loose EKG machine or OR lamp during heavy turbulence could wreak havoc.

Jack Nu stuck his head in the ward. "All ashore that's going ashore! We've got an injured diplomat to rescue."

Michael or Electra, usually both, had been at Chen Wang's since the injury. They had probed his body, measured his parameters, tested his blood and urine, and tried to lift his spirits. It was time to turn the case over to someone else.

Michael was not pleased by the specific someone else but counted on the great resiliency of the human body and its ability to withstand the diagnostic and therapeutic interventions of even the most mediocre of medical practitioners. He had long lived with the premise that a doctor, even a surgeon, had little to do with whether a patient lives or dies. Usually they'll get better with a modicum of treatment. When they are destined to die, even the latest and most expensive tools can't reassemble Mr. or Mrs. Dumpty. Eisenstat didn't really think that Dr. Fellows would kill his friend, but he did think that there was a greater chance of that than the possibility that he would do him much good.

Electra, usually emotionless, leaned over the gurney and kissed Chen on the cheek. Her eyes shined as tears formed. She said nothing. Chen spoke no words but his moist eyes said, "Thanks."

As Michael prepared to bid farewell, the door to the compartment opened and the Ambassador, the DCM, and the Political Officer entered in that order. Fairchild carried a leather folder that he opened a few inches above his Economic Officer's well-oxygenated face. "Chen, this is a Meritorious Honor Award. I know of no one that deserves it more than you. Your work on the economic status of Zinani was of great importance to us. And, by the way, it means two thousand dollars to you. How about that?"

Eisenstat, Grant, and O'Kelly were embarrassed but Chen Wang responded with class. "Sir, thank you. If I get through this, I'll make good use of the money. Who knows, by then there might be a Zinanian stock market to invest in. Ha ha."

Bernadette took both of his hands and kissed him three times, twice on the right, once on the left cheek. "Get better fast, friend. Take it easy on those Italian nurses." He grinned because he knew she wanted him to.

Ernestine, ever the professional, shook one hand of the man who she had spent more time with her than any other during her African stint. She whispered something to him that was inaudible to the others. Chen smiled because he wanted to.

The three left as they would after a funeral service.

Michael, in his career, had doctored many patients, probably several thousand. He had helped cure many by offering minimal care; he had watched many die in spite of everything that he knew how to do and everything that his many consultants knew to suggest. He knew that they usually died with dignity, as he was better than his peers in recognizing a patient whose time had come. He liked most of his patients. He despised several and loved a few. He loved Chen Wang. In this case he was certain that had made a difference. Chen would have died long ago had it not been for him, his hands, his brain, and his books.

"Gotta go now, partner. Gona leave you in the capable hands of Doctor Fellows, and these good-looking lieutenants. In just a few hours, you'll be bedded down in Italy and on the road to recovery. Just in time to put in a new bid list. Who knows, with this on your record, they might give you Hong Kong after all."

"Yeah, sure, Doc. My luck, I get sent to Yemen or Bangladesh."

"Don't knock Bangladesh, Chen. It's on my list. Not very high but it's there. So, my man, keep us informed. Make sure the staff there knows that we want daily progress reports. Doctor Fellows, you get the word to them that we are number one in need to know."

"Sure thing, Doctor."

Michael lowered his voice. "You know, you are getting better. You're going to get through this with colors flying."

"Doc, I sure hope you are right. But, it doesn't feel like you are. Something in me says that I'm not going to leave Italy."

"Where I'm from," he whispered, "that's called horse shit." He knew that in spite of what the numbers said, Chen might well be right.

"Chen, man?"

"What?"

"I love you." Chen closed his eyes and smiled so widely that you could see his big front teeth. Michael Eisenstat turned and walked away, forever, from the most meaningful patient of his life as a doctor.

XXXIII

"Tower, this is Jolly Roger."

"Go ahead Roger. This is Donolu Tower. How can we be of service?"

Eddie deQuervain was pleased to see his career as an air traffic control operator was nearly over. His record was nothing to brag about: one safe touchdown; one crash-landing with no survivors. He knew that takeoffs were easier and more predictable than landings. He figured that if Whipple could land his bird on 1500 meters of tarmac with half a tank of aviation fuel, he should have no trouble getting it up.

"Tower, have you deployed the fire trucks."

"Sorry Roger, we're all out of fire trucks. We can get six or seven people at the end of the runway with buckets."

"Do you realize that you are talking to an officer!" yelled Whipple with mock vehemence.

"I do, Sir. But, you are talking to neither an officer nor an enlisted man. I'm a Communications Officer of the Department of State, US of Fucking A. So forget the trucks, and gentlemen, start your engines!" Eddie laughed into the microphone, knowing full well that the four Pratt & Whitneys had never been shut off to mitigate the slight risk of their not starting up again.

Lt. Col. Jack Nu, rejected by both Jill and Lori, morosely went through the checklist. They had plenty of fuel to reach Sicily; all the needles on all the gauges pointed in the right directions. "Ready for take off, Colonel."

Four members of the official American contingent of Zinani were aboard.

First Secretary Chen Wang, his arms now free and bent at the waist, was cinched tightly into the operating room table, with an IV of B-negative blood dripping into his left arm, a second IV instilling a glucose and salt mixture into the right, a cardiac monitor pasted to his chest and registering his rapid but regular rhythm, and a catheter from his bladder to a plastic bag collecting amber urine. Next to him, buckled into awkward and uncomfortable flight attendant-style seats were the ear, nose and throat surgeon and his two nursing colleagues. Chen played solitaire with a pack of US Air Force-logoed playing cards.

First Secretary Conrad Prudholme, the putative HIV-positive Administrator, was one of two passengers in the separate cabin of eight luxury seats. He had abandoned attempts to finish the recent *Herald Tribune* puzzle, Sunday edition. He wasn't much on European and Asian capitals or old English literary illuminati. In its place, he studied the user manual of his office's new fax machine. He was confident that his trip would be brief and that the follow-up, high-tech test would reveal that he wasn't positive after all. He would surely be back in his office within a week. He'd have to deal with his girl friend on his return … but then again, if the test came back negative, he wouldn't have to tell her anything.

Jill Eisenstat, wife of the embassy doctor, sat across the aisle from the Admin Officer. He offered no evidence that he was aware of her presence. "Hi, Mr. Prudholme," she uttered barely loud enough to be sure that he heard. She had never, to her recollection, referred to him as Conrad or Connie.

He shifted his eyes toward her, without the slightest rotation of his neck. "Hello, Ms. Eisenstat." He quickly flipped a page of the user manual and continued reading. Jill reckoned that further attempts at friendly communication would be unrewarding.

She had never been an avid reader. Before Africa, she had been an inveterate knitter, but, since joining the Foreign Service with Michael, she had forsaken the woolly hobby where the temperature rarely dropped below 85 degrees. She pulled her tote bag off the stark, rubber-carpeted cabin floor and opened it, took out her needles and, for the first time since arriving on the continent, began to knit socks.

Unlike her fellow passenger across the aisle, she was of the strong belief that she would never set foot in Zinani, or even Africa, again. Sad as she was that she would be away from her spouse and best friend for weeks or months, she had not been a joyful expat in the third world. She had not, in her one-year-plus, accustomed herself to the heat, the filth, and the clamor of West Africa. She had made no new important friendships; she would probably never see anyone, with the possible exceptions of Chen and Ernestine, again. She very much looked forward to seeing her mother, her two children, and her dozens of California friends, knowing that she wouldn't quickly be required to leave them behind.

Oddly, Jill thought, she was not grieving over the death of her father, whom she had adored. She envied the many Latinos she'd seen on TV, and Africans she'd observed in person, for their ability to wail over a loss. She wondered how her husband, her mother, and her children would react if the aircraft did not make it all the way to Sicily.

The fourth American aboard was Peace Corps Volunteer Jenny Addison. Aside from the single suitcase allowed to the other three Embassy personnel, and the 22-inch black travel bags of the members of the crew, her simple wooden coffin was the only object in the windowless, gray shipping compartment that could have accommodated several heavy weapons and many dozen boxes of ammunition.

The jet engines whined more loudly as the 720, finally in motion, turned toward the taxiway. Jill stared through her window. At a distance, she noticed the diminishing smoke of the charred Libyan Lear Jet. The only humans visible on her side of the plane were the Americans under the barely protective shade of the lone neem tree. Like children on the banks of the Begoro River, the Ambassador, Deputy Chief of Mission, Political Officer, Gunnery Sergeant, Security Officer, Acting Administrative Officer, and her husband, the Regional Medical Officer, waved their right hands in unison. She returned the gesture, knowing that no one was aware that she had done so.

The 720, gunning its engines from the end of the fifteenth fairway, was airborne three hundred meters before the last set of white lines on the runway. They didn't need the fire trucks.

EPILOGUE

Chen Wang died. Dr. Eisenstat had made the right diagnosis. He had a huge abdominal abscess. The exploratory incision was made, not above the Mediterranean, but in a surgical suite in the US Naval Hospital in Sigonella, Sicily. Infection was everywhere. The young surgeon, right out of his residency at Walter Reed, cleaned out all the infection he could see. The antibiotics were of a wider spectrum and higher price than the ones received in the Abattoir. But the infection came back and came back again. Three operations later, the urine bag started to fill more and more slowly. Fluids and diuretics had no influence. His blood tests showed acute kidney failure. Chen refused the recommendations of several majors and colonels and at least two generals, all of whom suggested that he go on dialysis. He died, with none of his friends at his bedside and with his ex-wife en route to see him, in an airplane half way across the ocean.

Ernestine Grant was recognized as the fine Foreign Service Officer that she was. She was sent to the War College in Carlisle, PA, a tour offered to those officers destined for bigger and better assignments. Afterwards, she was paneled for the important task of Consul General in Capetown, South Africa, only to be elbowed aside by a white woman whose husband had donated heavily to the President's campaign. Grant is now working somewhere on the third floor in the State Department headquarters with assurances that she'll be named ambassador as soon as something appropriate opens up.

Conrad Prudholme's HIV-positivity was confirmed. He is on anti-retroviral medicines and doing well. Not eligible for foreign assignment with his diagnosis, he too works on the third floor, although he and Grant rarely run into each other. His wife, Peema, returned with the children to see her family in Bhutan, and has yet to visit the United

States.

Willie Anderson, returned to Zinani as Peace Corps Director after a short hiatus. Following a highly successful tour of duty, he returned to Virginia and was elected to the State Legislature, representing his hometown of Roanoke. He has no interest in professional football.

Beth Sinova was transferred from the country and reassigned to Micronesia, where she fell in love with and, after finishing her tour, married a native Islander. She works in tourism.

Angela and Trevor Addison, parents of the late Peace Corps volunteer Jenny, established and financially support the Jenny Anderson Middle School, in Korikono. Having taken French lessons, they plan to visit the school every year. The Peace Corps committed to assign at least one volunteer to the school at all times.

On the recommendation of Retired Colonel Whipple, Eddie deQuervain is an air traffic controller in Orlando. Whipple is often a guest on CNN when Air Force issues warrant it.

Jack Nu, promoted to full colonel, runs the ROTC program at UCLA. He is still single and often seen in the company of sophomores and juniors.

Lori Burkitt got pregnant. No one in the mission had any idea who the father was and she, as is her profession's wont, was not talking. She delivered a son on a short medical evacuation and returned to Donolu for a second two-year term. She is very close to the members of the ruling coalition. In fact, she regularly uses rank and file members of the PPD as baby sitters.

Ambassador and Mrs. Fairchild are celebrating their thirtieth year of marriage. Her threats to leave him after she was pulled off the plane were a bluff. They finished their tour, thanks to the skillful work of DCM Grant. He thought that his stellar performance in overseeing the transition to democracy in Zinani warranted a Deputy Assistant Secretary position or a higher profile Embassy. He was offered Equatorial Guinea but turned it down. He works in Foggy Bottom, on the second floor.

Oumou Kinsa is the President of the Republic. Less than one year after the coup, she won Zinani's first free election with nearly 85 percent of the vote over General Joro. Joro had quickly broken free of the primarily female PPD and established a new political party. President Kinsa is widely rumored to be on the payroll of the CIA.

The world community recognized the Republic of Zinani and the new government was quickly seated in the United Nations. They invariably vote against Israel.

Abraham Ibrahim Lassoso languished in prison for a year before his trial. Paying his bills with money he had been able to save in Switzerland, he hired a staff of the best French attorneys. In spite of his crack legal team, he was found guilty of 623 counts of murder and sentenced to death. Oumou Kinsa commuted his sentence, and he is now living near Biarritz.

Bernadette O'Kelly regretted that she had not extended her tour in Zinani. She found it a heady position to be the American Political Officer in a new democracy. She had declined, early in her tour, to re-up in Donolu; by the time she decided she'd like to continue her big fish/small pond routine, a Latino male had been pegged for the slot. She moved back to Washington, where she is spending a year in a think-tank, while still an employee of the State Department. She has had a series of relationships with mainly younger men but has accepted the fact that she will probably always be single. She discarded the wardrobe of African attire that was given to her when she left country and is usually seen in either brown or plaid.

Suleiman Sacco's body was never found. He has developed an almost Elvis Presley like reputation in his homeland, with sightings reported from time to time.

Michael and Jillian Eisenstat were apart for many months. Jill decided not to return to Donolu; Michael reluctantly agreed to remain unaccompanied. She made some extra money, which they didn't need by selling medical equipment. They figured that after a tour in a country in chaos, they would get a first world tour of duty. They had on their bid list London, Vienna, Bangkok, Warsaw, Nairobi, Jakarta and Beijing. Regulations required that their bid list had to include at least eight places. They added Dhaka, capital of Bangladesh as their eighth pick, but were confident that they'd get one of their first three choices. Michael and Jillian are now living in a luxurious house, next to the open sewers of Dhaka.

ACKNOWLEDGEMENTS

BAOBAB was an 18-year endeavor, starting from my earliest days as a doctor-diplomat in West Africa. Seeking adventure, my wife and I left rural northern California and joined the US State Department in 1991. We were stationed in Bamako, the capital of Mali, where I was the only native English-speaking doctor for 300 miles.

We were taken under wing by a small but incredible group of Embassy personnel, both American and Malian. Among them were Don Gelber, the Ambassador (nothing like Mr. Fairchild) and his Secretary, Pamela Ash; Peggy Blackford, the DCM and her secretary Sharon Amis; Mary Curtin, the Political Officer; Rob Merrigan, the Economic Officer; George Forsyth and Don Amis, the General Services Officers; Joe Hilts, the Finance Officer, Kerry McBride, the Intern par-excellence; plus the extraordinary Malian Political Assistant, Oumar Konipo. We loved the country and its amazing people; we're saddened by the tragic terrorist events that have befallen the nation since we left in the mid 90s.

The book project began some years later when I had been assigned to the position of Regional Medical Officer in Manila, Philippines. I was not thrilled by the first draft of *Baobab*, so I put it on the shelf and limited my writing to medical articles directed toward my health care comrades in the Foreign Service.

After further medical stints in Bangladesh, Washington, DC, South Africa, and China, I retired in 2006, and returned to America's finest city, San Francisco. In addition to teaching medical students at my alma mater, UCSF, I enrolled at the Fromm Institute for Life Long Learning at the University of San Francisco. There I signed up for a seminar in creative writing, and met the Professor, my mentor-to-be, Joan Minninger. She encouraged me to write fiction; as a result, I wrote and self-published, with modest success, *Philanthropist*, a San Francisco-based novel about aging. I removed *Baobab* from the shelf where it had languished for more than a decade, for a second look.

Joan and I joined a writing group, made up of a magnificent cadre of wanna-be writers: John Hudson, another retired Foreign Service Officer; Frank Stillman, lawyer; Hedi Saraf, learning specialist; and Amy Hosa, watercolorist. We meet every three weeks, sending each other tranches of our writing before every get-together. We spare no rods in letting the others know what we think of their work. They, over many months, helped me turn my Africa story into something of which I am quite proud. Thanks to all of them.

Thanks also to so many others, many of whom I'll surely forget to mention: to Ambassador Nancy Powell, who had led embassies in Nepal, Ghana, Uganda, Pakistan, and India, before becoming Director General of the State Department(DOS); to Joe Sullivan, one-time Ambassador to Zimbabwe and Angola; To Regis Sheehan, Counter-terrorist Official at the DOS, who critiqued my stuff, chapter by chapter, over many months; to Bob Kaplan, a film producer and close friend of more than six decades; to George and Sharon Gmelch, Professors of Anthropology at both U of San Francisco and Union College. All read and reviewed the work at different stages; without them, the manuscript would have been far less worthy.

Special thanks to my family: to my brother, Richard Hill from Berkeley who read *Baobab* through the eyes of an intellectual and uncovered several inconsistencies that required correction; to my son Trevor, investment banker in Tokyo, who read the book with a fine-toothed comb and made dozens of recommendations, nearly all of which I accepted; to my daughter Rebecca, swimming coach in Naperville, Illinois, for her consistent enthusiasm for my efforts. Particular thanks to both kids for their acceptance of their parents' temporary emigration when both were still in college.

And, most of all, thanks to my partner and spouse of 53 years, Terry. Having a background in editing from her days at the Asian Development Bank in Manila, she used her knowledge and perspicacity to read my novel twice, making it as error-free as possible. But more importantly, she accompanied me in my peripatetic career in rural Humboldt County, Asia, and Africa and was always able to create a stimulating, enjoyable, and productive life for herself – that's not always true for diplomatic spouses. I like to say that had I been assigned to a job on the Moon, she'd have found plenty to do.

Larry Hill, MD
San Francisco, 2019
chinadochill@yahoo.com